T3-BPD-786

The Stove-Junker

by

S.K. Kalsi

LITTLE FEATHER BOOKS, INC.
NEW YORK

Little Feather Books, Inc.

Library of Congress Cataloging-in-Publication data on file.

ISBN 978-0-9907790-6-3

Front Cover Design by LFB Studios

Dedication

To my parents, Surjit and Kanwal.

The Stove-Junker

For, behold, the day cometh, it burneth as a furnace; and all the proud, and all that work wickedness, shall be stubble; and the day that cometh shall set them ablaze, saith the LORD of hosts, that it shall leave them neither root nor branch.

The Book of Malachi 4:1

BOOK I

ONE

A winter owl hoots. *Hoo-hoo,* it says. Now the boughs of the old oak shriek across the roof like claws across a blackboard. Now something clatters to the floor, like a board or a bone and still that dog barks in some distant field. Short stabs. A suffering howl. Ancient. Atavistic. There's a rasp in its throat, the cold embedded in it. Embedded in the woods, nature speaks through the voices of animals. It's a sound that hurts my ears, such sadness in it. Such sweet sadness in it. What have the wild animals inherited but punishing weather, indifference to human life, insufferable appetites? What is a howl but the inheritance of return?

I am Somerset. It is night again. It seems to me that the roots of the trees spill their darkness into the winter sky gone black and starless. To secure a better vantage, I lean against the wall of my old master bedroom. The window, frosted in the corners, bears my warped reflection. What I see outside does not astonish me. At my age, seventy-nine and counting, nothing much astonishes me. A snow devil spins across the snow laden yard, a twig from the old oak falls unceremoniously, and still that dog barks, or is it a crow? The Emerson Bakelite radio softly susurrates (thank you, Armand, for the word) and I am attuned to things, my internal antennae positioned to receive messages from the dead. I am thinking, thinking back on my life… and what crossed my mind just now was this: thirty years is a long time away from a place you've loved; but here I am, back in the old, unfinished house, circumscribed by hills of astonishing greenery now gone white, back in Drums.

~

Since every end is a beginning, let me start at the end. I believe time is circular and so is memory. With the best years behind me, my mind spins back to the moments I lived the hardest, loved the deepest, and felt the greatest losses. Maybe *that's* just the effect of time on the brain, Armand would say. I wouldn't disagree. I'll get to Armand. I'll get to all of it. For now, let me think this: it is December and Mercury is in retrograde. I have returned to the old family Craftsman stuck in the corner of Luzerne Valley and circumscribed by the Poconos. This is all I have left now, my paltry legacy, besides my memories and my name. We were the Gardens, I say, formerly Van Gaartens. We *were* and not we *are* because I am the end of the family line.

~

At my age, you start to think a lot about inheritances. Legacies. Settlements. Because Mercury's in retrograde, the past feels more alive than the present with all these pleasant shadows. I like this time of evening, whiskey and nicotine my companions and the radio with Miki's voice flowing from it, oozing from its speaker like sweet cream. I like the sound of my own voice when soaked in whiskey and I like the feel of a cold, cold evening, though I know it's not good for me. At my age, seventy-nine going on eighty, thinking, remembering, ruminating, reminiscing on the vicissitudes of life, who am I but just a little washed-up man engaged in pleasures he has no right to? But what a day it's been, with its tumbles into the past and plans for the immediate future. How a single day can change your life.

~

I light a match. With the match I light my Hemingway cigar. By now the winter bears must be dreaming of the Chesapeake trout spawn, and by now I should be trucking in for the night. I should be asleep, but I can't sleep. My single-action Colt's tucked away in the tool chest, beneath the hammer and the hacksaw and a socket-set—a Colt with a single bullet in its chamber. My sleeping bag lies unfurled in the corner, beside the suitcase with its broken latch, and I wonder, as I regard the sledgehammer leaning against the wall of cracked plaster, cracks like floes of broken ice, and regard the kindling bundled in an orderly pyramid beside the hearth, and regard the pickaxe, or the shadows leaping from the axe blade's vicious camber, I wonder if I am not committing a final act of self-immolation? I wonder, am I not deluding myself in believing I still have time to put my life and this house in order?

~

Blowing smoke to the ceiling beams. Ashes fall, peppering my pants. Since I still have air to breathe, I will breathe it, and skies to stare up at and scenery to gawk at like a loon, and so I'll gaze up and out at that landscape of my youth to my heart's content and drink my Maker's Mark and puff my Hemingway and imagine and ruminate and talk to the landscape. Everything still exists so long as my senses don't fail me. Though this sea sponge of a brain has forgotten things it has no business forgetting, the tear ducts still remember, the skin remembers, and images of a past I scarcely recall buoy up to reclaim their place in my mind where memory sometimes blurs with dream and dream with fantasy. *What're you saying, Pops? You drunk?*

~

Sometimes Cole's with me, sometimes so near it's as if I can smell his breath. I have to laugh, and I laugh as if it were a prayer or incantation. Christ, what a good day it's been, eventful anyway. Though I am a little banged up from my accident and a little cold, despite the fire roaring in the hearth, though time seems to start and stop, the unaccounted gaps in it, and the Emerson sputters music, I... I'm alive. I'm home. I even managed to get a little work done around the house.

TWO

Last month, Nona died. Forty-years of marriage gone in a blink. For the past two decades, she and I lived in Baltimore, in a state of suspended animation, our days arranged like the letters in an alphabet, one simply following another to the end and then repeating. Traveling separate routes, we reached the same destination—a settled loss. Our directionless drift had as much to do with losing Cole as it did with simply growing apart. What held us together in the end but fear? Certainly not love, though I loved her more than anything, even until the last second.

~

One early September, amidst a heat wave—waves of hot air that wilted our garden, reduced our orchard with losses measured in wormy apples and shriveled lemons where shoals of gnats lifted from the soil—we lost our grip on the world. Cole's death—*No, never call it a death; he's just lost*—our loss, became the sole indestructible fact of our lives. Words left us then. Warmth. Order. The pattern of our lives lay scattered like ashes in the Chesapeake. No matter how hard we tried to conciliate ourselves with phrases we half-believed—*Cole's vanishing was for a purpose we cannot understand, according to a principle we cannot comprehend*—and no matter how we twisted the grammar around to convince ourselves his absence possessed a higher meaning, we became a couple siphoned into a void.

~

Light waned, music warped, space, emptied of everything but Cole's loss, magnified year by year. Eventually, Nona and I lost the feeling of distance—the proportion of time and space foreshortened in a way it seemed we could reach out our hands and caress the horizon's edge. So the last thing we lost was hope. For what was loss but the beginning of hopelessness? What was terror but the magnification of fear? We were lost to ourselves and to each other and to this town we called home. No longer a family of stove-junkers. No longer a family at all.

~

Now that I think about it, *lost* seems imprecise and precision is what's important. It's not as if I misplaced my son, like a set of house keys or matchbooks or eyeglasses, that someday I might find him again, hidden beneath the L-banister, behind the curtains in the den, Cole, wet and cold and exhausted and grinning, Cole, tucked away in the cellar, asleep, concealed behind the pantry shelves or in a closet. I'll cross out ~~*lost*~~ and replace it with…

Cole died!

~

Cole didn't die, I'd console Nona. He's just bumped his head and is stumbling about some town north of Nazareth.

Like Lazarus, Dutch? For a time, Nona accepted this reasoning as she accepted the fact of birds returning in the spring, because if there was one thing she knew intimately it was birds, their anatomy, habits, tendencies. I'll get to that.

~

Returning late in the evening to the Baltimore brownstone we shared for the last twenty years, I wouldn't tell Nona I searched Light Avenue hoping to find Cole, even following for blocks at a time boys of his age and bearing. I spent days threading Constellation Avenue like a madman. Like a madman, I spent countless hours peering through the plate glass windows at the end of anonymous streets, watching boys hunched over stacks of books. I wouldn't tell her that I pressed my hand to the plate glass and whispered, *Son*, only to be wrong. Again.

~

When I shut my eyes, it is Drums I always return to, and Cole in it—Cole, precious as the passing minutes—and remembering him returns to me his sense. *Pops, you always were sentimental.* Don't I know it, Son. I would think of certain winter nights when he wedged himself between Nona and me in bed, a furtive warmth embedded in his skin already tinctured with virginal earth and milk and possibility, or how that peculiar scent common to all small children before the age of five—sunshine sweetened hair, a nascent woodsiness in him exuding youthful exuberance—gripped us, suspended us weightless in the sense that our hope, our very survival, depended on the fulfillment of this child's dreams. How I took those years I spent for granted, believing them unalterable?

~

One morning, I awoke from my dream and Cole was gone and Nona's eyes had cracked around the edges. I found myself alone in a city that never wanted me. I fumbled about without words, overcome with an overwhelming sense that the walls of my life had collapsed around me, leaving me to pick through the rubble the sense of who I was.

~

And who was I? "Somerset Garden" was just a name invented for me, and you can't tell much about a man by his name. You have to dig deeper, mine the craggy tunnels. When I linger on the people we were, I feel my mind spinning as if in elliptical orbit, loss knotted at the center of my universe like a black hole. If I shut my eyes and calm my chattering brain, I spin like that snow devil whirling outside, spinning at the outer rim of a vortex, stretched by gravity—infinite gravity pulling everything in, my memories, my dreams, even my light.

THREE

I feel things. Pain, for one. Regret. Gladness? Hardly. Contentment? Never. My head throbs from the accident earlier, and my hands shake from the cold. My Emerson Bakelite model number 657 squats on the mantle. A bottle of bourbon stands on the sill, and a Hemingway cigar rests in my pocket awaiting the cutter and a match. I have matches. I have food and supplies, a survivor kit, and tools to get me through these next few weeks. When Armand comes, we'll set this old house right and get it ready for the spring.

Strange as it seems, I feel that I wasn't so much as drawn back to Drums, as compelled by circumstances beyond my control—compelled to this house, to these naked thistles, to the dead ivy, to the raven-haired creeks and silt-stirred ponds of my youth; summoned to this house built by my grandfather in this clearing bounded by woods that in the springtime offered up trees so verdant and air so thick with renewal it made one's eyes tear. Although you can't see them from this window, cornfields surround us with rows of tilled earth plumb as an arrow. There's no corn now, just empty rutted fields sheathed in snow and ice, but just before the harvesting, the corn blooms with purple blossoms tinged with green standing up from the earth like thousands of outstretched fingers. They were fields I would chase Cole through, where we'd play hide-and-seek. In the wind the corn speaks, whispers, sings, and the wind makes the corn swish like waves. Although you can't see it from here, perhaps just from the roof, if you look past the maple groves, you'll catch sight of South Main Street running perpendicular to the old Warrior's Trail. It's where Cole and Nona and I would stroll in the summers, Henry James trotting ahead. You'd see the steeple of Christ Church, just barely visible above a copse of stippled oaks. You'd see Whispering Pines Park. You might even see the lot where my grandpa, Obadiah, lies beside grandma, Geraldine, lying beside my father, Blake, and brother, Wally. How many times had I received the sense that no other street like South Main existed in the entire world? But I know better. I have seen similar streets up and down the eastern seaboard when it was just my mother, Pearl, and I.

You age, your mind alters, your heart tells you nothing exists beyond your town is worth its weight in salt, that other Main Streets in other towns and in other boroughs and in other cities—from the ragged coasts of Maine to the tan sands of Florida, from the snow capped peaks of the ice-blue Yukon to the wheat-hued Floridian coastline, and all that vast expanse of earth between east and west—ring false. My stomach growls. I light a match.

~

At Amber Daria's, Cole and Nona and I would wolf down CMP's, Amber's "world famous" chocolate and marshmallow and peanut butter sundaes. Nona would shine in the gloaming, the glow, the graft, the twilight, sipping red tea from a white porcelain cup rimmed with silver. Ribbons of steam would dissipate into the night air, still heavy with summer heat, and just as the silences spread outwards from us and into the woods, I took pause and nodded to my family in a fulfilled way. In those moments, that quietude took away my breath. You could smell the smoke of a campfire in Whispering Pines Park, smoke floating on the waves of guitar music and soft womanly singing and the thud of bare feet in a dance, and the smoke and the music and the dance wouldn't upset the late August fireflies blinking and blinking. You refused to believe in a town without the maple groves' adjacent Lantern Road, where under nights so pitch-dark and starless the graveyard trees shivered, lulling the nearby houses with their thrush. This was your town, your people, reflecting your heart and soul. *It was always about you, Pops, never anyone else.* Now, now, Cole.

Remember the days we spent at Angela's Park, swimming in the Olympic pool in the highest heat of July, or riding the *clickety-clackety* wooden roller coaster, Volcano Valley? Remember how I had you collect all those lost balls from the streams in Meadowlark Golf Course? It's all gone now. All gone. The markers of my youth are all erased. *I remember.*

~

This landscape, now white, and all that lies in it, connects me to a time that existed millions of years before my birth and, perhaps, will continue to exist a million years after my death, like a place of fixed absolutes. *Heaven, Pops?* What did I know about it, Cole?

~

Remember when I felt Drums was my own personal Eden, my Avalon, an ever-replenishing paradise bloated with both beauty and temptation? Isn't that what I tried convincing you? *Always.* The earth needn't be planted and tilled to bear yields, and the rivers ran ceaselessly with milk, and the fruit trees blossomed perpetually, bearing pears and oranges the size of a grown man's heart. Here I would find things dead or dying in the grass, beneath the trees or in them, awaiting resurrection, or new life in the creek beds, worms and crayfish, tadpoles and the clustered eggs of tiny fish. The sun rose over the hills and set under the hills and birds flopped from branch to branch and everywhere the virgin dance of beginnings and everywhere the rasp of endings. It was this Eden, always replenishing itself in a thousand different directions, whose center was everywhere and nowhere. Don't you remember? *I'm trying not to, Pops.*

~

Cole, there was always a discovery to be made: A flash of metal in Big Nescopek Creek turned out to be just the plop of a catfish tail upsetting the murk, a tail that plopped and vanished, sending water rippling to the banks in small concentric circles. Orioles perched on the bundled limbs of locusts and they sang northwards toward the Canadian Provinces. Birdsong spread over the thankless tundra, and farther north, I imagined those trills entered flightless birds, their fins like propellers spinning in ice blue water, birds that bulleted across the deeps to music that sent the arctic bears sliding over the snow. *That's some imagination, Pops.*

~

Where has the time gone? Where is the boy who spent his time making and remaking the world in his mind, a boy who climbed into the roots of a giant oak, heard darkness and made it his friend? *Me or you?* Me, Cole. If I knew then what I know now, that a man stripped of his family and his passions becomes a husk, I would stare for an extra hour at the textures in bark, observe for another hour time's unhurried pace leveraged by the falling of a leaf. I would do that, stare, taste, listen, feel, fill up my heart with the sheer sentience of the world.

~

Late at night, with the slow, soft hours bending me into a new dimension and the wind sloughing across the Baltimore harbor, igniting those wicked fire engine sirens and ambulance squeals that trembled the living room windows, and with the kitchen upended as if burgled, Nona gone and Cole gone and only memory to accompany me, and while a river of cars jostled for advantage toward Harborplace, with the morning sunlight revealing the skyline swathed in a pumice gray, I sat, pale as a ghost, my soft slow hand bouncing a pouch of Earl Gray into a chipped and steaming cup, my eyes heavy-lidded and head contemplating the shape and dimensions of a life spent dreaming the wrong dreams. While shadows crept into the corners and the lampposts clicked off one by one down Light Street, announcing the cool blue dawn, I returned to my Eden. I dreamt of my son and me, pretending not to know our names, not to know where we're from, like insomniacs having lost our memories, just so we could rediscover the world.

~

While crows collected in the telephone crosses outside my window, and while a radio blared noise and a baby wailed in the walls and while the steamy emanations of a world awakening just to establish itself for a few hours careered across streets thickened with false purpose, I cross-examined myself (*Who are you? Who have you been? Why were you? Did you? When did you? How?),* and how I felt nothing but astonishment then, that I could have loved so deeply, yet hurt so completely the family I had made.

FOUR

Forgetting that day was akin to forgetting your own name. September 11, 1985, Cole's eighteenth birthday and the two-hundredth anniversary of the Sugarloaf Massacre (I won't mention the Twin Towers. I'll honor those dead with silence, even as euphoria spread inside me while watching the conflagration).

~

Callie, Cole's girl, and Ivan, her brother, were to stop by for a small party. Nona's cousin, Mark, was driving up from Phoenixville with Lisa and Greggie, our niece and nephew. Mark's wife, Ivy, Nona's sister, had been dead for years (a suicide). Nona had already baked Cole a German chocolate cake, just like he'd asked her to, and I needed Cole's help in cleaning up the charcoal grill. The T-bone steaks sat marinating in the Frigidaire beside Nona's macaroni salad and a dozen or so long ears of sweet corn, still in their sheaths. The pop sat in a Coleman cooler. There were bags of salt and vinegar chips.

~

A delightful day. Gray as ever. I said a prayer upon waking (general thanks for good health), took Henry James for a walk in the woods where I found a birdling and held a little funeral for it down at the creek bed. My thoughts kept returning to Cole. He and I had fought that week (what does it matter now what the reasons were?). He had pushed me and I had pushed back, and fallen. Wanderlust, exile, rootlessness; these were his values.

~

Settling Henry James in his cage, I checked Cole's room. His bed was made and all his things stood in their rightful places. A glance inside might have told a reporter all he needed to know about Cole, but what to make of the stillness? His room felt different to me, a cold pallor to it, like an empty theater, every item staged and his absence fabricated for the benefit of an audience. The room still reeked of sweaty socks, of youth's sour emanations, but also of hollowness, like an old, dried-up well. His leather-bound journal sat on his desk beside his blue, fountain pen. His poetry and philosophy books leaned into one another in the bookcase, and in the corner on its stand stood his Epiphone acoustic guitar. A world map was tacked above his bed beside a framed picture of Jean-Paul Sartre. The map was old, faded, with deep crease lines. Red pins marked cities he hoped to visit: Madrid, Marseilles, Milan, the obvious choices; but also Bombay, Beirut, Baghdad. The curtains were undrawn. Outside, it was pale and windless. A single amber leaf waved down from the old oak's boughs. Over the western Poconos, three blades of pale light shot across the milk white sky. Cole's wind-up clock on his nightstand clicked.

~

It's the serenity that confounds you, the quietness of a room that despite the things indicating life, of dreams dreamt and plans made and passions stirred, seems bereft. His collared shirts, leather jackets, his engineer boots rested neatly in his closet, and on his nightstand, reflected in the mirror, lay those aspects of his life I never much understood, like a dish of pebbles, a robin's blue egg, that water-soiled copy of Heidegger's *Being and Time.*

~

Maybe he rode out to Nazareth to visit Callie, I thought. Callie was a dirty, dishwater blonde in whose lissome expressions, full of teeth, Cole developed a new swagger. The girl read poetry, had no higher aspirations than to work at a hair salon like Patrice, her mother. Maybe Cole had spent the night at Ivan's house. Like Cole, Ivan was a dreamer who failed to realize that his dreams would remain unattainable. We can't all be famous for something. Not everyone can actualize their potential. Some of us, like Ivan and Callie, were born to fail. Not Cole. Not if I had anything to do with it.

~

Downstairs I checked the garage for his Indian Scout. It was early-'30s in lush hues of candy apple red and cream, looking as if in motion even at rest. A few oil spots peppered the concrete where it normally stood. Cole's half-helmet was gone. The goggles which hung from a pegboard were gone; his chaffed leather boots and gauntlet gloves. Something felt undone.

Okay Pops, was the last thing he said to me the day before. I was in the barn, tinkering with a cast iron cook lid. *Okay.* We exchanged words and maybe I said things I regret saying, but a father has the right to be offended by his son's life. I could still hear his Scout in my head, those shotgun pipes roaring down the graveled drive, wheels thudding across the wooden planks of that old single car bridge. I pictured him at the bottom of a ravine, his leg shorn from his body at the knee joint while scarlet, viscous blood pooled around him like paint. No one but the woods to hear him scream. Nothing but the insouciant birds to feel astonished.

I found Nona lying supine in our bed.

Cole's gone.

Did you call Callie's?

It wasn't like him to miss his birthday after we'd planned so much, but we'd grown apart from each other. That was the law of late adolescence, with its secret handshakes and private language that excluded the adult world. The greater truth was this: he was a stranger to us.

~

By the time Cole turned thirteen, the summer of '81, his physical changes coincided with his emotional ones. He sequestered himself in his room, depositing his thoughts into a privacy we had no access to. Where was my son? *Gone away, Pops. Not even going, but gone. 'Cause you were never here and when you were here you were the color red. You were blue heat, Pops, you were fire.*

~

By the time he was sixteen, he would return home and retreat to the bomb shelter out back for hours—playing 33s on the wind up phonograph? Reading philosophy? Writing abstract poems about time, identity, memory? His life and interests were like Sanskrit, Aramaic, Pidgin, some alien language without reason or sense.

~

I never got a chance to tell him that I was proud of his sensitivity, proud of his depth, that the poems he crafted, though I didn't understand them, were good poems. *It's just surrealism, Pops. Ever read Baudelaire, Calvino, ever see a Dali?* Those things were part of a world I had no access to, nor reason to believe in. What did they matter or mean to a simple stove-junker like me?

After he'd been gone six months or so, I found a box full of those poems buried in the bomb shelter, behind a crate of turpentine. Reading page after page, I saw his inner life full of questioning the meaning of life, absence of God, and the nature of death that it broke my heart to read them. Blasphemy, I thought. Heresy. *Just playing around, Pops, like those ideas were fire.* I am not sure what I did with those poems, gave them to Nona, or threw them away, maybe buried them in the house? Now I believe a child is not just the father of man, but also his conscience, and conscience his tormentor.

~

Cole could be dreamy, shiftless, impudent. For the months leading up to his vanishing act, he alternated between anger and withdrawal. Moody. Aloof. Irreverent. He would skulk around the house, make short excursions to the creek, then return at dusk, roam the house and sit in his room with the lights off, strumming that damned guitar. *Were you any different, Dutch?* I would try to reach him with work—*help me out with that box, Son; give that old door a push*—remind him of the boy who launched rockets into the air one summer—*Just one, Pops*—the boy who ran around the tree dancing like a Brave, the boy who coaxed me into building him a time-machine playhouse. There I was laying all the evidence of his youthful exuberance at his feet in hopes to turn him back into my son.

Tell me how to make you happy, Cole.

His shrug would be enough to launch me into the sun.

Late at night, I would press my hand to his door and feel it vibrate with trapped tension.

I drove out to Black Creek Falls the day he vanished, parked before the single-lane car bridge succumbed by half a century of neglect. The bridge arched over the water as it snaked through the woods. Upstream, white rocks jutted from the black water like bleached bones. A pair of crows stood footed there, looking as if made of iron. They cawed, flapped their black wings. Just beyond the trees, the falls fell from a height of fifteen feet or so, casting silver, molecular sprays. Plump swirls of foamy water scattered into the currents, drawing downstream. The clearing was empty. I waited. No, I decided, Cole wasn't there.

~

How I spent that first day searching the myriad courses Cole sometimes took on his Scout, down Bishop Road to the Wagner Farm and back, winding down Black Creek Road into Black Creek Township and into Freeland. That day I made it to Jim Thorpe, cruised up and down Broadway, hoping I'd see his motorcycle parked at Seller's Books, Cole riffling through the bargain rack. I drove to Asa Packer's Mansion. Hard winds blew dead leaves across the museum's parking lot and a quick glance at the sky showed dark, bulging clouds. I waited. Every face was a threat. A tour bus pulled up, spilling lookie-loos, Orientals and Puerto Ricans clicking their cameras. Spits of rain landed on the windshield as I drove home.

~

Inside me floated that empty resonance when confronted by the mysteries of God and the magnificence of Satan, when my capacity to comprehend prophecy was overwhelmed by the sheer absurdity of parable: Daniel in the lion's den, Jonah and the whale, the ascension of the dead to heaven, or the fall of man into the devil's pit. I was still a believer then. Devout. I still believed God placed one in deep waters to cleanse and not to drown. I drove home, back to Nona and the silent house.

~

With the Mercury's engine rumbling in the driveway, I sat silent, my hands firm on the steering wheel (twelve and six), and I stared hard at the house with its brown shutters and half-dismantled porch, stared hard at the tarp covering columns of new black shingles for the roof Cole and I were to start on the following week. I tented my hands in prayer to a God who I did not then know had already abandoned me. That night, we waited. Rain on the roof was the loneliest sound.

~

The following day, while the house dripped and Nona lay in bed with a migraine, I scoured the house, the barn, the old bomb-shelter. Even then it was a storehouse for rats and spiders, the sodden emanations of neglect. Then I drove up to Hazleton, cruised North Broad Street, turned into the Ten Pin Lounge, and questioned some kids I thought Cole knew. They snickered and stared at me as if I were dredged up from the sea. I searched the back roads leading into Eckley, circled The Great Swamp, tramped the trails by Four Season's Lake where Cole sometimes drifted alone. He could be anywhere, I thought, lying in some rocky pit at the bottom of the minefields, trapped at the bottom of Beaver Pond. I plunged my feet into waters which held memories, waters in which Cole once swam. I climbed a notched pine in which Cole might have sat and I remembered times we nested in the limbs of the old oak like birds and gazed out at the shifting landscape. I scoured the length of Big Nescopek Creek, tramped across sodden fields whose dirt Cole would eat as if it were chocolate, cupping my hands around my mouth like a megaphone, shouting his name. *Did you, Pops?*

~

Cole, remember Pete Reznor? Pete ran Black Crow Cycles in Drums off of Mundies Road. *He sold me that junk Scout.* Yes. He suggested I look into Nate Grayson out of Jeddo. *What a laugh.* A hoarder, Nate's four-acre property, limned by pine woods. His goddamned yard was littered with nutty deer dung, broken furniture, rusted car parts, truck tires. He looked curious enough, what with his strabismic left eye, lily hair and saffron beard that fell to his waist, a sort of Rip Van Winkle who quoted the Koran in a place where the Bible was king. Twice a year, Nate roamed into downtown Conyngham in his ancient Edsel and held congress with the butterflies and bees at Memory Lane Park, or waded naked in Big Nescopek, sour smells lurking about him—grain mash and wet, wormy earth. But eccentricity alone didn't make you a criminal. My ten-minute interview with the man proved inconclusive. He was completely deaf, feeble, didn't even know what a Cole was. *A boy you say? Never heard of it.*

~

The next morning, I left your mother standing by the stove, the kettle screaming, her face austere. I recall her hair pulled tightly into an auburn tail, and I traveled the length of the endless hallway when suddenly space and time lost their resonance. It seemed spatial distance and relation of bodies to one another had lost their definition.

~

Cole, your mother, cool as glass, smiled at nothing, pure distance in her expression. She searched my eyes. Courage. She wanted my courage. Stoicism. She demanded my strength. She wanted to hear from me things I could not promise, like we'd find you like we always did, that your little disappearing act was just a game you played to test the limits of our patience and love.

I want you to beat him good when he comes back, she said.

Remember how he skipped out of the house and roamed the woods? Remember when he skipped school and we worried, because that's what parents do, and we scolded him when he showed up a day later, his clothes wet and dirty as if he'd been dredged up from the bowels of a swamp—*I remember, and you*—and we locked him in his room. But that sinking feeling, now hard as a stone in my chest, seemed impossible to dissolve. Maybe Nona felt it too. I know she felt it too. Earley's feet creaked in the ceiling. I sucked on the cigar, having forgotten it in my hand. I relit it with a match. Slivers of blue smoke curled, formed punctuation marks in the air, collided with the ceiling beams. Asthma sang in my lungs, that gritty, dry sensation of sand. The air in the house had changed.

Something feels wrong about it this time, she said. There she was, citing parental instinct. We both still had the right.

You think this has somethin' to do with the fire? I said.

That what you thought, Pops? Earlier that summer, late May, Sheriff James Earley had caught you reeking of kerosene while Christ Church almost burned—*Jerk had no proof, Pops.* What about your confession, Cole? *Coaxed. Wouldda told him anything for him to shut-up.* I posted a two-thousand-dollar bond for you, out of our retirement savings. There was still a hearing, psychological evaluation, a visit from Pastor Robinson.

We're out of milk, Nona said, shutting off the stove burner. The kettle's whistle waned. She cast about the room with her tired eyes and thin smile. Her hands shook. Those were some fine hands she had, an artist's hands.

Every year Nona exhibited her paintings at the Wilkes-Barre Fair, offering them for sale, leaving her card for private painting lessons. Fame, ineffable as starlight, was always beyond her reach. Her life seemed settled then, like sediment in a lake. I had stopped wondering how different her life would have been had she never agreed to marrying me. What if she had achieved her dreams? Your mother was a good, honest woman who lived a good, decent life. I suppose that was enough for her. *You never really found out, did ya, Pops?* I suppose not.

What was his mood like, I said, *as far as ya recall?*

Fine, Nona said. *Quiet. He's been awful quiet.*

I thought of the boy who stood in my barn a few days before, the boy who said, *Okay, Pops* while my hammer went *clonk-clonk* against a cast iron lid. *Did you tell Ma about what you said, Pops, like that last part?*

Quiet. Did yas exchange any unpleasantries before he left? she said.

He came into the barn where I was working and said "Okay, Pops," ordinary like. Then I heard his bike start up. He took off before I had a chance to see what he wanted.

She nodded gravely. Did she suspect me of something? Blood surged through my forearms. I looked down at my fists, the knuckles bone white. In truth I couldn't remember. I couldn't remember what we had said to one another. I just remember being in the barn when he came in and said, *Okay Pops.*

~

We both sort of stayed silent after that. Shadows pocketed themselves in the creases of her mouth, the hollows of her cheeks. *Something'll turn up,* I said, half-convinced. *Something always does.*

FIVE

Ninety hours passed. A group of twelve, including two deputies, one of our local historians, and other volunteers, like the kid who ran the lunch counter down at the mission house, all combed through the woods in a long, arching row. We tramped down the hot grass, releasing clouds of gnats we inhaled or which settled on our wet faces. Spores of dust caked our foreheads, turning to glue in our nostrils.

~

Someone's machete slashed through tall bushes and the shining leaves bloated with sun flew up like explosions. Someone swung a scythe, another man chopped at brambles with an axe. After three hours or so, the tight twelve-man line lengthened and drifted apart. A wasps' nest released a black swarm and we scattered, shrieked like girls. We dug up mud and slathered our faces with it till we looked like clay effigies. Eventually someone shouted *Hey! Hey! Over here!* Then all of us, even that cross-eyed imp who ran the lunch counter, ran toward the hollering voice. Except for a muddy boot and a muddy baseball cap, that I decided didn't belong to Cole, we found nothing. The day darkened into evening and we disbanded for home, returning to pickups and service vehicles, cars, and vans, returning to wives and sons and daughters, cats, caged birds, and dogs.

~

Nona and I spent all night making up fliers. We printed them up on Cole's computer printer which we had some trouble with. I woke before sun-up, drove around Conyngham, posting those fliers on lampposts and the sides of mailboxes. The fliers had Cole's grainy picture and statistics on it: His height and weight (which we guessed), the color of his eyes (field green) and his hair color, which I was convinced was russet and Nona was convinced was chestnut. Downtown, I knocked on doors, shouted his name into the woods by Knorr Road. I plastered fliers on the stoops of churches, pinned fliers to the corkboards outside liquor stores, tacked fliers to the message board outside the public library, even on the doors of the YMCA. I returned home and found Nona slumped in a chair. She was wearing Cole's leather bomber and the look of diminished hope.

Come to bed, I said.

I can't smell him anymore, she said. *All I smell is that pine cologne he wore too much of, but I can't smell him.*

Don't believe for an instant we don't leave traces of ourselves in the things we—

Shut up, she said. *Just shut up.*

~

The next day I called the *Standard Speaker* and took out a full-page ad. MISSING and REWARD, it said, with Cole's specifics. *Last seen wearing…* Meanwhile, Earley and the two Hazleton deputies searched farms, abandoned barns and outhouses. Earley even called in a copter to survey Beaver Pond. It flew the length of the two Nescopeks, circled World's End Lake and all the ponds. Clancy Huff's fishing boat skimmed the scummy surface of The Great Swamp, stabbed the cloudy bottom with a flag pole. A Deputy Cowper picked up a drifter but let him go after a few hours. The man said something about an encampment by Jeddo, where a boy about Cole's description was seen. Except for a few charred stew bones, a deer's skull and ash markings that looked like something from a Satanic ritual, that abandoned bivouac, littered with dented beer cans and a pile of cinders, was empty.

~

Calls came to our house. Claims of sightings. Someone had seen a boy resembling Cole at a truck stop down in Phoenixville, a boy matching Cole's face riffling through a trash dumpster. On the outskirts of Pittsburgh, another version of Cole was seen thumbing a ride. Each time I called Earley, and we would set off to investigate. Someone said Cole was in the minefields. Luzerne County was an expansive territory, thickly wooded, heavily isolated. There was no telling where Cole might be.

~

Six-hundred seventy-two hours passed. The calls stopped coming. It still amazes me that your mother didn't cry, not once, as if the fact of you returning was all but guaranteed. I still held her at night while her body trembled, threatening to break at the seams. I held her in the late–mornings, when screaming your name with such fury I feared her lungs would collapse. *Did I put you through all that, Pops?*

~

Cole, on Halloween, a month and a half since you vanished, a letter turned up in our mailbox. No return address. Presumably written by you, the writer said you'd gone west, to San Francisco. The writer cited the reasons for him leaving: *We wear masks of propriety, civility, decency, fearing the truth. God is a fiction, love is a lie.* And so on. The writer could not accept that we lived a meaningless existence, a Sisyphean existence that bore no fruit. The writer stated a hatred for the weather, for the crass religiosity, unbearable boredom, a desire to wander, for freedom, to discover meaning in a life that held no meaning, and so on. It almost sounded like you, that adolescent warbling on the true nature and true purpose of life. All there. Had the writer not used words you would never use, words like "incarnadine" and "concatenation" and "Sisyphean," I might have believed him. I asked your mother if she knew you to use such words and she shook her head no.

It's not even his handwriting, she said.

No.

I would know. I'm his Ma!

But Earley believed in the letter. He said to wait because in time Cole would return, he told us. Would he? We would wait because faith and hope and love demanded it. Did it?

Kids like Cole, free spirits pulled outta here with dreams of finding meaning out there, always come home with their tails between their legs. They come home because all the meaning they wanted was right here, under their feet, around, above, in family, friends. And ya know what we do? We accept them, because there's no shame in failing, we'll tell 'em. Because God puts us in deep waters, not ta drown us, but ta save us. Ya did ya best, we'll say ta them. Let's help ya pick up the pieces because that's what we do.

~

I'd like to say we received gifts of condolences: jarred strawberry and lingonberry jam, bowls of pickled peppers and pig's feet, boxes of venison jerky, enough colorful cards and monogrammed letters to fill a storehouse. I'd like to say a few of Cole's friends came by, kids with that air of highbrow conceit—upturned noses and pithy smiles—I had never met, smelling of tobacco and beer and musk. And I'd like to say they left mixed bouquets on our porch steps, effusive poems, even going so far as to make a shrine of pictures and wreaths by the old water tower. But they didn't. None of his friends came by and we wondered if he ever had any. It was as if Cole didn't exist.

~

Nona lit candles at the church, but I didn't, and when shopping at Boscov's for tea towels, toiletries, conducting our daily routines, Nona and I met with hushed tones, sidelong glances, curious stares, nervous "hellos" and "good days" and "glad to see yas." We may have stopped being Somerset and Nona then. We became a condition that had lost a son; it was as if we had done something to deserve your vanishing.

~

God's justice is an all-consuming fire, said Natty Nussbaum after one Sunday service—*Crazy bitch, Pops!* A Moravian, Natty equated human tragedy with biblical prophecy. She told us she saw you burning high above the earth—*Bat shit crazy!* She said we should count our blessings you had not suffered that your end was instantaneous. Hogwash! What about *our* suffering? Natty smiled and said something about the wages of sin and all that and Nona's face blanched. I dragged your mother away by the arm to save her from tearing that old crow to pieces.

Truth is hard, hard medicine, Natty shouted from her ancient Ford pickup, her finger stabbing the sky. *God always delivers retributions for sin, yours and yours and yours.*

Truth, what did any of them know about it, Pops?

~

Cole, ninety days after you disappeared, late-December or so, one morning I awoke to an empty bed. I found Nona in your room, leaning against the window glass, pinching a curtain pleat. In the half-light of the blue morning, she appeared shrunken. Your mother's hair, once long and flowing like the plume of a copper barbet, was gone. I missed its slow tumble to the small of her back, missed the shimmers of light in it. The moon shone feebly across the nape of her neck.

I can't sleep, either, I said, entering.

~

She blew her breath on the window. Erased it with her palm. How would I know then that her changes came as abruptly as blinking? How could I know then that your absence would mutate her purposeful life into a system of refusals—of light, air, food—because your loss not only obliterated her vanity but erased her matriarchy? Soon she would stop painting birds. She would bathe and sleep, bathe and sleep, directing her sorrow to the water, hoping the water could cleanse some unseen stain from her body. *He comes to me in my dreams, Dutch. Cole and I talk like we used to and he tells me about gravity.* Like a ghost, your mother drifted through the house, like a cold breeze emptying itself through the hallways, ruffling the edges of picture frames, her bathrobe swishing the floor. She would float back to our room and slip into our bed, cold and shivering and smelling of wet earth. And for me food lost its flavor, color waned, and every sound, no matter how faint, jarred like gnashing teeth. Even the air jabbed at me, each slight breath felt like needles piercing my skin.

~

Nona blew her breath on the window. Rubbed it away. While the birds tangled themselves in the trees, it slowly began to dawn on me that I was not inculpable. I had said things to you and I had refused to believe I had said them. Maybe leaving the house would be my reprieve. Maybe leaving would help me forget.

I reached her. I held her in my arms and dug my chin into her shoulder. She turned from that window, like turning away from Drums, and stifled laughter with both hands clasped over her mouth, shaking violently in the throes of some personal joke.

What's so funny?

Nothing, she said, her entire body leaning into her laughter. *Never thought he'd… Who does that? What kind of idiot just disappears into thin air?*

Nona, please, I said.

We didn't have enough faith, Dutch. You know that? Natty was right. That's why God did this. That's why there's no one to point a finger to and say, 'You did this.' We sure as hell can't blame God, can we? Can we?

I had no words. I waited. Nona moved to Cole's bed and sat. The blue-black of the violent morning pasted behind her from the window, reflecting her shape in the room as a warp.

Everyone always comes home, Nona, sooner or later. Like the cuckoo. She flies south for the winter and returns.

Nona offered me a tiny smile, made for the moment, the only gesture she could muster.

Boys aren't birds.

~

We lay on Cole's bed then, tangled up in one another's arms until late that afternoon. It felt good to hold her, our hot breath mingling at the edge of our lips. I drew her closer. I suspended my belief of this small ruin that was my wife. Cradling her in my arms, I ran my hands over her neck. Her skin felt coarse as sandpaper. Her hair felt brittle. I rubbed her back, tumbled my fingers across the ridge of her spine, over the shoulder blades, across her ribs which jutted like corrugated stone.

You're so cold, I whispered, rubbing her arm. She placed her hand on mine and said, *Where's your wedding ring?*

I must have misplaced it somewhere. You know how this house loses everything. Nona and I had a habit of losing things. We lost small things, cheap things, large things, fancy things. Things like spectacles, magnifying glasses, camera lenses. We would lose lamp bulbs, boxes of matches, candlesticks. Sometimes we lost time itself, the hours flitting by in a blink when engaged in the routines of life. Sometimes we lost space. The house seemed to shrink and expand, like a beating heart.

Let's leave this place.

Where would we go?

Maybe where there's water? Somewhere where things wash ashore for us to find them.

Treasure.

Something like that.

~

I kissed my wife and told her I loved her more with each passing minute. I told her my love for her would never change. I drew her closer, fitted her into the curve of my body and with her fell. How could I know then what was to come, that losing Cole would transform us, make our hearts inaccessible?

SIX

In the morning, Nona was still beside me, but edged to the corner. My hand softly palmed her thigh, softly, so as not to shatter her dream, but maybe to pierce it a little, just a little to lift her out from under it. I have always loved the theater of her awakening, the sound of her gentle moan, the feigned distress, the moist oval of her mouth as she yawned, then rubbed her eyes with the balls of her fists. Mornings returned us as children. I thought of water then, how it healed, and how, here, in Drums, even on the warmest, hottest afternoons, the water resisted color, rejected heat, flowed to unnamed tributaries, exhibiting only the properties of cold and colder and frozen. I longed for different water, older water, water as vast as an unmapped ocean, and I agreed to Nona's suggestion to leave Drums behind.

~

We drove east, then, Dutch, remember? I remember, Nona. We moved to Baltimore then, into Kelsey Morgan's brownstone, just a stone's throw from the Atlantic. Kelsey, our friend from Hazleton, had taught music at West Hazleton High, won the Penn State Lottery, and moved away. We arrived at her brownstone shell-shocked, and Kelsey must have seen the distress on our faces. I recall cups of peppermint tea in the anteroom—*It was coffee and it was too sweet*—and Kelsey said things to Nona while I stood outside on the porch smoking a cigar.

~

The brownstone, a three-floor structure of ruddy brick, stood gloomily beside a chain of row houses on West Lombard Street. It rose stiff as a private in a regiment, but where was the privacy? Windows looked down onto neighboring yards. If you sneezed in your bathroom, your neighbor might shout *Gesundheit!* from his living room. Bedroom windows offered dark views into dining rooms. Family room windows peered into someone's library. Overlooking the crowded street as if in a state of shock, each window rippled with oily distress. The front door was as weightless as cardboard. There was no land, save a small fenced in yard with a roofless doghouse.

~

Returning inside I asked Kelsey for the bathroom. Upstairs. Down a narrow hallway. No grand views of the Chesapeake Bay from the upstairs windows, just a scene of peaked or flattened roofs, of bunched up row houses and post and beams. I washed my hands in a porcelain sink, bisque, like the color of an old Chambers' oven door. I stared at the face of a man who looked about as tired of life as one could be. Downstairs, I plugged myself into Nona and Kelsey's conversation and before I knew it I had agreed to Kelsey's offer to stay.

~

Trading green hills for gray high-rises, pockmarked trails for traffic snarled streets, creeks bounded by pitch pines for graffiti-stained culverts, we never realized we were on the losing end of loss. There and there and there we tried to reconstruct ourselves by picking up old routines. It wasn't long until everything about the city deepened our despair, extending our slow drift from one another. Five years passed, and then a decade. We grew solitary, invisible to one another. Turned inside out, we turned further inward, further afraid. By then, we were neither married nor divorced—*Don't say that, Dutch*—neither together nor apart. *I suppose we were waiting*—always waiting, Nona, for something to happen, for Cole's return, for some magic bullet to kill our loneliness, lulled by the distant wrack of water breaking against the quay. I imagined Cole's voice skidding across the waves. His voice on the waves, in retrospect, would seem unbearable. The years passed and we waited. The decades passed and we waited. *You never told me*. And we waited.

SEVEN

I have bundled regret in layers of secrets, silences, obsessions, and eccentricities. One of the things I never told Cole was that I born in '33, or '32, maybe '34, because no one kept my birth certificate. What he knew of me was that I plied my trade here in Luzerne Valley as a simple stove-junker, where I spent my time fixing broken things.

~

Now I am a broken thing. Of my ailments, asthma, a leaky heart, clogged veins, and a bit of narcolepsy, I suffer from the vertigo of having lost time. Now all I need is the validation that comes from having lived a decent life. If possessions are any indication of value, then my life's been worthless. But I have my memories and my stories, and these warm me.

~

One of those stories is this house. I've returned to make amends. I've returned to settle my accounts. After all, it's November 26th and planet Mercury is in retrograde. *A time to reflect,* they say. *Time to take stock of one's life.* It's the season of hearth fires, wood smoke, roasted chestnuts, snowmen. Halloween has passed without my having celebrated it and the roots and branches of the surrounding trees lie buried in inches of snow. A quicksilver quilt spreads toward the horizon, signaling a blizzard. The clouds, urgent and silver, have returned, brewing mute disasters across this ashen sky.

~

Let me get comfortable. Let me lean against this wall and lean into the winter. Let me collect my thoughts. *That better, Pops?* That's better, Cole. *That good?* That's good. I have the bourbon and that's good. The smoke from the cigar is good.

~

The Bakelite still susurrates (thank you, Armand, for the word). It effervesces and squeals, and DJ Miki's voice provides her hourly update. She has dispensed with the time and weather report (it's six p.m., six degrees and falling), and turns toward the daily news: *Sandusky's in jail; Our Lady of the Sacred Ascension burned in Wilkes-Barre, killing the organist. Investigators charged a fifty-two year old man from Romulus, New York, with his son's murder over insurance money. In what appeared to be an accident*… and so on. As I see it, it's all prologue for what's coming. The doomsayers predict these are the ending times, these last days The End of Days. A funny fact: In a little under a month, I turn eighty, December 21st, coinciding with Armageddon. Let it all end. I'm looking forward to it.

~

The Mayan Calendar has predicted the firmament will split open, pouring upon us fire and brimstone, blood and ash, locusts and frogs. Plagues shall sweep across the lands, they say, blackening the winter. They say the saved shall be saved and the damned shall be damned. I have to laugh. It's quiet now. Cold. My teeth chatter like a ventriloquist's dummy.

~

A quick check outside reveals things. Just beneath the Poconos, the sun turns in for the night—coppery fire hovers on the horizon like an afterburn. To the west, steam from the Berwick Nuclear Plant coils upwards over the powdered hills like plumes from a fire, and that feels right. A lone jet thunders overhead, halving the sky. A crow rises over the treetops. How it must be made of metal to survive such chill? It lands on a snow mound and caws in that dry, woodsy way and pecks at the ice cover. I'd feel lost out there. Good.

~

Losing myself interests me. The fertile topsoil interests me, sprawling beneath a light dusting of snow, and the snow that crams the trunks and branches of the pines and elms and redwoods, having frozen up their roots, subdues me to consider life and death. What lurks beneath the ground? Surely dead seeds and frozen worms reside deep below that earth, and surely all those presentiments of life lying dormant, dead or dying, scattered and mute, like memories. They yearn to be reborn, unleashing their salvos of death.

~

Now the wind howls and the branches of the old oak scrape the roof, pealing like thunder. Formed out of glacial rifts, Sugarloaf Mountain heaves up from the hoary earth like the hump of a prehistoric whale, my little Ararat. So this is my winter Eden… Am I being sentimental? So be it.

I know things. I make lost connections out of things. For instance, moments turn infinite the longer you dwell in them. Just now, down by the old fence line, something yelped while whiskey colored leaves sprayed the lawn. The house jostled in the rising wind and the walls, though altered by dust, still look familiar, yet seem so different, and I suppose that's what the Hindus mean by *Samsara.* Illusion (Thank you, Armand, for the Vedanta lessons). Armand might say I am not even here. I have to laugh.

~

I suppose the noises I attune to, and textures I regard, and the gelid air I breathe define a landscape as much as a life. I inhale the cold, dusty air, breathe this old home into my body. If I were hungry, I might take a bite out of its walls. But no. This cold, dusty air, surfeit with the scent of home, nets me in a spell I don't wish to break. Seeing the white world there, I wonder where are the arbors of my youth, those orchards and coverts where I used to flush grouse with a slingshot? Where is my past if not buried here? Still here, somewhere out there, but rendered velvety white. My memories of those experiences seem built on the scaffolding of absence.

In Baltimore, I would hold firm in my mind those long June days where each seed pollen set adrift in the air so resembled snow as to make it seem as if winter had arrived early. And now the landscape blanches and the air hardens into a dense coldness, distilled so crisply as if it were a painted landscape, less topography than the undulations of silent music. Not a single bird sweeps across this sky. Not a single star stirs. All is quiet now. But is this snowy landscape, and the frigid air, the painted clouds in a painted sky, my image of heaven or of hell? I can't decide. It is snowy, cold, and absolutely at peace, a wasteland as much as a heaven. It is almost mystical. Armand, quoting one philosopher or another, might say, *The mystical is not how the world is, but* that *the world is,* and I might say in kind, *I couldn't disagree.*

~

Somehow, nature always filled me up when everything else emptied me out. I sip from the bottle. I drag on the cigar. I recall larches exploding from the branches with such velocity as to leave the bowers trembling like tuning forks, notes of flight ringing across the fields gone gold and green with stalks of corn. They were pitches of ascent you could tune a guitar to. *Earl ate dynamite, Goodbye Earl.* So, Cole, why would we leave? This is our home. *I'll give you a good reason to, Pops.*

A town of dairy farms and corn farms and fields of kale, here there's an inventory of hills of such rich variety regulating our town that it staggers the mind. How the spring thaw returns the chevron geese, honking in the alabaster sky like parade cars. Is that worth sharing? On summer nights you feel the murmur of crickets in your chest. Should I remember that? Autumn multiplies its colors across the hills when the air turns cold, then the cold multiplies itself and turns bitter winter white. I remember trees sprinkled with spots of color the hue of rust or lemon or ash, rising from this great, green earth, their boughs hissing in the wind. They were trees of infinite variety, the mind conjuring up Eden in their scope. But perhaps Drums was no more "edenic" than any other little town surrounded by an outsized geography.

~

I wanted to believe that ours was a singular place, special, imbued with that quality of richness and decency, goodness and mercy that could awe a skeptic. I tried convincing Cole as much. *Jesus, Pops!* I tried convincing you what was good about this place: friendship, honesty, purpose-driven work. These values meant a man didn't need to live to accumulate possessions to be happy. Maybe I couldn't admit to myself ours was just a little nowhere town you passed through to get to somewhere else—to vacation homes in the Poconos, to ski-lodges, to timeshares, to the Manhattan skyline two-and-a-half hours to the North, or to Philly two-and-a-half hours to the South.

~

If Pont Du Lac, Wisconsin was the luckiest town in America, then Drums was easily, if not the unluckiest, a place where a man needn't luck to live at all. For what is luck, like talent, but an unearned gift? People look upon lucky people, or geniuses, as if they're imbued with magic. To touch them is to touch a rabbit's foot.

~

Travel west on Route 80 and you could make it all the way to San Francisco by way of Pittsburgh, and maybe that letter we received was right. Maybe you did. *Maybe.* But Hazleton seals us in, a colloquy of twinkling lights high on the hill. Once I pointed out to Cole its faint, golden glow hovering at the mountain's edge, an amber reaching to the heavens.

Son, someone's pulled down the stars and set them there.

Who, Papa?

God, I suppose.

Why? you asked, posing the central question of all five-year-olds.

For what other purpose, I thought, than to instill in us the belief that reaching for the stars could be as easy as driving into any city, our city, Hazleton.

~

After church on Sundays, you would find me on our plywood deck, a rye and ice in a tumbler in one hand and *The Standard Speaker* rolled up under my arm. *Ain't that the truth.* If I shut my eyes, I still see you splayed in the cool pockets beneath the southern windbreak. There I am, planting myself in the wicker swing. I tune the radio in to WAZL FM 90 out of Wilkes-Barre on the dial. Tapping my foot to the music of Voorhees or Dorsey or Slim and Slam during *The Classics Hour*, I read the headlines and shake my head, amazed by the stupidity of God and man.

How is it that God, in all His benevolence, could punish the innocent and reprieve the guilty? I say to Nona, to no one.

Nona slips behind me, rustling a bag of salt and vinegar chips.

It's not our place to judge these things, she says.

Who's to say we can't also judge God? Cole says.

Don't you think those things, I say.

Don't we have a right to keep Him honest?

Stop this nonsense, both of you, Nona says.

I blamed your mother for your loss. If she hadn't been so loose with you, so lenient, I would think, so yielding, unharnessing the ropes with which I bound you, to protect you, Son, from yourself, you might still be here. *If you hadn't bound him so tightly with your damn rules, Dutch, squeezing him 'til the air left his lungs, then maybe—*

Nona, He didn't know what he wanted.

Then perhaps—

Perhaps, Nona? There is no perhaps. You can construct new worlds based on less speculation than ours.

Go on, Pops.

I blamed Drums, this picaresque town whose peace felt as stifling as any weight.

And on.

I blamed God, heartless and imperfect God. Have I said that yet? Have I told you I came around to your way of seeing things?

~

After accepting that you weren't returning, I turned my blame toward God. Your skepticism took root in me. *Pops, what was God except a projection of our own fantasies?* Son, what was that religion I clung to all those years but *His* handmaiden? We offered our prayers to *Him*, our hopes to *Him*, our good deeds to *Him*, suffering like lambs to the slaughter, and what did we get in return but a howling silence, then death? *You really do sound like me, Pops, except you can't blame something that doesn't exist.*

We never deserved you leaving for good, but who ever deserves what they get? Now I find the weight of loss—*Never call it a death, Dutch*—my defining principle. Your absence, and now Nona's, and the absence of the man I used to be, breaks my heart.

Go on, Pops.

In a minute, boy.

EIGHT

Your mother's mantra late in life was this: *Forgive but not forget.* But how could I forgive God for taking you away? For who else can I blame? And forgetting? How could I forget, as if I had a choice? The hands that cupped your small bright face have withered, the drop of my coat has lengthened, the trousers hang a bit baggier now than last year. I have to cinch my belt two notches in. See how my presence in the world has diminished? A stooped posture has replaced that once plumb frame. Add to that a slow shuffling walk. Add a menacing scowl. Add to that a mean, guttural voice like a waterlogged motor. My natural expression is a grimace. Children shriek when they see me coming, babies howl. Young girls turn away their face in disgust. What a monster, they must say. A man of my age has little purchase in a world owned and peopled by youth. *You've always been old, Pops.* Yes, even as a young boy, I beheld the universe with an ancient soul.

~

But aging is regression. Old age is a circle back to infancy. Nowadays I shake my fists at people who walk too fast and who speak too fast with nothing to say, people too quick to passion and too slow to cool. Who am I to rage against them, a man guilty of never having completely understood time? Look at my face. I am no more than a set of trembling expressions and cracked, quivering lips. I am the sense of ageless regret, for isn't regret the punishment we offer ourselves for failing to live up to our potential? We flog ourselves with regret. Regret assaults my posture. Regret slumps my back. I drool. I mumble. I toddle when I walk. I regret I wasn't more than a man whose contribution to this world was as useless as water-rotted wood. Staring at these cracked eyes returning my gaze in this window, I am wholly given over to time.

~

I strike a match. The flame sizzles. Smoke slivers up like a question mark. The Bakelite buzzes. From the single speaker's grid comes static, then Miki's sweet, husky voice pieces itself together… *it's poet William Cowper's birthday today and Bruno Hauptmann's birthday. On this day, in 1949, a new, old nation was born as India…* and so on. Sure Miki, I like a little history, but let's go farther back.

~

Alpha began with the second birth of Adam in a manger, a birth accompanied by the presence of a shimmering star. Also incense. Also myrrh. *Whatever that is.* After dispersing Nona's ashes into the Chesapeake Bay, I watched the Bible-thumpers perform apocalyptic monologues down by the Baltimore Harbor. A crowd gathered around men in cowboy boots and overalls, some in military fatigues with epaulets on their shoulders. Fat-hipped women in loose black jackets with their towheaded children waved placards: THE WAJES OF SIN ARE PAYED FOR IN BLOOD; REPENT YE SINNERS; GOD HATES SODOMITES. How could I not laugh?

~

A man in a brown bomber jacket and unkempt beard twisted into a single braid sprayed the air with his bile. With the King James firm as a knife in one hand, he stabbed at the faceless crowd.

~

Do not participate in those components of Satan's spiritual structure, in yoga, eastern religions, astrology, tarot cards, scientology, meditation, vegetarianism, vampirism, lycanthropy, public bathing, earth worship. Do not… and he went on… *Sinners…* and he went on… *Satan!* I had to laugh. Lunatics. They've been predicting the Apocalypse since the day their Messiah left the earth. They have their opinions and I suppose are entitled to their dumb beliefs. We choke on freedom!

The match extinguishes. I light another.

NINE

I am no lunatic. When I imagine the end, I picture cyclones. They jetty into the sky like drill bits into metal. Carbolic smoke, a profusion of mist creeps like black death, swallows up Sugarloaf Mountain, the doddery water tower across Deep Hole Road, and the two lean-to sheds on the outer edge of this property. The dark mist, like pharaoh's fog, seizes the outhouse with its broken roof, overwhelms the denuded apple orchard where Nona spent so much of her time and the Dutch barn where I spent so much of mine—*There you go again being melodramatic, Dutch.* So be it, Nona. So be it.

~

When the Apocalypse arrives they'll cancel Christmas. Gifts will remain unopened, prettied up in their silk bows and crispy wraps. Our computer systems might plummet into a shock of disorder. The clocks might cease ticking, or spin backwards, and fault lines might gape and swallow our coastlines whole. Giant waves high as Jericho's walls might wash the continents clean—*And the planes, Somerset?* Armand, planes might fall like shattered birds from the sky. Suspension bridges might plummet into the deeps where walls of brick, concrete culverts, water wheels, steel silos might wobble in the currents. Blackouts might plunge us in darkness so rich it turns us into cannibals. Nursing silent tumors, our financial systems might burst, and a general all encompassing putrefaction might spread through the world. That's what *they* say. *They* have passed their judgments. *They* say we are sinners and so deserve this end. Let the Four Horsemen ride over our ashen skulls. I have to laugh. Maybe I should be building an ark instead of fixing up this old house? Maybe I should have packed my bags for Eden long ago?

~

I won't paint my storm door with goat's blood, or is it the blood of a lamb? When the end finally comes, settles like a shroud over this county, I'll meet it shirtless and shivering. I will fling the front door open and say, *Come in!* I'll stand by the window and gaze upon a world slowly consuming itself, watching the giant fire tides burn this landscape clean. *So let it be written.* Let the grains in the hourglass trickle and raise their sandy heap. So let the sky split open. *So let it be done.*

TEN

My head hurts from thinking of the end and it hurts from the accident this afternoon. My '56 Mercury Montclair in mint green and cream, still sits in that ditch outside, its bubble roof flattened, safety glass cracked like a spider's web. The car flipped over once, exhaled, and then gave up its ghost. But by some miracle I'm still alive.

~

Like corpuscles in the back of an eye, one of the lenses of my progressives is fissured. My watch also shattered in the accident, the hands stuck at twelve and six. My nails look shattered, but that's how they always were. I have to laugh. A hot ache throbs in my left temple—a knot of heated blood. I return my glasses to my face. Let the broken world remain broken.

~

I light another match. With the match I light another Hemingway cigar. The smoke smells fine, the flavor nutty and bitter with hints of chocolate and leather. I know I shouldn't smoke, because of the asthma, but in spite of it I smoke. The attacks come in fits, a claustrophobia that feels like a caboose on my chest. I'll gasp for air, choking like a fish on land, then my fish-eye view of the world warps then shrinks to pinhole proportions, like a sheet of pinpricked stars. Nona would stroke my cheek when my chest seized up, minister a care that belonged more to pitying nurses than to wives. I forgive her. *Thank you, Dutch.* Now there's no sense in forbidding myself anything. I am too old to benefit from abstinence. Let's have a good time.

~

A good fire burns in the hearth, a fire I made with my own two hands, these hands, palsied, gone febrile from the cold. Suddenly I wish to roam the snow, build an igloo, perhaps a snowman, but there's time for that tomorrow.

I blow a cake of smoke. Slowly it curls like steam from a radiator. Suddenly I am tired and my body aches. My makeshift bed in the corner awaits, a roll up mattress, a patchwork throw, and a pillow. How it astonishes me that I am here, alive. Alone. My past also astonishes me. The fact I am witness to this winter and these ending times astonishes me. The fact that I managed to return to Drums all by myself, without a map, without a talking navigator, managed to return and carry out this final act of understanding, is an astonishment of the sincerest kind.

ELEVEN

I passed the last few days alone, reacquainting myself with the house. I ate. I slept. I made plans. This insouciance, bred from old age, is a type of work. I believe you have to reintroduce yourself to a house, flirt with it, walk through its empty rooms, climb its dusty stairs, palm its banisters, tap its cracked walls, softly stamp its floors. You have to get the sound and smell and feel of it inside you first. You have to approach it like a lost friend and then wait for it to tell you what it needs. What does it need? Everything. A new coat of paint just won't do. I believe this.

But now I am not alone. A boy sits in the corner of the bedroom, cross-legged like an Indian scout. A towheaded boy. Long limbs, long tapering fingers, nails like half moons and laced with dirt, as if he's been digging foxholes. Odd boy. His face glows white like a porcelain mask you see in Kabuki theatre. I am not sure how he got here. *Just sorta fell outta the sky, did ya?* He wears a gray hooded sweatshirt and his raggedy jeans are dirty and so are his sneakers. Where's his jacket? His mittens and scarf? He's a vampire. He's a werewolf. I have to laugh.

I found the boy in the barn, tucked in a corner of the loft. At first I thought him a mouse, issuing those soft scrabbling sounds of rummaging through paper. How long he'd been there I couldn't tell. For days he must have studied me flitting about the house like a lunatic, staring from the window, lighting matches.

It might be mid-afternoon. Maybe. I haven't checked in with Miki on the Bakelite. As the fire casts shadows across his face, he seems both young and old, an old man shrunken to the size of a twelve-year old boy. Now he rocks himself back and forth, mewls, the little lunatic. He's a boy made of white lightning, blue smoke, blue ice. I don't know. What I can confirm is this: Though the fire burns liquidly in the hearth, and the bourbon coats my belly in delicious heat, the boy's pale blue eyes chill. Now and again his throat pours guttural sounds. Now and again he pants like a dog in heat, licks his bottom lip. His eyes tear into me like a slowly spreading fire. I am sure I am not imagining him. No, I can't be sure.

Still not hungry?

He shakes his head no.

I don't know his name. He said he forgot his name. I don't know where he's from. He said he forgot where he came from. Having no concept of time, he said all he remembered was waking up on the banks of a waterway a few miles from here, said he scrabbled up an embankment, crossed fields where the shoots from some past harvest stood out of the iced earth like bent cables. Said he ran until his lungs hurt. Finding this house with its big sheltering tree, he said he hoped to find a home where people lived, a place where they served hot food and had the heater or a fire going. But he was scared when he entered. He heard someone talking to the dark and ran out. I had to laugh.

Flung into its own desolation, this house is far from a home. How the evidence of loss multiplies: The yard, hard as a sheet of marble, the driveway, an obstacle course of rocks and ruts and flutes like open graves, the rickety porch, the boarded-up windows, the peeling clapboards and the busted up barn, these are all signs that this house is far from a home.

Want a drink? I say, offering him my bottle.

He shakes his head no.

He's either a liar or an amnesiac or just playing games and I'm too drunk to call his bluff.

The future, I guess, he finally mumbled after I badgered him. *I guess I'm from the future,* and I found his statement agreeable.

You guess?

And you?

I guess I'm from the past.

Abandoned here in this old house, we are two time- travelers, the past and the future collided. I have to laugh.

He lifts himself from his spot and moves toward the fire. He moves in that somnolent way of sleepwalkers, delivered to me from a netherworld where children lost or abandoned roam about dreamily, move aimlessly, stuck on the notions of deliverance.

I had entered the barn to relive a memory. I had lit a match when I heard something scrabbling in the hayloft.

What the hell you doing here? I said when I saw him, and he touched his cheeks with both hands as if uncertain he was real. A golden forelock lay against his pale forehead like a question mark.

You deaf or just stupid?

I don't know, he said, wiping his lips with the back of his hand. His breath smelled fecal, of rotten mushrooms and damp rags. He stepped toward me and I stepped back but still he managed to touch my cheek. His fingers icy; hands smelled like cold, deluged earth. In the nervous light of that single match, his eyes, so shimmering, so blue, seemed like coruscating stars. Eyes of a murdering angel.

I don't know how to get home.

Did I see contrition on his face, shame, guilt? I would like to think so, giving him the benefit. A scab the size of a finger curled down the right side of his temple, a raised scar hardened there like the glistening consistency of strawberry jam.

Know how you got here?

No.

Don't know much, do you?

No, sir.

Come on up to the house and I'll fix you something to eat, I said. You'll catch your death down here. Come on up to the house where it's warm.

Thinking back, this statement may have been a malignant joke on my part, because the house was far from warm. The boy brushed past me then. My body trembled. A transference of cold. His body emanated cold and his clothes were cold and sodden and he smelled as if freshly fished from the sea.

Now when I talk, the boy makes no motion I can interpret as understanding. Just shakes his head no. No. Refusal. Is this insolence? All he does is stare. How he stares. Into me. Through me. Like I'm some spirit dredged up from Nescopek. There's something vaguely familiar about him, though, someone you see in a park, maybe crossing the avenue, or in line at the Quick Mart, someone who you swear you know. A doppelganger. You snap your fingers in the air as they pass, cluck your tongue, search the pavement or the sky, attempting to place them. You might even blurt out a name, *Jimmy? Burt? No, Fenrus. Fenrus, is that you?* No and No and No. *My mistake. I apologize. I'm just a sentimental old fool.*

Maybe I've seen his face on the side of a milk carton, on a flier for a lost or missing child tacked to a lamppost? *Call anytime, day or night—* I can't be sure.

Now and again he coughs into his fist. Is he ill? That's all I need, a sick boy to tend to when there's so much to do. Is he shamming? He won't let me get close enough to check. He keeps his distance. I keep mine. We don't trust each other. Fair enough.

Like to hide do you?

He shakes his head no.

I rub the head of a matchstick with my fingers. Smooth as an egg. Now and then the boy trembles as if afflicted with some paroxysm. But the room feels warm. The fire is a good fire. The room smells like apple-scented, hickory smoke, courtesy of Lottie or Leda or Lena's fire-logs. Now and again the burning wood issues terrific squeals. Those are water bubbles trapped in the wood. I sip from the bottle.

Must be hell not knowing who you are.

He shakes his head no.

I light the match. The flame spurts. Holds. Cupping the flame in my hand I say, Cole used to hide. One time we found him in the stove, tucked up in the oven like he was a Christmas roast. I'd walk past that Home Comfort and what I thought were mice scrabbling around was actually my son. I'd pull him out by the arm. Stand him up straight in front of me. Get set to give him a tongue lashing. Then he'd look at me with his sad little face gone pathetic at having done something he wasn't supposed to, big brown eyes welling up with tears, face smudged like a little coal mine canary, and I'd start to laugh.

The boy coughs into the crook of his elbow. Now and again he clears his throat. The match flame fizzles. I pocket the stick.

Hear what I said?

The boy shakes his head no.

I light another match. It spurts. Holds. I snap my fingers, Hey! The old annoyance rises up in me. Hey! I clench my jaw. Let's get something straight, I don't like being ignored. When I say something, you say something, okay? And don't look at me like I'm a ghost or some crazy old fool.

Does he nod? Does he raise his head?

I don't like complainers, so don't complain if it's too cold. I'm not your grandpa. Don't like laziness, late sleepers, so when I say get up you get up. And don't ever talk to me about the weather, or your health, or sports, or dreams, or routes, like how you got here and what the traffic was like. No one cares. Don't talk to me about money, like how much you have or haven't got; it's crass talk. And while I'm on it, I hate TV commercials, hip-shaking, foot-stomping, screechy music. I hate love stories, war romances, none of that Ernest Hemingway crap, or modern dance and all that. Don't like politicians or psychologists and don't trust people who don't say "please" and "thank you." That is to say, I hate rudeness. I hate gluttons, vain people, angry people, loud people, and salesmen. How I hate salesmen. I hate religion. I don't like clowns, slapstick comedy, mobile phones, fast cars. I don't like the homeless. Don't like monkeys that clap cymbals, nor ships in bottles, nor modern cars, snot and nose pickers, sloppy dressers and sloppy eaters. Know what I hate most? Little boys who sulk in the corners of dark rooms who can't remember their names.

You talk funny.

The match fizzles. I pocket it. Though the boy's harrowed expression makes him appear angry, and anger makes him seem old, and though he breathes, a rasp that sounds like the scrape of saw-teeth raked through heartwood, the collapsing darkness between us erases the shape of his breath. But not its smell. I can smell his teeth.

How'd you get here again? I ask.

You first.

TWELVE

It takes three and a half hours to get from Baltimore to Drums, three and a half hours, give or take, and one hundred and eighty-five miles on three different expressways. On the 309 Turnpike, I kept the radio on and my driver's side window cracked open, this despite the chill in the air. The seeped-in air held that familiar density of memory, despite the cold, or perhaps because of it, because Luzerne's air is unlike any other. Its cold possesses a kind of attitude, like its heat.

I thought these thoughts while driving here, glancing at the dash now and again where I kept a collage of Cole in various stages of youth. Here he smiled. There he laughed. There, he cried or looked meditative. *Thanks for taking me along, Pops.*

Hadn't I promised you a family trip one year on the Loneliest Road, clear across the country? And what a journey that would have been. A family on the open road, travelers finding adventure in every small town we happened upon. We would stop at diners and eat our fill of Southern fried steak and eggs, walnut pancakes, buttermilk biscuits slathered with white gravy, watery eggs, and we would love it, love those aromas of bacon fat and coffee and air tinged with cigarette smoke. We would take in the Sears Tower, the St. Louis Arch, cut through Kansas' sunflower fields. We would fill up at service stations where a guy looking as if made of battered tin would come out of the station's shadows and pump your gas, wash your windows with a towel, perhaps wax poetic about the weather and the prices of things. He'd fill your tires with new air and smile his beatific smile as we set off again, journeying toward clay pueblos in the red desert, lulled by the evening heat and the glorious sunsets over the Grand Canyon. *That was another broken promise, Pops.* One of many, Son. We never left Drums.

As I drove, the tires humming over salted asphalt, the sense of nostalgia for a life never quite past held me suspended in a warp of time, the memories of home rising to the surface and ever-present, like shadows ever-present even on sunless days. If I closed my eyes, I might have felt myself tunneling backwards through time.

As I drove, I wondered how much of the old house remained? Would it still be there, or had that giant oak finally collapsed the house to a pile of sticks and shingles? Had the forest's roots finally pressed through the foundation, pulled down the walls? Had time and weather undone all those years of upkeep and repair when it was just you and your mother and I?

I paid the toll at the turnpike, three dollars in quarters, nickels, and dimes, dropped them in the tollbooth operator's hand. He was a bourbon-skinned, black-bearded turban-type. *A Sikh, Pops.* A dour looking man. He reminded me of Shashi, the bearded bourbon-skinned man who sold me the Sunday Times in the Inner Harbor. Shashi, with his rosewater smells, incense, a good man, had traveled from Lahore to Baltimore with just a few coins in his pocket and the dream all immigrants dream: home ownership. A regular Horatio Algiers, Shashi had saved his money and sacrificed his time to provide for his family. He wanted to send his daughter to Harvard Law, but the girl was more interested in boys and fashion than in torts and compensation. A decent man, Shashi Singh. Salt of the earth.

I tented my hands at the toll booth operator as Shashi had taught me to do, and said, *Namaste.* The man flashed me a smile full of the warmth of ancient suns.

Sat Sri Akal.

I smiled back and said, *Back atcha.*

Shashi left Baltimore and returned to India after the attack on the Twin Towers. Beaten to an inch of his life by black boys who thought him a Muslim, a case of mistaken identity or ignorance, or a combination of both. So much for that dream. Over the decades, I have learned that one bad group of people doesn't damn an entire race or religion, though I would like to tell them all that their God is a lie.

Shall I go on?

No answer.

I'll go on.

Driving north, the forests occluded a view of the whitened fields. The trees, though denuded, formed thick nets that trapped darkness so furtive you could cup it in your hands. Miles later I passed a clearing in the woods. Redwoods torn from their roots, flung like broken matchsticks a thousand feet in every direction. Was this prologue to the End of Days? How storms settling over Luzerne always attacked with fury, summer *derechos* poured their rain and wind, winter blizzards pummeled mighty oaks, forcing the blue maples to shed early their summer crowns. By spring, what remained of the fallen trees and upended bushes was nothing more than things reduced to trembling. I pictured a grim-faced giant, face like Porter, Nona's conure, crushing oaks in its talons, scooping up the untilled earth, flinging barns over three counties to land crushed in hay bales, shattered in creeks.

In May of '85, a few weeks before Cole tried to set Christ Church on fire, just four months before he disappeared, no fewer than forty tornadoes swept through Luzerne. They ripped homes from their foundations and sent fence posts into the air like rockets. Entire grain silos formed of solid steel landed two counties away in tractor barns or silt-stirred ponds. Cole and Nona and I, and even Henry James and all of Nona's caged birds hunkered down in our bomb shelter for what felt like a year, but may only have been a few days. We sang songs in the rank darkness, while the birds nervously chittered in their cages. While Henry James sprawled on the floor, rested his chin on his paws and slept, I regaled us with stories that had neither beginning nor end, unfinished fables that began with *Once Upon a Time*, and ended with *Time Upon a Once*. Nona yawned and recited a story from her youth, of swimming in the Pacific with Robinson Jeffers' wife, and how the cold clamped onto her ankles like a vice. Cole played his guitar, hummed. He had a sweet voice, angelic even. We ate beans and soda bread with salted butter under the flickering lantern light, and later we lay in our bunk beds while the storm raged above. The shelter's lid vibrated in the wind, like a sheet of struck tin, and we felt the wind lowing through the concrete walls.

Pops, Cole whispered at me in the dark. *If you could do anything you wanted, what would you do?*

I'm doing what God intended me to do.

We didn't know then that Cole would leave us. It seemed we were a family then, finally. Maybe if I had answered him truthfully he wouldn't have vanished? If I had said, Son, I want to be an astronaut, like Buck Rogers who gets stuck out of time, maybe he would've laughed a little and maybe felt the word "father" was not something abstract, like the principles of meteorology, physics, the axioms of non-Euclidean geometry.

Ten miles from Harrisburg, I stopped to refuel at a service station. It stood at the entrance of a strip mall where a Gould's, an Ace hardware, and Sweetie's Diner stood separated by a parking lot the size of a small lake. After filling up, I cruised into a stall by the air and water pumps. Beneath the grocery store's plate glass windows stood a row of shopping carts in a trough. A sign there read WE CARE BECAUSE WE LIVE HERE TOO. Was that not the extent of compassion? What would the Indians have to say about that, some version of *do unto others*?

The pneumatic swish of the front doors accepted a mother and her daughter, both in matching outfits, yellow galoshes, gray sweatpants, gray sweaters, yellow scarves and knit caps, mittens. They passed by as if I were made of vapor. A police cruiser circled the parking lot. It flashed its lights and chirped its siren then shot off onto the expressway. I pulled a cart free from its queue, pushed it past a row of newspaper dispensers.

Each headline screamed the same scream: disaster, war, bloodshed, corporate greed. Violence makes people money. Journalism is a pessimist's franchise, trafficking in suffering for suffering's sake. Where there's no tragedy, they'll invent one; where there's no shadow, they'll create one. For once I'd like to see them write something pleasant, a human interest story, maybe a personal profile of a Regular Joe. But where's the money in that? Headlines make you feel like there's no good in the world, and maybe there isn't. They make you run to the church to put in your prayers to a God who's too busy trimming his cuticles.

Shall I go on?

No answer.

I'll go on.

White light poured down from the ceiling. Soft music. *Silent Night* sung by blue-eyed Bing. A few shoppers pushed carts down the aisles, lackadaisical expressions. Wheels squeaked and clicked and the glare off the linoleum looked about as harsh as the Day-Glo sun. The smell of baked bread, misted vegetables, and coffee. A wicked tang in the air like burning fruit. A yellow sign tented on the floor in the bread aisle said CAUTION, WET FLOOR. It showed a stick figure, slipping.

Everything can kill you. The elements, wind, water, sun, cold, heat, everything is dangerous, coiled to strike your heart. I entered the medicine aisle, surrounded by shelves of fever-reducing pills and cough syrups, diabetic foot creams and salves for insect bites, joint braces for sprained wrists and ankles, and wraps for bruised knees. They had every remedy, for everything from chronic flatulence to dry eyes, sleeplessness to foot odor, gum disease to earwax, but what about loss? Maybe St. John's Wort, maybe Stinging Nettle, maybe a cocktail of B-complex vitamins and fish oils? They offered you power bars to build muscle, testosterone pills for a lazy libido, vitamin-infused water, lotions that promised to liquefy your skin, making it buttery soft and impervious to the harmful sun. They offered ointments for psoriasis, stress packs and fiber powders to regulate your bowels. Simple solutions to complex problems. Even the words of their Lord offered simple solutions: *Turn the other cheek. Love Thy Neighbor. Observe the Golden Rule.* I had to laugh. We are so weak, it's a miracle we survive at all. Even our laws are weak. Everything that holds us together is diaphanous as smoke.

There are no easy answers. Only deep questions. There are no packaged resolutions. Only mysteries. No time-release capsules can serve as a cure-all for what ails the human heart. I selected a bottle of Tylenol—*It's all that ever works, Dutch*—and moved into the liquor aisle.

I consulted it my Marble Memo. It's a mnemonic tool I picked up from Armand (he carries one, too). *In it you write down what you want to remember, no matter how trivial, and it'll help you trigger your memory,* he said, and I took him at his word. A four and a quarter by three and a quarter inch booklet bounded in a black marbled cover, it barely weighs an ounce. In it I collect samples of my life, snippets of conversations I hear, the descriptions of landscape, the colors of certain flowers whose names I like—hellebore, dragon's breath, larkspur—and the effects of the changing weather on my moods. I jot down people's qualities, their expressions, gait, sometimes bits of poems and interesting or mundane facts of this ending time. Everything manages to find its way in.

Research permits. Visit housing and planning. Choices of wood: maple for that apple core brightness; birch, darkly stained, that hints of Mexican chocolate—a Hershey's factory floor. Floor—engineered or laminate??? Look at Mullican Knob Creek, hand-hammered pine, Caesarstone vs. Silestone/Differences? and so on. You could almost sing it. A hidden cadence, an acoustical quality to the language, like a bird tapping rhythms on bark.

If I die. When. If someone finds me dead in the house, frozen solid in this bedroom, people might know certain facts of my life. They might know what Somerset buys and the things that occupy his brain. They will certainly know the price of coffee and chocolate donuts at Pinky's Mini-Mart last month. Perhaps, in an attempt to decipher him, they will speculate on the reasons why his handwriting drifts off the page mid-sentence, mid-word, mid-thought. What might they think? It is vanity on my part to think someone would care. *Vanity, vanity, all is vanity,* page 32.

Even now, as I sift through this house like a ghost, spilling my thoughts into the ears of this mute child, I think that, long after I'm gone, I'll have left traces of myself: A skin fiber left on a bus seat here, a stray white follicle there, bits of me drifted down from my scalp to the pavement, thrown by a hot wind into a corner to collect in a heap with bottle shards and brick dust, plastic candy wrappers and globules of snot, *because we leave traces of ourselves.* A droplet of my sweat misted off my weathered arm in a summer heat wave might have mingled in the humidity, inhaled by a newborn boy pushed along by his mother in a stroller down the pathways of Federal Hill. My cells of skin might at this moment be adrift in the atmosphere over Drums, settling on the faces of bare leaves, shaken loose by winds, only to be consumed by a cricket. If only you could collect those random bits together and reassemble them, what would emerge out of the bits and scraps of my discarded matter but an abomination?

Is that your sniveling little laugh? Shall I go on?

No answer.

I'll go on.

The scribble that fell off the page told me nothing about buying liquor. *Buy multi-grain wheat bread,* it said. *Buy denture tabs. Mints.* Imperatives. Sure as the sky is starry, it was my handwriting, though I barely recognized it. Now large and loopy and messy where it used to be so elegant, so fine. *Buy long stemmed matches.* Who wrote those words? Some other Somerset for whom the need for disposable razors was more important than what was once the need for Nona's kiss. Who was this man who wrote, *It is sanctionable and right. Always be ashamed of being sad,* page 12. From where in the hell did he get that?

If my vision worsens (when), I'll have to read through a magnifying glass. *Buy Peter Pan peanut butter,* the list commanded. The list said something about grape jelly. I put away the notebook and filled my cart with things that seemed in keeping with the spirit of this ending time—four bottles of Maker's Mark, to keep my liver and lungs warm. Then I rolled down each aisle, filled the cart up at will.

The cashier who rang me up was a large-breasted woman, not quite a midget, but perhaps a dwarf (Lilliputian just the same). I adjusted my progressives and took her in. She sat before the register on a high-backed swivel stool. A mole above her left nostril looked as if a fly had landed there. Obese, she eyed me up and down with her heavily painted eyes. You should've seen her. Her thin lips, no more than lines, and painted a garish tangerine. I emptied my cart.

Welcome to Gould's, she said, her voice small and grating, as if she were speaking through a voice box.

A blonde permanent, generously rouged cheeks, a wattle figuring prominently beneath her chin. Her hunter green eye shadow, generously applied, faded expressively into electric blue. Her blue irises sparkled as if with flecks of glass. Pretty eyes. Thick lashes. Fakes. Some women have no concept of vanity, turning makeup into a mask. I felt suddenly sad for this woman, Lottie or Lonnie or Leda. I wanted to throw a bucket of water over her head.

Two by two, I placed the items on the conveyer. One by one, her small, portly paw slid them over the swath of electrified black glass without any respect for time. The register beeped like a heart monitor.

Gettin' yerselves ready for the blizzard, she said.

Beep.

Is that what it looks like? I said. You are what you appear to be, I thought. You are the image you project onto the world. You are hand lotion, hair color, eye cream that promises to reduce the black half-moons beneath your eyes, and you are your calloused hands, your painted fingernails in those shades of fuchsia, burnt umber, corvette red, and you are your waxy lipstick, and your ashy breath, and you are the discount clothes you wear that smell of cramped, dusty rooms—shoulder wraps and shawls and sweaters dredged up from a discount basket in some second-hand store. You are the nylons that make your calves itch, leaving rashes behind your knees, and your heels that pinch your toes into a triangle.

Beep.

Where youse from?

Youse, I thought, plural, just as it ever was. Are there two of me, one invisible, that only small children and dogs, the insane and Lilliputians can see?

Nowhere, I said. *Everywhere.*

Ain't youse a funny guy.

Been known to be.

I had forgotten how they sound, Northeastern Pennsylvanians—that reedy mix of Pennsylvanian Dutch and Polish, an Irish up-tilt of the syllables, and that blend of English and Eastern European influence replete with small town kindnesses. Did I still sound like them, or had the two and a half decades of life in Baltimore turned me into a city man?

Beep.

Got family in town? she said.

None of your business what I got, missy, I said. *At Gould's We Care*, I thought. *Because We Live Here Too.* Suddenly I realized the assumption behind the phrase. *We do not care for those who don't live here.* Maybe all compassion is local, extending no farther than the borders of one's town. We limit our mercy. We limn our charity.

Don't stare, honey, said a voice behind me.

Beep.

That mother with her daughter in the matching outfits, who brushed past me at the entrance, had slid behind me without me noticing. The woman placed the rubber divider between my groceries and hers. The little girl stared up at me as if I were made of some other material than flesh and blood and bone, as if I were made of smoke or stone, straw or dust.

S'posed to be barrelin' down soon, the mother said to me. She smiled through fatigue. A worn face. A soft bruise fading against her right cheekbone. Her eyes looked swollen and I thought of Nona in those last few months, Nona, wracked with insomnia, like me, unable to remember, to relate to the meaning of her life.

The girl, her eyes large as saucers, held a bag of candy in her hands.

Can I please?

To my right, a tiered shelf of sundry mints and candies, cheery colored plastic bags of suckers, sugar corn, and Sen-Sens in a red packet. A blue bow-tie ran diagonally across the lower right hand corner. *Breathtaking Refreshment.*

Beep. Beep.

I loved those, Pops. The plastic bag crackled under the child's grip like fire and I thought of you, Cole. How you loved those braided bits that turned your whole mouth black, like you were chewing on a lump of coal, A *sugary bitterness that stains your tongue a lovely purple,* its radio commercial promised.

No, put it back, the woman said. *No, no, no!* you had said, some forty years before.

No, you can't have it, I told you.

Please?

No, Son. No.

I barely remember that, Pops. Surprised you do. You were four or five years old. Your mom unwell at home, nursing a headache. A migraine tearing up her vision. Lights off in the master. Curtains drawn. Nona moaning. A cold, wet towel draped over her forehead.

Sleep it off.

Get me a gun.

No painkillers in the medicine cabinet. Me, downstairs in the foyer. Me, bundling you in galoshes, a red sweater and a black scarf. Me, already in galoshes and a sweater and a scarf.

Later, on Butler Road, in the Mercury, swerving to miss a truck loaded with timber. Blaring the car horn.

Later, at IGA. Me, pushing a shopping cart with a squeaky wheel. You inside the cart, arms dangling out the sides. Passing a candy rack. You rip something from the shelf.

Stop.

This? You say, your eyes wide as saucers. *This?* An astonished expression on your face, the bag crackling like fire in your hands.

No.

Pleeze?

No.

I want it.

You splash to the floor. You fold over at the waist and bang your head against the floor so hard the cereal boxes rattle.

Stop it, I say, subduing momentary rage. Look at me, the picture of calm. *Stop.* I am refusal. *Stop it.* I am calm refusal. My refusal is a powerful force, I think. My refusal is a choice levied against what you want. You don't know it's not good for you. Don't know what's good for you.

I reach for you. You squirm away. You caterwaul. Your wail opens a wound in the air, tears holes in space, shreds time. My top lip beads with sweat. Waves of heat pass down my back. Heat circles my neck. Heat flushes my face. So I unfurl my scarf.

Shake him, choke him, throw him through the wall of cereal. Kill him. These are not the thoughts a father should think. He's my son, my child, my baby. What kind of father thinks such things?

Papa, I want it!

You'll split your skull open. You'll kill your brain cells. You'll be no better than a turnip. *Come on, Cole,* I say, my voice barely above a whisper, gentle as if coaxing a monster from its cave.

You writhe, all muscle and bone. It's like handling a shrieking piglet. Your mouth roars. You laugh when I buy you the candy. Diamond-shaped droplets on your cheeks on the way home. You laugh and hum and suck and chew the candy. By the time we reach home, your tongue is already black.

Maybe it was then that you figured out something about me, little as you were, that if you dug your heels in deep enough, you could get what you wanted. And maybe I discovered something too. That if I were not careful, I could easily turn into my father.

Beep-Beep.

Mister, you gettin' those or what? said the cashier, Lulu or Layla or Lottie. The world snapped back. How long had I stood there, staring into space like a lunatic?

What's my damage?

I paid her then left.

Shall I go on?

The boy shrugs.

I'll go on.

Crossed the parking lot. Lay the groceries in the Mercury's backseat. Sank myself into the driver's side, lit a Hemingway, opened the day-old Sunday Times. EIGHT YEARS AFTER TSUNAMI, VICTIMS FORGOTTEN. A photo of a Ceylonese woman, her head wrapped in a black tunic, dark face knotted in grief, seemed the very definition of agony. She had lost everything in the tidal wave. Two tears, like thin black braids, crept from her eyes and collected in her frown lines. Images of the disaster: Hulking waves fifty stories high, soupy rich, thick with detritus—lampposts, cars, cows and pigs, all the bric-a-brac of civilization hurled toward the mainland. A goat's horns bored deep into the flesh of a shark. A tiger rolled in water the color of cinders. Hundreds of thousands dead and this poor woman's entire family among them. Even after eight years the losses were still being measured.

How did one go about measuring innumerable lost livelihoods, measuring displacement, measuring devastation? Where would you begin? What tools? What words had the Hindus or Muslims or Christians, Buddhists, and all for *that* quantity and quality of suffering? Was suffering still a form of *maya*? Did calling something an illusion rob it of its weight? Even if you could measure them, the losses could yield no statistical fruit. You could measure facts: hundred-foot waves raging across the Indian Ocean at over five hundred miles per hour, bending freighters in half like paperclips, plunging steel hulks tall as five-story buildings to the bottom of the deeps, damning them to rust. Perhaps.

Crazy Natty Nussbaum might blame this woman for her suffering. *She didn't have the right faith*, she might say. *Prayed to a false god.* Maybe the Bible-thumpers down on Constellation Avenue, stabbing the air with their misspelled placards, would call this woman a sinner. Perhaps they would say she deserved her loss. Look how merciful is *our* God, they might say, sparing this woman's life just to teach her a lesson on the Almighty's immeasurable power.

It's the survivors that matter. My true kin. Each tick of time, each intake and outtake of breath, perpetuates their losses a thousandfold.

Staring at the woman's picture, I had to believe there was some reason for her loss, that her suffering was not in vain. But maybe there wasn't and we are fools to believe there is.

Pressure built up behind my eyes. I swallowed hard against it. I wanted to reach into the photograph and hold that woman in my arms and whisper to her, *You're not alone. We can draw strength from each other.* I turned the page.

Famines. Tsunamis. Cyclones. Hurricanes. Earthquakes. Terrorists. Planes plummet into our towers, raining bodies onto the pavement a thousand feet below. Gunmen, fueled by insanity and warped ideology, enter our kindergartens and spray our children with bullets. Has the End of Days not already come? Still the faithful pray to Him and beg for miracles of salvation. What do they get in return except pithy expressions of promises of Heaven through The Golden Rule. *Prove yourselves,* He demands. *Follow My Commandments and obey My Eternal Laws,* He orders. *Observe the imperatives of My Holy Will.* It's a cosmic joke. *Sounds like what I once told you, Pops.*

I told Armand once that when it was my turn to finally meet Him (if He exists), I would convene a hearing on behalf of all the innocent dead. I would collect everyone who had died meaningless deaths—babies of dysentery, malaria, or famine, those belly-bloated children pecked by vultures in some godless African desert, and schoolchildren sucked into tears in the earth from Indonesian earthquakes, and mothers swept into flooding rivers—and I would subpoena God for His crimes.

God, I adjudicate You guilty? I would say, slamming down my gavel. *Where were You when innocents died? While a sniper's bullet tore through the skull of a little girl playing with a bicycle tire in the streets of Tel Aviv, where were You but grooming Your beard? Paring Your fingernails? When that 747 exploded over the coast of Northern Ireland, hurling bodies into the sea, where were You but fattening Yourself on our misery? Did You unleash Your furies, Your heat waves and floods, Your earthquakes and tsunamis, just to make us see one another again?*

Drawing on my Hemingway, I turned back to the front page, gazed deeply into the weeping eyes of that woman, her skin ruddy and leathery from the sun, and I traced with my finger her expression of absolute grief—knees crushed into a silver beach, ashen sands littered with the detritus of people's tragedy. Though I couldn't speak her language and she couldn't speak mine, loss connected us. We existed on an equal plane, as securely linked to one another as did all those anonymous sufferers stretching into history. Was that the point of God's retribution, that is, to bind us once again? Was *that* the point of suffering on such a grand scale? How You must enjoy watching us scream and drown and bleed? Do You laugh at us? Do You laugh?

A tear fell without my consent onto the page, spread like a bruise over words that held no sense. If the spiny fingers of loss could reach us even in Drums, where the air on certain days was so still and so rich with chlorophyll that even the slightest breeze was a gift, and if loss could do more than merely tap us on the shoulder, it could reach into our very chests and crush our hearts, then what hope did the rest of humanity have? We are born losing, time, cells, memories. But is our suffering due to God's retribution for *our* sins? *Sins, Pops? What sins?*

I folded the paper up and set it beside me on the empty seat. I jammed the key into the ignition, kissed my palm then touched each picture of Cole stuck to my dashboard. Cole's eyes, rich with false life, his expressions, smiling, victorious, somber, naughty, his gestures, his poses, leaning against the Scout like James Dean, staring into empty space, reinforced in me the desire to change the old house.

The sky looked like boiled ash as I entered the onramp. A police cruiser's lights spun far out ahead.

THIRTEEN

Secrets kill us. No? Not ready to talk? No? All right. I'll say you don't have to pass through Hazleton to get to Drums. Could take the 81N direct. Drive past the Lebanon/Shuylkill border, pass Vulcan Hill Road, pass Laurel Junction to Route 81N till you cross the Schuylkill/Luzerne County line, then take the 424 to the 309 turnpike into Hazleton. Routes are lives. You travel their lengths and through their circuitous turns and bends, you create a life. The ever-changing routes change you.

Approaching White Haven, I passed cliffs of crimson-hued rock, like the marbled red of sliced beef, and that was surprising, never believing our hills yielded red schist. How much of Drums still existed, or did it exist only in memory? Passing ponds frozen like glass, I slipped into Hazleton.

You felt your arrival in the air. There's a slowness to things, some faint transition in attitude. Even the birds seemed slightly altered, confused, indecisive, turning toward a branch then turning back. People brake softly here, speed down the street only to return to their houses. They use their turn signals. They yield their right of way. Politeness is a gift.

Soon I would pass Downtown Joe's, where the beer taps always suffered from faulty pressure. At Friendly's Ice Cream parlor, you could coma yourself on a banana boat sauced with chocolate, and at

Leader Store Luncheonette, you could order up thickly cut French fries doused with malt vinegar. Lounging at the Top Spot you could sip a Yuengling from a chilled mug, so that the frost steamed up the sides. Strike up a talk at Jim Perry's while you fetched a paper, you could, and skedaddling into Pietro's for their world famous pepperoni pie, you could turn your kidneys to stone. Where was Jelly's Donuts? Where was Uriah Weaver's Ford dealership and Big-Jay McClain's tire store, where Jay himself, in his candy-striped suspenders, treated the locals to a secret sale?

Hazleton, Pennsylvania's highest city, city of failed dreams, named for the hazel bushes that sprouted in the hills. Hazleton's "magic" anthracite once fed the furnaces of the steel mills in Bethlehem, New Castle, the big Carnegie mills in Pittsburgh. Hazleton's industry forged the steel girders and suspension cables of the Brooklyn Bridge, the Golden Gate, fueled the formation of the steel beams and iron trellises that raised the Empire State. A misspelling turned it into "Hazleton" instead of "Hazelton." The details are important. You'll see.

Broad Street, a terrific spine stretching north to south, emptied into the nervous system of the city's outer limits or spilled down into the valley. Choked with disappointment, the city, drab and in perpetual decline, even the air here smelled bankrupt. Wind, gelid, howled down pavements, scattering plastic bags, rolling silica into gutters choked with bottles and cans and shards of glass. The wind in the empty lots swirled disenchantments as easily as dead leaves. There was that sense of defeat spilling onto church stoops, defeat riding the backs of subzero air, defeat dragging down the light. I drove on.

To whom did these city grids now belong? Who owned the clapboard row houses, the city buildings tilting up to the long, lean afternoons, the five and dimes? On North Broad Street, a car beside me honked. I turned toward it. It was as if looking through an ice block. A blurry face mouthed something. I threw up my hands in a gesture, *What do you want?* The figure pointed up. It was like trying to decipher an alien language. The light was green.

I drove past a row of sparse trees supporting, it seemed, crenellated walls of brick, and pockmarked false fronts that had stood for a hundred years. Sunlight swirled beneath shop doors laden with frost. Torn ribbons hung from empty windowsills. A stray dog, its ribs like piano teeth, trotted down an alley. I am witness to a failed dream. I am witnessing the loss of hope. Who could blame Cole for leaving? *See what I mean, Pops?* The failed returned swathed in the kind of disappointment that distorts a soul beyond recognition, and Hazleton had warped them, enfolded them into her mouth like a Venus flytrap, decomposing their bodies as much as their dreams. The failed hoarded familiarity like warmth, pieced together the fragments of their former lives like picture puzzles with half the pieces missing. You would buy them a round of suds at Shenanigans and sit back and listen: *It wasn't my luck*, they'd say. *Times ain't like they was, when a bootback or any fool with an idea could make something of himself.* You leave Hazleton, either in death, or in war, or because having nothing left to lose, you might as well go. *Might as well.*

What would Ardo Pardee say of his beloved city? Would he blush at what it had become? On streets where the Carnegies and Mellons, Rothschilds and Rockefellers once strolled, picking bits of duck comfit from their teeth, their pretty daughters and pretty sons skipping over the pavements ahead of them, what would they think? My hope for Cole was his transcendence, that he might transcend the limitations of this city and make it great for us, for all of us. I drove on.

Now came the great outcropping of stick houses and frame houses, colonials, gothics, those row houses surrounded by institutions in stone and steel, crosses of brass or gilded in gold. A city of churches. Religion comprised Hazleton's genetic code. But it was wrestling and football the city and its citizens truly worshipped. Those were some great battles between Eddie Koloski's Wildcats and the Bulldogs. It was a dream of mine to see Cole as a star player. *Jesus, Pops, that stuff wasn't for me.*

Then came shops lit from within. A harsh light, neon or fluorescent. Plate windows displayed words in a foreign script, Spanish, Korean, Chinese. Restaurants advertised fried, oily fish, their snow-dusted tables crushed against ochre walls. Packets of sauce lay mashed, scattered on the sidewalk like black blood. People milled about the pavement, their breath steaming, some huddled in a bus stop. Down a lonely alley a transient tore apart a corrugated box. I drove on.

I took a left onto Elm Street. A quiet street. Frame houses, boxy colonials and clapboard ranchers. Strapped to one another, each structure seemed to support the next in its misery, chained to the other like a long concatenation of defeat. Forced togetherness here, one borne out of an embarrassment of confusion, or egalitarianism of the worst kind: the equality of sameness. No one had anything left to impart, nothing to bequeath, except to serve as mirrors of paucity. Their pocked walls and slim porches protected mediocrity, in fact stockpiled it. Shameless, rectangular yards, ordered with spindly hedgerows, divided one property from the next—such permeable borders.

On a house, much like mine, faded yellow paint clung to the clapboards like jaundiced skin and dead vines spilled from pots dangling from rafter beams by wires. In the yard of a house with a façade of brick, a tricycle lay upended in the coppery weeds. Life was thin here. Life looked leeched of weight, of color. Flag posts stood empty. Trees had withered and flowerbeds had withered, and even the once great oaks looming over once proud streets seemed as if in the throes of decline. If the pavements could talk, they would scream through their cracks. Even the dead branches stuck to trellises would scream. Even the light would scream. Complaint. Provocations. Cavils. It hurt me to look at windows like weeping eyes. It hurt me to consider I demanded Cole inherit this. What would Cole say? I knew what he would say. *I said it.*

The boy sneezes.

Bless you. Do you want a hankie? No? Very well. Just don't wipe your nose on your… sleeve. Animal.

At the intersection of Polar and Broad, a billboard advertised English lessons for Spanish speakers. A white woman held a Spanish girl in her lap. Both were smiling. *What a man needs to recreate himself is a new grammar,* Armand once said. That could be applied to places, too. Give Hazleton a new grammar and she'll spring to life again. Return her misspelling to her original name, and she'll glow with possibility. But who would do it? Where were Hazleton's great thinkers, its great musicians and composers, its artists, its architects? Which poet would dignify it? Long before Athens laid the foundations for our modern physics, Constantinople was once the seat of learning, possessing the greatest library in the ancient world. Where were Hazleton's storied music halls, opera houses, the sanctified public spaces, the museums and parks and pleasure gardens? Where was that bastion to cosmopolitanism I had convinced myself of? No schools of great reform sprang from Hazleton's soil. Work and working, suffer and suffering, redemption in the grave, the city existed on those principles.

I drove past empty schoolyards, gray as wet cement, and turned right at a stop sign swirled with graffiti, re-entered North Broad going the wrong way. *You're a hellion, Pops.* Rolling down my window, cold air poured in, flat and sour, like curdled milk. A car swerved to miss me, its horn blaring. I grinned. A van swerved to my right, ran the curb. I swerved to avoid hitting a commuter bus, then turned a sharp right onto a side street.

Up ahead was a construction zone. The rake of machines, men hammering metal, a crane whined. I passed men in neon yellow vests, hard hats, eyes grim from the winter. Words could lose themselves in this tangled noise. Ideas could falter. I stuck my elbow out the open window as if it were summer, pushed down hard on the gas pedal and ran the Yield sign. Someone shouted *Hey!* I accelerated, coveting greater danger, a collision, the slip of tires on black ice, coveting death, each block I drove I coveted greater and greater risk.

Reaching Top of the 80s, the junction of 80 and 81, the intersection like a great tributary at the Old Warrior's Trail, I shot through the traffic light. Horns bellowed. Tires shrieked. Hidden behind the marbled clouds the sun, flattened, shone like a bulb behind a reflector screen, and behind walls of shimmering fog, stretched the silent Poconos. The valley, bordered by the overflow from the sky, tilted upwards to the flat-topped hills where miles deep in the earth and perhaps impossible to reach, lay an ocean of anthracite.

Speeding down the hill—*slow down Dutch, slow the hell down*—down the long left-leaning switchback—*faster, Papa, faster*—I turned down the lazy right hand chicane, grinned at the thought of fishtailing, colliding against a redwood old as Jacob Drum's grave. A wild gust shook the Mercury's roof, wild air with the metallic wetness of cold, air bombastic, choked with the rime gliding off the spruce trees. Riding a road into a woodsy tunnel, I was reaching home.

FOURTEEN

I'll tell you that Woods Path lane and Rock Glen Road were names of streets I once knew. Not now. Not for a long time now. I drove half-remembering things. A rusted water tower flashed in my mind. The glistening black waters of Big Nescopek Creek, fireflies glittering over Whispering Pines Park, the winking fields of kale wet with dew, all flashed in my mind like coruscated starlight. Laughter rolled into air hardened by smoke. Glass shattered. The quick movement of feet tramped over Missy Petrovich's azaleas. That was a day I found Cole walking by the roadside, a mile or so from the Conyngham Historical Society, his face wet. His eyes shimmered like sparkles in creek water.

Need a ride?

Hi, Papa.

Edges of Cole's photos fluttered in the open breeze—*Papa, I can see our house from here and Mama says there's a bird that can remember faces.* A crow sailed high above a frozen pond on my right, reflecting the ashen sky. Pine scented air kissed my face, this air minted from new snow. Everything rang vibrantly as a plucked string.

A new shopping plaza on Route 93 surprised me, its gleaming windows incised into red brick. Further along, several old businesses were boarded up, their roofs ripped away, their entrances posted with *No Trespassing* signs—*Forgive those who trespass against us*—and that surprised me too. The Bank and Trust was gone. IGA Grocery had changed to Safeway. A new Mobil service station. A new insurance building. A new law firm—Fishbone and Scheer, LLC. A new this, a new that. Where were the familiar markers of home? Where was Vesuvio's? Gennaro's Deli? What had become of Casey Pulaski's Trading Post?

A man with an enormous backpack tramped down the shoulder. He looked beaten from the cold, his face ruddy, hair matted and beard wet. Ahead of him trotted a mangy dog, thin as a goat. I thought of Pearl and me adrift, living like mendicants. I conjured the culverts we slept in, the doorways of churches whose wood in the late winter reeked of sweet flowers and those empty days of starvation when I ate mud for dinner and Pearl stole apples from a fruit cart or loaves of sour bread or picked through trash bins for scraps—*Being poor means God forgives your thefts, Somerset.* There were nights when we walked the miles in silence where the landscape never changed. *Did we see that tree already, Ma? Is that the same pile of rocks, Ma?* She filled my head with stories then, myths of ancestors. *Somerset, you were named after the great Iroquois warrior Somerset True Feather.* Lies. We had nothing but tales to tell one another, nothing more than the stars to guide us by. Our movement across unknown valleys on unnamed trails we filled with songs and our songs reached the heavens and altered the universe and those melodies returned to us, rained upon us in the clatter of night birds, fireflies, bee swarms, the shrill of crickets. We slept in ruined barns. Sometimes a ditch cradled us, or a Cypress tree's moss-laden roots. We nested beneath the starry blackness.

I veered onto the shoulder, set my parking brake and sat. How had I come to embrace the sedentary life? How was it that I came to call Drums home? When I dreamt of Pearl, I dreamt of motion, peripatetic motion, slow, insufferable motion. Before returning to Drums, long after Pearl's fire burned up half the woods, an event launching us into the world like two fugitives, Pearl and I traveled from town to town, city to city, living off the land. When we dried up the earth's hospitality, we moved on. Pearl found work occasionally, wherever she could, at the Hershey Factory packaging chocolates one year, at the Yuengling factory stirring the beer vats another year. Accused of petty larceny we moved on. We were always running, from people, from place to place, from town to town, suffering hunger and thirst and inclemency of weather—drenching storms and whiteouts so fierce they made our cheeks febrile and our hands numb. *Let's go somewhere warm,* Pearl would say, her teeth chattering and her knees knocking, and I would nod yes. Running her bony fingers through my brittle hair, she would say, *I'm turning you into a snow boy.*

Mama, maybe we can go south for the winter, like the birds do? And she would nod yes.

The vagrant with the backpack and mangy dog approached my window and said something and I waved him away. I had no time for him. He pushed on ahead, turning once to regard me with eyes less furious than sad. Where would he go? What would he do? What did I care? Everyone makes his own life.

Pearl and I entered towns whose names sounded as if invented, places composed of a few ramshackle buildings and a general store: Firetown, Connecticut; Monks Misery, Maryland; Hell Hollow, New Hampshire; Little Heaven, Delaware; Neversink, Pennsylvania. Outcast. Free. Adrift, caught in a tide of discovery and wonder, we traveled up the eastern coast.

Like a knife into butter, you pass into these towns, step through their quaint village streets, their bedroom communities, converse with people unknowing of their own history. An old man at a bus stop might relay tales of minor drunks who lofted to mayorships, then ask politely for a dime. *The world is a book and those who do not travel read only a page.* Buildings, clapboard, or brick; homes, Georgian Revival or Queen Anne; inns and cottages, Victorian or Colonial or Stick; general stores, Cape Cod or Prairie or Mission; even these simple structures, though pulled together by careful haste, meant something more than their increments. Let's say that in Hartford, I learned about the Dutch settlers, or let's say that in Kennebunkport, Pearl and I ate snow cones on the gray beaches during summer. At Nathan's in Coney Island, we sauntered up and down the sea-starched boardwalk, eating stolen frankfurters slathered with spicy mustard and kraut and pickles whose tang puckered our lips. Chewing stolen saltwater taffy, we watched the white sailing boats bobbing across the blue-black harbor and we wondered how much of the world we would never know.

We hitchhiked turnpikes, climbed into pickup beds whose straw reeked of pigs. Once we walked south to East Virginia, rode on a tractor into North Carolina, then a mule-driven cart piled up with chicken cages into Myrtle Beach. The smell of water intensified as we walked, slaked with thirst, followed the camber of dirt roads arching into spruce forests where the trees looked like ash—ash forests where porcelain streams riffled through dense groves, where even the birds angrily shot from the trees like bullets. By night we bivouacked in weedy clearings and in the morning we moved on, our soles eaten away by the roads. We found outposts in towns with unpronounceable names, Punxsutawney, Towamensing, Wyalusing. If history had been written by the powerless, then Drums might have been Kanatio or Teueikan or Mistikwaskihk, and it's only the legacy of Jacob Drum that it wasn't.

Back then, if the word "family" had any meaning it meant "duality." Family meant Pearl and me. If the word "Mother" had any meaning it meant movement. We were never still, it seemed; no, we were never still. I set my blinker and turned back onto the main road.

The match fizzles. I toss it aside and light another. Shall I go on?

If you want.

When the dark thickened around me, it was toward Pearl I directed my light.

Mama, why can a boat float when a coin can't?

'Cause, beneath the boats there's balloons keepin' them up.

Mama, who made the Lord and why did He make us, and when will the sun stop shining?

Slow down, slow down. One at a time.

How come birds can fly and we can't?

'Cause in their wings they got magnets that pull in the wind.

Mama, why'd we leave home?

Home ain't a place. Home's a journey.

Walking across railroad tracks somewhere, nowhere, Pearl put her ear to the rails and held her head there and said, *Listen,* and I would listen to the dim vibrations in the metal. We felt the train before we heard it, heard it before we saw it. Gouts of smoke. Black billows. We would run down an embankment, throw ourselves behind bushes and watch train cars stuck to rail cars in a long concatenation of clatter and brash. Faces peered out of windows, women in bonnets and children in sailor's hats and men with long waxed mustaches. In dinner cars, couples sat at white linen tables, regal-looking men and fancy-looking women sipped tea and ate biscuits by candlelight. Once I saw a boy my age, who might've even looked like me, and I wondered how many versions of me were there? I imagined that somewhere in the world there existed another version of me, a rich little Somerset who enjoyed all the benefits of affluence, a boy whose image mirrored my own in every detail right down to the teeth. He rode horses and sipped his hot milk from a marble cup and lived in a mansion. His life was attended to by servants and tutors. There were pleasure gardens, marble fountains, horse stables in which neighed champion stock. When I slept, I dreamt of woods I had never seen, clear waters whose surfaces I had never broken, blue hills and blue skies that I can only attribute to a shared consciousness. Sometimes I felt sweetness in my mouth but no sugar ever touched my tongue.

Mama, I asked her once, *Where was I born?*

You weren't. I found you beneath a willow tree up on Sugarloaf Mountain.

At the end of one long day, our march across the landscape accompanied by crickets tambourining in the trees, we walked on and kept walking through roads overhung with branches whose shade provided no comfort. We kept walking until one day we stopped. I am not sure where we were, between somewhere and nowhere when Pearl turned to me and said, *Time we headed back.* She turned around and walked back the way we came. It took us another month to return to Drums.

The match fizzles. I finger another.

As I drove through Drums, I was struck by a thought, that somehow *that* glade or glen or *that* copse of eucalyptus trees or even *those* clouds above, *those* bulging gouts of atmospheric pressure, I had idealized in a way that no sky ever was. The urbanite seeks in agrarian spaces his own Eden. He scents the attitude of labor in hewn stone, cut planks. In the stink of hogs and cattle, in the sour liquors of fertilized earth, he witnesses the evidence of true life. *What's true, Pops? what their God tells 'em? You gotta laugh.* A farmer's chapped hands return him to a past where men owned their work and took pride in it. A man's chapped face lures him closer to his primal condition. His sore back provides evidence of virtue.

I light the match. I draw on my Hemingway. Sip from my bottle. The boy picks at a crack in the wall with his fingernail.

And what did *you* see when coming here? Did you see those signs nailed to the same old trees that offered old warnings—BEWARE OF BLACK ICE, DEER CROSSING, NO HUNTING—and did those feel like a welcome surprise? That's right, you can't remember. For me they did. They were words to cling to. Seeing them was like remembering faces you hadn't seen in decades. I almost waved to them. Almost said, "Hello." I rolled up my window finally, my arm already smarting from the cold.

You drive on?

I drove on, over a cantilevered car bridge, its planks drumming beneath the Mercury's wheels. I passed South Main Street leading into downtown Conyngham, missing the turn in. I passed Knorr Road then Mundies Road. I took a right onto St. John's Road—*Don't ever converse about routes, Dutch, 'cause no one cares.* So be it Nona. So be it. Little by little, the seed pines, conifers, elms and poplars—*And nature talk, Dutch, bores me to no end*—receded to a familiar view of brown fields frosted in patches of gleaming ice. Here and there, the cold had sealed in a hard minerality. It was like inhaling witch hazel, that rubbing alcohol smell that cools your insides as it burns. The fields, corn farms in the spring and summer, now swelled and dipped in their former saddle-brown profusion, then they rose whitely, mutely, savagely toward Sugarloaf Mountain.

It made of sugar bread?

Wish it were. I always thought it a mistake of language as much as perception to equate that knobby mound with anything more than a hill, but there it was, a dome of silence whose sidewinding trails I traveled one summer and dissolved into a willow tree. *Brahman*, is what Armand might have called that feeling I felt. Bliss. That was some day. From my perch, high in the willow's boughs, I stared down through the tangles, down at the sprawling landscape of patched brown, green, and gold, seduced by patterns of reaping and sowing that repeated mile after mile. *I belong here*, I had thought then. After years of rootlessness, I needed to claim this landscape as home.

Where moments before the tall trees limited the view of horizon and sky, now came fields. This is our farm country, stretching either to the base of the distant hills or swallowed up by the distant woods. Browns Road became Kisenwether Road and I followed it up past desolate lots. I reconnected to St. John's Road and followed that for a good ten minutes, then took a right onto Deep Hole Road. I passed Dietz' old farm. Some barns that looked as if melting into the earth, roofs weighed down by ice. Reaching the rusty water tower, I slowed, veered onto the shoulder and my heart raced. Up ahead a milk can stood half-buried in a scorpion hedge. I spun my head around. To my left the water tower leaned on its side, succumbed to rust. Playing Hide-and-Seek, I would find Cole stretched flat on its narrow gangway. I would find him staring up at the shifting, colliding clouds, perhaps wondering what else there was to the world? *Neptune is a place where the people are fish, Papa. True? No, son, not true.* Once I found a bicycle leaning against one of its posts and I took it as a gift. I rode it till my calves cramped and my chest became spasmodic, as if I was breathing flames. What did these little memories mean? Collected together, they still offered only an incomplete picture of my life, like pieces of a puzzle spread out on a table, each shape implying another shape, each corner capturing a separate view of the whole. A crow cawed above. The Mercury's engine rumbled through me. What a faithful and trusting machine, its resonance vibrating the hairs on my hands.

FIFTEEN

I'm hungry.

In a minute.

Okay.

Steam from the exhaust billowed behind the rear bumper, fogging the rear window. Sensing fledgling heat, a crow descended from the lower boughs of a walnut tree and settled on the car's hood, it flared its wings. Its thin claws clicked across the metal—*Mama says there's a bird that can say your name.* I palmed the horn. It let out a wheezy, watery sound, like a punctured lung. The crow crooked its neck, in that jaunty way that makes them seem like toys—*Eye of gleaming obsidian. Oily pelt, blue-black.* The crow cawed—*Caw-Caw*—its call like a hack, thin and reedy, then it fluffed away.

A crow?

A black bird. A single crow could read you, pick you out of a crowd even two years after. *A memory bird,* Nona had said once. *Black as pitch, bird of death, your obsidian eyes pull the soul inward, you scavenger, you rat of the winter skies.* Easy, Cole. Straight ahead, at the mouth of our graveled drive, my old driveway spilled out onto Deep Hole Road. My heart pounded. I needed oxygen.

Induced memory, Armand once said, *is when a place triggers anxieties you cannot control. Entering a room you haven't been for thirty years and terror grips you. Rooms contain memory, like a glass holds water. A room holds memory in its objects, in its jambs and frames and floors. The ceiling pours its terror back into you.*

Short of breath. I reached into my overcoat for the Albuterol spray. Gave it a pump—*Mama is better than Papa and Papa is bigger than Mama but when Mama cries Papa makes her so and when I cry it means Papa loves me*—and the powdery air settled my lungs—*Mama smells nicer than Papa who smells like burns.* My breathing eased. My lungs have holes in them, small pinpricks and traces of metal fill the sacs. A veritable trove of cheap metals there. At courthouses I set off metal detectors. I have to laugh.

Come on, Cole, I said, my voice bouncing from the windshield. *Let's see where this old road leads.*

~

Ice in the ruts. Patches of gravel. Sharp stones. The road shot through a field once clustered with hazel, sloped upwards and then rolled downwards into a declivity. Trees. Lovely raggedy trees. Cole had tied a rope to a tire and tied the rope end to that tree's branch there (or was it that tree over there?) and from that makeshift swing, he swung like a pendulum in a grandfather's clock. Was he eight? Nine?

The driveway, deeply eroded and dusted with snow, curved up a narrow hill. Dead weeds wagged in the wind like the tails of leaping fish. Naked trees shot up from the snowpack, poplars, as if drawn in pencil by a child's crude imagination. The denuded bushes like crowns of thorns seemed to crackle and hiss like conflagrations. When the car's front end dipped, one of Cole's pictures slid under my seat. Snow and gravel jangled in the Mercury's wells. Every camber, every arch, every limb, every stone, every twig, every leaf, every dead berry, and every dead bead seemed argued over, chafed, ruined somehow. Everything held a threadbare solidity. A single chorus consisting of a million thin, disparate voices chanted *Die! Die! Die!* Shrieked *Die! Die! Die!*

As if entering a rampart composed not of stone but of ice branches, ice bushes, long boughs filigreed with long knives of ice, the Mercury crashed through brittle branches. Needles shaped like goats' horns battered the windshield. The transmission whined. The car lurched and lifted as if powering through waves. The woods, wicked as a repeating nightmare and etched in white, encroached from every angle, like a mouth with big teeth—*Better to eat you with.*

Scary.

I know. Having forgotten how steep the initial climb, having forgotten how the road flattened out, then swooped left in a downward bend, I wrestled with the steering. The Mercury banged into holes the size of wheelbarrow scoops. By turns the rear wheels lost traction, slipped and slid then regained their grip, finding insecure purchase on icy gravel. I gritted my teeth. I pressed down hard on the pedal, followed the bending road.

Pops, isn't this what you wanted, for you to stay and me to go? I could make out the roofline of the old house. I remembered Wally up there, shimmying down—*Hey, Somee-set, you think you can fly like me? Come up and try.* Then the single-car bridge had held, the boards thrumming beneath the wheels. The water below it had hardened, trickled oily blackness, and its small embankments were packed with snow. *What can ya do with a catalyst and a match? That's if you're not chicken, bakaaak*! Almost home, I thought. Almost.

I used to drive this last bit of road with my eyes shut, even in the dark, having committed it to memory. Coveting danger, I shut my eyes. I felt as if gliding, all contours gone, just a smooth straight line that led me in all directions at once. When the Mercury's tires juddered, I opened my eyes. A log like a body leaped into view. I pumped the brakes. Nothing. Just a pneumatic hiss. Just the clack of the pedal against the well. The wheel when I turned it hard right screamed, like metal teeth grinding in an iron mouth. The car slid. The earth flipped up. The white sky turned white earth and white earth turned sky. Sky earth white earth and white sky, all of it spun.

SIXTEEN

Did you die?

I'm here aren't I?

So then?

Then all was still. Steam whipped from the radiator. The acrid smell of oxidized fluids: brake fluid, viscous transmission liquid, coolant, green as milky moss, returned me to my senses. The car horn's dispirited hiss. Windshield cracked, a hundred-point star. The right lens of my progressives cracked; the thin line dividing near sight from far, fissured. My watch face cracked. Red wetness, hot and coppery, spilled over my mouth while heat collected at my temple like a weight. I patted my limbs for broken bones.

Stupid, I said, banging my palms against the dash. All Cole's pictures spilled onto the floor. *The risks you take are more than you can handle, Dutch.*

Shut it, Nona. Not now!

I cranked the starter. It whinnied like a beaten horse, then it grabbed. Pressing hard on the gas pedal, the engine whinnied, then ticked like a clock in double-time. A busted gasket shot into an empty cavity. Ping. The high squeal of a loose flywheel.

I shifted the gearbox into first and then eased off the clutch. The car lurched forward. Its rear tires spun, spitting floes of ice and snow into the air behind the tailpipe. When the front end dug deeper into the snow wall, the belt snapped and spun off its crank, ripping into the air a screech like a grating wheel. I switched off the ignition. A final death rattle.

I managed to open the door. Below me, small tracks from some wild animal, muskrat or fox, tattooed a clean course into the woods. In disbelief, I stared hard at the car. Broken, it was no longer mine. My suitcases lay twenty yards away. The car had expelled my groceries, scattering everything. The box containing my two-burner stove lay a few feet from the bridge. I eyed the four bottles of bourbon near a hacksaw and picked one up, unscrewed its cap and sipped. With the liquor sharp in my gullet, I trudged up the remaining length of driveway.

And then?

Whatever the picture I had of it in my mind all these years, the house and property failed to match the facts. Abandoning the house to time, I had abandoned it to its fate. The house, with that old oak's branches twining the chimney, looked like a paltry thing, but it still had the capacity to surprise you, not with its stature though, for although two-storied with a fine mansard and a peaked roof, it was a simple country house on a historical site clutched in a centuries' old violent dream.

I swigged from the bottle. *Can you hear that, Dutch? Pops, are you listening?* A dog barked. Cold wind moaned through the deciduous trees. I stood and…

Where did you go?

I'm sorry. I drift away now and again. Where was I?

A crash.

That's right. A gust, cold and sharp, cut through the pines and cut through the bramble bushes. It cut through my clothes, turning my breath to iron. Wiry thickets and wiry blossoms pushed out of the snow-dusted yard—bushes in whose dead patterns you could make out anguish. Dead creepers crept up the clapboard walls, a dead web that seemingly held the house together. *Did you miss me?* I said, addressing the façade, and as if to answer, a branch broke off the old oak and slid down the snowy roof.

Was this my inheritance? A foundation, four walls, a roof? Was this your legacy? Weeds? Ruin? The broken barn and the denuded orchard and the torn up strawberry patch? *He would have inherited a house reined in by woods of astonishing greenery, Nona,* my young voice said. *He would have inherited my trade, inherited the understanding of the working life, if only he hadn't gone.*

Two pier posts still supported the lee, now bent askew. Two transom windows opposed a shattered bay front window off to the left of the batten, windowless door. The knocker was gone, once a ring of leaded brass. I pried away the boards nailed to the front door.

And then?

I didn't want to appear too eager, so I lingered on the porch. Slid my feet across the old boards. Stuck a toe in through the front door as if I were entering a pond. No, I'll just pretend I stumbled onto you by accident.

Stepped inside. My authority over the house had changed. Here I was, an interloper, a petty thief, looking to steal away the hours. Cold lurked inside. Musty defeat. Each room held the absolute rapaciousness of time. If it could speak it might shout, *Leave me be!* I often wondered about you, I whispered there in the dark foyer. You, pushed up against the trunk of a giant oak as tall as a skyscraper, pinned to it like a barnacle to a ship's hull, no, you were never far from my thoughts. You were a repository of memory—Nona's bird cages in which cockatiels or macaws, or the two lovebirds (Tippi and Rod), or that single grim-faced, green-cheeked conure she named Porter, sang soliloquies in the mornings. You were the scent of her center-soft raisin scones, the creak of the maple floorboards in the upstairs hall, of sunlight cutting across your bayfront and shimmering like a golden blade across Cole's freckled face while he drew horsemen, whales, lions. You once delivered to us the quality of watery air that had breached your outer walls during a surprise summer storm, or the wind that fingered through a loose window sash, or the snow, fine as felt or dust sifting through cracks in the attic. And I want to tell you that I am sorry for having left, that you meant the world to me, though I may not have said it often enough. All I want is to help you reclaim what you've lost, piece you together with my own hands, because if you let someone else work on what's yours, you lose your claim on it.

I stamped my feet in the hallway. *Hello?* My voice faded into rooms, then bounced thinly back. I scanned the floors, the walls, the ceiling. There was a time when you had a look of unyielding heft—your wood floors were real wood, not that cheap laminate they sell by the square foot, and real brass on the door pulls and knobs, and real stone counters—and that sort of reality felt like lost virtues. Above the standalone sink, carved from pebbled stone and set atop a base of four iron legs, stood our manic Frigidaire, which, because of a solenoid or a bad fuse, kept shutting itself off just when we needed it most, like during a summer heat storm, and opposite that sink stood grandma Geraldine's ancient Home Comfort. A wood burner, it tinged every bread or meat with smoke, until I retrofitted it for propane. Somehow, apple pies and blueberry tarts and raisin scones, even roasted beets, still tasted faintly of burnt hickory or pine or blackened oak.

Above the center island hung a trellis of copper pots and cast iron pans, their handles looped by iron hooks. Cole would shoot rubber bands at them, just to hear them ping and clatter like chimes—*Stop that racket*—and there were times I laughed with him—*It's like Papa's barn door.* We would leave the window above the sink open in the summer and treat ourselves to the valley breezes wafting in—of heather and mint and honeysuckle. Sometimes in winter, Nona left it open to evacuate the smoke from grease fires, blackened bacon—*I can't get a handle on this stove*—and when the smoke dissipated and the air cooled to a hardness—*Just keep trying, Nona*—in tramped the smells of the oak's icy branches.

A red painted door in the corner led out to your pinewood deck. Blackberry brambles climbed the trellis and bloomed in the summer. Ivy twined the porch rails, scattering green leaves across the lawn that shimmered metallically in the sun. The back stairs led out to a row of privets, then to an arbor, and stretching beyond the green garden lay our dew-beaded lawn, our Dutch barn, and five full acres of the family lands. I turned and entered the den.

Cole marched in with muddy shoes once, tracking mud and wet leaves across your hardwood. That disrespect for you was enough to tear off the top of my head. There were other infractions—bedwetting, cursing, tantrumming, lazing it up 'til late in the afternoon. There were other violations—crumbs on the dinner table from half eaten bread rolls, fed Henry James table scraps, failed to wash his armpits or brush his teeth or comb his hair, and when older, he disappeared for hours at a time, losing himself in the woods. *A bad boy*, Blake would say of him if he knew him, *Needs a good ass-kicking to beat the bad outta him.*

I passed the basement door. A supernatural chill crept through my body. How many nights had I spent down there alone? Blake, perhaps to break my dependence on Pearl's memory, would throw me in. While outside, the night spread motionless beneath a moonless sky, I buried myself inside the small sharp emanations of a world that looked as if assembled by a madman. Junk heaps: Crates of moonshine bottles, and all the cheap objects Blake stole when junking took over his life, broken things—rusted Huffy frames, rear view mirrors, hubcap stacks, tube tires, tin signs. Lack clung to those objects like stink. Shivering from fear, I would crouch in a corner, knees to chest, rock back-and-forth, Blake's handprint burning across my face while, above me, Blake warbled drunkenly about Armageddon. *Come and see. So I looked, and behold, a pale horse. And the name of him who sat on it was Death… to kill with sword, with hunger… with death, and by the beasts of the earth. Amen, Wally? Amen.* Sheltering in the rusty, dusty air, deep beneath the decades-old sleep of the cabinets' peeling paint, I wedged myself inside junk caves, their sharp elbows and jawless shards and bony thicknesses abrading my skin, and I covered my ears and wept.

In the morning, the pale light of a Pennsylvania summer crept through the lunettes, grays casting thinly across stacks of porcelain signs, mailbox heaps, old bird feeders, and the gray waned across those old radio tube transistors and broken clocks—that veritable archaeology of useless things—and I hoped for courage then. *Sit quiet. Be still, little man. Light a match. Think of me.* While Blake sermonized to Wally—*And I saw a star fallen from Heaven to Earth, to him was given the key to the bottomless pit and he opened the bottomless pit, and smoke arose out of the pit like the smoke of a great furnace… Listen, shitface!*—I stilled and quieted my mind and made myself so small you could fit me between the hands of a cuckoo clock. I would slip past and under the hour and minute and second hands. *Climb, you small figment of a child's imagining.* I would scale numerals and lie supine in the wedge of a "V," straddle the double columned "II," flatten myself across the back of a colonnaded "III."

Hours passed. Night into morning into day into night. What could I do but wait while Blake raged on? *But the woman was given two wings of a great eagle, that she might fly into the wilderness to her place.* I sat absolutely still while the blackness seethed, argued for its own power—*a hundred forty-four thousand anointed ones!* Little by little the blackness crept into every corner of the room. Like ink, it oozed from the ceiling, dripped blackly from the walls, bubbled up from the concrete floor, oozed across the floor. It hissed and in its trembling voice I heard Blake's voice—*Ssssoommerssssett*—the venom of his tone pooling, spreading its poison inside this locked space, that sickness spilling out and into the house, through the house, the hissing and the blackness thick as bitumen making me nothing at all—*Did ya know?* The voice said. *Did ya hear 'bout Suicide Ridge? What's now Bonser Road, in Ross Township, used to be the Sullivan Trail. Was tough times when yas were born. Depression and all killing off a man's livelihood, and many a man and even a woman or few took to their solution at the end of a noose. Daddy and son Werkheisser hung 'emselves, one after the other, from an old pine overlooking the ridge near Sober's Meat Market. Shhh, ya can still hear the creak-creak of a taut rope swangin' in a no-wind, or hear 'a the crunch-crunch 'a boots on a no-snow, and other small boot feet crunchin' after and without no footprints at all.*

What was his purpose but to instill in me fear, fear meant to break my will? I would clasp my hands over my ears and shake my head no and curl up in a corner, but I could not shake his voice. A match would kill the blackness, I thought. A single match to light my way—*Bee-cause Somer-shit is angry like fire*. I rolled my eyeballs back into my skull and hummed *God is Nigh*, mimicking my mother's lullaby tone and I shut my eyes and the night passed. A week passed, or what felt like a week, and I thought of Pearl. *When all is lost, light a match, and think of me.*

I sniffed the air below. From the darkness rose the smell of burning hair, skin, nails. There was nothing to find down there. Things won't un-burn. Things won't un-die. But still, Wally wouldn't stop *bakaaking me in the dark.*

You talk funny.

I have to laugh.

And then?

So I took a long pull from the bottle. So I crossed the hall, the floorboards creaking like old bones. So I thought of archaeology.

What's that?

People who dig up old things, sure. What would future archeologists say about us? Perhaps that we were resourceful creatures, that we mimicked the tertiary existence of ants and mites. Jealous of the birds, we created flying machines. Envious of fish, we crafted boats and iron lungs. We crafted things of utility, tools to create other tools, machines to form other machines, other comforts, other objects whose value faded as quickly as their shine or novelty dulled. Perhaps they would find us restless creatures, forever seeking improvement, sacrificing present time for a future when all theories and practices ceased. They would ask themselves, scratching their oversized eggheads, where did their desire come from, this will to improve? When their things no longer served their purpose, when they replaced old things with new things, better and faster and shinier things, they discarded them as easily as shedding the past, filling basements as easily as landfills with the weight of their restlessness. They discarded people too. Abandoned them in graves, or death houses with lofty names—Summerlane Gardens, Lazarus Memory Care, Vintage Retirement. They filled their minds up with things that had lost their value, making their minds into landfills of broken thoughts. They invented new narratives and recast themselves in new roles. Their sin was not guilt, they might tell each other, their eggheads vibrating language. It was not lack of this or that, but something else: Want. They had infinite wants but few needs and had confused the two—*Shall we continue in sin so that grace may abound, Somerset? Answer yer Papa!*

I don't understand.

You don't have to.

My fingers graced the newel posts of the banister leading to the upper floors. So I took another swig from the bottle and felt that sharp descent into drunkenness. I tested the first step leading up. It seemed to cringe beneath my boot. What would the Indians call that sensation, also *maya?* I took another step up and then stopped as if I'd smacked into a wall. A floorboard snapped. The house shook on its foundation, throwing me off balance. No. The house wasn't yet ready to accept me back. *Then I ain't ready for you, either. Let's just get a good look at you first.*

I like how you talk to yourself.

So I stepped outside. The wooden siding, once white, no, not white exactly, exactly bone, stretched in lengths of five or six feet across the outer walls. Remember how, when the raw winds blew, you would shift and moan as if you were a living, exhaling thing? *Remember.* Wind had stripped your roof, exposing patches of tarp, and in the four corners, your gutter spouts curled up like bent tongues. Ivy had withered to veiny filaments, but your trellises remained, so fragile now they could have crumbled beneath a whisper. Something had taken chunks from the lower corners of the outer walls, as if some rabid animal had sauntered there and feasted, then carried pieces of you with it into the woods to build its own nests, line its own caves, build its own dams and dikes.

I circled to the back. Your chimney, once a red brick column, stood leeched of color—the filaments of a wisteria long dead still gripped the mortar. Although yellow nutsedge once grew along your wide-bottomed base and the privet hedges Nona and I planted one year were gone, your chimney still held its shape, not a single edge chipped.

Fifty-yards from the old back porch, its roofline laden with snow, stood the old Dutch barn—*Papa, are you here? Mama says to eat.* I steadied my breath. Shut my eyes. Drifted. Cole enters. *About time you thought of me, Pops.* He pads the floorboards as if with cat's feet, and he passes a man he calls "Papa." This "Papa" wears chafed boots, blue overalls, a denim shirt, and a pageboy cap. The man he calls "Papa" hunches on a swivel stool, burnished by the light from a tungsten bulb, more yellow than white, a "Papa" who hammers the dents out of a cast-iron cook lid. *Tink-Tink-Tink,* his hammer falls. Occasionally a spark arcs in the darkness and fades.

Cole climbs the loft steps with a sketchbook and a charcoal pencil. He settles himself into an old canoe the "Papa" keeps suspended from the rafters by two guy-ropes. The Bakelite plays music, serene music, horns and strings, and the "Papa" paces about, jabbering to himself. While Cole draws pictures—ships balanced on the waterspouts of giant whales—the "Papa" scribbles equations into a notebook. While the "Papa" bangs and cobbles together an old cast iron stove, barely aware of the son's presence above, Cole folds the charcoal stick into his sketchbook and sets it on the gunwale. Cole scoots down beneath the plank seat and he shuts his eyes, folding his arms over his chest like the posture of the dead. He has seen corpses. He has been to a funeral where the air smelled like candy corn and people were crying, seen the pale stiff body of the woman his mother called sister, whom he called aunt, a woman whose name on a cardboard sign said Ivy Jo. He did not dance or sing with Greggie when the organ played a song he remembered from nowhere. Cole, lulled by the hammer's fall on metal, shuts his eyes.

Maybe an hour passes, maybe two, and then, like a distant bell, Nona's voice rises into the meadow. *Co-ole! Du-utch!* That Doppler voice, rising in pitch then falling. *Sup-per!* With the "Papa's" hands aching and his brow clinched in sweat, he sweeps the crowded room with his eyes. Everything seems in its rightful place. His precious vintage stoves stand in neat rows, just as they always do—faithful, attentive, awaiting his admiration—and his tools sit against the wall or lay in their rightful drawers and cabinets. He knows the mother will not come to fetch him, because a sign on the door says KEEP OUT WHEN CLOSED. A MAN IS WORKING. He feels annoyed at her voice. Hasn't he told her a hundred times not to shout while he's working? But a "Papa" must also eat. And this "Papa" is hungry.

So he clicks off the radio and silence seals the room shut. The "Papa's" eyes survey the room a final time. The sketchbook edged on the gunwale falls and clacks against the floor. The "Papa" looks up and there, in the canoe, a tiny arm dangles over the paint-peeled boatswain. The "Papa" climbs the loft ladder. A church mouse skitters into the shadows from the bay hales. Then, down on his haunches, he watches the little stowaway. Asleep. He nods to himself, barely able to breathe at the small perfection of this boy's form. *Cole,* the "Papa" whispers, unable to say any more. *Cole,* a single word, a single syllable, a name that must mean *this* boy. Like an old man roused from a nap, the boy the "Papa" calls Cole opens one eye, makes his mouth into a circle and yawns.

Is it time, Papa?

And the "Papa" nods and the "Papa" smiles. *Stop your shamming, son,* the "Papa" says. *Shop's closed.*

And then what happened?

Above me the sky pulsed with snow. The jonquil sky, topped with cloud towers, resembled the masts of ships. Rising from the snow-flecked earth rose the flanks of the old oak tree—old when I lived here and now looked older still—*Papa, I'm going to Saturn to spin on its rings.* The tree's dun drab limbs, olive brown here, jacketed there with neon green lichens, quivered. There we are, Cole and I, staring up at the crown of leaves. *We can build it there, right?* In its thick cross-section of roots, I always saw more struggle than pattern, in its carapace of puckered grooves and folds, its trunk looked more like an argument than bark.

Remember how Blake and I, and sometimes Wally and I, and years later how Nona and I and sometimes Cole, decorated the oak with strings of blinking bulbs during Christmas? *Ruby chains, emerald strings, sapphire and diamond lace.* But all efforts to dress it up and make it look cheerful only made it look foolish, like we had dressed up a monster for Sunday service.

With Nona's oils and horsehairs, Cole once painted the trunk saffron and crimson and salmon pink, colors so bold and discordant that the trunk looked like a patchwork quilt—*Jester in your skin tights of lozenged lavender and gold. Harlequin clown.* Reaching the trunk, I traced several delicate marks with my finger. The old tree always accepted its punishment, inhaled its embarrassments, accepted knife notches to mark height, absorbed our initials, and digested those penknife scrawls Cole carved to time travelers in case they might appear. The tree became a beacon then, permeating into the upper air an invisible light. Nona feared that disembodied souls, maybe aliens, might even come. *You think that's where Cole's gone? Abducted by aliens? Traveled back in time? Do you think that, Dutch?*

Its scars had outlasted the hands that had scrawled them. Cole's growth chart, right there, still, his height and age carved in some alien hand—*Papa did I growed? Did I growed?*—and the remnants of that paint—silver, blue, red, the faded stars and stripes of the American flag, were still there, trifling as confetti.

Up on a branch, thick as a grown man's arm, stood the remnants of the treehouse we built. Cole was ten going on twenty then and the double treehouse—*the rocket ship to fly me to the future*—was Cole's time-machine. Together we tapped the root tangles with our feet. Together we knuckled the bark. Tugging at my shirtsleeve, Cole whispered, *Papa, you could be Buck and I could be Twiki, bedee-bedee-bedee.* And so we built it, united in the singular purpose that summer to build Cole a treehouse/time machine, because to grant a boy his wish was what fathers do.

I circled the old oak. How many nights did Cole and I sit up on the treehouse's star deck, marveling at the stars, naming and renaming the constellations? *Hydra is the water snake*, I would say and Cole would say, C*etus is the whale. Aquila, the eagle. He's a star child*, Nona would later say. *I read somewhere that certain children have a connection to the stars. They're half-human, half-gods.* I thought of Pearl, Pearl in whose eyes I glimpsed the universe, Pearl *The Rocket Girl* of the Wilkes-Barre County Fair.

Stars?

Shooting stars. Comets. Remember when things fell so quiet that any sound—a whisper, a footfall, the flapping of a crow's wing—sounded like a signal that the world hadn't yet ended and taken you with it? Things fell from that treehouse, leaves, twigs, seeds. Cole fell out once, almost broke his skull against the roots, and I scooped him up and cradled him. In my arms, his heart stopped. I hammered his tiny chest, screaming *Breathe! Breathe!* and when he sucked in his breath, I wept and I held him tight to my chest, hoping my heart's strength would infuse his with new power.

Ice nettles. Fingers of ice hung from the old oak. I saw myself from above, like a black stain against the white earth. There you stood, the bourbon bottle in one hand and your whole body trembling like a leaf. You closed your eyes, pressed the heels of your hands into your eyes and your eyes witnessed stars and black shapes tearing across the sky, the sun drinking down the hills, remaking the sky into a chamois quilt. A damp breeze drew down from the Poconos, catching speed as it circled Sugarloaf Mountain. The cold wind scattered white drifts—*Pearl set the fire and she ran off into the woods then down Deep Hole.* Snow fell around you, on you, salted your crinkled brow, melted on your hawkish nose, rolled off your ruddy cheek without an ounce of heat in it. And a sound reached you from the darkening woods and you turned to the crumbled fence line, just thin spines at the yard's outermost edge. The woods beyond looked thicker than ever. As a boy, Cole would enter through the gaps between the trees, thinking them as doorways into enchanted places. He thought them portals into new lands where whales swam in the air or where sweet-toothed sharks lived out their dumb, dense lives on the flanks of sugar mountains. But now, not a yielding space remained. Nets of ropey vines bellied up and down and walls of bushes like small exploded suns sprayed the etiolated earth. But that sound? What was it? *Remember.* Beneath birdsong, above the electric chatter of chipmunks and a crow's reedy squall, between the barking of a dog somewhere in a distant field, you heard the trickle and patter of Big Nescopek Creek—its bituminous bed forming waters black as a nightmare—*Do as I say and not as I do. Drink it up, shitless!* You recalled a birdling you set adrift on a funeral barge. You thought of paper boats, paper lanterns, a paper effigy of Cole, his feet swallowed in mud on the banks. One night you chased Cole into the woods, and you wondered what Cole saw in the water that so mesmerized him? Angels and devils battling in the white crests of foam? A beast with seven heads and ten horns and on his horns ten crowns? A woman clothed with the sun? Your mother's face, a woman he never knew?

Crows barked and the glacial wind blew and the trees shook with fury. You wondered, how long would it take to fix this place? When was Armand arriving? Did you imagine him saying yes? Though it was freezing, though your breath steamed before you, your ink-spotted finger hooked away a trickle of blood from your nose. Chains of sweat leaked from your arms. Where would you begin? How could you have the strength to repair this place, at your age, nearing eighty and the world soon ending, nearing eighty when you've already tumbled headlong into decline? *Papa, the crickets are screaming. Dutch, the locusts are shrilling in the trees. Somerset, my son, look how the night is solid as a plate of metal, and just a shard of ceramic, the moon. Mother, Mama, Ma, I see a star leashed to its left. Son, that's no star. It's just Mars or Venus or perhaps Mercury in retrograde.*

Go on and collect your things from the snow. Go on and place the suitcase in your old bedroom. Go on and unfurl the bedroll, settle the groceries you bought at the mart and lay out your tools. Set up the camp stove in the kitchen and the propane canisters before gathering up all the evidence of your life. But you moved no muscle. You stood in the center of the yard. You felt your lungs tighten and your head lighten—*Someeree-set struck a match, he did, and he done burned the moonshine and Wally done went up like a match*—and you squatted, dropped onto your haunches while snow fell around you, on you, falling inside you like a storm of atoms crushed by gravity.

Is this how the end begins? *I'll show you what endings mean, some-an-a-bitch!* You reached for your inhaler and sucked in the life giving dust. Held your breath. Exhaled. And you let your heart settle a little. *Breathe. Baby, breathe, breathe. Wally breathed in fire and burned himself up.* The sky thundered and the blackened hills undulated like sea swells in the distance. Frigid wind as familiar to you as your own name greeted you like an old friend, caressing your body like death, tingling your face like death, like death caressing and chilling you.

SEVENTEEN

I pump the inhaler as I make for the stairs. The boy follows behind. We pass spaces in which dusty wood and plaster bits lie in heaps. I navigate the staircase as if I'm also made of dust.

I cross the hall. The floors bend and flex. Have the beams rotted through? My hand grazes the wall. Have the pipes rusted? Passing through the threshold, I slip from darkness toward a darker black, from cold to a deeper cold.

Outside. The boy is behind me.

Smell that? I say, inhaling the air. It has teeth. The cold air feels like peace distilled.

The boy inhales. A mimic. In the distance, the dog barks, still.

Hear that? That's a dog. Cruel to neglect her, to ignore her needs. She's a good girl and just wants to be inside, sprawled on a sheepskin rug by the hearth, gnawing on a pork hock.

You talk funny.

I laugh. I relight my cigar with a match. The flame sizzles and the cigar tip glows red, like a distant semaphore. Wind rises out of the bowels of the earth and lashes the trees. Sounds, smells, textures, images surround me, waiting acknowledgement (isn't that all memory is?) and so I shut my eyes and acknowledge them—*It burns, it burns. Hate is a scar that never heals, little man.* I breathe it in. Exhale.

Let's take a walk, I say.

Why?

Walking's good for ya.

Okay. But I'm cold.

Sometimes when the night is starless, dark and very still, tongues of old fires course over my memory walls like an ascension of water—*Help me, Son. Please. Untie these ropes.* A blur of legs kicks up gray dust and crickets rub their legs and fireflies swarm, like cinder sparks overwhelmed by a gust of fierce heat. Shooting through the air, a star explodes into a million streams of streaking ash. My son is laughter then. He is that light edging across the horizon. The hairs on the back of my neck stand on end as if someone—*Papa, no!*—has slipped a blade of ice between my ribs. Now I'm a boy, entering my brother's room and my brother—*who is not my brother*—lies like a piece of bent iron on the bed, his legs bandaged and his face bandaged except for his eyes which are blue and watery and bulbous and do not blink. My skin crawls under the cold thin watery blue-black touch from his bandaged, blackened hand—*the pain, stop*. The snap of a tinder box. A crystal shatters to the concrete spilling fire water. The finality of a struck match. Into air stiff with a no-breeze climbs the hiss of sulfur. Smoke freezes. A question mark. Smoke struggles, shivers, becomes a cloud. The visions explode. Dissipate.

You okay, mister?

My chest heaves and my heart grows weary, so heavy, that my ribs ache. How so much of my past leaves me dizzy and thirsty for meaning that I wonder if I'm inventing my life by remembering it? Perhaps I am. Perhaps imagination is a compensation for what I cannot remember. Perhaps tale-telling to fill up the time and ease this heart is a compensation for what I cannot remember. Maybe I am imagining being home, imagining the Dutch barn, the cold air and this boy. Maybe the dog is not barking and what I think is real is just imagination? Nona might be in her room, or in the kitchen downstairs beating eggs for a Christmas pie. But to put a life right you have to start somewhere, either in memory or in imagination or in its blending.

I'm fine, I say. Come on.

The boy and I pass the barn, cross into the woodlot. A tree trunk curls upwards from the snow like a hooked finger. My feet ache.

Let's sit a second. Let me catch my breath. That's good. That's better. Isn't that better? When Nona and I moved to Baltimore, we tried to make peace with our past and with each other, but on nights like this, so cold and so dark and so desolate, I would tumble out of bed like a drunk and pace the halls of our brownstone like a man on the brink of collapse. Words—"defeat," "malice," "guilt"—clung to me like lichens to old bark. I would stand by the double windows in the den and part the curtains and reflect on those sensual evenings when I sat on my porch swing here, the soft concussion of the maples blown by a late summer breeze ringing in the evening like a chorus of muted bells (Nona in the kitchen or upstairs in her studio and Cole disappeared somewhere in the folds of the house) and I would smile to myself, glad for my life. Some memories glow with the warmth of small suns.

The dog barks. The boy crouches. I light a match and with the match I light a cigar. I would remember Henry James, our faithful Shepard-mix. How he could huff and bark up a storm long into the night and at what? Shadow of a black bear, a trembling thicket, a quorum of deer? I would leave the window and take a seat at the bistro table and stare at the moldering grease clinging to the base of the kitchen's walls and imagine laughter seeping from the boughs of those poplars there. I would try to collect their names in my memo-book and net them and hold them in my little brain. But the moment I tried, my words faltered, because all around me lay the progression of decline.

Sitting there in that kitchen, amidst the clutter, surrounded by newspapers stacked up to the ceiling, and towers of books, dusty and unread, and the soda cans attacked by ant swarms, I would switch on the table-top Bakelite in the corner and listen to music, remembering those ancient songs sung by my mother Pearl. Colloquial expressions sprang into my brain—*All good? All good! Keep the fire guessing like old Virginia Bradford*—terms that once spilled from my father's tongue like tobacco juice. These were scraps of the past that had no purchase in the present, that music and those voices, then other shreds of music drifted on the waves of smoke fuming from my Hemingway, something by Cole Porter, or the melody to *God is Nigh,* my mother's favorite song.

In those slow, repentant evenings, in whose slackened rhythms you could feel the pulse of your blood, I wept like a child pining for home. Nona never knew this. Or if she knew, she never asked me why I looked as if I hadn't slept in years. All those memories had weight, I would tell her if she asked. They pulled you down to the bottom. All those qualities of life pinned you to the floor. They kept me from leaping off the Chesapeake Bridge, leaping off the dome of the Basilica or jumping into the speeding MARC, Balto-Penn line, number 502.

Baltimore screamed, *Leave!* Each wan color, every thin crack, each wild prickly weed that needled up from the edge of broken sidewalks fueled my hatred of time. Inside I felt… Christ, it's impossible to know. I suck hard on the cigar. I blow smoke. Perhaps I felt as if I were inside a prism, the view out of each facet beautiful yet distorted. Certain prayers, certain trees, certain buildings, the mélange of certain events, became the fragments of a shifting kaleidoscope whose meaning made little sense. I had become impressionistic, composed of dots, like one of Seurat's people lounging on the banks of *La Grande Jatte*. No, revisiting my yesterdays wasn't at all like stepping into a river, as Armand once said. It was rather like being consumed by a fire, the epidermis peeled away to singe my bones, boiling my marrow. Let's go back. It's cold and getting colder and I'm not sure why I came out here. Okay?

Okay.

We walk back toward the barn. You know what I told Armand then? I told him that I wanted to be a traveler in the town of my birth, and he said, *Go on and try.* So I told Armand what I believed, that memory was an object you could manipulate, like a puzzle, like something to lose yourself in for a few hours as easily as you could in a painting of a landscape, or in music, or poems. It's like your consciousness becomes one with the infinite and you become the ground, the air, the light. *It's what the Hindus call sarvajna,* he said. *Omniscience,* adding, *Go on and try.*

No, that's the barn, I say. We can't go in there yet. Let's just go on up to the house and we can eat something.

I'm hungry.

Me too.

We walk. The boy loses his footing in a groove in the earth.

Careful. I offer my hand but he shakes his head no, as if I am to blame for him falling. Digging an irrigation trench to feed water to Nona's hydrangeas the summer Cole turned ten, he and I unearthed a small wooden box we thought contained the remnants of an ancient time capsule. But the box, with its crumbling lid and rusted latch revealed just four objects, a tusk-shaped mirror shard, an arrowhead made of flint, a chipped seashell, and three kernels of blackened corn (which we both mistook for rotten teeth). We also unearthed two or three chipped arrowheads, a blood-speckled spearhead, several cobalt blue ceramic beads—*What happened to them who made these, Papa?* With county names like Tunkhannock, Towanda, Nuangola surrounding us, those objects reminded us that we lived in Indian country.

Then Cole said, *Papa, there's pirate's treasure buried here.*

Where's the proof?

Here, he said, offering me the box.

That's no treasure.

I feel it is.

Feeling's a sort of hope, isn't it? A sort of faith?

Paa-paa, he said, the Doppler Effect of his tone piquant, as if to say by intonation alone what he had no words for then: *There you go again, overthinking everything.*

Treasures found are unearned gifts, I might've said. I might've said that the objects of memory are treasures too. I might've told Armand that if we could make of old and ruined things something useful, then we could restore them to their former value and I might've told Cole the same. *Could we not, Cole? For the things discarded had use once and could so have again?*

Cole might've nodded, looking befuddled. He might've thrust his hands in the pockets of his overalls and said, *Can't I just play with them?*

Just put them away in a safe place and look at them now and again.

I am not sure what he did with those objects, reburied them, or threw them away, but I do recall Nona wearing a necklace once with an arrowhead dangling from gut.

We climb the short embankment. My lungs already tired. The cigar glows dimly. The boy behind. His breath steams. The trees surrounding us shiver in the wind and I tighten the scarf around my neck. Strolls through Baltimore's Constellation Park, or Reed Bird Island down by Potee Street, the cherry blossoms nicking their branches, reminded me of the click and clatter of Cole shooting marbles on the front porch of our home, this home, and the waves lapping the shore brought to mind wind in the evergreens. What did those memories mean except that I wished for another chance to relive them? If Cole were here I might remind him of what was good about this place. If Cole were here I'd—

Where is he?

Here, I say, pointing to my head. And here, I say, palming my chest. Son, I might say, I am awash in regret—of the things unspoken, of the actions untaken, of the ideas and feelings I never fully explored. Son, I am but a speck of ash floating in a pocket of hot air, meandering from a crackling fire that brings no warmth, no heat, no comfort. Son, here I am as if by some miracle. I would have liked to tell him so many things. *Start with sorry, Pops.*

Go on and try.

We reach the crest of the embankment, the house dark before us. Wind. Cold. Heavy as heat. A faint glow reaches up from the south.

Downtown Conyngham must be a good five miles from here. Might take me half the day to reach it now. If I tried someone might find me frozen stiff, mid-step in the ruts, looking just like a snow effigy, teeth gritted, glasses snowed over, and someone with a pickup might take mercy on me, throw me in the backseat with the heater on defrost and drive me all the way to Florida. I have to laugh.

You talk funny.

At the end of South Main Street, perpendicular to the old Warrior's Trail, the houses always looked serenely solid, their calm persistence hardening them. Just simple clapboard country ranchers or colonials with yards blending into neighbors' yards with the occasional privet hedge or flowering bush serving as a border—*unadorned, simple, drawing no more attention to themselves than ordinary faces.* They could be built on any little street in any little town in America, their porches blighted beneath coats of paint behind which the tertiary damage was already done. The ranchers, the two-story homes with weathered, gabled roofs signified something, perhaps lives tuned to a lower pitch. Mansards, porticos, porch lees, mail slots constructed according to conservative, functional values, reflecting the functional, conservative values of the people living inside. You could almost hear chants for God and Country, God and Guns, God and Liberty chorusing inside like the buzzing of bees. With surnames stenciled on mailboxes you could trace back to The American Revolution—Shilhamer, Lung, Yerty, Hewe—mailboxes Cole took a baseball bat to one year when he was fifteen. He's leaning out the passenger side of Don Zions' Firebird, slugging away, letters exploding like fireworks and storming upon the asphalt like sliding, slumping bits of ash.

Did I ever contemplate passions stirred in rooms decorated like country churches? Did the old crimson-faced witches rocking in their grand rockers ever crush a heart or kill? Everyone has secrets. Guilt. Regret. You never know whom you're dealing with. Every heart is inaccessible.

The boy and I enter the house, stamping our feet. In the kitchen I light the lantern with a match and turn the knob so the flame glows bright.

Isn't that better?

It's still cold.

It is. Think of a warm place and you'll feel warm. When I'm cold, I think of Cole. Son, circumscribed by the Poconos, we lived in this town named for Jacob Drum, in this two-story Craftsman I inherited from your grandfather Blake, a handyman. ~~But let's go farther back.~~ Before this was our house it was Blake's, and before it was his, it was your great-grandpa Obadiah's place, and before that it was an Indian burial ground, so Blake said. When it was Obadiah's house, it doubled as a Christian worship house for some of the earliest mining families who lived in our patch towns. Before a candle caught a curtain on fire one Christmas Eve in 1913, burning the building so completely that all that survived was the front door, a few charred posts and beams, our rose up on land once peopled by savages. When the church burned down, no one was sure why. People needed some explanation. Foul play was suggested, for the Good Lord's house didn't simply burn up without good reason, and that, too, on Christmas Eve.

Some claimed that spirits of Captain Van Etten's platoon (he of the Sugarloaf Massacre) rose up out of the earth like a congealing mist and assumed various shapes—of mayflies, fireflies, dragonflies. People claimed to see snakes, hooped like ropes, rolling down Sugarloaf Mountain. Vipers uncoiled at the base of your feet and hissed. Some claimed that certain farm houses held rooms so starved of warmth that even in the heat of summer you could see your breath freeze. Unable to furnish natural explanation, people invented superstition. It's their right. Man, after all, is also a mythmaking machine.

Some said Obadiah was a pederast, but there's no proof of it. They said that the alms he collected in the donation plate financed his fornication and love of grain alcohol, but that's hearsay too. So God had made retributions, they said. God's thunderbolt struck the steeple just to send Obadiah a lesson. That's one of those myths people tell one another.

Growing up, I recall no fences ever limned our property, leaving in doubt where our private property ended and the public domain began. Big Nescopek Creek seemed a good enough marker as any to determine the private from public, for no one owned the creek. As a child, I would stare into its riffling waters, black as pitch, black water yielding nothing behind its surface. Sometimes I wondered about the water's source—from which mountain, from which river did it flow? Wondering also where it ended. Which creek did it course into? Did it meet some larger tributary? Did it empty its dim jostle of waves into World's End Lake, or other waterways, the Susquehanna River or the Chesapeake, increasing its volume and depth, to disappear or falter into a sea? I liked swimming in its blackness, unaware that, below me and around me, populations of small fish, networks of thin worms, flukes slim as threads, and larval banquets bustled about. Fording its waters in summer, I felt it slicken my skin like a foreign substance, perhaps blood, perhaps oil. A water snake angled across my heels once and I rushed from its shallows, kicking up sprays of water, molecular in the half light of the gloaming. With my heart in my throat, I ran up the embankments and into the forest, crying *Devil!* Settling into the roots of a tree, I slept, but not before watching the colors in the sky turn beautiful. You could lean into this land then, sink into it, let it swallow you up.

In the winter, like now, the creek banks whiten and the black water hardens and the landscape morphs into a citadel of ice. When the water thaws and the heat of early summer spreads across our valley, Cole and I would dig for crawfish in the creek's muddy bed, critters we collected in lidded mason jars. I would hand my jar off to Nona so she could cook them up. For a week or so, we could sip crawfish soup and spoon up crawfish corn cakes and fork up crawfish salads. But Cole collected his crawfish jars on a shelf above his bed, still with a little muddy water left in them. Fascinated by their clicking and clacking distress, enamored by their hard, black armor, he would measure their changes, hour by hour, week by week. That was a hint of something.

If the ground wasn't spread with frost, like now, you could make out the traces of the old church-house's understructure in the front lawn. A slight depression might still spread along one narrow edge, indented lines shaped like a cross. Those planks that survived the fire,

Obadiah repurposed as beams and crossbeams for the new house he built. This Craftsman. A few spare planks, blackened at the edges, he refashioned as a worktable and installed it in a corner of the Dutch barn.

As a boy, I would enter the barn, its cool darkness scolding me, and I would slide my hands across the old table, fingering the dark grooves and pustules running its length. I believed then, as I believe now, that wood retains something of its past, like old metal, that the salvaged planks of the old church that made up that table and parts of the new house still held the memories of sermons, baptisms and funerals, late night catechisms and prayers, perhaps even exorcisms. Sometimes, late, late at night, I would lie in bed and hear noises issuing from the old wood, the original beams and crossbeams whispering, singing, screaming. Once I heard a jumbled chorus of voices—voices that seemed to tell me things only children are privy to, though I never shared these thoughts with anyone, least of all my brother, lesser still Blake.

I'm hungry.

A little soup will do us good. And bread. Though Blake suffered from religion, he also suffered from hatred and prevarications and hypocrisy, and when he wasn't reciting scripture to me and Wally, or working as a miner for the Hazleton Railroad, he was tinkering with bottled ships in the old Dutch barn. There was a time I thought he could fix anything—a leaky faucet, a squeaky shower door, cracks in the wall—for he had a talent for tinkering. His precise fingers manipulated masts and lifeboats of intricate variety, slipping them inside glass bottles once used for rum or shine or whiskey. He sometimes made little people too out of straw bits, boys in sailor outfits, uniformed captains with Napoleon hats, Davey Crockets and Benjamin Franklins, and imprisoned them in bottles. It's a sad fact of Blake's life that he didn't amount to much more than a goddamned drunk.

Blake was bad?

I believe every devil has a little good in him, somewhere. Even Satan was a talented musician before his fall. I suppose I took it on myself to bring that ounce of decency out of him. But no amount of patience and love, obedience or submission, could change him from what he was. Some people, like some stoves, are ruined beyond repair.

And this house, it testified to his ruin. The past was lost in Blake's house. Unsentimental, he kept no mementos of my mother Pearl, nor of Obadiah, nor of Geraldine. There were no pictures of grim-faced uncles decorating our wooden walls, no aunts murdered by disappointment at having to carry our surname. There were no photos of spirited nephews and delighted nieces playing stickball on bottle green lawns and no bonneted babies in cribs fringed with taffeta, and certainly no sharp-eyed granduncles and grandaunts with that touch of scorn edging their lips so common in our family.

Do you like the soup?

It's good.

I'm glad. I'd like to forgive Blake for his sins of purpose and omission, because making amends is about forgiving your transgressors. How he transgressed. Blake was never a father to me, more like a troubled distant relation. Like his words, his presence in my life was a half-truth—a broken man clinging to his old world Moravianism like a castaway clinging to driftwood after a shipwreck, and that might excuse him. Or it might not. He taught us to wrestle, and pitted us against each other, dispensing Old Testament punishment on Wally and me to, as he said, *train us on the belief that life's cruel, heartless, intolerant of poverty and feminine weakness.* He drew with powdered chalk a central circle on the back lawn, a passivity zone, dressed us in singlets and leather headgear and lightweight shoes. He first positioned me on Wally then Wally on me, and while Wally scored takedown after takedown, receiving points for exposure, winning by falls, and bloodying my nose or lip, Blake scolded. Later, while palming the King James Bible in one hand and a leather belt or a switch in the other, he punished us to correct our form, quoting Revelations or Leviticus or some verses from Psalms—*The wicked prowl on every side when vileness is exalted among the sons of men.* Rooted to this land like the old oak tree outside, Blake seemed as if molded out of the Pennsylvania earth, and it still hurts me to remember him, this pain now searing my head and cleaving my brain.

What about that bread?

Sorry, I get carried away. Rummaging through the shopping bags, I find a bag of potato chips. Here, I say, tossing them to him. This should do you fine.

Taking a seat on the floor, I stretch my legs. The boy sits across from me, just a shadowy shape amidst the collected shadows. The bag rustles in his hands. I light a cigar.

When I got lonely or sad, I'd think of Pearl.

Your ma?

If eccentricity has any definition, then it surely applied to her. A circus performer before she was a wife and mother, and before she was mother and wife, a wanderer, a stray.

Like me? Like you were?

Sure. What led her to marry Blake, I will never know. Some mysteries must remain so. If I were to speculate, I'd say that she also saw in him the possibility of reform, tried using love to heal him. Blake, still handsome then and fresh from the Navy, was released before seeing action in the Great War. A training accident in Biloxi cost him his left eye, a backfiring rifle turned it to stone. He had dreams once, of rising above his lot in life and inventing things. I even found some sketches in a notebook, sketches done in his hand, regarding new, efficient engines powered by the sun, or water, or wind. It's not hard to see why Pearl left us, caged in a house whose history produced more than its share of ghosts, ghouls, for the free bird must fly.

You like those chips?

The boy nods yes.

Cole liked them too. Those were his favorite, salt and vinegar. Just like him, salt of the earth and vinegar in his blood. I have to laugh. I never told Cole that Pearl and Blake met at the Scranton Fair one heat-stricken day in late July, in '29. Pearl was just sixteen. An orphan. Launched from a cannon in a cloud of blue smoke, her form through space was plumb as an arrow. She drifts over the Indian and cowboy clowns circling their wagons. She sails over *Arno The Strongman* shouldering a heavy metal ball. A net catches her. She springs up, bounces, and lands on the ground. Applause explodes. She beams delight at having soared over sixty-three feet, breaking the previous record set by Artie Gumshaw back in 1910. It made the papers. And Blake, looking neat and trim in his white uniform and cropped hair and black eye-patch, watched her from the crowd, his bottom lip loaded with chew, never dreaming that The Rocket Girl of the Scranton Fair of 1929 would one day be his wife.

In my vision of her, Pearl's in a fringed lace tutu whose pleats curve out from her legs like the petals of a rose, and a glittering red blouse, and tight, white leggings, and ballet slippers. She's pulled back her hair into a tight bun and her face looks polished, argent, powdered white as if with baker's flour. Two red blush marks circle her cheeks. Bright red lips. She's lithe. She's strong. She's graceful. Demure, a little lady whose eyes shine with hope.

She sounds great.

That's how I like to remember her, not like the last time I saw her—hair ratted, ripped away from her scalp in clumps to reveal swatches of pink flesh, her right eye swollen shut; Pearl, crumpled in the corner of the barn, her torn dress muddied with pebbles and straw.

I draw on my cigar. I cough. My chest feels heavy. After Blake died and my brother Wally died, I lived in this house alone until I married Nona, an art teacher at West Hazleton High and would-be ornithologist, and, I might add, the best baker of key lime pies in all of Luzerne County—*You'll make me blush with that flattery, Dutch.* At the age of seventeen, Nona left Drums, in '55. We met as children once. We met again while I briefly taught wrestling at Rock Glen Elementary. *Come and meet the new art teacher, Somerset!*

Modeling herself after John James Audubon, whose book, *The Birds of America,* she carried around as if it was The New Testament, Nona's talent for drawing established itself early. By the age of ten, she had already pen-and-inked a lithograph series so stunning in detail she had them displayed in the Hazleton Town Hall.

"Remarkable," people said of her drawings. "A genius." But she was "just a girl." At the age of fifteen, she had already published in the *National Geographic* under an assumed named, Norman M. Hawkins. Expert in her use of color and perspective, imbuing each bird, be it owl or hawk, titmouse or grouse, with a personality, she even pulled attention from the likes of Grant Wood and Andrew Wyeth (Nona showed me their correspondences, praising her gifts). Truth be known, I hadn't a clue who they were.

By the time she left Drums, Blake died of a heart attack. I found him curled up like a shrimp in the center of the barn and left him there, returned to the house to cook up an egg sandwich. While Nona rounded the peaks of the San Gabriel mountains, pursuing red-tailed hawks, I buried Blake in the old family plot. While Nona sketched falcons in Sioux City, I took up the mantle of Blake's former life as a handyman and stove-junker. By the time Nona was hobnobbing with the likes of Moses Sawyer, Edna St. Vincent Millay, Dorothea Lange, I spent my hours alone in this house, determined to reinvent this space that held so much hurt. Friends dropped in now and again, guys going off to Korea, like Jerry Fitzgerald and Joe Sanko, but I stayed. My asthma prevented me from serving my country.

I sustained myself by working on the house and following her climb to fame. Still drunk on her memory, of the day I saved her from drowning in Four Seasons Lake, I tacked her articles above my bed, beside the notices and invitations to her various exhibitions, because from the moment I met her that tumultuous summer day, when we were still children, I fell in love.

Nona would never admit to it. She wasn't the type of woman to tell me she loved me—*Aww, Dutch, you know I did.* Even now, I still think it strange, why such a talented woman chose me for a husband and not some artist or poet or musician who matched her talent, was a miracle of fate—*'Cause you were real, Dutch, the realest man I ever met.*

Nona's series on the mourning grouse she followed up with one on magpies, then a series of cubist-style paintings of ravens that John Updike panned as "derivative." She spent five years chasing California birds, ending her journey in Big Sur, where she hoped to glimpse the condors soaring over ancient cliffs of golden rock. It was there, on the shores of Carmel, where she fell in love with Robinson Jeffers' poetry, swam in the Pacific with Cole Porter, lunched with Langston Hughes, roamed the grounds of Hawk Tower with Jeffers until his wife threw her out.

Nona returned to Drums in the spring thaw of '62, a week shy of Jeffers' death, having witnessed a side of the world I could only imagine: Hills more gold than green, forests of ancient redwoods, starry skies in which the moon, low on the horizon, looked like a silver planet.

They are totems, Nona once said of birds. *Birds are metaphors. A hawk signals the hunter spirit; an eagle, courage; a sparrow, togetherness; a robin, childlike wonder. You have to see past what a thing looks like to get at the real thing,* she would say, then quote Jeffers' poems. So a bird was a symbol, Nona? *Everything is a symbol of something else, Dutch.* Did this definition also include me? I'm still unsure where she got those notions, perhaps from poets. A blue jay was a "talkie" and a crow, like a ferryman, carried souls into the afterlife. *If you find a feather on your path, know that an angel guards over you. If you see a blue jay, it means to remember to take life less seriously. Dutch, you have to laugh.* When Nona held a fleeting bird in place, for admiration's sake, she defined it. *That's what painting does, Dutch; it freezes time.*

We married in the fall of '64. A quick ceremony, a church in Hazleton near City Hall. After three years of trying, we finally had a son. We named him Cole Jeffers Garden because Nona loved the music of Cole Porter, whose lyrics to *Be Like the Bluebird* she could sing by heart, each syllable slipping from her tongue like worship music, and we named him Cole because we lived in coal country, in the heart of the heart of Luzerne.

EIGHTEEN

Why don't you get a little sleep and we'll try and figure out what to do with you later.

I'm not sleepy.

No?

Tell me more.

About?

Cole.

I was nearing forty and Nona was twenty-six when Cole was born that September eleventh of '67. It was the two hundred fifty-fourth day of the year, making him a Virgo, not that I believe in astrology. Nona did. Patting her stomach she said he'd be cautious, earthbound, stubborn. It was a hard pregnancy, with Nona complaining of shooting pains in her legs, and the surges of electricity that coursed through her stomach, both fascinated and terrified me. A woman's capacity to endure pain is superhuman. It was a pain I envied, for it excluded me.

Cole was born on a Tuesday, on that day nearly two hundred years before, the Sugarloaf Massacre of 1780 defined this town long before it was a town at all. Luzerne Valley was where the coal grate (Wilkes-Barre's Judge Jesse Fell's famous invention) single-handedly crushed the whaling industry, so I'd like to think, saved many a Moby Dick from the end of a harpoon. Luzerne honored, if not produced, Jim Thorpe, half-bred Sauk and Fox and descendant of Chief Blackhawk.

Even that beloved cowboy-actor Jack Palance made his home right here in Drums, shopping for beets for his Halupki at IGA. I said this to Armand once and he said *hiraeth. It all sounds like a hiraeth.*

Hir-a-what?

A little Welsh word that means pining for a lost home.

And Armand's your friend?

My only friend.

Can I be your friend?

I have to laugh. Armand's a storyteller, a regular Ishmael or Marlowe. A retired professor of Linguistics, Dr. Armand Kalla taught at Johns Hopkins University, dealt in semantics, roots, dead languages like Sanskrit, Azari, Aramaic, Norn. He's a good man, a decent one. *A grammarian*, I said to him once, to which he said, *A grammarian's just a fancy term for paper-grader.* I had to laugh.

Life's the value of seem, he once said while we cruised the halls of the Air and Space Museum. He might have been quoting some poet. It took me months to understand what he meant. Honestly, I'm still unsure what he meant. *It's nothing more than grammar,* he said of life, reducing it to a system of punctuation, syntax, codes, and that seemed odd to me. While we perused planes staged in various angles of flight, bombers hanging from the ceiling by piano wire, he taught me that a word means nothing without its context. *Context is everything*. I nodded then, sheepishly, pretending I understood. *You can literally remake your life by using words in new contexts.* I'd remind him that some words, like "loss," never altered their meaning. *And death?* I said. *What new context could change its definition?*

At the end of our coffee discussions, I'd call him "professor," abashing him, to which he'd reply, *I profess nothing.* Armand prefers the term "philologist." It's a title carrying with it connotations of dour scientific scrutiny. No, I can't say I understand what he does, or why, because trafficking in dead words seems about as futile a way to make a life as fixing stoves. But who am I to judge? Armand enjoys futzing with words and that's all you can say. But what a pair we make: A tonsured, ivory-tower institution man matching wits with a baldheaded blue-collar, closet intellectual.

Besides being doppelgangers for each other, loss is primary in our souls. We've both lost children too soon. Armand once said that if it wasn't for Anil's death, he might never have agreed to take on sprucing up this old house in the dead of winter. No, I am not sure who convinced whom.

Your hands are shaking like a leaf.

Can we go upstairs where it's warm?

Let's.

We climb the staircase. The house creaks. Armand's snowy head swirls in abstractions, but he's not afraid to get his mitts dirty. He flutters back to earth from his tower from time to time and fuddles around with engines. If there's a combustion engine in this world, past or present, Armand has taken it apart, recombined it, set it to humming again. It was Armand who said, *The body is a machine* and *food the fuel*, quoting some eco-philosopher or other. *Work keeps up the internal combustion in the lungs.* What an "Armandian" expression, I thought, coining an adjective. Now when I look at my hands, I can hardly believe in the implied wisdom there Armand always talks about. I do believe in work. I do believe if we work hard and work honestly, then the work will reward us. I believe this.

We enter the room. It's balmy as an oven. The boy takes to his bedding; I, to the window.

What was I saying?

Something about work. Hands?

Yes. What I also believe I can't say, for words sometimes fail me. I know there's more to a man than what he says, much more, much more than what he even thinks and certainly more than what he does. It's only a matter of luck or painful scrutiny that we set down our words as deeds and deeds as truths to share—our truths, small, imperfect, yet somehow absolute—ours alone.

With my senses dulled, ears clogged with wax, nose whistling like a flute, with my dumb fingers unable to caress a leaf, let alone pick up a screw, the world, ignorant of my bearing, still lifts like steam to meet my dulled touch. There's a wind outside. It makes cuneiform patterns on the snow. Letters. A snow devil spins.

Let's get some sleep. There's much to do tomorrow.

Okay.

You might even help me.

Okay.

NINETEEN

It's been several days since I arrived and I have barely left this room. I worked on the house a little, not much. It seems I've grown lazy, content to dither like a fool, anticipating Armageddon. The fire in the hearth still burns hotly and shadows still dance on the ceiling and the walls. There is no boy this morning, December 2nd, a sort of palindrome. Did I scare him off? Good. I'll sit here and wait for him and watch the shadows dance. The shadows are a silent music. I'll shut my eyes.

I awoke later than I should have. Now it's late afternoon, almost evening. I didn't get to work on the house. I didn't dismantle the porch or tear out the old floor in the downstairs hall. Remembering and drinking, sleeping, smoking, took away all my energy, took away all my time, because somehow I still don't want to appear too eager to work. I'm playing coy, hard to get. Renovation, after all, is partly foreplay.

I light a cigar. Where's the boy? That blasted dog howls outside. Poor thing. Maybe she's Mesingw and I ask myself *What's that?* and I answer, Oh, just a monster living in these woods, *What kind of monster?* Oh, just something we scared our kids with to make them behave like good, God-fearing children. The boy enters.

Who're you talking to?

Myself.

You're funny.

Is that dog barking or am I dreaming it?

There's no dog barking now. Maybe before.

I sink into the blankets. I draw deeply on my cigar. I feel insouciant. I look toward the door. There is no boy. In his stead, I scent burning sulfur, that old metallic reek of blood.

If only I had had more time with Cole, I would have told him that down by the old Wagner farm, human blood had stained the earth pink from that old Sugarloaf Massacre. On moonless nights, you could hear the boughs in the woods squeal, the jangle of utility belts, bridles, knives unsheathed and bayonets slipped between ribs like the swish of a spade in sand. *The Bloodstained Field.* We erected a marker on Walnut Street:

> Near this spot occurred The Sugarloaf Massacre. On September 11, 1780 a detachment of Captain John Van Etten's Company Northampton County Militia resting at the spring was surprised by a band of Indians and Tories led by Seneca Chief Roland Montour.

Let's go farther back—*Farther further mother murder.* In the winter through fall of 1779, the Five Nations of the Iroquois and a band of Tories attacked pioneer settlements along the Susquehanna River. Under orders from Old Wooden Teeth, George Washington, himself, Klader and his fifteen men marched by foot into the Luzerne Valley. They tramped down through the Old Warrior's Trail under the oppressive heat of our Pennsylvanian September. Overcome by exhaustion, the militia camped on the banks of Little Nescopek, napped, snacked on deer jerky, apples, sang a song or two, and while swimming or sleeping, the Reds crept up through the bushes, flew down from the trees. They scalped, slashed, stabbed, strung up entrails of Van Etten's contingent from the seed pines. Those who survived scattered, but some were tortured, many drawn and quartered, most killed.

I might have told Cole how history tells us Washington was a hero, the founding father, a boy so honest he couldn't tell a lie. But history failed to show his thirst for blood and hatred for the Indians. A man is a verb, I would've told Georgie Washington, not a noun. A man's as good as what he does, not how nature colored him.

Every five years or so, we held reenactments of the massacre down in Whispering Pines Park. Armed with wooden rifles, wooden hatchets, dressed in uniforms our wives sewed out of old curtains, scraps that made us look like a ragamuffin regiment, we play-attacked naked-to-the-waist neighbors, their faces smudged with war paint, heads donning homespun wigs and chicken-feather headdresses. You'd think we were playing it up for a camera hidden somewhere among the hedgerows. You'd think we were on some soundstage in an honest-to-God Hollywood studio.

We slashed the air in slow motion, missing noses and jaws, our animate fury bypassing necks and ribs by a distance of a foot or more, yet we still managed to stain the poppy field red with crimson soda paint. Later we hoofed it up, hopped up on giggle water—ale, shine, Colonel Yuengling's homemade mash—while Clancy's Revolutionary War ensemble fluted and trumpeted and snare-rolled deep into the evening. We lit hay bale bonfires, reclined on the knolls, sang while smoke billowed into the darkening night, a night alive with the rasp of crickets. Sometimes Nona and I took part in those plays.

One year, I played Klader and Nona played Queen Esther, the Iroquois leader of some great significance. Nona had the long auburn hair and high cheekbones for the role, the wildness in her eyes for it, the freckled ancestry. The director, Penny Super, Conyngham's resident dramatist and perpetual scholar of Greek tragedies, had decided, in a burst of inspiration or whimsy, I couldn't decide, that to restore justice to Klader's fate she had him skulk through the scenes of march and arrest as a disembodied spirit, explicating events as they unfolded. But the Hazleton Historical Society's committee of truth, accused her of communism and protested her decision. They summoned Penny Super to a hearing. So in a stuffy room attended by none but the play's cast and crew, the peer jury, and a few curious kids, Penny rigorously defended her artistic choices, standing as if on trial at the center of that salty room. Creaking ceiling fans billowed up hot juicy air.

Though my play is an attempt to transform our collective recollections, my choices are protected by artistic freedom. I am not sure I am remembering her words accurately, but am sure of her intent. Penny's speech lasted a full forty minutes, leaving most of us perplexed. She cited all the crimes of injustice against art, accused the committee of witch-hunting, narrow-mindedness, pettiness, crassness, and so on with such poetic wit and innuendo it stunned us. The committee members scratched their tonsures, adjusted their bifocals, jotted notes in their legal pads, furiously worked their pens. They conferred with one another in low tones, gingerly sipped their glasses of water, excused themselves to render a decision. Forty minutes later, they returned, decided the show must go on. Many of us who took part in the play didn't share Penny Super's ideals. Our goals were less political, tilted toward summer pleasure, simple family fun, something for a bored town to do on a late summer day.

Maybe for some of us, Klader represented hope, blind trust, even if he served Old Wooden Teeth's evil directive, and I still wonder if that excused his culpability. Only in his mid-twenties and with a new wife at home in Albany, Klader's death spoke to our collective consciousness of injustice. Maybe by disembodying Klader, Penny Super had resurrected him, his spirit at least. Maybe Iroquois magic had transformed him into Mesingw, the cantankerous creature who haunted the woods near the Water Gap and surrounds: Klader as Mesingw, eater of children, Luzerne Valley's great boogeyman. I had to laugh.

Mesingw crowed in the woods and unleashed its gringles on children who failed to finish their peas or creamed spinach, children who soiled their bed linens, brusque children who defied their elders and who refused Jesus in their hearts. I suppose the Mesingw myth compounded the mystery of a borough where nothing much happened—where an abandoned house in the woods drew rumors of spirits, or a widow's nightmare of devils caused tongues to wag, or a deer struck and flung into the boughs became cause for murmurs of monsters at Cuz N' Suds. People would claim to see flickering lights rising from the Clay Hole, images not attributable to any wind or play of moonlight through the locusts, but perhaps it *was* only foxfire, or a boy playing with matches, or swamp gas, or perhaps what they thought to be the chaff of Mesingw motoring in the woods was just the burp of a big throated bullfrog.

The branches of a weeping willow became Mesingw's claws, and his roar in the woods reverberated in your chest while you lay beneath your covers. Our children obeyed us under the duress of Mesingw's shrill screech. I would use Mesingw against Cole, but he would shrug it off like the tall tale it was. A born skeptic, that boy, doubter of things mysterious and inexplicable, like the miracles of Jesus and the existence of God.

How do you say it? Mesin—

Muh-sing-uh. A Lenape mask spirit, living solid face, a powerful monster, master of games. It came to men in dreams. Some said it balanced nature. Some said it was Bigfoot. Sasquatch.

I ain't scared.

I have to laugh. It's just a story. It doesn't mean anything. Or maybe it does. There were all sorts of stories about this county. In Canadensis, you'd find the ruins of a half-built castle, rumored to serve as the final dwelling place of an exiled Marie Antoinette. Some said Marie, prisoner number 280, Antoinette Capet, had escaped her beheading in 1793, traveled to America in the bowels of a slave ship, dressed as a commoner. Who's to say? The castle seemed more a ruined stronghold than anything else, so resembling the felled structures you would find in the pages of books on Franciscan churches as to mirror them. Imagine, Marie Antoinette alive and well in the backwoods of these northeastern woods?

Some said the stones themselves issued bloodcurdling screams. Some claimed the quarried walls, rough hewn and roughly mortared, laced with dead ivy, trickled blood; yet no one could say for certain if it was blood or just the rust stains from old iron pegs. Hard to conceive. Hard to swallow.

I ain't scared.

In an abandoned house on Sherwood Road, the one with its roof caved in and windows boarded up, there was a lawn tilled in jagged rows and planted with hundreds of crosses. In that same house, they said spirits of such awesome fury oozed like rancid gas from the cellar, levitated across hallways where children chased their puppies into daylight dens. The gas entered a child's room, animating the glassy eyes of dead dolls, flicking lights on and off, circulating ceiling fans, opening and shutting closet doors, and then, like a watery wind stinking of sulfur, it meandered down the staircase and into the kitchen, opening and closing drawers and opening and closing window shutters, thus altering the shape of a life. *Papa, do ghosts know they're ghosts?* I am not sure they have consciousness as surely as they have will. Were they subject to the rules of determinism and chance just like the living? *Papa, when do ghosts die?* Cole, how I miss your questioning.

I still ain't scared.

I have to laugh.

You see, boy, it's the small moments that take my breath away when I remember Cole, moments I focus on to recapture a sense of lost magic in life. It's the shine on Cole's hair when he cannonballed into Big Nescopek Creek, that sense of laughter spilling from his body after having climbed all the way to the top boughs of the old oak. Once, when Cole returned from some long excursion in the woods, he came home scratching his arms. A red trail of pustules topped white spread up his shoulders, his neck, his cheeks. He scratched his crotch and I said Stop! and he said, *I can't not!*

It's poison oak, Son. Scratching'll only make it worse, I said, and he said, *I can't stop!*

Calamine lotion. Powder. I slathered his hands with salves and fitted them with mittens, duct taped them to his wrists—*Don't scratch.* Still, he almost tore his skin apart.

Later, it was the smell of earth on his breath, later, of cigarettes on his skin when he turned twelve, later, the odor of liquor in his mouth. I raged with disappointment.

Don't be in such a hurry to grow up, Cole!

I can't not.

I watched him grow into an adolescent, then into a young man who found himself further at odds with the world. I objected to his obsession with motorbikes and fast cars and gave in to his desire to own an Indian Scout, because Nona said to let him enjoy a little freedom, because her authority over me was her love and benefactions of her affection. How can I forget the way he seemed that final week, lying supine on his bed, his legs bracing the wall. Asleep. A beam of light shot through the parted curtains and illuminated him. There was a book flattened on his stomach. Picking it out from under his fingers I read, *April is the cruelest month, breeding lilacs out of the dead land, mixing memory and desire.* I lay the book on his desk, beside his leather-bound journal, and inched the door shut upon leaving his room, unbelieving that soon he would be gone, lost in that vacuous ocean of the world that claims everything. Yes, it's the smallest things that render a life complete.

Let's go down and see if we can't break a wall or two.

I don't feel so good.

What's the matter?

My stomach hurts.

Quit yer bellyaching and help me out.

I can't. Maybe if you talk more I'll be better.

We'll never finish if we don't get started.

Please?

Some things are never finished. Like my fatherhood, and like this house, some things go on unfinished. One day you're a child chasing bluebirds with a slingshot, or dragging a hope chest by its leather strap down a shimmering, dusty road, or you're sheltered in a culvert with your mother while a thunderstorm passes overhead, and the next you're staring into a window at an old man barely recognizable as yourself.

Like me looking at you?

Like you looking at me. I'll admit now that I wasn't so different from Cole. Maybe because I saw in him what I most wished to overcome that I turned him into my enemy. I never told him that as a child I also practiced geophagy, ate dirt, also bore witness to silences, silences that evaporated my sense of self, silences that turned me inside out. I was also observer to light overwhelmed by the shadowed redwoods, old as petrified bone, attuned to stillness routed by the sheer presence of blue elms and willows, the spotted spruce woods and the piebald forests, whose bark always reminded me of zebra skin. For me, perhaps like Cole, those trees of a thousand varieties sheathed in ancient secrets never failed to astonish. Part of this project then, I told Armand, is to restore the sense of wonder for life, to recapture my *Sarvajna* (was that the word?) and to enter that infinite space where I lost myself, that space where I could still be astounded by the simplest things, like Cole.

Where's Armand?

When Armand gets here, I'll tell him of the things I've seen and try and attach meaning to them. I'll tell him of the wounded buck that flashed over a trail sheathed in ice one winter and how I thought I had witnessed the tail of God. Of God! Ha! I will tell him of the simple fact of Sugarloaf Mountain rising in the center of our valley, lifting from ancient green earth like the hump of a giant whale. Maybe I'll tell him about that fleet of red-tailed raptors that wheeled in the sky one spring, maybe fifty years ago, or was that in a poem by Cole I read? You could just about smell the clouds pushed down from their wings. One summer, maybe a million fireflies lifted from the woods abutting Whispering Pines Park. They blinked into the air like cinder sparks. So I put two and four together and thought the world was ending.

Like now?

Like now. One winter, when Cole was still a toddler, just learning his alphabet, someone sighted a rabid wolf near the shoals of Big Nescopek Creek. Frankie Shattock and I led a small posse through the woods that day and hunted it for three days and three nights, but we never found it. At night, you could hear it howl over the wind, and Henry James joined in, barking and barking. The wolf bawled for a week or so and then quit. What did its voice tell us except that the mysteries of the woods ran deep as men's dark souls? Still we kept a close watch on our daisy cows. Homer Danforth even locked up his prized Clydesdales. We locked our doors and left our porch lights on.

Feeling better?

No.

Just sleep it off. I'm getting to work. Leaving the boy, I venture downstairs and take stock. I cross into the dining room. Observe the wainscot. The crown molding. There was always some project to do. There was always a new wall to build, a new leak to plug, a new hole in the roof to patch. The house needed hands to rescue it from oblivion, to transform it into a home where all reform ceased, because that was Jesus' promise of Heaven. I suppose being the kind of man I was meant to be, letting actions serve as surrogates for speech, meant letting the hands talk. Sure, let the things the hands produce say all that needed saying. Looking back, being a stove-junker held about as much capital in the modern world as a typewriter or a payphone or a grandfather clock.

Keep the hands busy and the mind going. Idleness is a sin and indolence a defect of one's character, I would say to Cole. I would say these words to Cole because, decades before, Blake had said these words to me, and I suppose that words, in the end, count as a kind of inheritance, and I suppose another gift you can bequeath is memory.

When Cole should've been outside being a boy, skipping rocks across the surface of Angel Lake, tossing a baseball, practicing his grounders and knuckleballs and curves, instead I had him practice wrestling moves, or had him work. We spent many a summer day working on his throws, his submissions, or fixing broken pipes, repairing fissures in the ceiling, tamping down bubbles in the floorboards. We rejoined broken joists, tacked insulation, pink and fibrous, in the attic that left molecular deposits of glass on our skin. I drilled him on multiplication tables, long division, had him read the dictionary and memorize words. I pulled him up by his shirt sleeves when I caught him dozing on his desk, and forced him to work on the house. Things would be fine for a few weeks, but it seemed that disorder was the house's natural state. A few days after patching a hole or plastering a crack, a new hole would appear or a new crack. Soon as he learned a word, he forgot it again, or used it wrongly. Plug one leak and two more appeared. Rewire a conduit, cap the ends, and although the lights in the kitchen blinked on and off just as intended, just as they should, the entire second floor lay plunged in darkness so syrupy you could ladle it with a spoon. This house, like Cole's mind, remained intent on undoing our efforts to fix it, even as it gave us a purpose. It remained, like Cole, in the end, unchanged.

The boy enters the dining room and says something and I ask him What? and he shrugs.

I asked what you did with your life.

I was a stove-junker, as I said. That's a piece of honesty right there. I suppose being honest is still a gift I can give myself.

What does it mean? Stove-junker.

What does anything mean? Armand once said that reworking the definitions a man lived by could be a start to reassessing one's life, at least account for it. I couldn't argue. If time has taught me anything it is this: Sincerity is a foundational principle, like gravity.

What you say, as much as what you don't say, can destroy a life, I told Cole once, and he said, *Why?* And I said, *Because words are weapons,* then his lips moved without sound. *What?* I said. *Say again?* Then as if I were made of vapor he walked through me. At the end of the room he offered me his back, his posture stiff as a pillar of salt, then he mechanically gyrated, turning to face me facing him. He regarded me with that mix of insouciance and understanding that never failed to annoy. But that was just a dream, because in the next instance he crumbled into a heap, then seeped through the floorboards and into the marrow of the house.

I move into the hall. I stop to regard the stairs leading up. The stairs are a spine, this banister, the house's backbone. I shut my eyes.

What're ya thinking now?

Cole could run up and down these stairs as if he were made of electricity. He could slide down the banister at a velocity that would hurt me to watch. I never raced him up the stairs because I couldn't keep up. Nor did I follow him down the banister, sliding where God split me. All I ever said was No. No. No.

People take your temperature by the words you say. Maybe I'm guilty of not saying what needed saying that last day. If I could enter a time-machine and return to that Monday Cole left us, what would I say? *I love you*, for one. *I apologize, I didn't mean it, sometimes my words are weapons.* Or perhaps the inevitability of each moment is this: We are who we are and cannot change a thing. Armand calls that *fatalism*, a fancy word for the expression, *What will be, will be*. Maybe I would have done exactly what I did that day, nothing, said precisely what I said, everything.

Go and get my shovel upstairs. Let's pry up the floor.

Okay.

TWENTY

A new day. We worked on the floors yesterday, the boy and I, or I worked and he watched. It's tiresome work. My joints creak and so does the house and also that old oak outside. Now the room is warm. The boy's bed empty. Where is he? Has he gone? Was he ever here, that little ghost? I also feel like a ghost. My feet ache.

My contact with the world begins with this floor barely felt by these stupid feet. Stuffed into two pairs of thermal socks and one pair of leather work boots with soles like teeth, I shuffle about the room like a long-distance skier. My black work pants are made of some heavy, blended material, like nylon and polyester, and this morning I fitted myself into a red and blue flannel shirt, and over it I wrapped myself in a gray woolen scarf, its two tongues tucked into the lapels of a black overcoat. I look heftier than I am, squeezed into this costume like ground meat in sausage casing. A ski cap warms my scalp, covers my cabbage ears. My old work gloves, bourbon brown, I wear out of habit but not for warmth, their leather cracked and mottled like the skin of a reptile—though I can't decide which kind. I pat down my forearms, drawing blood into them. My brain seems to work fine. It seems to work fine. Work fine. Fine. I have to laugh.

After a breakfast of dry corn flakes, I spent the better part of the morning inspecting the house and grounds. I shouted for the boy, but he was nowhere to be found. I made notes in my journal. I stomped up and down the porch steps, stood in the center of the yard, reasoned, deduced, nodded to myself in silent understanding of what needs to be done: strip the shingles, tear down walls, rip up the floorboards. Renovation begins with destruction.

I pat down my legs. Now and again, the vein above my left temple throbs. Now and again, pain shoots into my cranial wall like a hot knife. This is memory, I tell myself. Memories press against my skull, bulge my forehead. When my brain hurts, I focus on something, the weather or the landscape, and then I am garrulous as a blue jay, remembering things maybe I have no business remembering—A rope swinging over Nescopek Creek, a splash, a tumble of watery waves cresting silver then fading to black. What does it all mean? It's all *maya* anyway.

Where is the boy? I cough into my fist. Am I getting sick? This year I forgot to take my flu shot. Didn't forget. Forgot on purpose. I have no one but myself to blame if I get sick. Who else can I blame? Surely not God. I am the product of poor choices: Fatty foods, pickled stuff, fried fish, smoked meats, bourbon, cigars. Somehow even breathing this air feels like a vice.

Where is the boy? Between the trees, running and playing like boys should? I never jogged for pleasure or health, haven't bicycled since I was his age, what is it, twelve? Now death, like a pattern of whorls that shape-shift in the dark corners of dark rooms, caresses its cold hard hand against my cold soft cheek. Sometimes I imagine rakish things in those corners, shadows blacker than the surrounding shadows, like an eyeless boy girdling his head, or a double-headed crow, cawing. A slip down the stairs and a good hard tumble to the landing could send the shadows pouncing. Listen how I sound, paranoid and agoraphobic. Armand and I might just be two loose screws in a drawer after all.

Except for Armand, no one knows I'm here. This fact should frighten me, but it doesn't. Winds rise. The old oak's bough scrapes across the roof and the house moans. The tree knows I'm here. I think it wants me to acknowledge it. It's just a tower of gristle with a chandelier crown, its bulbs burned out. The winds rise and laughter spills from the branches, mine or Cole's? I clear my throat.

What are you thinking? The boy says.

Where'd you come from?

I can't remember.

I didn't mean that, I meant... never mind. I light a match, cup it in my hands. That's an old oak, over a hundred years, I think. When I was a boy, I decided it was apoplectic, that is, sick, or dejected, or just plain sad, like it'd lost someone it loved, or maybe it never wanted to be a dumb old oak tree and just wanted to be a boy that got turned into a tree because of some magic in the universe we can't quite fathom. When the autumnal winds blew through the woodlots, shaking the pollen from the stalks, its old trunk trembled and rocked the house. When blizzards battered the countryside and encumbered its roots in ice, powdering his branches with crystals of snow—*snow daggers, ice knives, mails of glass*—it would moan and tremble, ready to crush the house or cradle it, I couldn't quite decide. When the spring rains drenched our valley, overflowing the creeks and transforming the farmlands into silt lakes—*silt pools upon which bobbed patterns of the sky the color of cinders*—the house shuddered and so did the old tree, showering the roof and our back deck in a spray of wet leaves and cones and seeds. Nona and I would hear the plop of a wet branch colliding against the kitchen's bayfront, the crack of a branch end snapping off and landing on the lawn with a thud. All that clatter seemed to make me think the world was ending.

Let's go inside.

In a moment. Sometimes, I'd find Cole staring absently out the kitchen window, out at the old oak's leathery trunk, and he'd see pictures in it he'd draw in his sketchbook. He'd watch the oak shiver, or weep, or laugh, its bark bleeding amber sap and say, *Papa, what would it say if it spoke?*

A tree can't talk.

But what if it could?

The pots hanging from Nona's pot rack would tinkle sibilantly when the old oak bowed and flexed, then I would marvel that it hadn't toppled over by the roots and taken the house with it. Some nights it groaned like an old man—arthritic and cantankerous and foul-mouthed. Alive, angry, terrified, it creaked discontent and moaned complaint and I felt both it and this house in my heart united into one living, breathing thing.

Come on, let's go inside.

Okay.

Upstairs, I place my hands close to the fire, so close it's as if I mean to scoop up a cinder. The heat is good. I feel color return to my cheeks.

Come here and help me with my boots, I say. The boy doesn't stir. Is he still afraid? What's there to be afraid of? Come here, I say.

Something scrabbles in the ceiling—small feet, a tumbling as of dice. Rookeries of mice in the attic, and crows, perhaps, their wings caked in speckling bits of ice. Maybe it's the crow that landed on the hood of the Mercury when I arrived, or maybe it's just my mind playing tricks. I want to ask the boy if he hears it, just to corroborate what I hear, but I don't and the noise doesn't return. I hold my breath. Count to five. Exhale. Some animals must understand the winter best, because I surely don't. Winter always seemed like something to suffer through. But we made the best of things. Winter united us. One winter out of the long claws of ice that collected in rows from the eaves of the front porch, Nona and I snapped them off and pulverized them in the sink with a ball and claw hammer. We squeezed maple syrup on the shavings and scooped the ice into cones to eat by the fire after supper. That's when the house was so still you could hear your heart. The ice brooks, frozen solid, I'll visit tomorrow, after I work on the family room, or the kitchen, I haven't yet decided. Because it *is* decided that I must. *So be it.* But that is tomorrow.

What do you want to do now?

Lie here, I suppose. Finishing off these long days with the hearth's heat like arms spreading wide warmth through the bedroom, I'll stand by the window for a bit longer and study this landscape and write in my memory book and remember or daydream or invent. Lean into the pane and drink till the bourbon is gone. Light another Hemingway. Let the smoke commiserate with those snow cyclones outside. This landscape still amazes me. Argent. Ivory. Heavy as forgotten dreams. The winter is stunning.

BOOK II

ONE

Several days have passed and no sign of either Armand or the blizzard. Miki said it's December 10th, so it must be. She said it was eight-fifty-seven a.m., and so it was. We awoke to another day whose whiteness blinds. The hearth fire ticks like a metronome, flicks electric shadows across the broken plaster, over the broken ceiling, transmits my shadow like a Rorschach stain across the broken baseboards. A great webby crack, like that in broken glass, spreads like lightning across the wall adjacent the window. Funny how I hadn't noticed it. The old iron pipes in the walls peek through the holes I made with the sledgehammer yesterday, and a welt, perhaps from a burst water pipe, squints at me like an eye. Perhaps the house is past the point of repair, but I must try. Who would I be if I didn't try?

The boy enters.

Remember who you are yet? I say.

He shakes his head no.

It'll take time. Things reveal themselves a bit at a time. I light a match. On certain afternoons this room filled up with a brassy light that felt solid, I say, like something you could turn over in your hands, and I think how it never pooled but seemed to lift the textures from the house. The drabness it revealed climbed over the throw rug, rose over the feet of the armoire, the legs of the credenza with its framed photos recording the starts and stops of our lives. There, the drabness revealed a still life—golden apples, blue plums and ruddy dates, a feather quill and inkwell, a burlap bag of golden wheat, each object shining against a black background, lit by some unseen light. How that painting's impressionistic blues and golds mimicked the blues and golds in Nona's eyes, mimicked the blues and golds of morning light—light that seeped through the window's white taffeta curtains. *The Lord's light*, Pearl might call it—*Light that Lazarus must have felt summoning him toward the Lord's voice*—and I might've said, *Ma, are* people also light*?* and she might've said, *People are constellations; you can travel by their light.* And the drabness it revealed swirled over the nightstands on which stood our beaded lamps, the mouse-eared alarm clock, a photo of Nona, of Cole, of me in my younger days clutching a fly rod, then it curled like smoke over the dresser atop which sat Nona's vanity tray (perfume bottles, face brushes, skin creams), revealing swirls of dust frosted across the framed full-length mirror that once leaned there against the corner wall, and the drabness inched toward the hurricane lamps and the candles in their glass cups, and the drabness crept over the antique books on ships and nautical maps and pulp novels and metaphysics and religion standing in neat little rows with their spines facing out on the four-tiered bookshelf, and the drabness softly rode over the face of the cuckoo clock on the wall, its hands frozen at twelve and six, revealed the bowled glass of our wall sconces, the wall ledges, and the drabness licked up all the small evidence of our small lives. The room would awaken this way, piece-by-piece, disclosing the ever-widening gulf between disaster and rescue that united us. The match fizzles.

What time is it?

Why do you want to know? Where do you have to go? What do you have to do?

He shrugs.

I'm not sure of the time. It might be after nine or so, or it might not be.

With my cutter, I clip the end of a Hemingway. The butt rolls across the room and bumps the wall where the boy sits with his feet outstretched. I light the cigar with another match from the matchbox Armand gifted to me at Nona's funeral and I take a few deep draws. The tip sizzles, glows red as a coal.

What does the smoke taste like?

Mind your own business.

I palm the matchbox, weighing it in my hands. How light it feels, yet what power it holds, each matchstick possessing the force to save or destroy a life. What strange substance it is: I am talking of fire. Neither chemical nor… Christ, what is it? Controlling fire put you in a league with God.

Can I see it?

I toss him the box. That's General MacArthur on the cover, I say. In full salute.

"I Shall Return" the boy reads.

Very good. You can read. That's something.

I didn't know I could.

I. Shall. Return. How serendipitous (thank you Armand for the word). When Armand gave me the matchbox I touched his shoulder with my palm. Outside the funeral parlor, near by the flag post, we shared a smoke below a NO SMOKING sign.

Blue smoke spires from my lips and my throat dimly burns with notes of leather and Dominican earth and deep, sweet wood.

Why do you do that?

Smoke? Because it's bad for you and sometimes what's bad for you is what's good for you.

You talk funny.

The first draw reveals a simple layer, but the longer it burns, you get new essences that fuel your imagination. I blow a plume of smoke to the ceiling. It clatters and fans. Ancient faces revealed in the smoke, strange words and funny letters. The smoke is a tool, like a hammer or a saw.

Smoke, the Indians say, helps a man remember. *You shouldn't smoke, Dutch. What'll I do when you're gone?* I shut my eyes. Nona, here's what I'm doing now that you're gone.

End of October, we held Nona's funeral at Silver-Dippel's parlor. It was time for closure, to tell her the things in death I couldn't tell her in life. Even now, when I think of her, my heart swells with love and admiration and pride. How such a fine woman decided to be my wife and for so long is an achievement I cannot take credit for. The fact I held on to her as long as I did says more about her than it does about me. What she endured. How she carried me along, even on those days when our marriage was less a direction than a destination.

While she lay in her casket looking strange, hair feathered blue, face waxen as a porcelain doll, lips drawn down and cheeks hollowed and reddened by some awful blush, I touched her hand. Cold as plastic.

No, this isn't Nona, I said, recoiling. *There's been a terrible mistake.*

They had leeched her veins and injected her with embalming fluids. The fluids made her skin smell like lemon rinds and castor oil beneath the powder and the lilac perfume.

Where's my wife? What've you done with my wife?

The night before she died, I pushed open the double-pane to let in the night air. Outside spread a city moving away from us, receding into the light. The red taillights of cars glowed like the tips of burning cigars, and a frosty wind pushed a newspaper and flattened it against a chain-link fence. Something rattled below. A soda can rolled along the sidewalk. Mewling sounds. Across the alley, Eunice, our neighbor's teenage daughter, gyrated in her stepfather's crotch while a bass drum thrummed through the walls. A baby wailed from next door while a woman's voice screamed obscenities—*Fuck it! Fuck my asshole! Suck my cunt!* The madness of crosstown traffic. The maddening people. The maddening chatter. Everything my eyes swept over saw inured pain. How could this waste not prove the death of God?

How long had we convinced ourselves of our innocence, Nona, cloistered here for the past two-odd decades with our curtains drawn, our lives rationed to small conversations amid cartoon tigers and toucans glaring at us from empty cereal boxes? Dearest, our bedroom is a wasteland of broken things—lamps and radios and tattered books piled in the corner or at the foot of the bed, soiled napkins under the curtained sill. Snot rags. Scum in the shower tub. Piss stains. Egg shells in the cupboards. Spores of mold cling to the ceiling fan. See this wasteland? That ruined garden? The other dark room? I wanted to tell her these things, but I didn't. By then, time had taught me to spare her feelings, whereas before I could be so cruel. I turned sixty, then sixty-five, then seventy-five. Instead of shouting or stamping my feet or throwing a book across the room, I just rubbed the throb between my eyes, inhaled the metallic air and said, *Time we did something about this place.*

There was inside us another life. A secret life. There was a time when entering her life was like entering a brightly lit room, where the air was fresh and healthful, scented by wild places where wildflowers grew from stones shaped like fists, and each object was ordered, arranged as if in a museum, displaying that quality of beauty that time could not disarrange. That other Nona, the one in my dreams, was immortal. This Nona, who slept and wept and shuddered, held congress with ghosts the last few months of her life. She spent entire weeks sequestered in our bedroom, scratching circles in her drawing pad, sleeping with the radio on to some trebly, nervous, abstract music with its tinny trumpets and shrieking strings and timbales trembling, drowning out the vacuity of life. While flutes blared tortured phrases and cymbals crashed like shattered glass—"*The Apocalypse Symphony in E-minor," Dutch. It's by*—I attempted to draw her out, rapping at her door—*Nona, we need sugar, butter, we need bread. Are you coming out?* Hours after I gave up, retreated to the den with a newspaper or book, she would resurface as if from a nightmare, the music still blaring behind her. She mumbled things to herself and I said, *What? What is it? Speak up?* Her eyes held vacancy. I would snap my fingers across her pupils and she would snap back and say, *I forgot who you were.*

A week before she passed, she took my hands in hers and blew upon them and said, *Remember how you held them that first time?* She shrugged me away when I tried to draw her near. Turning away from her oystery eyes, quickly welling with salt, I said, *How could I forget?* and I left it at that.

She looked lovely that last cool morning with the streets decorated with hobgoblins and bed-sheet ghosts. Spider webs dripped from trees and lampposts. Pumpkins, lit by candles, grinned on stoops. That morning, Nona's appearance almost hurt to look at. It was like looking into light. She looked present. Her red-rimmed eyes looked clear, and her voice, for years bitter as a blackened gourd, softened. She leaned against the sink when I entered the kitchen, drawing herself a glass of water from the tap.

I've been lovely all morning and you weren't here to notice, she said.

What? I said, stopping in the threshold as if punched in the stomach, watching her watching me for reconciliation.

I said, she started, then stopped. *Forget it.*

Having finished doing the hard things, like falling in love, making commitments and relinquishing them, raising our son, grieving his loss, our lives had turned surreal. We had left the familiar roads I could drive with my eyes shut, even in the pitch of night. Now time had revealed us as strangers to one another. We were coarse as sandpaper. All our past tenderness calcified. Maybe I should have complimented her that morning, but I didn't. My tongue froze in my mouth.

I'll take a glass if you're pouring it, I said.

(Pause)

I dreamt. She shook her head. *No.*

(Pause)

Go on.

Who were we in the end? What? We shuffled about the brownstone in our nightclothes like ghosts observing the routine habits of things, commenting on nothing, upsetting nothing, leaving the dust to settle where it may, a sentence to die. Sleepwalkers, we bumped into each other and into the furniture, staring out of windows while dreaming of home. We were conscripted into silence, such silence, folded into a quietness transfigured into a din. We doled out benefactions to each other in wan smiles and slow nods of the head. Still she remained, for those final months, weeks, days, devoted to one thing: Cole. She stood guard over his obsolescence like a sentinel, guarding her secrets, still an observer of things lost and past.

(Pause)

Never mind.

Where was the soft arch of her cheekbones, the delicate curve of her breasts, eyes that softly blazed? Maybe I am being too harsh. But where had she gone? *You never touched my soul, Dutch, you know that? Even Cole said you were incapable of knowing what anyone really needed.*

(Pause)

She moved to the electric stove and rounded the coils with her finger. I poured myself a glass of hot water, shook in a little salt from the saltshaker standing against the backsplash, then gulped it down.

I'm meeting Armand at the aquarium later.

When do I get to meet this Armand?

(Pause)

My eyes circled the kitchen. Layers of filth. Boxes, soda cans, bottles, newspapers two years old.

He doesn't make house calls.

(Pause)

Honestly, he just might be a figment of your imagination.

Honestly, I just might be his, I said.

(Pause)

In the bathroom I performed my toilet, fitted my dentures. I cried out to Nona, my voice in a tone of distress.

Just oatmeal this morning, Nona. A little honey in it if you can manage.

I dressed for the day. Slipped on my newsboy cap. Dabbed a little polish on my shoes, buffing them to a mirror-like shine. Returned to the kitchen.

Nona sat at the bistro table, looking like a marionette with all her strings cut. Her head was slumped forward and her arms hung down by her sides. The water glass lay in her lap and a dark stain spread across her thighs, down her left shin, the hem of her nightclothes dripping water.

I changed my mind. I'd like a hardboiled egg.

I stood before her. Expressionless. Her deflated form collaborated with that inhuman silence that settles over a space where someone has just vacated. A baby wailed from next door.

Stop your shammin' and get up, I said. *I'm in no mood.* I compressed her shoulder with my hand. Clammy. Rigid. *The hell's the matter with you?*

She did not swat my hand away. She did not spring out of the chair and complain, scream, weep. She sat slumped in that metal chair, in that godforsaken kitchen, still as a statue, as if sleeping.

I crouched before her, took her mute hand in mine. Removing my bifocals, I rubbed away the pressure built up behind my temples. Her hand in mine felt like nothing at all, the bone and tendon and sheath of skin like absolutely nothing. I could have picked up her body with two fingers and thrown her into the clouds.

You never really knew me, Dutch.

And I never really knew you, Nona, and that's the tragedy of life. She was right. Even when we share our lives, share love, compassion, even hate, misunderstanding, the intimacies of loving and the defeats of the heart, even after a lifetime together breathing the same air, weathering the same storms, we remained as distant from one another as two planets in separate constellations. And now there she was, a burned out star, hoarding the greatest secret of all.

TWO

We don't experience our own death, Armand told me. It's for others to experience. So there's at least one experience in life we have no words for. Where language fails us we invent stories. We manufacture Heaven and Pearly Gates and a bearded old God to embrace us with a light like love. We never truly understand our identity or our lives' value and we are made and remade under the eyes of others. Others define us, strangers categorize us, friends determine us. Our meaning is always deferred.

Though Nona and I offered glimpses into one another's lives, how I mistakenly believed our barriers were slipshod, that the walls we built to conceal the world had not concealed ourselves. I mistakenly believed that the fact of our affections were not random, that the horny emanations of youth were not the product of accident. I believed we were necessary to one another's survival, like light to shadow, cold to heat. So then, what to make of the end? What to make of the cheek-to-cheek kisses upon waking? *If that.* Or the unuttered sentences that left one another suspended in a chapped silence? Or the atrophied embraces we kept up for others' sake? What to make of the unfulfilled sentiments arising from one's small needs ministered by another?

There was enough blame to be cast, and for years I blamed losing Cole for ruining us. An easy scapegoat. What would our lives have been like if he hadn't left to teach us a lesson? *Is that what he'd done?*

Would we have been kinder to one another, more forgiving of our small differences, less prone to anger and blame? Who would we have become?

But that *thing*—what to call it? That *monster.* What to call that charged silence suffused with accusation and confusion, thickened with memory of the people we were? I believe, in the end, memory has the capacity to kill.

~

The night before her viewing, I laid out her funeral clothes, draped across our bed her navy blue dress with its single row of three brass buttons, hem of white lace and lace sleeves and lace collar. In a leather bag, I placed her favorite book, *Selected Journals and Other Writings* by John James Audubon, then her cosmetics and I handed the bag to Mrs. Dippel as if I were handing her parts of Nona's soul.

Make sure she looks honest, I said.

We have the finest embalmers in all of Maryland, she said. *She'll look asleep.*

Beside her open casket, a photograph of Nona stood on an easel—Nona with her hair glossy blue, wearing those plastic bifocals that exploded her eyes. Her ear-to-ear smile looked cheerful as a cricket. The photo stood on a table draped with a white cloth, its ribbed pleats falling to the carpet and fanning outwards like waves. A guestbook where you could sign your name lay open beside a vase of white carnations.

Standing over Nona while the seated funeral party watched, I pinched the edge of her lace collar, fingered the center brass button on her dress, in disbelief. It occurred to me that the word "wife" seemed destitute of meaning. I flicked a curl of her hair with my finger, that hair sprayed stiff as wood, and almost recoiled at the glitter that made her crown of white look like a powdered, sparkling wig.

What have they done to you?

While *The Loom of Time* droned over the loudspeakers, faint notes like drops of crystal falling through open space, my stomach churned the watery eggs and undercooked sweet sausages I had cooked for breakfast that morning. To settle that sour feeling, I thought of Halloween—decorations having turned downtown Baltimore into a city of ghosts and ghouls and goblins. While the air in that room spilled the stale breath of friends and acquaintances we seldom ever saw, I imagined crowds of costumed children teeming the streets with plastic shopping bags or pillow cases, their laughter rising in the chilly air like the chatter of birds. Air furtive with candy, thick with joy, dense as cream. Children, happy as larks, flitted from house to house and screamed, *Trick or Treat, Trick or Treat, give me something good to eat!* and maybe Cole was among them, a father to a petulant, pretty child. Moment by moment, I became less aware of that version of Nona lying in the casket, Nona absent of all her air and noise and light, as if the flowers and the music and the powder and the piss-stale bacon fat emanating from the commissary, and the sermon and psalms and all those plastic decorations—flowers and electric candles—stood for items in a recipe for respectful grief. A formula. I had hoped to conclude our final moments together, drift downwards into that long, amiable, interminable sleep. But that was hope, and hope by then was a depleted substance. *Oh, puh-leease, Dutch.* Forgive me, Nona, I'm being maudlin. Again.

While the weeping sounds tore apart that parlor, a room as dim as a benighted place, with its pale green walls and sea foam carpet and the air clouded with radiated heat, there I sat, stiff as a pillar of salt, ready to vomit on the floor of death's house, surfeit with overwhelming sickness over the sheer absurdity of life, life deadened by ritual. I wanted to get in my Mercury and drive someplace far away where the air was clean and vistas clear. I wanted to feel un-regarded, un-staged, invisible.

I should have returned Nona to Drums years ago, lit candles and sent them adrift on Big Nescopek, set Rod and Tippy free, and the aria of canaries, and Porter, that grim little conure that clucked like a chicken. That would have been more appropriate. Not this. This stage play—*If that*—hardened into an institution.

While Mr. Grimes took the lectern, I bowed my head, fighting the urge to vomit. My hands, busy on my knees, tapped muted rhythms. I bounced my leg like a third-grader holding back his bladder, tapped my heel to music only I could hear—festive music, music to confound this sense of insult. Trumpets blew in my head, their pitch bright as sunlight, and the swish of cymbals, and the pop and dull thuds of a snare and bass drum, and the candy hard syncopation of congas while

Grimes stood at the lectern prattling on about community loss and familial strength and personal redemption, expressing opinions, saying how Nona's soul was at that moment soaring with her angels toward Heaven. St. Peter would accept her through the Pearly Gates and "Win-nona" would laugh and sing and dance for all time. If he only knew.

I nodded silently, contemplating something Armand had said to me just a week earlier in the park. *Retrace your steps, fix your house. When it's finally your time, you'll want to have something to show for your life.*

A legacy, I said.

Call it that.

While Grimes pontificated about walking alone in shadowed valleys, I thought of Charlie Alsace. Charlie Alsace died for an hour and fifteen minutes and returned to life in the morgue, bringing a tale of the afterlife with him—*It was a tunnel and there was a voice, like sunshine, and it called me by name, and up I went to that voice, so like a sweetness, it was, and there were figures in the light, too many to count and no smaller than dust spores but no larger than planets, and I wasn't scared because the voice, that sweet sunshine voice speaking my name was all love*—but what Charlie Alsace felt might be no more than the brain winding down, and the light he saw might be nothing more than the brain dying, like a star exploding before it collapsed into black. And the tunneling? The tunneling into the light might only be the vestige memory of birth, convincing us that time is circular, like memory. Charlie Alsace was a boy I knew in high school, in '46 or '47.

Having survived the viewing, I stood near the front door and shook strange, warm hands, accepting feigned warm condolences, accepted studied words and practiced gestures that rang like false notes. I am being harsh, I know. I am being cruel, even. I knew the people we called friends expected me to cry, but I didn't. Couldn't. I knew they wanted something more from me, to show them I was human and not some monster. With faces like masks of propriety, who could blame me for passing judgment? Maybe it was the howl of beef gravy and burnt coffee emanating up from the commissary, or the miasma of old bacon fat that had frozen my expression, turned my face to stone, for it seemed so inconsistent with grief. Even as I said, *Thank you. I appreciate your concern. I'll let you know if there's something I need,* I fought back the urge to spill my stomach.

The creak of the ceiling fan, the organ music, sonorous as the void, the crackle and hiss of the loudspeaker as it fizzled, and light, gray as curdled milk funneling from the windows onto the floors, was grief turned absurd. I wanted to be outside, to smell clean, candied air, to feel the clean, cold breeze, to run among the masked children and chant, *Trick or Treat.* I must endure this, I thought. For Nona's sake. Give them something, a jerk of the shoulders, a few hearty sobs, put your feelings into action and placate them. So I removed my progressives, rubbed the bridge of my nose. I exhaled thoughtfully. Hands traveled my shoulders. Hands touched my hands even as I scanned the faces for Armand.

While the hired pallbearers carried Nona's casket across the wide green lawns to the crematorium, a long, rectangular, flat-roofed brick building the size and shape of a train car, I mustered up the strength to endure watching Nona burn. While they fitted Nona's casket onto a set of rolling tracks that led into an oven I could scarcely afford, I contemplated a return to Drums.

I steadied the pressure building behind my eyes. I waved away Grimes when he asked me if I wanted to say a few words in parting. Tina Bussard, James Batista, Betty Minot, Derek Cline, Jennifer so-and-so and her husband Dave or Mike or some monosyllabic thing—strangers, acquaintances, so-called friends—all waited, dabbing cheeks with napkins, blowing wet noses, holding silent council with their own memory of Nona, who was not there, not anywhere.

There's nothing I can say she doesn't already know, I said.

Grimes nodded, checked his wristwatch, wiped his nose with the back of his hand, and then, smug as a carny, rushed through the rest of the sermon. I almost shouted, *Take your time, asshole. Though I might not believe in your old Lord and Mighty anymore, aren't you trained to honor my dollar?*

Grimes lay his fat hands on the Bible. *Lord, we beseech Thee, in the tenderness of Thy great mercy, to have pity upon the soul of Thy handmaid Win-nona Josephine, cleanse her from all defilements which have stained her mortal form and give her inheritance in everlasting salvation. Amen.*

Amen.

Wake up Nona. Sit up. Stand up. Walk. Dance. Twirl like a dervish. Flap your arms. Beg me to save you from falling and drowning one last time. Embrace me. Kiss these parched lips. Nona, let's forget this absurd theater and return to the brownstone, pack our bags for Drums. Nona, let's go home. Work on the house. Remember. Dream. Invent.

A row of open windows overlooked the cemetery plots. A sheet of light fell from the silver sky, scintillating in its fury. Tuning out the watery trees aglow in the setting sun, tuning out Grimes' chattering, ignoring the few artful gasps and sobs escaping this weepy little flock, I thought everything had become intrusive. The ceremony reeked of vanity and I wondered who was this ceremony for? Certainly not for Nona. For me then. For me to prove that I was still capable of loving my wife in death even as I loved her in life? I had a good mind to tell them all to go to Hell.

Doors opened. Nona's casket entered a cave of blue flames. With the prayers spent and Nona's body turned to ash in the furnace, we convened for lunch. They would serve us meatloaf that tasted like cardboard, certainly not meat, and they in their wisdom, to mask the blandness, drenched it in fetid beef sauce that tasted medicinal. A side of creamed corn, watery as soup, and bread rolls crusted with sesame seeds that resembled birds' eyes. I threw down my fork and napkin and said, *Enough!* then walked out.

Later, in that mourning room, after all the well-wishers had left, their condolences still ringing in my brain—

She's in good hands.

The best hands.

She's in a better place.

With loved ones.

—it happened, my stomach emptied out of me and onto the carpet. A woman smelling of grape jelly, I can't recall whom, led me to a chair. She wiped my mouth with her handkerchief. A man with veined, muscular hands, reeking of chocolate offered me a glass of water.

I'm fine, I said, my hands trembling.

Busy hands rubbed my shoulders.

I'm fine. Please. It's the nerves, Somerset. Tell them it's all catching up to you. Tell them that to bear the loss of your wife of fifty-odd years is akin to half of your better soul dying. Tell them…

I'm fine, I said.

I scanned the room and spotted Armand. I nodded. He nodded. Excusing myself from those hands that moved across my back, patting my shoulders, hands touching my wrists, hands patting my knee, I said, *I'm fine, please, leave me the hell alone.*

Armand sat against the rear wall in a metal folding chair, a plastic cup in his hands, and I reached Armand's shoulder with my hand, and I touched him, and I said, *I am in no mood for your excuses.*

I have no stomach for funerals, old friend, he said. He smiled wickedly. *Seems neither do you.*

My upper lip curled in a half-smile, glad for the one friend who understood the depth of my suffering. His hound's tooth, pageboy cap, which never left his head, sat at a jaunty right angle, covering one brow so that half his face lay in shadow. Without his spectacles on, his bulbous eyes, dark and watery, projected a kind of alien knowledge.

I've been thinking, I said.

Thinking is good, he said.

Have I gone crazy considering going through with your idea?

What idea? I forget.

Should we go and fix that goddamned place once and for all?

He cleared his throat twice. He swirled his coffee. I felt in his gesture something mechanical—a pivot, a drop, a settling, like the arm of a locomotive.

Aren't we blind as mealworms to the importance of things? he said.

It's a trick of language to think we're not, I said.

THREE

Mister? Don't be sad. Mister?

I'm fine, I say. The boy sits by the hearth, half his face in shadow. The cigar in my hand is cold. I relight it with a match.

One evening, a few days after Nona's funeral, I sat all day in the same chair where Nona had vacated life. Another evening, with Nona's ashes already scattered into the wild Chesapeake, I lay all day in bed, staring up at the ceiling fan's blades. And another evening, perhaps a week later, with the air still furtive with sugar, I wondered, *Who can I share my feelings with? What angel would hear me?* Everything hurt then. Every pore screamed. Loneliness, sharp, angular, cut into me like a shard of broken glass. I wanted only to sleep then, but how could I when the noise of filth collected from years of bad decisions crowded this false home? So I decided to clean out the brownstone, throw out everything—*You can't extinguish a life just by*—and it was then I discovered aspects of my life I had forgotten. Finding in the corner of my secretary a velvet black pebble that smelled faintly of sweet creek water, I wondered, *Why had I kept it?* What did that stone signify if not the idea that in these random facts of existence littered about these old humorless rooms, lived a past that had gone unaccounted?

I grit my teeth. Smoke pours from my mouth. Each sliver of smoke rising, blue in its curling, looks like Pidgin or Aramaic, perhaps Chinese or Sanskrit or Kitchen Kaffir, certainly an alphabet to some dead language. Its secrets draw upon the assumption that self-truth is too heavy a burden, so we hoard our secrets in words that mean little—mean little words that mean nothing. One of those secrets is a love constant beyond death.

My mouth feels gritty. I extinguish the cigar against the floor—*Maybe I'm one of those secrets you kept, Pops?* Maybe Cole or maybe not.

What's a secret?

It's who we are. It's something that's kept hidden from others, like us from the world. We're secrets. I never suspected Cole of keeping secrets, or Nona, certainly not from me, but cleaning out the brownstone one day, I discovered that objects conceal a private life. I found wire brassieres fringed in black lace, in a cup size I couldn't have reckoned, or pink linen pantyhose I never remembered Nona wearing. Finding a pair of sequined dance slippers stuffed in the pocket of her raincoat, I wondered, *when had she danced?* In the back of the hall closet, I unearthed a small velvet box stuffed with costume jewelry (rhinestone rings, earrings of black teardrop glass, charm bracelets with turquoise seahorses) she never wore, the price tags still affixed to rope chains and black pearl rings. In the kitchen, beneath the garbage disposal, I found books I never figured she read—Emily Dickinson's poems, for one, poems by Rumi, paperback erotica. I found a Ouija board under the dresser, tarot cards, moth eaten scarves in a sheer material like chiffon or silk that smelled faintly of peaches. Between the couch cushions, I found a silver bowtie (not mine), a set of black garters, three dull pennies dated 1926, and a nearly empty bottle of lavender nail polish—fragments of life lived, abandoned for me to discover, to bear witness to, to feel berated by. Even in death, Nona could still find ways to confuse me.

In a manila envelope buried beneath her nightstand drawer, I found half a dozen photographs of Nona—*Dutch, that ain't me but my doppelganger*—in the throes of a youth I barely remembered. Faded black and white four-by-sixes clearly showed Nona modeling in an atelier, but whose? Where? When? In one photograph, she parted wide her legs and the dark coarse hairs between her thighs looked like an ink stain. She grinned for the camera without an ounce of shame. I traced the contours of her breasts with my finger, the large dark nipples, rolled my palm over the curve of her hips, unable to reconcile this woman turned into an object of lust from the wife and mother and painter of birds. In another photo, she peered into the lens with a voluptuousness I did not understand, or had forgotten.

Shuffling through the photos, focusing on her expressions—by turns uncertain, circumspect, seductive, coy, the rhythms of her face alternating anger and grief—I sat on the floor astonished at those poses of recline or torture, revealing a woman I had never known, or perhaps known once but had lost access to. Who had taken those pictures? One of those eccentrics that lingered about the Tor House?

I know my wife, I told myself. There was her passion for painting, for her charcoals and pastels and pencil sketches, of course—how she painted the most detailed birds, expert enough for a science manual—and I could name the two or three pies she cooked to my utter delight— apple cobbler, blackberry—and her collection of hat pins, and her stuffed birds—loons, larks, robins. I knew her darkness and her light. I could pinpoint the day her mind shifted from the world into the sanctum of grief and regret that reeked of madness. Toward the end of her life, how she hoarded things as much as her emotions. But did I know her? And how much did I know my son, my flesh and blood and bone? How much did I know myself?

After laying aside those strange pictures of a Nona I never knew, a strange woman with wild eyes and expressions dripping with concupiscence, I turned to the dresser in the corner. Beneath a pile of bed linens, neatly folded, I found Cole's first baby book. The cardboard cover, some dim shade of yellow, depicted a cartoonish, rosy-cheeked newborn, asleep in an embossed circle. Balloons drifted up the page in aggressive shades of pale blue and pale green. A small pocket inside the front cover, the kind where you place note cards for a baby christening, held a lock of Cole's hair, fine and coppery, like saffron threads, and I rubbed these between my fingers, and I inhaled their dull scent of paper, and then I placed several in my mouth and chewed.

Inside the book I found details about Cole's life I never knew—the date of his first walk, the hour of his first words, even the moment of his first tantrum. Nona hoarded these facts and set them down without my knowledge, just as she'd kept from me the sensation of him kicking her bladder and tumbling in her womb. Did I know that *Bonnie and Clyde* was the number one movie in the theaters the day Cole was born? Did I know that the price of gas was twenty-five cents a gallon, the same as the price of a Sunday Times, or that a Shasta can was eight to ten cents each? Miguel Angel Asturias had won the Nobel Prize in literature that year, a name without sense. All these facts, and others, turned Cole into a puzzle.

His birth certificate, neatly folded in thirds lay at the bottom of a box marked LEGAL. It produced other facts of his life I had missed—his birth weight (seven pounds, six ounces), his length in inches (twenty-two), his blood type (Type-O Negative)—and these facts felt like mysteries, too, like I had never known my son.

Amid those mementos, I found his first baby rattle, his first nipple, his first bib, and also his middle-school yearbook signed by his classmates, children I never met: *Always Stay Sweet*, wrote Connie Brannon; *Have the bestest summer ever*, wrote Nathan Stein. The caption beside Cole's photo conveyed his age's fleeting interests—*building rockets, collecting rocks, riding my bicycle, swimming, painting trees, roaming*—and those, too, transformed him into a riddle. But how could those collected facts, collective knowledge, compare to my feelings for him? I loved Cole, even if I never understood him. Wasn't that enough? Wasn't that everything? I swallowed his hair and coughed.

FOUR

Y*ou're a mystery, Dutch,* Nona once said. *I still don't know who you are.*

What's mysterious, Nona, is that you still don't know who I am, a stove-junker.

In two rows against the eastern wall stood my Gasco-Crawfords, then my ship stoves. Along the southern wall, stood the quirky Glenwoods and those sensational Magic Hubs. Cast iron chrome emblems—O'Keefe and Merrit, Chambers, Gaffers and Sattler—names like estates, or like the founders of great industries: steel, cement, automobiles. Each curve of the bull nose, each squeak of the oven door or rattle of the regulator when the gas pushed through, each chafe of the oven racks had some story to tell. In the peerless black of gunmetal, you could almost hear the whispers of kitchen conversations. In the ruddy blues and stippled hues of ten-pound oven doors, you'd scent the glorious past. Run your hand over a cast-iron hot plate, you might picture thick-hipped women stirring pots of rabbit stew, might glimpse the fiber lifting in the air from torn burlap bags, white beans or wheat or kidney beans pooled on the floor, might smell the century's air thick with homespun cheese, heavy cream, arrays of Kugelis or Halupki or Italian Easter Pitz. Nona would call me a poet of fire, a heat poet, playing with flames the color of water—*gas blue, bottle blue, a color like a conundrum, because ice is also blue, because when the temperature of water dips low enough, glacial blue, ice burns paradoxically like fire.* I spent the better part of my life playing with fire, twisted my back over those old Crown step stoves, Gasco Crawfords, Franklins, those perfectly scrolled Triple Effect parlor stoves, coke ovens, salamanders. A Magic Standard, built in 1800 in gunmetal black. Convictions in polished steel trim. Decisions in the deft scrollwork, the top hob so sturdy you could park a Ford truck on it. Mechanical clocks whirred and clicked, temperature dials whose mercury never lied, these were all statements of belief, their facets holding me suspended in retroactive time. That's all you needed to know.

Up before dawn with the air blue and the sky black and the sun just a whiskey impression behind the eastern hills. Black coffee by lamplight and then in the barn by six. Sweated there in the summers until well past the locusts swished and the crickets screeched and the sun dipped behind the western hills. Sleeved in monkish silence, I tinkered, I toiled, immersed in restoring inarticulate junk into objects that could steal your breath with their beauty. I confronted puzzles, turned over riddles, followed mysteries. I asked myself questions, formed arguments, worked to solve the effects of time and reverse obsolescence. At the end of the day, I needed to feel so tired that I couldn't remember my own name, so tired that the only thing I felt when tumbling onto my pillow at night, Nona dreaming her own dreams, was the feel of my throbbing hands and my back stiff as iron. That meant a good day. An honest one. Closing my eyes, my chattering brain kept chattering, puzzling over some unwieldy Brown Stove burner whose flame refused to burn blue. Then a voice spoke to me from within the folds of a language not my own and I felt in conversation with ghosts—*Did yas check the red wire crimped to the circuit junction? Down in the pedestal there's a screw tip lodged itself in a cranny. Gotta remove the float bowl to get to it. And Jesus H., use a magnet*—and the next morning, I attacked the puzzle again, a tar-black coffee poured in a chipped mug and cradled in my hands. But the mug would shortly sit abandoned on the workbench, collecting the floating motes.

With the Bakelite playing the Classics, inspiration, intuition, experience, guiding my hands, I worked, convinced I was doing God's handiwork—*What's it doing?* I would ask myself and then answer, *Ah, you got a warped float; it's off by about a millimeter. Check it and get back.* I would check it and get back. *You're right, you son-of-a-bitch,* I would say to myself, to the sparrows perched on the rafter beams to the air and hollow space. I could pinpoint the health of a flame by scent alone. Spoiled eggs, sour-musk, oil-sludge reeking like burned leather, those smells held meaning. Too much oxygen. Not enough. Dysfunction was a sound like troubled breathing. Insecurity was a rusted burner tube. A mutilated hinge, a crippled foot-peg, these said as much about the injury as it did about the user. Those old stoves, tarnished and tattered and breaking apart, felt like grief on display. God knows where they are now, used, used up, piled-up in a junkyard.

While Cole like a brave ran through the woods, while Nona sat in her parlor painting birds, while the sun rose and fell and the seasons changed, I fiddled with stoves. I rebuilt broken timers. I welded shoddy manifolds. I hand-painted oven temperatures on die cast metal knobs. You could spend decades just admiring the quiet upheaval of metal on which, embossed like a signature, danced the dialects of old artisans, their vernacular of glyphs and ideographs in daisy petals, flowering ivy, olive stems. Standing at a distance and drinking the stove up with my eyes, I would wonder, *From which parent language was born this magic lamp?* Twist a knob, release the fire, release the genie imprisoned inside. Who did that make me, Scheherazade? I have to laugh.

At the end of the day, alone, I would prop the windows open and breathe in the air swifts scented with apple trees and licorice, kale and mineral rich sod, and while the Chairman crooned over my Bakelite's speakers, I tapped my toes, might even have danced, my lips puckered in a whistle. Now that man feels like another man, that time feels like another time. *The world may have its mysteries, Dutch, but everywhere there are clues to its solution,* I would think to myself between deep draws of a cigar, and I'd whisper, *I'm master of my own destiny.* Exhaling blue rings that widened into ovals and dissipated into the surrounding trees, I would say, *I'm a good man 'cause I have a purpose.* I would extinguish the smoldering inch on the heel of my boot and think pleasing thoughts of my family, believing I worked for them—to provide because providing was love. Trudging up to the house, past the old oak, I looked for Nona and Cole, hoping to share with them my day. But they wouldn't understand, or couldn't, or didn't care.

That's so nice, Dutch, Nona would say. *Help me set the table.*

Okay, Pops, Cole would say. *Meeting a few of the guys up at Twin Lanes Alley. Can I have a few bucks?*

I draw on the cigar. The dog howls again, so I drag on my cigar, because the dog howls and because it is cold I want to put the damn thing out of its misery.

Did you ever get the feeling you're living inside someone else's dream? I say.

I don't know what that—

That's right. You can't remember.

This room smells cold, if cold has a smell. It smells like dust, too, years of dust and of something else I can't put my finger on, something wet and silvery, like mercury, if mercury has a smell. I sigh.

The house creaks and moans and I think I hear footsteps clopping up the staircase, but no, no, I am alone with this strange boy and it is good to be alone, because it is cold and the liquor warms me and the dog barks. For now. Soon Armand will come and we'll pull down the ceiling and move the walls about. Soon we'll make everything like home.

FIVE

People use each other as markers for what's real, so you can't be alone anymore. Solitude draws suspicions. Now they have cameras in every goddamned place, stealing your privacy. You can't be alone anymore. The modern world cares nothing for your personal space, nor for silence, certainly not for privacy. No, you can't be alone anymore. There's always an eye watching, a lens, always a phone ringing, always someone waiting for you to notice them. You can't be alone. Planes roar along the skies and cars scream across the expressways and sirens shriek and bells clatter. People plan parades, then boom their drums and crash their cymbals and blow their noisy trumpets. Ships moo their horns. Planes thunder. Rockets scream. Even the silence of a church, officiated by mandates from the Lord, scream. Give me silence. Crowds collect on the pavements, confabulate like bees. Give me peace. Distractions, diversions, destinations all corrupt your time and confound your sense of self. It's no wonder we're confused, embittered, impatient, scornful. It's no wonder I wish to die as soon as possible. But I can't do it myself. I won't give the world the satisfaction. I still believe in things. You see, I believe you can commiserate with nature to discover yourself again, even in the winter. Especially in winter. I believe this. No, these days you can't even be caught dead alone.

I suppose I'll make myself a cup of coffee, I say. What do you want?

I'll take salt and vivinger chips.

Not for breakfast.

Why not?

No one has potato chips for breakfast. And it's Vinegar. *Vin-eh-gur.*

Please?

Christ, who am I to set limits? What do I care? Go on, stuff yourself.

While the boy shovels fistfuls of chips into his mouth, I spoon the instant coffee into a mug. While he moans agreeably, I set the kettle on the twin-burner primus and wait for it to boil. I turn to the dormer above the sink, draw on my cold cigar.

There's no moon outside. The dog is quiet. The wind's not quiet and not still and no snow falls. If I close my eyes I can almost hear the ancient ramparts of glacial drift, a deep cracking sound of the land eaten up by ice, or the wail of arctic wolves, or the lowing of a polar bear. I have to laugh. Soon the blizzard will come and transform my winter paradise into a frozen brash. I say let it come, the blizzard, the bite. Armageddon can't come soon enough. Soon Armand will be here to help me and together we'll see this project through.

It's ready.

I know. The kettle screams so I shut off the burner and pour the water into the mug. I like my coffee dark brown, dark as Armand's skin.

When the Hindus wrote of reincarnation, Armand said, *I recognized the principle at work in Anil.*

The picture Armand presented me the afternoon we met at the Air and Space Museum, was of a boy with brown hair, round eyes set in a finely chiseled face. He looked every bit like Armand himself—a lissome expression to him, something sneaky there as well, something feline, right down to the teeth.

Who is this Armand anyway?

We met last year at the Lindbergh exhibit. The place has its twin-engine bombers and air gliders and Wright Brothers' replicas. When I saw a man strolling the halls, hunched over and mumbling into his hands, I recognized something oddly familiar about him, as if I were watching a movie of myself. Looking neat and ponderous in his brown three-piece suit, brown leather oxfords, and that brown hound's tooth pageboy cap, I found him beneath the Spirit of St. Louis, his face tilted up.

I asked him the time and he asked me if I was lost and I almost burst out laughing.

I was about to ask the same thing of you, I said. I hadn't planned on striking up a friendship, but it turned out we had been born the same year, '33. Strange how we shared the same height, five-foot-nine, and possessed the same slender build and frame. If you saw us from behind, you might even say we were twins. But whereas I had lost most of my hair, Armand's hair looked vibrant, thick, white, shiny as oiled cotton.

We chatted, a little small talk about the weather, and just before we turned into the cafeteria, he said, *I may not remember you next time, because I forget things, and sometimes when I forget I invent,* and I took that statement to be not wholly ironic.

Absence is a powerful thing, he said sitting at a table with a coffee and a maple scone. After asking me my name, about my family, he said, *Absence creates its own life in ways you can't imagine.*

I know, I said. I lost my son.

I could tell. There's a mark on those who've lost their loved ones. It's an anointment.

We walked together, passing a video screen showing The Spruce Goose turning huge, elegant circles in the sky.

Anil died in an accident, Armand said. He blew his nostrils into his handkerchief, repeating the word "accident" without any ascription of blame. *There was a bomb in the luggage compartment of the 747. I could tell you the baggage handlers were culpable, or the ticketing agent, but what's the use?*

Later I researched the event, using the public library's microfiche. The reporters said that of the three hundred twenty-nine people on board his flight, no one survived. The victims, experts said, displayed "flail patterns", an indication that their bodies blew from the aircraft at high velocity from an altitude of twenty or thirty thousand feet, then buffeted apart. Of the recovered bodies, many victims displayed signs of hypoxia, or of explosive decompression, and some by asphyxia. You could choke in air, imagine. Some survived the blast and the free-fall only to drown in the ocean. Of the one hundred twenty-nine bodies they recovered, many were so bloated and so blue they were almost unrecognizable.

Anil was passenger 26C. A window seat. He was on his way to London to study Greek tragedies at Oxford. He became like Icarus.

There were reports of sharks in the area. The bodies that were neither eaten nor found, simply vanished, either reduced to ash by the explosion, or drifted down to the bottom of the sea. The airlines released no names to the public, but one of the victims was an eighteen-year-old boy named Anil Kalla.

What God would allow that to happen?

I gave up God years ago, I said.

I could tell. I often wondered what Anil would have felt had he survived the explosion and then the plummet? What goes through a mind? In dreams, I would see him thrashing his limbs in arctic air, blue air, blue light, flailing his cold, blue arms as the sea rose up to vanquish him. Once I dreamt him swimming toward the hint of a shoreline, jet fuel rainbows glazing the silken blue water. A body goes through such trauma, plummeting from that altitude. The wind can burn just as easily as fire. Air can crush every bone in seconds.

It's like being chewed up in a mouth, I said.

It makes me queasy to think what he suffered thrashing through those clouds whose solidity is a lie. What he must have felt, tossed about in air currents like a rag doll. A body can endure only so much.

And of the people who planted the bomb? Was there justice?

What justice?

SIX

A day or two passed. It might be 12/12/12, for all I know. I am not sure. What is time anyway? I haven't turned on the Bakelite. It sits in the corner collecting dust. I should turn it on. I should. I might. For the moment, ignorance of the present pleases me.

The boy plays outside and I play inside. I am inside and alone with the house. My thoughts feel splintered because life is fragments—insects crushed in a corner, the veins of feathers, sparks from burning embers. *There is no unabridged life. It is all piecemeal, fragmented,* I write my memo book. *We are incomplete. And to that incompletion we add the loss of a beloved son—a senseless ending to a promising life that abates closure. No, for the nights to collapse they must in their darkness, their awesome powers, reveal the fevers of what we dream, hide but envelope them, revealing to ourselves and each other, like the inarticulate shapes in mist.*

As if struck by lightning, I think of Pearl. She had once kneeled near the banks of Big Nescopek, kneeled as if offering supplications to the Lord. How her eyes that beheld stars once, in whose reflection I saw every possibility, looked, that final day I knew her, as vacant as a corpse. How her thin arms hugged her waist and how she rocked herself back and forth, moaned while her temple dripped blood, a gash there vicious as a fishhook. What was she doing but waiting for ichthyic grace? John the Baptist also stood knee-deep in a river, cleansing souls. Water purified one's sins. The Great Flood washed the sinful world clean. Renewal was always under the threat of drowning. While fire transformed, water renewed. While fire destroyed, water cleansed. Despite his father's warnings, Icarus flew too high to the sun and crashed into the sea, his end a transmutation by fire. Pearl turned to me, *You can't go where I'm going, boy. Not this time.* And then she waded in.

I rest my pen, gaze up at the ceiling. Maybe one of our chief purposes is to collect those fragments and knit them together from frayed fibers and invent a new self? Rediscovering our memories requires imagination, but then why does the act of rediscovering myself leave me confused as to memory's value? It's a little like stumbling upon foreign bank notes in an old suit pocket, the paper has dulled, the monetary value no longer holds the same old value, the profile of some leader you cannot name written in a language that has no meaning except a new one you ascribe to it.

No, Nona said once, turning to face me as we sat on the couch, her in her corner and I in mine. *Wheel of Fortune* flickered on the Zenith screen.

The Maze of Memory, she said, offering the answer to the wall puzzle after a contestant, a pasty portly woman with a furious overbite, had bought a vowel, an "A." Armand might phrase it in another way: *Memory is a labyrinth of false turns and dead ends.*

It's when I remember my family that my heart aches for the people we were, then I curse this creature I've become—feeble-brained, dimwitted, blind as a sea slug. Return me to the man who reeled in ten steelhead one Memorial Day forty years ago. Bring back that boy who pinned butterflies to a cork board, the boy who dove after a bird he mistook for a girl, a boy naked as Adam who kissed that girl naked as Eve on the shores of Yardley Lake. Return me to the man who once spun his son in the air like a propeller—*Wheee! Again. Papa, again!*

I turn to the window. Snow has erased the contours of the yard. Snow clings to the barn's roof maybe three feet thick and above the roof stretches the boughs of maple trees. Beyond, in the blue light, the fir tops look as if underwater. The limbs dance in the cold breeze and above the branches stretches the silent sky, the texture of white lace in which patterns of spring trees bursting with vegetable health clump and lengthen and clump again, mocking this snowy landscape. Like rhythmic music, the landscape undulates. Like a dance, the contours of each blanched pleat signal the progress of your desires—each rib and depression are convictions. *Everything is as if arranged by some silent arithmetic.* My breath collects on the window and for a moment I believe I can write a message there. Breath on glass. A life made visible by the strokes of my finger on frozen glass. The impermanence of it seems oddly right.

The woods outside have become a catch-all of memory. The hole Cole once dug to bury his time capsule, his toy shovel and sand pail toted behind him in a cart, might still be there, but blanketed beneath snow, and the white oaks, whose bark Cole carved with poems to the woods might still be there, or there, at the base of the old boulder that looked like a goat, Cole and I constructed an effigy out of hay and twigs and twine, and there and there and there… The larks will sing old songs in the Spring and play in the treetops.

I would love to run, not sure where I am going. I would love to run and leap, maybe even dance, maybe even cry out like a savage, making a celebration of being lost. Kick the snow. Pull down a snowy branch. Punch a snowy bush. Is that what Cole felt when he left us and roamed? *To be lost is to be free, Pops.*

I'm ba-ack!

In here, I say.

The boy enters. His face febrile from the cold. *Whatcha doin'?*

Nothing.

SEVEN

Another day passes. Another night. Another morning arrives. Another afternoon. Another evening. It might be mid-December. Through the window's cracks, seeps the scent of frost and pine so authentic to Drums in winter. Where have the days gone? Where has this life gone?

Outside that dog still howls. It seems she will never stop. It is night. Late. My head hurts. My joints are stiff. I move about the house as if in a perpetual dream of the house and I bump into the walls as if bumping into dream walls. The fixtures on the walls look soft, as if I could mold them into new shapes. A house, every house, is malleable.

I can almost hear the walnut trees shiver, those trees there limning the outer edge of our property. Even the deadfall shivers. Something in the house clatters and I think it's the boy again, doing what boys do, the little animal. Things grew wild here, or turned wild, and we tried containing them. Animal, raccoons, squirrels, crows, always breached our property, because here everything grew big and wild, boisterous with bad intentions. Sometimes I'd joke to Nona that you could bury a dead man in our soil and in half a year he would return, alive as the day he was born and thirsting for blood. *Like Lazarus*? I draw in a deep breath, filling my lungs with air that has no business being breathed, air tainted with the past. Nutsedge and wheat grass once sprouted beneath the front porch, topiaries of privets shaped like mushrooms and orchards of apple and tangerine spread for half an acre out back behind the old Dutch barn. You could plant your broken heart into the earth and it would piece itself back together. Your tears could water the roots of dead weeds and they'd sprout roses so red you'd think they were congealed love. *Lazarus land?*

The lemon grove, Dutch? Yes, Nona. Our lemon trees produced misshapen country lemons resembling baby squid, if you can imagine it, and those drew out the yellow jackets, and I would chase them from our kitchen and smash them with a clap against the windowpanes with a rolled up newspaper. You'd make the finest lemon meringue I'd ever tasted, Nona. *Dutch, there you go again.* In the spring you could hear the whine of magpies, oriole songs, robins robinning and blackbirds blackbirding in that grove. Rising from the gardens was the whistle and whoop and scrambling of larks collapsing into the warm gusts, and it was a kind of magic to behold them. *Bang! Bang!* Cole would shoot off his air rifle at them, pumping the damn thing like he was Jack Palance playing Sam Clayton in *God's Gun.* It's all gone now, even the conventions of sparrows swelling the trees, swooping down from the locusts to the strawberry fields. One year a fleet of black crows convened on our property and a shadow like a giant wave darkened the house. I turned to Blake and pointed up at the sky. *Is it the devil?*

Blake giggled then, because his affections for me and Wally had not yet withered. He jangled the ring of keys that hung from his belt, spat on the ground a thin stream of tobacco juice.

That's a murder. Looking windblown, his eyes shriveled to horizon lines. *That's prophecy that the world's soon goin' ta end.*

I was eleven years old in '44, and what I feared more than Blake and torture and death was abandonment. By then, Blake and Wally had driven Pearl away. By then, I already feared the world, with its privations and shadows. The world made you hungry and cold, and it made you skinny and weak and sick. The world made your mother sacrifice her body to feed you. You watched drunken men slobber her skin, seduce her in dark rooms, behind buildings, in outhouses. I feared the world more than I feared Blake even if from his body emanated the rankness of darkened taverns. The smoke of gambling dens and spilled liquor and ten-cent whores wafted from his hair like a curse. He said he sinned to test his faith in the Lord. I had to laugh. In his eyes, you saw forbidden conversations. In his cracked teeth, you saw spent rage. You saw hypocrisy.

Hey, shitless, ever taste a murder?

I held my breath and shook my head no. Unsure of what to do with my hands, I stuffed them in my pockets. Blake followed the curve of the crows as they sailed into view, took up positions in the old oak, and then he spat down at the ground, curling a finger across his lip. Then he tramped toward the barn, his shadow long in the long dusk, the curve of the murder's inky shadow pools, sails blackly over the roof, and where am I down on the blue lawn, slack-jawed, fear and disbelief having turned me into stone.

Kill 'em, Wally said.

My eyes flashed to my brother, three years my senior and naked to the waist, his skin blanched and neck florid as a crab's claw. Wally chewed plastic spoons. Wally climbed trees like a monkey. Wally trapped muskrats and skinned them and fed their entrails to the no-name dog. Now he aimed his left hand in my direction, pointed his finger, and then closed his hand into a fist.

Pow!

And it was Blake who entered the barn, the dim space where he toiled hour upon hour with tools in whose delicate purpose lay mysteries, and Blake himself a mystery—a silent man, a man of prevarications and half-truths, of deep convictions over the nature of evil and a just yet vindictive God. I see him, tall and angular and sharp, like a sheet of schist, bent among the fuselages of machines in various states of assembly, tattooing with his small hammer messages to some other world—*Clink Clink Clink.*

And I hear him say, *Get in the goddamned house!* A voice, resonating with the timbre of judgment, thin and sharp and angular as a sheet of struck tin. An iron door croaked shut.

What did I say, shitless?

I turned toward the house. Wally behind me said, *Pow-Pow! You're supposed to fall dead when I shoot.*

Blake's boots thudded against the hard earth, and the belt loop of his jeans rang with hundreds of keys—for deadbolts and padlocks and gate locks—jangling like Christmas reindeer. His life was a bawl. When not junking, he spent it peering into the darkness of his own soul, armed with his holy book. *The book of all books. The best of all books.* What did he find in them but mysteries? All his sermonizing, demonizing, agonizing of himself and us, produced no answers.

I would have told him, had I the words then, that to travel into the depths of the soul was to carry with you light, from whatever source it came. But Blake, my father, my monster, had no light. Even "the book of all books" could not mend him. He twisted its parables and fables and turned them literal. He used Christ's words to shroud his moral sickness, clinging to him like sweat, like dirt, like grease. *Shitless, go on and get me ma Remington!* That week, Pearl Harbor had been attacked. It was 1944 and the papers screamed war—*The war of all wars.*

I look outside and, like the skin of an albino trout, the sky shimmers. The earth is coconut meat. The trees are sheathed in cream. A few crows spindle from the old oak and climb the air. They jape at each other, jabber, return to the bare branches. With the gales rising up from the lungs of the woods like a long exasperated breath, lifting from the orchard a gray, glacial mist, I shield my eyes with my hands and I see Blake and Wally, and I see spindling crows.

From downstairs comes a terrible whoosh, a chorus of *Caw-Caw-Caw.* Has the center of the house collapsed? Has anarchy been loosed upon us? The shovel leans by the hearth.

Boy?

I cross the threshold, dragging the shovel, and navigate the staircase. My heart rages with that excitement of children seduced by bodies of water in which to swim and drift. A crow flies over my head. I swat the air—*Ain't nothin' but flyin' rats.*

Boy?

They're here. All of 'em.

Crows swirl like bats, clog the hall like fat smoke. The boy stands in the center of the kitchen, twirling like a dervish. Grins like a clown. A murder picks apart my rations. Crows and ravens, their obsidian eyes and sharp black beaks specked with light, glide about the halls, into and out of rooms. Their claws clack the counters. *Har! Har!*

Raising the shovel I swat the air, swing it like a baseball bat, swing for the fences. *Caw-Caw-Caw.* Crows flap their wings, circle the room, roil like a black mist. Several dozen shoot into the hallway. The hard shovelhead collides against a soft bird, clangs against its black body, sends it spinning to the wall. The boy screams, *Don't!* I am Somerset's rage. I am Somerset's heat. I won't stop, I will not stop, I cannot.

Get out, I shout. *Caw-Caw-Caw*! A stygian chorus.

Blood, black feathers, broken beaks. Small black rags writhe on the floor, necks twisted like corkscrews. I chase them outside. *Caw-Caw!* Some, their eyes ignited by terror, storm up the stairs—*Shoo, shoo, Papa, the sound they make hurts.* They squeeze through the slim spaces between the wall gaps.

Soon everything returns to quiet. Against the floor a few dying crows rustle, twist, flop, flare a broken wing. With the head of the shovel I smash them, one at a time. There are tears in the boy's eyes.

Why'd you do that for? Why?

Why?

Guano, bird feathers, blood. The crows have ruined everything: the boxes of Minute Rice torn apart, oatmeal bags blend in with the dirt and wet straw, making a sort of insect gruel. They've reduced the bread rolls to ends and crumbs. The coffee spills across the floor, oily black grinds that resemble dead, black ants. Everything has been pecked, argued over, trampled, regurgitated. Without food, a man cannot live, without food and water he might as well give up the ghost.

Look at this mess.

*They were just…-They…-*The boy folds over from the waist. Bawls.

Jesus Christ! I have no energy for his tantrum. No patience left. I want to kick the boy. I want to pull him by his earlobes and throw him outside. Go on, then, and be gone, out, away, go, leave me be. The hell you doing here anyway? If only I had the strength. I am winded.

What's your problem? I say, because I still have the energy to scold. Didn't I tell you the rules? What did I say? Answer me you dumb son-of-a-bitch!

The boy sobs and I want nothing from him but his contrition, not his recalcitrance or magic tricks, but a simple apology, not his defiance and shiftlessness, but his regret. Don't you dare justify them being here. Don't you dare—*You're always holding on to your anger a little longer than you should, Dutch. You're always holding on.* How can I forgive what I can't forget? Nona. Tell me. How? I feel a pang of conscience. Sympathy even. Even a monster can feel sympathy. I move toward the boy.

I'm sorry I said that.

I don't care.

Scavengers always return. They get a taste of a free meal and risk their lives for it, I say. *Caw-Caw!* There's a crow still in the house. I would shoot it to bits if I had a rifle. I think of my gun.

Where you going?

I make for the stairs. I enter the heated room and find the toolbox. Rummage past the hammer, the ratchet set, the screwdrivers and box of six-inch nails. Pick out the Colt, wrapped in a chamois cloth. Unwrap it. It gleams. Check the barrel. One bullet. I should have brought a box of shells.

The wind gusts. The wind sprays the window with pellets of ice. Pellets of ice tattoo the roof. It sounds like gunfire. Bullets quiver through the air. *Pop-pop-pop!* A thousand wings flap. *Caw-Caw-CaCaw-CaCaw!* The dry cacophony of a thousand crows. The air smells thick with the stench of blood. Has the murder returned? Stuffing the Colt inside my belt loop, I step out of the room, then out of the house.

Outside, I round the deck pile, making for the old oak. Crows and raven carcasses scatter across the yard, wounded crows, broken ravens, their wings crushed, some with their black beaks blown off. They writhe about like black rags blown by the breeze. Speckled with blood, patches of rust glow thickly near the base of the old oak's roots. The snowy earth sprouts new grass, furtive, green weeds, box hedges glow in which bloom strange pink flowers. Things look strange. Resurrected. The old oak shrinks to a remembered proportion. Limbs and branches recede, sport showy leaves where moments ago the oak stood frozen against the white sky. Now it appears healthful, young again, even the treehouse reassembles itself from molecular deposits of light.

Where is the winter storm? The cloudless blue sky is an absolute discovery. The sun beats in the corner, bright and high and fervent. Even the air fills with liquid heat.

My feet are strange. Small. The strap of one of my sandals has broken off. I have to drag one foot across the grass, swishing it like a scythe. My legs, thin and wiry and hairless, seem convinced of youth. My hands, small and fine and muscular, light a match, toss it still flaming to the grass.

Har! Har!

Caw-Caw-Caw.

Pow!

Twenty feet from the old oak stand Blake and Wally, while a spiraling mass of crows settles on the old oak's branches. Blake, bent at the waist, jabs his Bible hand in Wally's face, a Colt, my Colt, the one moments ago I held in my hand, rests in Blake's other hand. Wally stands beneath him simpering like an idiot. His hair matted to his forehead, eyes wet.

...*How can Satan cast out Satan?* Blake turns in my direction and says, *How can a house divided against itself stand?* Impossible, I think. *No one can enter a strong man's house and plunder his goods, unless*... I freeze in my tracks. I make no sound, no motion of having heard him at all. Blake raises the pistol into the air, aims at a crow and says, *Be not weak or meek, Son*. He blasts off a shot. A crow plummets to the ground.

Shitless, he says to me. Go on and *wake up ya mama.*

Wally snivels but I am frozen stiff with fear. Unlike Wally, unlike Blake, I have no taste for this mindless violence.

Shitless, you deaf and blind as well as dumb? Wake up yer ma!

A chord snaps inside me. I am Somerset's rageless fear. Wally, shirtless, his cheeks reddened with heat, laughs, cries, *Bakaak! Bakaak!* My legs are not these old stodgy things and my heart is not this weak little contraption whose valve leaks blood, no, it is 1944 and I am eleven again. I run into the house. The memory of wet rooms and long, dry roads still inside me. Where is Pearl? Is she asleep under the covers in Blake's bed? Has she finished sleeping? I am Somerset's confusion.

My lungs are in my throat as I run up the stairs and down the hall, shouting *Mama! Mama!* I shout. I shout because Somerset needs her protection. I shout because Somerset wants Mama to feed him a new memory of a past that never was, sing to him of angels and stars. Somerset tries the knob to Blake's room, but the door is locked. I am Somerset's dilemma. *Ma,* he shouts. *Open up, Blake's killing birds and Wally's crying and laughing and calling me names.* Somerset want to tell her it was a mistake coming home and that they should leave. *Ma!* There is no answer. He knows by instinct that Pearl lies under a heap of blankets, spent from their journey home, and it's her right to sleep. Sleep will heal.

Somerset runs to Wally's room and sits on the floor, because he soiled the mattress he shared with Wally that morning, and he spills himself onto the floor and rocks back and forth like a pivot. He searches his pockets for the matchbook and lights a match. If he focuses on the flame, like Pearl had said, if he concentrates on the tiny yellow cone, he can settle the rising ache in his chest and things will be whole again. The flame will take away the dark, take away fear, it'll make Pearl wake up and it'll make them leave this house and it will make everything better.

But outside the gun goes *Pop!* and Wally applauds and crows still slam against the window. Somerset wants to sing now, "God is Nigh," but he can't remember the words, and outside there's just the *Pop-Pop-Pop!* of gunfire. The match fizzles. He lights another, because if he lights another match Blake and Wally will go away and he and Pearl will be back on the long road. The shooting stops. There's a deep silence, like the yawn of God. The back door creaks open and slams shut. Heavy boots chomp the stairs. Heavy boots eat up the hall. Heavy boots shatter the door. Framed in the threshold stands Blake.

The hell's the matter with youse? His voice has altered. It's not the shouting voice from last week when they returned to this house, not the screaming Bible voice he used on Pearl for going away all those years ago. There is no Leviticus and no Psalms and no Job in his voice. It's a nice and soft voice, a voice you could sleep to.

It ain't no big thing to kill a crow, he says. *They're no better than flyin' rats.* He moves inside the room and takes a seat beside Somerset on the floor. His gentleness reeks of stale liquor, tobacco, wet roots. He extends the Colt and says, *Go on, it won't bite youse.* He presents Somerset with the pistol. The nozzle smells of burnt hair. *Youse take it?*

I am not plural, Somerset thinks. Yas, Youse. I am *I*. You are *you*. Pearl is *Ye, Thee*. God is *Thou*.

Prove yer somethin' and not nothin' and pull the trigger.

If he takes the pistol and shoots a crow, then will it make him proud of Somerset? If he kills, then will it make Somerset his son? Will it make him Wally? If he takes the gun and shoots, will Pearl wake up and take him away?

It's no big thing to kill. Shit, yer ma done it.

Mention of Pearl returns Somerset to his senses.

Why?

Youse not a single, boy. Yer half a double. There was two a yas in the beginnin'. Know that? A twin that come out a few minutes before, screamin' and kickin' like hellfire. Wally was just three then.

Somerset stares at the dwindling match flame. The soft glow of heat singes his fingertips.

We named him Adam, 'cause he was the first, and you we named Somerset 'cause you both were born in a manger in Somerset County.

Is this true? Is it? What is true? Am I half of a twin? Where is my brother? My true brother?

So one night I wake up to cryin' and Pearl's by the crib and she's leanin' over it with her hands stuck inside it like she's scrubbin' a pot an' I goes over and see she got a pillow over Adam's head and his little legs are kickin'. But you're cryin' like all hell's broken loose. An' I push Pearl away an' she looks at me, her eyes all wet an' wild.

You're lying, Somerset says.

Sure as I'm sittin' here, Adam's buried out there by the old zebra oak, by Big Nescopek.

I hate you, Somerset thinks. Blood surges into his neck. The tips of his fingers glow with heat. Pearl's words return—*I ain't nothin'. Never got to be the somethin' I wanted. So you have to do the best with what you got, and sometimes all you got is bad, so the trick in life is to stand it and by standin' it you turn it around.*

Mama, he pleads. Somerset's voice, the boy Blake calls *Shitless*, the boy who Wally calls *Bakaak*, after the sound a chicken makes, pleads with the space between him and Blake. And his Mama replies, *Every little thing in life is a monster, but you can make your monsters your friends by giving them what they need,* and Somerset says, *What does a monster need?* And she says, *Love. Love your monsters and you change 'em.* And suddenly Somerset realizes her implication: A father is a terrible thing for someone to be.

You're lying, Somerset says to Blake.

Don't have ta believe nothin'. But your mama's killed a baby and that makes her a sinner, and I tried ta fix her with the Lord's good words, but that didn't take. And so she ran off and took youse with her like a sinner, and now we's aimin to do what we have to do to clean her sin. He runs the Colt's muzzle up and down my arm.

No, Somerset says, his voice choked with hatred.

Now, youse be good boy and take a hold of it, Blake whispers, a voice like maggots writhing in Somerset's ear. Somerset can smell his pickled breath, soured with summer shine. *Shootin' them's like shootin' flyin' rats. That's all.*

I am a lamb. I am a sacrifice. Somerset shakes his head no. This is his only defense, a small twist of the head—*no*—a tiny twist of the head so imperceptible that Blake doesn't even notice.

Lookit here, Blake says. He places the muzzle to his temple and presses the trigger. *See? It ain't nothing at all. Youse try it.*

Can't.

Sure yas can, Blake says, laying the pistol on Somerset's thigh.

I don't want it. Fear shakes Somerset's hands. He hears his heart. Afraid Blake might hear his heart and slip his hands into the boy's chest and crush it, Somerset holds his breath, because if he holds his breath he won't hear his heart. A rivulet of sweat runs down Somerset's back down into the crack where God split him in two. Blake's neck glows with heat and the overflow of blood and Blake presses the Colt's muzzle to Somerset's temple and says, *On three we'll test yer luck.*

The cold muzzle pins Somerset to this moment. It is what is real. The only thing. Before he can leap from the floor, run from the house and lose himself in the woods, he's pinned down by the weight of this moment. In Blake's eyes, Somerset witnesses greed, sickness, that enchanted look of demons before possession. *You gotta love your Pappy,* Pearl once said. *Love those beyond loving and love till it kills you.* It takes courage to love a monster. Where does one find such strength?

One. Two… and Blake squeezes the trigger. *Click. See? It ain't nothing, right? Easy as sassafras. Just like playin' a game. The trick to winnin' is ta get ta the end.*

Somerset is his refusal. He shakes his head no. He wants to scream, but hatred, fear, nausea have murdered his voice. He wants Blake to hit him, kick him, twist his arm, because a blow to the face or a broken wrist would be a reprieve from this slow diet of terror.

Wanna we try again? Blake grins wolfishly, jerks his eyebrows. The wolfish smile on his mealy mouth could easily devour as it could kiss. He rolls the barrel. It clicks like a clock winding down.

Where is my real father, Somerset thinks, the one I imagined while Pearl and I stayed in some backwoods town? Where was the father I dreamt of? Father of dreams. Where was the *real* father who read me bedtime stories, wiped smudges of dirt from my cheek with his spit and his thumb? Where was my hero? The white-hatted cowboy on his mighty white horse? The giant of wisdom, the fount of knowledge, the bard of these black brooks?

Blake lifts the muzzle to Somerset's temple. *One and a two and a…* and he presses the trigger. *Click.* Somerset shakes with fear. *Now what's the matter, youse ain't scaredies?*

Somerset weeps soundlessly. Maybe if Somerset cries Blake will take mercy on him. Somerset shivers. Maybe if Blake sees Somerset is cold, he'll leave and then Pearl and Somerset could go back to the big world. Tears roll from his cheeks and hit the floor with a staggering velocity.

A silly little laugh overwhelms Blake. A child's giggle. Maybe laughter is a defense against this fear? Maybe if Somerset just laughs things will turn out fine? Laughter is a hope and Somerset tells himself to hope. But Somerset cannot stop the tears. Paralyzed. Somerset turns small. If he makes himself smaller and smaller, if he can just slip through that crack in the floor there, if he just makes himself the smallest piece of thing in the universe then maybe Blake will leave him alone.

Shitless, Blake says. *That's what you is, just scared shitless.* He lifts himself from the floor, his keys jangle, and he rises to the heights of the sky. His shoulders disappear into the clouds. Ogre. Monster. Mesingw.

Not even ma real flesh and bone, not like Wally. God knows whose youse are. Wish youse was never born. You'd be better dead. Blake spits on the floor.

The sentence releases Somerset. His insult shatters Somerset's eardrums. I am not his son and that seems right. I am Pearl's son. My real father is somewhere else and Pearl and I went to look for him. Now Somerset lights a match. Draws strength from the small flame. Now Somerset seizes on the idea he wants to hurt Blake, take something of his away—*'Cause it ain't no big thing to kill a rat.*

Wally is a rat. Somerset wants to take Wally away. Somerset's lip twitches. The pistol hangs loosely from Blake's monstrous hands like a flaccid prick. Blake clomps toward the open door. The keys on his belt loop jangle.

Come an' think a it, I ain't sure who we buried out there under that zebra oak, youse or yers twin. So here, he says, placing the Colt on the dresser by the door. *Just leave it here fer youse to ponder it.* He clicks the door shut. Boots churn the hardwood. Stomp the staircase. The patio door creaks open then bangs shut.

It takes several minutes for Somerset's heart to settle. Several minutes for hatred and fear to dissipate. Somerset stares hard at the pistol, its handle of pearl, the barrel notched exactly like the grooves of indented fingers. The long, cold barrel receives glints of sunlight through the open shutters. It seems too heavy to lift. It has no place in this room of maps and charts, of stamp collections folded into books, of rock collections, no place in a room whose windowsill will shortly crowd with empty matchboxes depicting playing dice, card games, ten pointed bucks, a whale blowing a double arch of water through its blow hole—*Little Sailor, Federal, Golden Fish.*

Like the animated dead, Somerset lifts himself from the floor. He reaches the pistol. He raises the pistol, measures its weight in his hands. Without reasoning, Somerset places the nozzle to his temple. He cocks the hammer back just like Blake had done. He shuts his eyes, counts backwards from ten. This is not the life for me. This is not the life for me, son of a junkman, a handyman, roped to a monster man who spits tobacco and smells like sulfur, a man I share nothing in common with but a surname. He's not even my father. "Father", "Papa", "Poppa", "Pops", what do those words even mean?

Somerset's eyes blur and the wall before him shimmers as if deluged by deep water. He squeezes the trigger. The pistol clicks. He waits for either courage or fear to return, two emotions that pivot on the fulcrum of a vanished childhood. Time is what I need, but I have no time. Hatred has stolen time. Fear has eaten the hours and days. Soon it will eat the weeks and months and years. Soon I will be an old man staring into a window contemplating the meaning of the past where events recede, fade, falter, blend, a no-time, in a no-place, where the past melts into the corner shadows and my hands transform into the jittery hands of a tired old man.

A blast explodes in Somerset's brain like a firecracker, such a small, anemic noise, and his mind contemplates the recent past when his and Pearl's journey began. Pearl bounds through a cornfield. Twigs snap beneath her slippered feet. Crescent dark circles beneath eyes thick with anguish. Somerset runs toward Pearl. Behind him gyrates smoke. The woods behind him are aflame. *Mama, wait!*

The present snaps back. The boy is before me, and the boy mouths words I cannot hear because I am Somerset's distant past. Now the cool dark basement of this house drips water, and in the center, circumscribed by heaps of junk and crates of moonshine, Walt twists and turns like a spiraling gyre, and I am frozen stiff while he burns and I am smiling because he burns. The air turns supernatural, not quite dawn or dusk, but something in between. There's a pall to everything, a midnight sky over a Day-Glo field. Now a rocket careers across the sky, so slowly it might as well be a gliding falcon. Tattoo of gunfire. The acrid smoke from muskets. Bullets scream through the air like whizzing mosquitoes and then the rocket explodes. A mangled doll falls into the locust trees, a doll of disheveled hair and blood. Sparks descend into the blackened woodlots like the burning bits of rockets, falling like ebbing flames. Parabolas of light and fire. Sparks extinguish in the night's pure darkness. The present as dream or memory recedes.

My hands are those of a boy again and I am in my boyhood room again, and once again I stand by the closed door with a Colt in my hands that feels as heavy as God. Somerset checks the Colt's barrel: A single bullet still left in the chamber. He lifts the pistol and fires at the window. *Pop!* The glass shatters. The murder died that day. The rest of them shot by Blake with his Remington.

EIGHT

How this house remains, like those woods, after all these decades, a catch-all for memory. Open a door and you see the years buoy up, not the years literally, but the scorched scent of our family history. Our past, like a texture woven into the fabric of the hummocky carpet, our past, left behind in oil stains streaked across the garage floor, in nail holes where our family pictures once hung. A house, in essence, is a repository of time.

I took apart the floor in the living room today. The shovel worked expertly in the grooved spaces. After an hour I managed to reduce the space to something after a mine disaster, splintered wood, heaps of it. A cloud of wood dust. Later, having gone over the family room walls with the sledgehammer, I managed to burst through and make a few large holes. The boy watched me. He did not help. That's progress, I said to him and he shrugged. I wish Armand would get here soon. It's these moments when you anticipate things happening that the silence is deepest. The solace agrees with me. That's enough.

Now in the feeble light of the gloaming, with a fire roaring in the hearth, the master bedroom smells like progress, but also of hickory. The fire produces a thin ticking melody. The wood burns sweetly, pops, hisses, screams, releasing trapped water. I could use a little music, I think. I should check in with Miki on the Bakelite and see about that winter storm.

The boy drifts in and out of sleep. When he awakes, he coldly stares up at the window from his bedding. Now and again, the old oak groans, shakes the house, and then the house returns the bawl with its own. In the silken dust pulled from the eaves fall bits of the broken ceiling. In their floating, I imagine some wild struggle for order. The dust spores rain onto the floor, these broken bits of matter barely visible, and just as I reach out to touch one, it disappears.

I dial in the radio. Static. I light a match. I shut my eyes. The match fizzles. I sleep and dream of a clear sky. No clouds. Sky blue as water.

I awaken. The boy beside me staring into my face.

What's the matter?

You stopped breathing.

I rise. The joints stiff. An image of the stove fire, warped and capering, seizes in the window. The bottle of bourbon near my elbow anticipates my fumbling, and beside it sits an inch of cigar.

I reach into my breast pocket for a Hemingway, my cutter, and the matchbox, and my fingers graze something small and angular, that pebble of anthracite I found that day I found Nona's secret stash of pictures. *It's another one of those sentimental attachments to the past,* as Armand would say. One side is dull and the other shiny, like clotted oil. I palm the pebble and shut it in my fist. I want to think of… But I am tired of thinking. I am tired of my reflection, my face, warped as it is, tired of my speech. I am tired of my clothes and words. I am tired of this house and the coldness that infects everything and tired of my memories. I want new ones. Better ones. I don't want this face anymore, or this body. I want some spirit to possess me, animate me, to turn me into someone else. But whom? What? An Eskimo. I have to laugh.

Armand once said that the Eskimos have a thousand different words for snow. Imagine that. *They can feel things in a way that we can't.* Their contact with the world is altogether different, so removed from ours they might as well be aliens, dropped down here from some alien moon to fish for salmon in our ice rivers or whatever it is they do. At the end of the day, they warmed themselves on stories, and the stories they told lifted into the arctic air and became part of the world. I imagine their stories clinging to the ice mountains, sentences stretched across river bottoms, phrases wrapped around the muzzles of arctic wolves. Stories could change the quality of the weather, so that the bitter wind, which, moments ago, had chilled them to the core, now warmed them. That's the power of tale-telling. I would like to be an Eskimo, telling stories to his tribe late into the night while the sky burns with the Northern Lights, the bitter wind scorching my face flat.

I light a match.

Once upon a time—Just a week after the first snows, sometimes as early as the first week of November, Cole and Nona and I would make a fire in the hearth. We would tell each other stories, casting the people we knew in Drums as heroes or victims or villains. *Jennie Finch got rabies when Donnie Kervich kissed her and she went around pissing on daisy bushes and barking at trees.* I have to laugh. I'd think of the birthdays we'd attended over the year, the baby christenings, the two or three marriages that swelled the churches with lilac perfume and sweat, the pews groaning while the church organ played "The Wedding March," and I'd think of the two or three funerals in the same churches, the chandeliers above softly radiant like explosions underwater, my mind's eye returning again and again to those cycles that defined a life—*Pop, whose got time to sit and chat it up like old friends?* I worked—*in a land*—while Cole grew into a bigger version of himself. I worked—*far, far away*—while he turned away from us, swallowed up by the fiction that I had destroyed him, robbed him of his vitality.

Once upon a time—And one year Bud Dietz ran his wife Janice through the fields adjacent to our property, and she arrived at our door in a tangled mess of torn clothes, Bud's knuckles imprinted on her cheek. Nona sat with Janice in the anteroom while I spoke to Bud outside on the porch, clasped him by the shoulder and said, *Let's take a walk.* Into the woods we went. In silence we sat and smoked a cigar by the banks of Big Nescopek, and we nipped from a flask. We watched the creek water riffle past us and said nothing.

My life didn't turn out as I planned, Dutch.

Whose life does?

Aw, Jesus.

I sat and listened. Bud wanted to play trumpet for Dorsey's Orchestra, because if he dreamt at all he dreamt in jazz.

Jesus, I was good and all, really I was, but marrying a woman you don't love changes a man. It sucks out what makes him himself.

Bud took a long pull from the flask, tossed the cigar into the water.

He could have played for Shep Fields and his RKO Orchestra. He could have fronted his own Big Band.

Look at you, Dutch.

Look at me.

Look at you.

Yeah, look at me.

What could I offer him except a platitude? *Man proposes and God disposes, Buddy.* His eyes, wet with the paucity of his life, turned to me imploringly, and in them, I watched everything crumbling.

You believe that? he said.

I believe a man's family makes him who he really is.

You really believe that?

We averted a tragedy that day, but the truce we brokered between Bud and Janice didn't hold. Bud burned his home and himself in it not a week after our little chat, killing himself and his family—his two setters and those two beautiful daughters, what were their names? His blackened trumpet still hangs on the walls of the Conyngham Historical Society next to Penny Super's script of *The Bloodstained Field.*

And—*Once upon a time*—when the winter snow finally cleared, Nona and Cole and I would go tobogganing. We sledded down icy slopes when everything surrounding us looked bright as a brass flute. In February, we formed snow angels on the back lawn. We staged snowball fights. In March, we tramped our initials down in the snow with our squeaky galoshes. One year, early April, while the threadbare trees still stood up from the fields like frayed matchsticks, we built a snow family in our front yard. We dressed the dad in plaid sheets and rumpled trousers and the mom in a straw or felt hat and the son in a fireman's helmet we found lying in some dark corner of the house. We made their eyes and smiles from Cole's rock collection—black creek stones, small lumps of anthracite—and we made their arms out of twigs from the old oak. And as the month tumbled toward late spring, releasing us from our cold hands and cold feet, we poured hot cider in mugs and returned to our routines. We helped Cole with his homework, painted canvases, and worked on stoves, leaving behind that snow family. They soon melted into cold pools of straw and felt hats and sodden trousers—cold pools mirroring the shifting clouds and enlivening the new grass. *Once upon a time* the springtime replenished us. In the riffling brooks, breaking up their late winter ice, I heard the crackle of reconstitution. That's worth remembering.

Mister, you okay? The boy shakes my shoulder.

Fine.

You stopped breathing.

NINE

Shadows of the tools flicker against the ceiling beams—the sledgehammer, the axe, the handsaw with its single serrated edge. They seem like stage props and this seems like a stage play, and if it is, then I'll cast myself as a villain: He's vile acts, because his nature demands it. He cannot stop. A pitiable creature, he's unafraid of fire and covets the heat like a lizard splayed on a desert rock. Where's his cape? His fangs? Where's his coffin? I have to laugh.

Can we work on the house today?

Later. Later. Did I tell you that, one year for Halloween, Cole fashioned wings out of an old bed sheet, glued feathers to it that he painted black, and then made a kind of helmet out of a box, rounded off the edges, stuck a beak he formed out of a scrap of tin he found lying around. That was a frightful costume. Nona and I took him around to the shops downtown. His long cape of wings reached past his ankles and brushed the sidewalks. He bobbed his head as he walked and went *caw-caw,* his black beak, like a crooked finger terrifying the neighborhood cats and the smaller children, babies dressed as monkeys, rabbits, and penguins. He skipped along the fences of Arn Kovich's house, his grandpa a lecherous drunk, and that was a house we wouldn't enter.

Why, Papa?

Bad jujus, I said. *Has eeee-vil in it.*

Ghosts, Papa?

That too. And Arn's daddy hacked up his family with a hatchet, chopped them up into little pieces and made a BBQ out of them he fed all the townsfolk.

Don't scare him, Dutch, Nona said. Cole turned to her for protection, his eyes wide as dishes. Nona touched his shoulder with her hand.

Daddy doesn't mean it honey.

You scared, little man? Bakaak!

No, sir.

Good boy, Nona said. *That's my good, brave little boy.*

Somber, he fluffed his feet across the sidewalk and, before we reached the end of the street, he said, *I wanna go home.*

But your bag isn't even half full, I said.

I wanna go home.

The curtain draws. The floodlights dim. A spotlight reveals a monster collapsed on the second floor of a ruined house with a boy in the corner and a winter storm brewing outside. A radio sputters noise. The monster huddles close to the fire. He is a light-scared trilobite of the forests deep, a shriveled prune dredged up from some stink bog. He shuts his eyes and remembers himself swinging from the trees like a capuchin monkey before the gods turned him cruel. How he used to bound up the stoop of the Markle building, taking three steps at a time, agile as a chipmunk. He used to ford Nescopek Creek, power through its murk. If his son were here to see him, he might laugh—*Pops, you look abominable, a regular abomina-man.* I have to laugh. So I do, son. So I do.

The monster leans his shoulder against the wall, stares out the window. Perhaps he waits for a friend, or perhaps he waits for the strength to continue fixing a house that may already be past the point of repair. He doesn't know this. He cannot know this. He must believe that he can recover what was lost.

The monster might appeal to the fates for help. The Olympian gods would scrutinize him, arrange him like a chess piece upon a board. The monster's lover has died and this loss disfigures him. Cursed to live in cold caves, he becomes a troglodyte, this Grendel, Caliban, swamp thing, eater of frogs and fish and worms. I have to laugh. I light a match.

You talk funny.

The fire's a stage fire, plastic sheets cut in waves and lit by a red bulb from beneath. The moon's made of tin foil and the clouds out of pillow stuffing and the sky out of a black plastic canvas in which stage hands have pricked holes, lit it from behind by lanterns. The tools are ready for use, like Perseus' shield, Minerva's owl, Neptune's trident. Whatever I receive by the fates, either punishment or penance or redemption or renewal, I deserve to see this play through.

Deserve? You deserve your anger, Pops. You deserve your loneliness, you deserve my loss. Yes, son. I could easily deserve punishment as well as reward for my life. But who's to say? Good and bad are not for me to judge. Right, Nona? What I deserve is to have everything God or nature can hurl at me. I want the pleasure of the attempt, the pleasure in solving the problems arising from work and working. I want to feel sweat dripping from my chin, maybe suffer an injury, but nothing serious—a stubbed toe, a twisted finger, a broken nail—suffer cold so punishing it scalds my synapses, but just for a little while. I deserve my soul crushed under the weight of bad judgments—*Melodramatic, sentimental, maudlin.* Yes, Nona, there I go again. But I won't disagree. I have always been a little melodramatic. *You're a teary old man, Dutch, you cry at commercials of starving African babies, at puppies whimpering in cages, always ready to write a check… at…* And so I do. Testing my body against the elements and the siege of this house is also a test of stamina and will, or, as Armand would say, *A test of stubbornness*, and I have plenty of that.

Enough thinking about thinking. *Enough!* Let's get something done, I say. The walls lose my voice.

TEN

It looks precious.

The boy presents me a silver ring with a ruby. It was my wedding ring, one I lost decades ago. I had Clayton Meleski, Conyngham's resident jeweler, set that ancient ruby, first Obadiah's, then Blake's, into the band of silver himself.

Where'd you find it?

Inside the wall.

I dig my fingers into the hole and wonder what else I might find in the walls, whose cache of jewels? Would I find Cole's box of arrowheads, marbles, misshapen rocks? Maybe his time capsule, maybe his mason jars of crawfish and doodads. I wonder how the ring made it in there. Maybe Nona had buried it?

I slip the ring into my pocket.

Hey, it's mine.

It's in my house, ain't it?

Finders keepers.

Let's play "Simon Says."

I don't want to play any games.

Say, "Simon says give me the ring," and I'll give it.

I ain't Simon.

You could be.

I don't feel like a Simon.

How would you know?

You talk funny.

Say it.

Simon says, give it back.

Not so fast. Let's give it a story. Let's say it's a beacon. Suppose when the end of the world comes, you just hold up this ring for the folks from Eden to see and they'll come and save you.

Really?

Would I lie? Let's say you'll have to find a clearing where there's rows of zebra oaks, a place where the storm can't reach. That's where the Eden folks'll land and you come and fetch me then. Okay?

Okay.

I hand him the ring. He beams, slips it into his pocket.

Thanks.

We really need to give you a name. But not Simon.

Okay. He runs off. He slips out the open door, marches toward the barn. Suddenly he slips into the earth as if into a rabbit hole.

The hell?

Something rattles out there. The tin roof of the old bomb shelter perhaps? It's where my son would hide—*To think, Pops, because inside the earth you can think things through.* You'd hide in that shelter, sequestered in moldy darkness that dripped water. Nona would coax you out, her tender promises of protection that would not hold. She would lead you back to the house and I would stand and watch you both from the kitchen window, your tiny hand in hers, your tiny shoulder leaning into the pleats of her summer dress.

After one of those flights and rescue, I sent you to your room, and I recall a tense dinner, just Nona and I, and I threw down my napkin and paused before your empty place-setting and I tented my hands, thinking, really mustering my courage to look into your eyes made tragic by my anger. I climbed the stairs and entered your room and whispered, *Son, are you awake?*

No, sir.

And I sat on the edge of your bed and tried to shake my fear of you, because I feared you, because childhood was as fragile a thing as love. I assumed the role of the comforting father then and I said, barely able to control my breathing, that when I spanked you, I did so out of love. I said that when I took a switch to your bottom, I did so because I worried for your eternal soul. When the skin on your buttocks welted because I had lost control, the pain you felt was just sin leaving your body.

Son, you listening?

My hand found your head tucked beneath the blankets and I said, Son, *you're a good boy and know that I love you and always will. But try harder to listen. Try harder to be good.* Turning to the open door, I caught Nona's disapproving mask as she leaned against the jamb, her arm folded across her stomach like I had slapped her, too.

Cupping your chin in my palm, I said, *Son, you know what the Lord says about forgiveness?*

You shook your head no.

Forgiveness frees the forgiver.

Okay.

Do you forgive me?

A slight nod of your head, almost imperceptible, was all it took to release us from distrust.

Now I make for the bomb shelter, its lid luffing like a sail. I know down there that darkness is an absolute entity and its presence still frightens me. I know the boy isn't safe down there.

Once I ran from my bedroom and into Blake's room for shelter, chased by some succubus or incubus or bug-a-boo, and Blake threw me out again—*Back in yer room, shitless.* In the morning, my bed sheets soiled and my nightclothes reeking of piss, I crawled into the corner and rocked. That was all the ammunition Wally needed to pounce on me—*Little bedwetter, little bastard bedwetter!*

I lift the bomb shelter's lid, light as paper. The cavity stretches into eternity, this frozen abyss. I swallow hard. The old oak moans. It's as if he doesn't want me to go. I have to laugh.

Each step flexes and creaks. Something clicks, like time winding down. Voices, scared, starved, hurt, menacing, I cannot control the eruption in my brain—*The unholy blackness breathed, rolled skyward like a black river, and in it, slight as flukes, waved gold ribbons frayed at the tips: red, orange, gold. Not the autumnal hues, no, wet fire, fire like a splash of ice water against your cheek, sharp like broken glass.* And the voices seethe: *The thirsty fire drinks even the bear, even the hawk, rabid and screeching, pulling out air in them lungs our merciless God made.* And from those voices I see Pearl, beautiful Pearl—*Pearl lit the candle. Pearl walked into the woods holding a firefly. And I followed. And I didn't follow. And I traced the light with wet eyes and runny nose and I waited—waited for the blood-hot heat to return to my neat hands, watching that firefly dance down past the old Dutch barn. But I'm scared*—of the dark, of losing. Scared of speaking the wrong words, feeling the wrong things, taking the wrong turns, because Blake and Wally are there to adjudicate. I fear the future. I fear the past. I light a match.

Reaching the stony floor, I recall a set of wooden steps far up ahead, leading up to a storm door that opened into the barn. Now they are not there. If it was daylight outside, the steps would lead up to a pencil thin light, a light like a dividing line marking the lower edge of the ceiling. If it was day, the light would spill down the steps, forming soft penumbras—*I'm lost down here, someone please help. It's so cold and there's things crawling around, please.* If our eyes were the eyes of bats or owls we could see—*See-saw, hee-haw, Somerset is an ass, hee-haw hee-haw, and*—and from the cool dark rises the faint sound of dripping water. I clap my hand over my nose, protecting my lungs against the mustiness of two decades of poisoned air. A sound, dim as distant waves tumbles from the darkness—*wash-wash-wash*—it goes, like something treading water.

Hey, I say. My voice bounces, returning to my ears as a stranger's voice, thin and wobbly. Who's down here? Boy? That you? And the darkness answers and the darkness says, *Pearl lit the candle. Pearl walked into the woods. A thousand-winged serpent made of gold and red slinked across the hills, its gold tongues flicking at the sky, its black thousand-winged body pouring its thick black sheets of ragged black water into the sky. And the orange and red and gold made daylight under the stars. Did the sun fall down? Did the sun melt and spread its fiery fingers across the hills?*

It's a rat, maybe a flying rat—*What evidence is this? Of what? One night Pearl lit the candle with a match and walked into the woods. Pearl set the candle on a log by the black creek sounding like fire in the black and*—I take a tentative step forward. Gaining confidence I move toward the sound of swishing waves—*Has a name, confla-conflag, a name, say it, repeat it, the big word, no, don't say it, never say it!*

The match fizzles. The darkness collapses around me, ready to crush me in its fist. I light another match—*Pearl lit the candle and left it burning on the log by the black waters that sounded like fire. The fire is good, it warms, even that fire, built by the kindling of the forest, but don't say it. Never.*

Not once. Conflagration. Too big a word for you. Boy is father of fire. This boy has a name that sounds like summer, the setting sun of summer.

I freeze. My feet unable to move. A starless night that night and absolutely dark—a no-moon sky, a no-wind—and the old oak stretched its arms over the house and sheltered the house in pitch. The creak of a floorboard in the hall, a long, drawn note held, threaded through the dark. The creak spoke. It said *Wake up* and so I woke up. I went to see because the creak said so, but I saw nothing. Down below, the screen door swished open and clicked shut. The swish and click of the door told me to go and see. From the kitchen's window, a light, tiny as a firefly, stole across the lawn, sheltered in darkness so thick you could breathe it in like smoke. That single pin-light bobbed, a distant semaphore, disappeared.

Followed it, I did, because that pin light said so, and barefoot and still in my bedclothes I followed its memory out of the house and down the lawn's cool wet grass, sticky against my ankles, and then lost the light and found it again deep in the beyond woods where Wally said all times, *Don'tcha go in there if ya know what's good fer yas!* But the light said *Come, follow, follow me.* So I crept across the lawn like a cat, I did, measuring each heel and toe against the cool sticky grass. My eyes held onto that small pin-light as if my eyes were hands. Distant like a star in the sky, the only little light in all the big universe.

Then deep in the woods. Surrounded by silence like death, the shadows pooled, air sticky in a no-wind that bled a darkness of pure obsidian, as riotous and metallic as Nescopek in which no-stars burned, issuing no-heat, and just that single pin-light, not bobbing now, but at rest. The firefly landed, a star fallen to earth as if it were tired of its incredible bob and weave and swerve, and I still crept along, still crept like a cat whose paws touched down, light as air on petals, my heel-to-toe upsetting no-ground and no-leaf, making my airy body light as a windblown mote across the farm fields which had no-name, a mote so small you might breathe it in.

Pearl sat on a log with ladylike precision, composed as if for a painting—one leg folded over the other, her two hands resting neatly on one knee and back ramrod stiff, this strange Pearl looking not like Pearl but some other version of her I never knew—*beside a guttering candle, beside a flame in a glass that was once a firefly.* Before my mouth could speak, her head turned toward a snap, at me, as if she knew something followed her. I thought how pretty she looked—ladylike—not in her night clothes but in her full dress and black traveling jacket that fell to her shins, and her lace bonnet she wore to church on Sundays with Blake and Wally and me, and her black gloves whose finger holes she had once sewn up to make them look whole again. Why dress up as if for a trip and wait in the woods? What train stopped in the woods? What coach driven by what black mares?

Maybe I was afraid for her because she was afraid of something just beyond her sight and I knew she must have sensed something in wait—a wolf, a bear, a boy—

Perhaps she feared Mesingw, eater of sinners who sinned and lying children who never finished their peas. But before I could say her name, I dipped behind a boulder. I watched Pearl watching the darkness. Then Pearl turned away. What was she turning away for? What purpose did this night walk serve? If Blake found her gone, he'd be scared for her, and there's no telling what he might do because I am also not in my bed. I am here with Pearl watching Pearl, spying on my strange mother who is no-mother. She swivels her head and hums lightly; it's the song she sings, "God is Nigh," because it's my song, our song. Why is she sitting in her best clothes on a dirty log with a guttering candle in a glass as her only accompaniment?

Her song stopped. She stepped around and around the candle as if making a spell, but what kind of words were those?

But I stayed quiet, watching this version of a woman I had no recognition of, a no-mother, so distant. No longer holding in her eyes memories of soaping my body, spooning beans into my mouth, singing songs and comforting me when I comforted her when Blake got mad, the mother I knew who fitted me into the sticky, itchy clothes I wore to sit in the church pews and sing words I knew not the meaning of, and no explanation of those words either except that something called "God" loved me but would also punish me if I didn't finish all my oatmeal or do my spelling or know the difference between "further" and "farther" and "father."

Then a shadow moved through the woods. My throat went dry—dry as the bark from the old oak Wally always forced me to eat, bark with the black ants in it that crunched and tasted like bitter seeds—and I saw Pearl move toward the big shadow and then she became shadow, but smaller, and the two shadows, big and small, were one shadow and then the two shadows moved apart. Then they stood still. The big shadow held the smaller shadow a little farther apart and then the big one spoke things in whispers and then the big shadow turned back the way it came and I almost screamed *Wait!*

The little shadow stood still. She stood staring after the big shadow that moved back through the warm night of trees. The big shadow went into the black and the little shadow dropped to her knees and made the same sobbing sounds I made when Wally twisted my ears after beating me at arm wrestling or after Wally beat me at running, then slapped me for losing, or when Blake used his Bible palm on my face after I did something I wasn't supposed to—sleeping too late, speaking outta turn, getting sick when there were chores to do. Then the little no-mother's shoulders jerked and she moved toward the candle and the little shadow no-mother picked it up and she threw it against a tree. But she didn't pick it up again. She left her bag and walked down the forest trail in a no-light where the leaves of trees, faintly electric in the new moonlight streaking from the clouds, moved away to let her pass. I followed. I almost said, *Wait!*

Pearl entered the outer edge where the woods broke into the field beyond and I followed behind, making every step quiet as she showed me how, toe-to-heel, toe-to-heel. I followed her through the field slowly, not running, slowly not rushing and finally when she reached the main road I said, *Mama, wait!*

I was five all that summer, and because I was five and small and because Wally had made me eat earthworms that day before, and because I was not strong like Blake who always looked at me like I was bad while Wally was always good, because Blake would go to him at night and they would lie together, Pearl in the pale light of a summer moon turned towards me, her eyes wet. And when she looked at me she stopped me.

Ma?

My Pearl, my devotion, my salvation, my love, stared past my head and stared at the woods behind and I turned and saw something that hurt. I saw too what hurt Pearl. But I smelled it before I saw it. A thousand tongues of fire licked the woods clean, flames gnashed the dark. The forest was blood. And she ran then. Ran towards me. Pearl, my mother, scooped me up. And she ran and ran but not toward the house. Not back to the house and the barn and not to Blake and to

Wally and the no-name dog chained up and kicked for half her life. Pearl ran and ran down the dark, rutted road. She ran. She crushed my ribs into her ribs, molded my heart to her heart. I could hear the air going in and out of her lungs.

You're a stupid, stupid man, Somerset. You're delving into things you have no business delving into. Forget this restoration business. Return to the house. Pack your things and hitchhike to that little Baltimore brownstone. Watch from your window Eunice perform sex tricks on her stepfather. Watch the streets return to life after the dark, cool, quiet hours. Wrap yourself in a wool blanket and build yourself a fire in the hearth. Pour a whiskey and get it in you quick. Light a stogie and sit in your recliner and read the biography of Ralph Waldo Emerson. Spread warmth into your fingers and toes. By God, listen to music.

The match dwindles. My shoulder brushes against something hard and I turn the match toward shelves, laced with webs and caked with dust two inches thick. Hummocks left by rats big as raccoons. My boots crunch snail shells, coiled like candy wrappers, glistening trails. The oily swirls of larval life and dead slugs shimmer, the shelter breached by small skittering and stinging things. Rotten air soured with senescent rainwater and mold and decades old wet dust. Rotten stink of feces, urine, discarded fur, dead leaves, all these blended like the decayed liquors of a swamp. The match fizzles. I light another match. *Fear is just a symptom of language. Somerset.* Armand, if you never learned the word for fear, did it still have power? Cold sweat dripped from my brow and my skin prickled. Dim shadows flickered against the walls. I could call fear something else and it would still turn me to stone.

Hell or high water, I say. My voice a foreign substance, broken glass mixed with black pebbles, oil and mercury, melted copper and singe. I make my palm into a cold fist. In the darkness, all my vulnerabilities could be a defense. The darkness is my mask. If I feigned weakness, no, if I played it true to form, perhaps whatever awaited—*Mesingw, eater of children*—might take pity on me. It might be shocked to find me here, an old man with wheezy lungs.

This is not the place for you, Somerset. You have no claim on Drums. Soon you'll slip and fall and break a hip, because your bones are as brittle as winter branches. Can you even feel the floor beneath your feet? Your forearms might as well be attached to splintered wood for all the feeling that's left in your hands.

Wash-wash-wash, there it was again. I hadn't imagined it. No I can't be sure I hadn't imagined it.

The match fizzles. I light another. Hello? I say. Boy? Images of bodies draped over the limbs of redwoods. They flashed on the wall as if flashing on a projector screen. One year Hurricane Agnes swept through the valley. Black clouds shaped like anvils tumbled down from the north. Clouds expanded like squid ink spreading in water. Cole was five then, '72. Driving through the county, you witnessed things you could not forget, the surrealism of despair, like undergarments dangling from telephone wires, a snare drum squashed against a paling fence, a couch flattened on St. John's Road. A grandfather clock impaled in an elm tree, a cat hanging from a telephone pole, a typewriter in the muddy banks of Nescopek, bark in its platen. The storm turned everything inside out, revealed the best and worst of Drums.

Nona, Cole and I had prepared for it. We had storm-boarded the windows to protect the glass from whatever the wind launched at us—sticks and branches, seeds and stones—never once suspecting an attack of tractor parts, buggy wheels, milk bottles and textbooks, and we locked ourselves in the upstairs attic, tuning in the disaster on the old battery-operated Bakelite.

For seven days the storm drenched the valley. Gales blew the shingles from houses, turned weathervanes into spinning projectiles, snapped hundred-year-old redwoods in half. The sky shuddered and burst, released an ocean of water. Copious lakes formed in the valley's declivities and our shallow bike paths turned into waterways. The flood water drowned St. John's cemetery, drowned church cellars all up and down Valley Township Road, lifting sooty water up to second story windows. South Main Street folded up into a river through which people navigated their canoes, rafts, lifeboats held the planks and oars together by nothing more than glue and painter's tape and twine. Our own backyard became a brackish pond on which collected the detritus of leaves and waste blown down from the hills. The barn filled up with silt water three feet high.

The house groaned then. The old oak trembled like a dog throwing off water. And when the storm finally eased and when the sky finally shattered into salmon skin patterns of iridescent silver and pink and gold, like cave dwellers we climbed out of our attic encampment to investigate the damage. We went from room to room, estimating the cost of repairing a cracked wall, a cracked window. In the family room we found nothing much amiss, nothing in the living room neither, nor the kitchen. Our protections had held. We headed downstairs and smelled the upsurge of groundwater. Cole flicked the light switch before I could shout, *Stop! What if a live wire lay buried in the water?* But the power was gone.

Water, brackish water, poison water, had ruined our mementos—family photo albums, Nona's framed landscapes, their artful exaggerated colors resembling no known world, what with their sea blue fields and purple cliffs and effulgent yellow clouds. The water had ruined scores of books, Baer Almanacs with their antiquated advice on housekeeping, a set of Encyclopedia Britannica, cartographer maps. The water ruined a dollhouse, a set of knitted yarn dolls, porcelain vases, hurricane lamps. Devoid of context, such things were valueless, but we kept them anyway, those keepsakes for some future, unknown purpose.

A small pond had formed at the base of the first landing, black water shimmering like oil upon which shoes and boots with their tallow soles bobbed and bumped the corners of the walls like rudderless boats. Leaves of paper and tented books floated about like headless birds, clicking against one another. We found flower print dresses Nona never remembered owning, that perhaps belonged to Pearl, and a pale wedding dress in white lace, that looked like a floating ghost, that might have been Geraldine's. There, a derby hat and a small child's sandal, just one, and here, a collection of stamps, spreading in every direction.

The house's mysteries rose with the flood water, perhaps for us to recognize them, making of them more than a wedding dress in white lace, a child's sandal, a collection of stamps spreading like atoms in every direction. What was the point if all that disaster, but to make the invisible visible?

When the sun eventually broke up the clouds, dissipating the storm and driving moisture from the valley, people found corpses draped like rags from the elm trees lining Tomhicken Road. The stink rose into the furtive air, weighed upon the dripping pines and elms and hung about all that summer. When we piled the bodies up, doused them with kerosene, burned them, ash rained down upon us like snow. Gusts drove the ash east and north, clouding towns as far north and east as Providence. Cole asked me why it was wintering in summer—*and why does the snow feel warm and why does the snow not melt when it touches your tongue?* What could I tell him but that the Lord works in mysterious ways?

The match fizzles. I feel larval, cold, squeezed into a corrugated shell—*If it weren't for Pearl, if it weren't for what Pearl had done, if it weren't for*—Ah, shut up! Shut up! Shut up! The apertures of my eyes dilate. I strike another match. Still, fear tightens around my chest. In the frozen darkness, my heart still throbs, ready to burst. *Courage, courage, Somersssssset,* Blake hisses. *Ah learned that ta make yer devil yer angel frees youse from yer fear.* I inhale, exhale. My lungs whistle. My useless feet shuffle, scrape up the winter dust, decanting the stinging smell of creosote. Sulfur stings the air—*Now, if it weren't for Pearl, if it weren't for what Pearl had done, if it weren't for (a match, a log, a creek black as molten coal), if it weren't for the wind and the dry brush that hadn't touched rain in months and if Jonny Blessing had come like he was to (the colors eat up the dark, the warthog, the beaver, the tiny worms in the earth are screaming and the fire ants are screaming).* Please, shut up! Whose voice was it that was speaking if not the darkness? *And what would you say was the color of death? Is it white? Is it black? Red, like blood, or pink, like love. Love is what killed her, boy. In the end love is what kills all of us.*

Wash-Wash-Wash. There it is again.

Boy, quit your shammin', I say, my voice reverberating with a wooden timbre, as if spoken into a barrel—*Hee-haw, hee-haw, Somerset stinks like piss. Shitless!*

Now you cut out teasing Wally, little shitless, and stop it before I put my belt on your ass.

No trespassing, you hear? This is private property.

A shadow moves among the shadows. A shadow approaches noiselessly, as if gliding. The shadow hisses—*Pearl kept the boy two years then returned him home so, for the boy, matchsticks became another word for love, and sulfur the smell of cleansing and healing while love burned, yet it hurt the blackness and made the dark things go away but not for always, for in the light the darkness lives.* I turn from the shadow, from its iron teeth dripping acid, and from the shelter, run from it quick as I can.

BOOK III

ONE

For days, the Mayan prediction has come to nothing. *Papa, when will the sky break open?* Patience is a virtue, Cole. The sky has yet to burst, yet to throw down cold white ash and the earth has yet to fissure. Maybe Sugarloaf Mountain will erupt, and from it will pour the bones of extinct animals?

~

The boy lies on his bed in his corner of the room. Sweat rolls from his cheeks and onto the floorboards, staining them dark. His lungs wheeze as he breathes.

~

Mister, he says, *I don't feel so good.* He offers me his hands, palsied and veined, the hands of an old man, and I take them in mine and rub them.

You're cold as a corpse, I say.

I'm hot inside, he says, palming his chest.

It serves you right, running around outside when you should be inside helping me.

Can't stop shaking.

I retrieve a bottle of aspirin from my suitcase. I shake two pills into my palm. He swallows them. Coughs.

Let's get something straight: I can't be watching over you all day. Gotta show Armand I ain't been idling away my time. You hear?

His eyes flutter. His teeth chatter. I fetch him a blanket from my own pile and drop it onto his legs. He draws the blanket over him.

Just sleep it off, I say.

The boy coughs into his fist, coughs into his fist, and then rights himself.

I'm sorry for trespassing, sir, he says, his voice scratchy.

Damn right you are, sorriest kid I ever seen.

The hours passed. I slept. The boy slept. I awoke. The boy slept. I wrote in my memory book. I read. I ate. Slept. Awoke.

~

Now I watch tendrils of dust spiral downwards like thin worms. I wince. Something stabs my brain. I need medicine, but reach for the bourbon instead. I take a swig. I shove a cigar in my mouth, pat down my clothes for the matches. Not there. Where did I put my matchbox? In my toolbox. I find my Colt inside, wrapped nicely in its chamois cloth. Out it comes. It gleams electrically. I click its barrel. I aim the nozzle at the window. Pow, I whisper. I sweep the room, aim it at the hearth, Pow. I aim it at the boy, Pow! I press the metal barrel against my forehead, Pow! then smile, then put away the Colt. I shut the toolbox. I turn away.

Later.

I rub my temple, but my hands ache so I stop. My legs throb. My chest aches. I glance at the boy. He shivers and shakes. We're both in the ruts. Hurt defines us. Scrapes and bruises long forgotten linger in our bodies like smoke from some long ago expunged fire. Hurt, the pain from hurt, injury—concrete and abstract—each as tangible as the system of nerves dying, lives on. And on. It's the memory of hurt that carries in our voices, trembles like a plucked string that vibrates our bones. When remembered. Scars are nothing more than congealed memory. Old pain, the pain of our forbears, our forefathers, pain of things forgotten chokes our words when we attempt to speak, bends our backs when we attempt to walk, throbs up from our deepest parts and manifests itself in dreams and visions and nightmares. And what of our sanctuaries? Maybe they're also nothing more than pain alloyed by a hundred other elements. I have to laugh.

Later.

The boy stirs. I hear the creak of the woods in his chest. The fire's shadows dance across his body, pale shadows like muted colors animating his face into dreadful expressions. The seven deadlies are all there, distributed across his lips and cheeks. A sewer rat, an urchin, a goddamned little guttersnipe, his body dispatches the brackish odors of mossy water, smelling faintly of swamps and slithering things. I suddenly hate him. The blanket I gave him drapes across his shoulders and now stinks of wet, milky clay. I suddenly resent his presence. I have the urge to kick his legs and scream in his face and tell him he's breaking the rules by sleeping in. But he's sick. *Sick in the head.* He's an outcast. A stranger. I'll take pity on him.

Later.

He looks so peaceful, just like Cole did when he slept.

Later.

It's cold in the room. The fire has burned down to blue ash and orange embers, resembling the remnants of a meal composed of roasted meat. I add another log. Sparks shoot up into the flue, insects on glowing wings, fireflies. Maybe today Armand will come. Maybe later? The hell with him!

Later.

I turn on the Bakelite. After a bit of static and squealing, Miki's voice comes in clear. Nothing new to her report—different types of disasters, same in kind. She talks of the winter chill, chatters about the hoarfrost. There's infighting between the Shiites and Sunnis. They can't agree on a goddamned thing. Where's their Mohammed to adjudicate? I have to laugh. I need music now. I need coffee. My mouth itches. Cottony. I check my breath in the palm of my hand. My teeth feel loose.

Later.

Rise and shine, I say, nudging the boy's backside with my foot. A coffee steams in my hand. Rise and shine. Early bird gets the worm.

The boy stirs. Turns over. His red-rimmed eyes regard me with a grogginess that almost chokes me. A noodle of spit slinks from the corner of his mouth. He stinks.

Aren't you a sight, I say.

I'm cold.

Did you take that medicine like I said? I check the aspirin bottle. Empty.

It ain't candy. What's the matter with you?

He lifts himself up on one elbow then vomits on the floor.

For Christ's sake! *Look at this goddamned mess you made, shithead!*

Later.

I regret my anger, but my pride is too strong. I won't apologize, Nona. No, I won't. *You have to.* I survey the kitchen. Its renovation can wait. Enter the family room. With the shovel tip, I strike the baseboards, wrenching them free of the walls. Nails screech but the work is easy, and, I might add, effortless. I have a fount of energy.

Patterns of light and shadow. Ornamental dust. Decorations in the floorboards made by time, faded circles made by old furniture legs and feet. There are other marks formed by tracks of insects, of the motes that settled here over the decades. They form oblique paths. With my boots I erase their marks.

I cough. I pump my lungs with the Albuterol. Only once. I cross the room to the windows. A featureless world. No lights on the hill. No stars in the sky. The Poconos have disappeared. The yard emits few signs of life. Snow drifts across the fields. The porcelain sky above mimics the snow drifting across the fields. Leaning against the shovel, I settle my pumping heart. I wipe my brow with the sleeve of my jacket. The hairs on my arms prickle. The boy stands by the doorway and regards me.

You up?

No answer.

Hungry? I'm hungry.

No answer.

You cold? I'm cold.

I wish, he starts. *I want. To go home.*

You seen outside? Try to leave now and you'd die out there. We're locked in till Armand gets here. Come on.

I lead the boy upstairs. The fire smolders. I add a few logs to the fire. The climbs under his covers. He looks at me grimly, as if uncomprehending my purpose here.

Tell me a story.

Not much of a storyteller.

I like your funny voice.

I have to laugh. I stare into the fire. I scratch my head. Wally once told me that the fire has a smell and he'd know, and Armand said that fire is an exchange for all things and all things are an exchange for fire. Not sure where he got that from and I ain't sure what it means except that maybe fire changes everything. Armand's a card. You'd like him. He's always going on and on about the meaning of life.

The boy says nothing, stares at nothing, stifles a cough. The house moans. The old oak is awake, its frowning mouth sucking in air.

That's the old tree talking, I say. I wait for a response. That's okay, I say. You don't have to say a thing. Being the sort of quiet little person you are is a virtue. Ever hear that? Silence is a virtue? If Cole were to come up here and press his hand against the door, he might rightly feel the quiet inside. He might know intimately that the quiet he felt was borne out of a silence made by two people pondering things like the meaning of life. Sure, the quiet helps you think and I suppose that's what I'm doing here, thinking, because it was Armand who also said that the uncontemplated life isn't worth living.

Can I sleep now?

You don't want to hear me talk?

No.

TWO

Later.

Miki tells me it's December 13th. She tells me it's ten past ten at night. We're another night closer to oblivion. I cannot wait. The desire for nothingness, for that great chasm where even memories burn, is the non-state I long for. The bliss of nothingness. What's there in this life but loss? Let Armageddon come. Let this chattering mind stop chattering.

~

The shattered beams of the ceiling leak dust or bits of frost, and I peer across the room, through the bedroom door, and my eyes settle emptily on the rails of the landing sleeved in dust so fine it looks like felt, I cannot completely tell, and I think of the empty years of neglect it took to ruin this house. It held laughter once, mock-laughter; tears, mock-tears. Here the clamor of work and there the business of life. Birds sang in cages here. Paintings were painted there. All around me, plans were made.

~

The boy snores. Sleep is a luxury now, if it comes at all. Though the body winds down, it turns restless. I want to tell the boy that I envy how easily sleep comes to children. Their heads hit the pillow and they're gone, flying over clouds like dragons, tramping through fields playing hopscotch with Rin Tin Tin and Benjamin Franklin. I'll shut my eyes and drift for an hour and then I'm up again, bright-eyed, bushy-tailed, just like that white rabbit there, hopping into view—*Oh dear! I shall be too late!*

~

I rise from my bedroll. I follow the rabbit down the stairs. He's the flash of a tail. I cross the house. *Oh! Dear!* I slip out of the front door and find myself on the lawn, the white rabbit blending into the snow drifts. *I'll be late!* He shilly-shallies over the embankment and I follow. My hands feel cold, so I rub them. Where is the rabbit? I feel my shoulders stoop. Look at me, Neanderthal of the winter. A thin voice ahead, *Late!* Am I crossing time as I walk, returning to some primitive version of myself? *A very important date!* Am I descending into a wormhole? Lost in this white space, impossibly effulgent even in the darkness, the darkness feels so bright it blinds.

I pass the Mercury dead in the ditch, the hiss of its inner tube still releasing air. *No time!* The faint smell of motor oil capitulates. *Hell…!* A hard lingering look inside the windshield already caked with snow reveals a blurred shape. *Bye!* A man sits hunched over the steering wheel. *Weren't you always one for extremes, Dutch?* I was, Nona. I am. My nose turns watery.

~

The rabbit is gone. Steps to my right, pockmarked, holes as big as fists, might be from his tracks. There are craters in the snow, footprints from giants. What if the moon came down for a walk in these woods late at night while I was asleep? Or maybe I'm on the moon with only the cold view of black space for all I know. I have to laugh.

~

My boots crunch the snowpack. I cross through a threshold of low arching limbs and my boots crackle against the patched earth, the ice thin as a membranous skin. There's nothing human in the air. No scents of roasted hams, no apples roasted on spits, no wood smoke billowing up from distant chimneys. Pools of aspic in which small flukes lay trapped in coiled shapes draw out my laugh, and pools of ice reflect the evergreens. Winter flowers. Bushes with filigreed stems. Near a jumble of piled stones lies the carcass of a muskrat, its rictus frozen in death's grin. There is nothing but the smell of the frozen woods and icy weather and the sound of that poor dog, barking and barking. If Henry James were here, he'd be bounding through the snow, leaping at birds. If I shouted, "Heel," he would heel. He would circle me and sit by my side. But he's also gone. Having let him loose the day we left, he trotted after the Mercury till the end of the drive then gave up. *How he must have waited for our return.* No sense in thinking that.

~

The tops of the fir trees, the rounded crest of Sugarloaf Mountain, the scant distant crows, seem to pull the sky down. Scraps of cloud. Vaporous bits of mist, air argent, effulgent (thank you Armand for the words). The evening's light, silvery, casts its dull brightness onto the trees—trees gelid in this blue light of winter. But whiteness dominates with the pines and evergreens steeped in vibrant grades of silver. I hear notes in the mist, like silvery chattering, coins in a pocket, the jangle of keys. These trees look like ghost trees, figures from a dream barely visible, and those bushes look like apparitions, gnomes, trolls, witches with bent fingers. If I run up to them, will they vanish or would they cast a spell on me? The arrangement of limbs and branches, trunks and roots feel as inaccessible as the distant Poconos somewhere out there. Everything is strangely alive with discomfort. It's as if the world is weeping. Here birds returned from southern haunts and there the trees came alive with new leaves, their buds in whose bottomless green I could trace the routes of ancient rivers. Big Nescopek crackled on those first sunny afternoons, sending shivers through the ground. I want to tell someone that these are not the trees I remember. These are other trees. The trees I remember, incalculable, gelid, their winter bark like gooseflesh whose limbs chattered in the wind, knew me. These trees are older, inaccessible. If they had eyes, would they not see me as a shadow against this white enameling, emulsified, a shadow appearing and disappearing like the shape of a half-imagined thing? *If the sky was not plated silver, Dutch, I would think the sun is a moon.* No, Nona, that is not the sun you are seeing, I would say, but the moon, shimmering like a silver dollar in a pan of grease-fat, throwing molecular sparks. Perhaps here, perhaps now, between light and dark, sense and nonsense, is where the past and imagination merge. Perhaps Armand was right when he said, *The past is a shattered bit of a conversation in some half-remembered dream.* I shiver. If it weren't so damn cold, I swear the earth was on fire. The snow is ash; the mist, smoke.

~

Dawn arrives sooner than I thought, which means it's later than I thought. I tighten this noose-scarf around my neck, pull up the collar of my overcoat and toddle forward, one foot ahead of the other. I walk. I breathe it in, the mist. The mist and all the cold sunshine of hell, sits trapped in this insoluble, effervescing air, rises from the milky earth and collects in the trees, the trestles, the broken eaves, and congeals there, like the notes of frozen music. Are those windblown leaves I see? A frightful murder circles the distant fir tops.

~

I wish Cole were here to experience this with me—*Pa, I'm not always gone when I go away*—and not that sick boy I'm nursing—*I can't stop from coughing, Papa.* I stop at the wooden bridge and squat. I scoop up a bit of snow in my palms. *Pops, did you know there's more to life than fixing stoves?* Perhaps if I had been a different man than I was, I might have patted Cole's cheek. I might have taken his hand in mine and said, *Now, Son, there's a basic truth.*

~

I make for the mound. It offers me a better view of Drums. As the mist burns away, it reveals a landscape so pure and barren it makes me tremble. The neat avenues of tilled white earth, white furrowed land, dusted in the ruts by frost and the light snow that intermittently falls. If I were to scrape the ground with the toe of my boot, I might find veins of ice so pure it would bring me to my knees. Water transfigured to ice, buried beneath topsoil and invisible to the eye, would also endear me to the belief that life is the product of accident. God, the prime mover, moved nothing but our desire to create Him.

I can't feel my feet. My teeth chatter. I suppose it's time to get to work on that kitchen. Make a hot cup of coffee.

THREE

Three days passed. Miki claims it's December 16th and I won't argue. While the boy slept, I managed to tear apart the kitchen with my shovel. The demolition work was good. I made dents in another wall. I pushed shards of the house around and made piles. I eat, I remember, I scrawl messages in the dust. I count the days.

~

For the past three days, the boy slept. For the past three days, I gave him water and capfuls of bourbon, forced it down his throat at times. For the past three days, I tended to his suffering, patting his brow with a towel. I crushed Tylenol capsules into his baked beans, drew up a tall fire in the hearth and dragged his bedding up close. He muttered incomprehensible things while dreaming, his eyelids fluttering. His body twitched. His mouth, fetid as manure, coughed vile fluids. Now his fever's broken. A little color has returned to his face. He's awake.

Feeling better? I say. The boy shuts his eyes. So much for that.

I retrieve the axe leaning by the wall, leaning beside the sledgehammer and the shovel, and I swing it by the throat and palm it in both hands. Leaving the boy, I prop the belly-end onto my shoulder and its weight cuts into my bone. The axe bit points at the floor, the eye staring backwards.

Here I stand, outside in the cold like an idiot. The veins in my legs have gone blue. That signifies something. A lack of oxygen maybe. Work the outside, clear the dead weeds. Later maybe move up to the attic and see what's there. Maybe rip out the old bats of insulation, then maybe move downstairs. I'll strip the walls bare. I'll skin the family room. I'll tear open the ceiling and pull down the plumbing pipes.

I circle the house, dragging the axe behind me, searching for a vulnerable place to strike. A patch of gray wood between two broken shingles resembles the drabness of weathered skin. I lift the axe and aim for the spot. The axe head digs into a shingle—*Swing and a miss.* If Cole were here to help me, we'd give it the ole father and son try, but when did we ever give it the ole father and son try? I wrench the axe free. I lift it and swing again, aiming for that sweet spot. Crack! *Steerriiike!* I'd rather be walking through the woods. I'd rather be anywhere but here. Before Nona secluded herself in her room with the lights off and the curtains drawn, she and I took walks through the bustling neighborhood, where everything looked to have turned itself into a trigger of memory just for us to acknowledge it. I wrench the axe free. I lift it again, strike the house. Whack! *Steerriiike!* Fall of last year, we passed the storefronts on Thames Street. Around us, the paper lanterns in soft pastels decorated the cherry blossoms. We passed Faulk's Hardware Store. I lift the axe and aim for the same spot. Crunch! *Baaaalll!* Inside the plate window stood a mannequin family dressed in their Christmas best. The little boy mannequin held a model rocket, the father clutched a Craftsman toolbox, the mother held a horsehair paintbrush. *Now,* I said to Nona. *Who does that remind you of?* All that seemed missing in the background was a cast iron Home Comfort in pistachio. I pull the axe blade from between the shingles and before lifting it again, I remove my gloves. I slap my hands together and rub them. This past April, I strolled alone past Carver's Private School, stopped to regard children in their starchy collared shirts, kids young as ten squeezed into their blue and white uniforms, bounding up the brick stoop. Other children twirled about in the playgrounds, while others played hopscotch with a stone. I lift the axe and aim for the sweet spot. Thwack! *Steeeriiike Three!* Some of the boys swung across the monkey bars with that fevered pitch of excited birds and I thought of Cole at that age, free and playful as a robin, cheerful as a cricket, inviolable in his utter joy at being a boy running and jumping and bounding. Yet, I was not there for him. Having missed so much of his life and so much of mine, I must have felt to him like a ghost. So where was I but in the Dutch barn? Where was I? Curled up with a newspaper on the porch with the Bakelite relaying the news of the world. Where was I? In my study, the phonograph blaring sentimental songs. While Cole tore open his knees sliding for home, where was I but cruising the Luzerne Valley, hunting for an ancient Chambers stove. While Cole recited lines from *Hamlet* on Rock Glen Elementary's stage—*He was something, Dutch*—where was I but working. Working. Always working to keep a roof over our heads and the utilities paid, always justifying my life. *Yaaar out!*

I lift the axe. My arms are rubber. I lift my face to the clouds. Cole, I could use a little help. *So when did you ever help me?* Now I feel nothing more than embarrassment at this effort. If Cole were to tumble down from above, tramp on by, what would he say? *There's a guy who's lost his marbles.*

Footprints in the snow lead from the house into the woods. So he leaves the house and wanders, returning to the warm little room to sleep. Wind skims snow off the fields, shakes the trees. The wind whistles through the broken window sashes, rattles the rafters above. My feet and hands feel frozen solid. Winded, I drop the axe. It lays against the snow like a fallen god.

FOUR

Upstairs, the embers in the hearth glow red. Sparks shoot up through the flue. The wood crackles. The fire is beautiful. Real. Simple things provide the most pleasure. The boy yawns. I sense a pull of warmth, a slow degradation of heat that ends at the boy's body. I can see my breath as I breathe.

What was all that noise?

Just me.

What did you do?

You feeling better?

You smell funny.

I sniff my hands. I smell old. I want to tell him how Cole would dig up grubs and silverfish from beneath fallen logs, made his hands smell something awful, that he would fill up Coke cans with mealy worms. He brought them to school for Show and Tell once, terrorized Missy Hanson and Tammy Mooney by flicking silverfish onto their blouses. I got calls from both girls' parents.

Your son's a pest, said Mrs. Hanson.

A bully, said Mr. Mooney.

He's just a kid, doesn't know any better, I said, offering Cole's defense. No one had the right to criticize my son. At fourteen, when Cole skulked home from school, suspended for making a catalytic bomb in chemistry lab—*it was an accident, Pops*—I led him to the barn by his ear.

Take down your pants and bend over.

I'm too old for that!

I'm not playing, boy.

I took a steel ruler to his thighs that time.

This'll hurt me more than it'll hurt you. The sound of metal on skin, *Whack!* broke my heart. But Cole didn't cry. I'll give him that. He accepted his punishment as if accepting a reward.

That wasn't nice to do, says the boy. *If it was me, I'da run and hid.*

Cole ran. Cole hid. Maybe that last time he ran so far he forgot his way home. As a baby, he never once walked. Just got up from a crawl one day and ran—*Pops, you never told me that. What else didn't you tell me?* Son, your first word was "Go."

The fire ticks. In it I see shapes, blue and gold and orange memories. An image of Cole floats up on a sleeve of smoke, his toes, pink and bare, peek through the den's linen curtains.

Where are you? Come out come out from wherever you are.

Nona, on her haunches, thrusts her hands beneath the sofa.

Dutch, not here, either. Is he there?

Nope, not here.

Cole giggles. The curtains tremble.

I wonder where he's gone? Honey, check behind the TV.

Nona checks and slaps her palm across the top. *Nope, not here, either.*

Jeez, where's that boy run off to? I say.

Giggles.

Outside?

Maybe he's mucking around by the old tree?

Cole? Co-ole.

Giggles.

We pretend to tiptoe from the room. We circle back, each taking our positions on opposite ends of the window. *Gotcha!*

Noooo! Cole's cries pierce the moon. Shatter the clouds. Break apart the mountains. Why this desire to stay hidden?

The firewood pops. On the cones of the fire, I watch Nona and me tramping through the woods, calling Cole's name, shouting, *Come out come out from wherever you are.*

He takes things too far, I say.

He's always hiding, Dutch, always disappearing and I'm sick of it.

The fire ticks.

Sir? You there? The boy snaps his fingers.

During those awful summers, when it was too hot to breathe, Cole crept out of the house like a little night cat, quick and light-footed. I'd have to rouse him in the morning for school and he'd shuffle to the bathroom like the undead. *You look like you ain't slept.* He would shrug. And one night I caught him, followed him down to the creek trail. Keeping my distance, I slipped behind trees, ducked beneath bushes, crouched low to the warm wet earth. He became one of those shadows without detail—*Like Pearl when she lit the candle.*

Sir?

Reaching Big Nescopek he tore off his shirt and slung it over a branch. A little later he skipped rocks off the surface of Pulaski's Pond, and that was for a good half hour, then a little later he whistled a tune I don't recall, crouched on all fours and growled like a dog. Later he flushed some dark birds from the bramble bushes, partridges maybe. My throat tickled.

Sir?

By a row of beetle-infested firs, Cole slipped off his shorts and undershorts. Naked, he traveled the creek bank for a good hour and still I followed behind, my face tagged with nettles, witness to a secret life. He skipped. He danced. He stopped now and again, turned behind him, then kept on. Eventually, the woods increased in volume, just as the creek increased in depth. Near the Shacklewood farm, the crickets screeched, stopped, screeched again.

Sir?

Then came the fit. I coughed. He stopped. Turned. Choking, I said, *Okay, that's enough.* It seemed the world and the night birds died and the sky fractured like glass. Every star suddenly extinguished. Cole froze mid-step, became stone. His face was fury. He shot me a look revealing such hatred that I shuddered.

The boy slaps my face. His eyes enter me.

You stopped breathing again.

Did I? Oh.

The boy's eyes scan the room. He sighs. *I wish I could leave.*

If you're lonely you just have to think of someplace friendly, that's a trick of the imagination.

That's stupid.

Maybe it is or maybe it's not.

FIVE

It's been several hours now and the boy hasn't returned. He's outside. Somewhere. It's easy to lose yourself out there. It's also easy to find yourself. Follow a trail to a road then to a farmhouse. Someone's always willing to take pity on you. A locked front door never means what you think it does. Just knock. Just wait. Someone will let you in. The room feels viscid, heavy with heat.

Boy! I say. It's a matter of expedience that he needs a name. *A name is just a shell, a package, wrapping. Names are no more than a false choice. We are more than our names. Or less.*

I once awoke from a dream of names. Objects flew past me as I sped through a shining tunnel, and the spinning objects hurtling past my head had different names attached to them; so a tree was "quivxlou" and a rock was a "nrdajl." A terrible dream. I stumbled to the bathroom in the dead of night. Outside, the spring in full arrest crept toward summer. With the lights off, I washed my face in the sink, the tap sputtering foamy cataracts. In the mirror I saw a different man. I saw Blake. How had this happened? When? It was his nose, the same furious ears, the same dimple in the jaw. *I am Somerset,* I said. *I* AM *Somerset.* The name didn't know me; it wouldn't attach itself to my image in the mirror.

When I saw Nona lying stiff in the casket, I knew that bundle of qualities wasn't her. *Her!* People greet the wrap, console the wrap, embrace what you've packed yourself into. The years burn away, decades, then half a life is over and the wrap withers and you become a stranger to yourself. Experience changes you. The weather. Suffering. Joys. Romantic pleasure. The loss of it. The city with its putrid smells and vacuous people and delightful little parks changes you. The city, its manufactured experiences, its shopping malls where potted plants bloom to mimic the bloom found in spring meadows, changes you, and you cling to your old life like a withered leaf dangling from a dead branch, swaying in wind. In time you discover a new ache, a new joint grown stiff, a new coarseness. You awaken at the age of sixty, unable to control your bladder. At seventy, your skin turns sallow and spots the color of rust pepper your face. At seventy-five, your lungs whistle with each breath. At eighty, you look into the mirror and see reflected back someone you don't recognize, a man tumbling headlong into an abyss. The fall is steep and sharp and you abrade all your swollen parts. What name do you attach to that image in the mirror? Not the same Somerset.

At least Cole would never experience the ruin of age, of arthritic hands and diabetic feet, a pate and a wattle, a swollen prostate and insomnia. Pearl, too. She would remain timeless, caught in the net of my memory as a woman of twenty-eight: ageless, perfect, as abstract as the word "beauty," a perfect beauty, perfect and eternal and beautiful because of its eternality, because of her absence.

In the living room, a board covering the window has come loose. It flaps—*frup-frup-frup*—like a broken wing. Wind howls outside, pushes against the house and the board, *frup-frup-frups*.

Boy, you here?

Entering the foyer I turn toward the old dining nook. Boy? I say. You know what I said about roaming the house alone. *Frup-frup-frup*. The noise sounds familiar.

In 1982, Cole turned fifteen and his upper lip sprouted dark fuzz. He experienced a growth spurt that summer that raised him an inch taller than me. He was a loner. Had few friends except Ivan. Ivan's dad, Sonny, owned a motorcycle shop off of Route 91 and rode a black Bonneville he had speeded across the Salt Flats, losing the world record to Burt Munro and his Indian. That year, Cole took up playing the guitar, because Ivan played drums. They listened to brash music teeming with screaming voices and screeching guitars. They both wore jeans torn at the knees, rock T-shirts whose sleeves they tore off, even stuck a safety pin in their left ear. Like Ivan, Cole grew his hair long and pimples sprouted on his forehead and chin.

That spring, with patches of snow still on the ground and the air rich with the colossal mix of vegetable health, sunshine, and new rain, Nona, without my consent, drove him to Sonny's shop and bought him a banged-up Indian Scout out of our savings. I might have scolded her for buying him that pile of junk, but when Cole came around, promised to do good in school and do his chores, and cobbled it together in the garage, his darkness lifted.

Need help? I asked him once, poking my head in.

I'm good.

It only took him a few months to turn that junk-pile into a functional machine—*Pops, fifth gear slips*—It spat venom and fire, its torque capable of taking off the top of your head.

By sixteen, he looked like a gangly man-child. By seventeen, he was still caught in the grip of a disastrous adolescence that once again excluded us.

SIX

The curtain draws. The spotlights form white circles on the stage. I, the actor Jack Palance playing Somerset Garden, reach down, cup a handful of snow. The snow tastes metallic on the tongue—It ain't *nothin' but a candy drink that burns like hot sauce.* I've wasted too much time, wasted too much light. I want the voices to stop. *Stop!*

Clutching my chest I turn to the old oak. Tree limbs like frozen lightning spread over the house, like arteries, like nerves—*Ready to crush the house or cradle it.* I tap the oak's roots with the shovel and the metal hums in my hands. I sit, with my legs splayed before me, cradled in cold roots. My mouth is metal. I have tinfoil teeth. My tongue iron. *This here's a water like fire that burns like hot sauce on the tongue, little shitless, so you try it and go on try and stop bein' chicken, bakaaak, and try it otherwise youse goin' fight George Ripley again and this time I ain't gonna tell him stop before he quits on you.* My heart squeezes. My skin burns. Why is Wally inside me? Why is Wally coming out? *It's 'cause what you did, little shitless. You chased Pearl into the woods that night the woods burned. You stayed in the world two and a half years before she returned you home, here, to shack with Blake and me, before leaving again for good.* Wally believed what Blake believed. I was not their blood, but a half-breed shitless bastard. Wally felt what Blake felt, that to rid the soul of evil one had to drown.

How everything was competition then, for Blake's acceptance, to see who could climb the old oak fastest, throw a stone the farthest, hold their breath underwater the longest, or drink glasses of muddy water, or eat the most worms, or run their hands through a flame without burning. *You know why they dip witches in water? 'Cause water burns them up.* Woken up with an elbow to the ribs, made to wash myself under icy hose water. Twisted my ears, elbowed my ribs, kicked my liver. What had I done to deserve what he did?

Summer in full bloom that day and I am ten years old, and heat blooms like a white hot rose and it burns up the valley like a dry tinder under a match, and Wally says, *That goddamned Frigidaire ain't worked for a week, sputtering like a swatted housefly, and there's no water that's cool enough to take, and even the hose water steams like lukewarm piss. So,* Wally says, *Shitless, you're no good for nothin' but hottenin' things up and I figure I'd show you a thing or two. Come on if ya know what's good for yas.*

So I followed him.

Come on down to the basement, come on, it's cool down there in the basement and there's a drink we can take that'll cool us inside... No, Blake won't say nothin' 'bout you goin' down in the basement... I'm here, Wally, and I won't do nothin' to yas... the heat's killin', tearin' the land up, and if the heat weren't out, there there'd be no sense in goin' down into the cool, dark basement.

Wally doesn't lie because he's older by three years and the steps leading down are cooler than the floor upstairs and the walls are hot but not as hot as the ground outside on the grass. The cold's dark and the dark's good because it's cold. My head brews with revenge for what they did to Pearl and I want to punish him for the fear Blake gave me and I need to damage something dear.

Wally's turned on the light and the filament bulb burns yellow like a small sun, and he's right about that, too, that the light, though it shines, is a cool light, goddammit if he isn't right about everything, and it's cooler down here in the basement because there's big jugs and crated bottles stacked up against the wall, the big jugs with a word written on it that I'm told not to say, *Moon*, it starts then wraps around the jug. The moon is cool, too.

Ya believe that I'm water and Somerset's fire? Do yas believe? Nod yer head if yas believe.

Why can't I be water and you fire?

Because that ain't what God said. God said, Walt's water and Shitless's fire, so if God said it, then it must be true, right? Now nod yer nog if ya believe it, that Shitless's fire and Walt's water and nod if ya believe that water's stronger than fire.

His grinning teeth, you could not refute, his wide eyes, like those you saw in his comic books—eyes of lepers, creatures of the forests deep who terrorized weary travelers—and you could not argue with those vicious eyes, boring into the darkness like drills of light.

Am I culpable for what I did? I am not. I am not. I am just a child of ten. Just. *Stop!*

Wally uncorks the bottle with his teeth and the screech it makes sounds like a nail torn out of a plank, and he sniffs the mouth of that jug and he holds the jug out to me and he says, *Go on and take a swig. It's good fer ya. It'll cool down yer insides.* Now the basement smells like what's inside the bottle. A strong stink. Strong as camphor, like sulfur. It's what I imagine Hell smells like.

You first, Wally.

Skeered?

I ain't scared. But I *am* scared. If Wally sees me scared who knows what he'll do. So say you're not scared so Wally will believe it. But he knows I'm scared like he sees my scared and sees it like he's seeing into my heart.

Go on then, he says.

I take the offered jug. Cradle it. I smell the jug's lip and the smell screams into my face that it isn't cool and that it won't cool down my insides. But Wally said it would and what Wally says is true. Wally said that God sees into the hearts of men and makes men fishermen of other men and so I suppose it's true. Wally likes to fish. He and Blake fish while I stay home. I want to fish. Maybe if I drink they will take me fishing.

Tip it back, tip it back why dontchas, just like Pops do. It'll cool yas off, just like it cools off Pops.

It smells bad.

Plug ya nose if ya haftas. Plug ya nose up by pinching yer fingers and tip it back and it'll get you all cool inside. Don't you wanna be cool?

I lift the jug. It's heavier than the devil. I lift and feel the splash against my neck and then… Why does the jug slip from my hands? Why does it slip if the bottle is a cool promise? Why does it slip onto the floor and why does it shatter, spilling the cool hot water over the floor?

Nowya done it. I'm gonna tell Blake you broke it.

It slipped.

Yer not even 'sposed to be down here. What the hell youse even doin' down here?

You said.

If I said to jump off a car bridge, woudja? Woudja jump if I said jump?

At the tree's base, Nona and I planted flowers once, daisies, I think, something white and pink with black pistils like bent black wire. On the back lawn we celebrated our last Memorial Day with the Flaims and the Hansons and even the Gennaros came down from Mauch Chunk where they lived across from Asa Packer's Mansion, the smells of freshly mown grass laced with roasting meat and Nona's heady grill sauce (red pepper, black pepper, cayenne, honey), seasoning the late summer air. We lit sparklers on Independence Day and, once a month, late in the summer, we hosted a garage sale, posting signs on St. Johns Road and Butler Road and South Main Street, opening the Dutch barn's double doors to anyone who chanced to stop by. On Halloween, we decorated the barn's lee with strings of corn, or we carved jack-o'-lanterns and set them on the house porch, trailed webs of cotton from the porch swing's iron chains, once even making a family of hobgoblins from straw that Cole spiked into the lawn grass. How many Fourth of July's did we spend launching fireworks, my family lying supine on the grass, delighted by the tight flipper turns and noisy flat-hatting and the trails of cosmic rains, streamers taxiing to earth. Our eyes reflected Saturn ring eruptions and those tiny supernovas of mixed colors—gold, green, the metallic blue of the irony sky caught in a lake of silver. *Stop!*

You sure done done it, Shitless!

And Cole and I made snow homes one winter—*Iga-loos, Papa, just like the snow people from the North Pole*—that sunk from the weight of poorly planned geometry. We fortified ourselves against blizzards by boarding the windows and salting the driveway. How many winters did we watch the snowdrifts on the lawn, while a long, slender fire burned in the hearth? The house smelled like love then, love unalloyed by any other element. *Stop!*

The bottle's broke dummy! Dummy, the bottle's broke. The basement bulb blows out like it knows Wally and I aren't supposed to be down there and now only the darkness hurts us. The smell of grain alcohol and a foul, swamp-gas rotten egg smell lifts to the ceiling beams. Darkness upon us like a cold hard black wing.

Skeered? Bakaak! Like a chicken. Skeered a the dark. Bakaak!

Turn the light on. Please, Wally, please.

Bakaak! Bakaak!

In my pocket sits Pearl's message. Her gift. *Fire is magic, Somerset, Son, and when you're scared of the dark, you just give that match a strike and I'll be right there to light your way.* I remember the look of the matchbook before I feel it in my hands, a picture of a magician in a black top hat and tails and his mustache curled up like two half loops toward the sky, and I remember the smell of the flame before I feel its heat, and I remember the heat of the fire before I strike the match. *Fire helps us kill our fear. A small little flame to take away the black. Fire is our truth!* Wally is a lie and Blake is a lie and so fire could make them true.

The black whispers things and the black tells me Pearl set the fire to keep her secret quiet, that Pearl was evil, a black witch who played with cards with pictures of the devil, and that Pearl's the dark and that Pearl's the reason God doesn't love me. The dark whispers things, like Pearl is a whore. Pearl is the defiler of men, sucking from men their life's blood. But the dark is not knowing. The dark is not believing. The dark is not seeing, hearing, feeling. The dark is the devil and not Pearl.

Bakaak!

In the hot dark, Wally flops around like a chicken, splashes in the puddle of the cool hot water, wades in the cool hot water, laps at it with his tongue.

I light the match. My hands shoot up in flames and I drop the match and the light is good but the floor flames up. Light and heat. The darkness is gone but in the flames there's just Wally, his legs going up in flames, his hands, his face, his mouth swallows fire. He crashes into the crates of Moon… and he's breathing fire like a dragon and he's screaming fire, screaming, screaming, before he stops.

From the folds of my jacket, I find my memory book and pen. What Wally inherited was a tendency to, no, not tendency, I'll scratch out ~~tendency~~ and replace it with "capacity for cruelty."

My legs are numb. My body feels damp beneath my layers. My face beads with sweat and when the wind blows, blade sharp and bitter, I unknot my scarf. This is dangerous, I think. A risk. *Everything is a risk—breathing, walking, sleeping, thinking.* I might catch something. I deserve to catch something. I have flung my nets far and wide.

SEVEN

Huge banks of clouds roll in from the North. The sky has thundered most of the day. Miki says it's December 20th. It all ends tomorrow, but when, at the stroke of midnight or eleven-fifty-nine p.m.? Now and then, something clatters down the old oak or skitters down the roof, scrapes, chafes, snaps. Now and then, a branch or beam bursts. The boy, oblivious to the house dismantling itself, watches the changing weather from the window.

Is that it?

Is that what? I say.

Is that the ending storm?

Don't ask me things I don't have answers for—*Papa, what is infinity times infinity? Pops, define Da-sein, because the what that calls itself the they isn't much more than the is of now, which...* The boy turns to me with an expression of such sweetness it stops me in my tracks.

What does it taste like, I mean, the storm?

I have to laugh. A storm doesn't have a taste, boy.

Why not?

Because, I start, and then I search my mind for a reason—*There's the ontological dimension, Pops. Say what it is.* Cole had that ability to stop me in my tracks with his questions—questions borne out of wonder. And my answers were never good enough; they led to other questions. *Why? Why? Why? Papa, when does death die? Papa, can you hear the trees crying? Papa, why is the wind always thirsty?* Pops, *what's the real of the now as opposed to the real of the then. Pops?*

I move toward the boy. I reach out my hand.

What are you doing? His face knots up in fear and distrust, disgust even.

Nothing, I say. I'm doing nothing.

Then don't.

I guess the storm tastes like milk, I say.

What does milk taste like?

The storm.

The air feels different to me, some dark spark of unrest to it that wasn't there before. The air holds no light. What am I saying? What am I feeling? Have things altered again? Have the woods altered, thickened while I slept, turned, in this winter of memory and storms, into a citadel of ice? *Everything is as it should be*, says Cole. *We repeat our lives infinitely.*

Let's get to work.

But it's bad out there.

It's bad in here.

We are outside. It is later than it was but not as late as it will be. All is white. The snow falls steadily. The wind has not abated. This is good. Everything appears bereft of detail. A cloud bank pushes down from the sky, erasing the jagged tops of the evergreens. Sugarloaf Mountain is lost behind the dispersion. There is no heat left in my body and I find this fitting, because all is white as the snow falls in a big bad wind. Winter melts on my clothes, seeps into these old bones.

We are outside. The shovel sits in my hands. The boy tramps toward the old oak. Just like yesterday or the day before that, the wind passes through the denuded woodlots, tinkling in tin sibilance the blue ice. Stalagmites have formed on the back eaves, chandeliers with crystal drops sharp as daggers are stuck to the window sashes and door jambs and porch steps, and all above them the tree is stuck with fingers of ice, and in them, the sun forms shimmering spots like diamonds. The house is a white fortress. It looks so, *because I say so*, because with the silvery sunlight pouring down from the cloud gaps, it's made these last days solid. But the cold still bites and Armand isn't here to share this experience and in the distance the dog still barks.

We are outside. With the edge of the shovel, I pry apart the shutters. I swat at the hinges. The boy slips behind me and makes for the old oak, regards my efforts with a sidelong glance that sends shivers through my body. His eyes tell me things and I'd like to believe there's something besides veins and blood, meat and bone behind the eyes, that when I look into a person's eyes there is, if I stare long and hard into them, an essence, the promise of a dim golden spark that warms, a transcendent vitality. A soul. I can't be sure. It's an assumption to believe in things like that.

Care to help? I say.

No.

I feel animated because the boy watches me. Because of the flexing old oak, I feel regarded, as if performing a ritualistic act that existed as part of a tradition that no one seems to recall—*All the world's a stage, Pops.* Son, now isn't that a basic truth.

I lunge at the house with the shovel. Bulks of snow slip from the eaves. Scream like a madman. This is part of the character, the crazy old fool having returned to his old house to fix what's beyond repair. Stab the wall. Peel away the slaked boards. Rusty nails explode.

The sound hurts.

My blood surges. My lungs compress and my mouth reeks sourly of ash and liquor. The vein in my temple pulses.

Come here and help me gather this up.

Where is he? No one leans against the trunk and I wonder who I've been performing for?

The wind grows fierce. The snow falls, evenly, steadily, like flour dusting the white earth from a sieve. Shredded wood lies in heaps all along the base of the wall. This is good, I think. Armand will be happy when seeing this. It's progress. I glance up at the old oak and my glasses collect with snow. A shadow moves on a limb. A shadow swings its legs. There, high above, sits the boy, his legs dangling. He's tangled up in a snowy branch, quiet as a statue of a boy, quiet, and I think, quietly grinning.

You can't fix it, you know, the boy says. *The house I mean. It doesn't want to be fixed.*

Why don't you come down before you break your neck.

His eyes search the sky. *Is Heaven far from here?*

It's what Cole might have said, there's a familiar intonation in the boy's voice that could be Cole's.

Heaven's too far to see.

I see it, come look. It's so perfect.

Blake always maintained that the Kingdom of Heaven was a changeless place and thus perfect—*The future home of the redeemed and the Redeemer, the saints and the angels, the hundred forty-four thousand.* Change distorts lives, warps, deforms. Change provides the vicissitudes of joy and suffering, the ability to learn and forget what you learned, and so I suppose man invented Heaven as a reprieve.

Come look. Climb up. I swear I see God's face in the clouds.

But change charges life with meaning. It makes it purposeful, for what would our lives be like if nothing altered? A child grows into a man and a man returns to childhood in old age, and I suppose there's meaning in that. We change without willing it. We lose the capacity to do the things we love. We lose the power to love those we've loved. So if life was change then death must be changeless, so the mystics say. But if death exists out of time, how can we return to life? Now I wonder why the idea of Heaven forgot to consider change as one of its qualities? We're taught to strive toward an impossible condition, toward a condition where changelessness swallows change and so appears perfect. To me, a changeless Heaven sounds like Hell—*Be meek, be poor, be mournful, be merciful, be pure, be a peacemaker, be persecuted in your righteousness, for ye shall inherit the Kingdom of Heaven.*

Blake, Father, why should Heaven be a static place where nothing happens, where passions are dead passions and thus frozen? Father, if the Kingdom of Heaven is static and Hell is its opposite, full of lust and fire, then I prefer Hell to Heaven's interminable bliss. Father, my personal idea of heaven is a flawed paradise, where every fault, like objects in a glass display, sit mutely for museum-goers to admire, where even moral weakness is a virtue and every flaw shines as perfection. My personal heaven clatters and clangs. It is boisterous, bombastic, full of messy language, a salacious Avalon where the lakes freeze in the winter, a raucous Eden where the skies blanched white in the winter. Eden, noisy with imperfection, filled with rich little details and rich little cruelties and repetitions of chance. Father, it is time that provides us our meaning and so gives us our worth. Maybe that's why the Mayans calculated the end? *Pops, the fact that we are alone and finite renders all meaning meaningless.* Even the idea of Heaven requires consent. Does the fact we must create our values, by consent of others, invalidate the idea that we can achieve a sort of bliss in a heaven of our own design? Consent in matters of religion requires faith, and not just any little old faith, but the greatest of all faith, the one that banishes reason and sense. Faith claims reason is impoverished to comprehend God's true ways. What arrogance to assume we can comprehend God's true ways.

Are you coming up?

Father, what is the verb for faith? How does one behave one's faith? In good deeds, Father? Arrogance presumes to know what God wants or expects from us. Father, what of those revelations you preached? What of received wisdom whereby God spoke through His Son so that He may speak to mankind? Father, God, that entity possessing every virtue man incapable of, we've postulated out of the clatter of dust, the rage of sunshine, the clamor of a river, out of the desert heat and the winter cold, out of our fears and confusions and mysteries. And received wisdom, Father, is nothing more than the imagination spiraling upwards at the sheer absurdity of existence, throwing up its hopeless arms. God is an invention, Father, like a gas regulator or a combustion engine. We charm ourselves on His myths so that our lives might mean something more than nothing. Father, what ego we have! What guile!

Sir, you listening?

I am aware of the shovel, the house, the tree, the boy. I am defenseless against this reality. Now I want something more than reality. Something less real. I want myth. Magic. Aiming my life in the direction of perfection, I made my life an arrow, attempting to strike an invisible target. It was work that tethered me to the idea of restoration, and by extension, redemption, so then why should God and Heaven not be a place that you could also fix*?—'Cause it wouldn't be Heaven then, Dutch.*

Sir?

Who implanted in us our ideas of Heaven? Who? What silly little troglodyte in some desert cave scratched his pen across a parchment scroll and declared this the final word? Why exclude renovation from our concept of Heaven? This new Heaven, then, what name to give it, for you couldn't call it by its old name. It would no longer be eternal. Its rivers would no longer flow milk and honey and the untilled fields would no longer bear fruit of astounding variety and health—at least not forever. Heaven would evolve just like we do and spin, just like the earth spins on its axis and wobbles around the sun. In Heaven all things would be born, live, age, and die. Heaven would be earth. We would see our Kingdom here, protect it, love it, cherish it, build our cities around the concept of Eden. The snow falls. Quietly. There is that wind again.

Come on down, I say. Please.

Come up and see. Come on.

I fold my arms across my chest and I make for the house. The boy scrabbles down the trunk, jumps to the snow with a hard thud. Reaching me he says, *You should've come up. It was nice up there.*

If only I could, I say. My heart pounds, like a piston pumping stale oil. Inside, I have half a bottle of this rye to get through and a Hemingway in my pocket awaits the cutter. I cling to these vices. Bad habits die harder than stars.

The attack arrives suddenly, violently. Try to breathe, I tell myself. The scenery pulses like a living heart. I rise, fall, break apart. The world loses its oxygen and falls apart. The light splinters in a million small suns. I drop the shovel. I fall, knees to snow, plush snow. My chest seizes up, like a vice around my lungs. The world recedes, spins, collapses. Like vapor floods, words steam from the earth, lift into the sky in a rheumy coil and congeal into a black bruise that swallows up the world. Blackened, hardened, roiling, the bruise churns, bursts, showers upon the earth broken letters—the curve of an "f", half of a "u", and the broken letters collect in heaps and pools, rippling coins and discs of silver, and they riffle through rivulets, collect in the ruts of inky roads, embedding themselves like daggers in creek beds, jetties, brooks, combine and recombine into a manic dance of shattered language—words lash, plash, spit, rush, tremble, and tumble through meadows, upending grass and weeds and flowers, rolling to the edge of borders, and they lick the edges of tree roots and plant stems and flower pistils, crash through fence posts, gather like dust spores in pulpous masses and form other, nonsensical words, new words—nonsense of sift and gravy soot, bleached sand, river roots, sky sticks, larynx leaves, suckle stems, breaching the borders of sense, breaking like waves on moss addled rock quays, and this frothy spume of language bastes the porch steps of my old house and cracks apart the walls, and like wood beams splintering, these words flap at my feet like fish, such a rippling dissonance, a cacophony as mad as the wintering sun. My inhaler isn't in my pocket. Where? Why? I might die. I will die. I want to die. I am dead.

The boy, shadowed by the tree, his face an alabaster mask, reaches out his alabaster hand.

Is this what you want? I am aware of the inhaler in his hand but it's too far to reach. The inhaler means things— "salvation" and "power" and "breath". Deliverance.

It's what I need, I say.

Simon says?

Give it.

You didn't say 'Simon Says.'

Si…

The boy places the inhaler against my lips and my lips part greedily. He presses the plunger and releases the blast of cold, powdery air. Another. Then another. Once more. Eternity passes. The bruised sky spins at my feet. Breath settles. The house groans like the prow of a sinking ship. Everything is noise. *Buzz. Clatter. Crank*. My ears ring. My tongue swirls in noise. *Creak. Clonk. Snap*. My eyes are blinded by noise.

My lungs settle. Like darkness exiting a room, the weight in my chest dissipates. My breathing eases. I exhale. My breath sounds wheezy, a watery whistle.

I owe you one.

I know.

Suddenly I am thankful for him.

~

Later.

He has led me into the kitchen. He has poured me a glass of water. I have told him he needs a proper name, that I can't just keep calling him "boy".

What kind of name is "Billy"? It's stupid.

Crushing the cup in my hands, I toss it into the hole in the counter where the sink once sat flush against the tiled top, the fraying fibers of grout still visible beneath the dust. There are pipes snaking up from the wall. There are holes in the walls where the cabinets once stood. The holes look like waiting mouths.

You okay? The boy asks.

What? Yes. I'm fine.

You went away again.

I clear my throat. I spit a glob of phlegm into the corner then say, I do that sometimes.

You do that a lot.

Do you like Jack Frost?

What does it mean?

Why do things have to mean something?

I ain't a thing.

That's right, you ain't. You're just lost.

I reach into my jacket and he reaches into the folds of his shirt. I pull out a Hemingway and he pretends to extract a cigar. I light the Hemingway with a match. He flicks his thumb and pretends to light one too. The smoke cakes in my mouth in the inward draw, then lazily leaks out. The boy watches me, sucks on his imaginary cigar, blows imaginary smoke. I blow a ring to the ceiling and he pretends to do the same.

It's not nice to mock people.

What's "mock"?

What you're doing.

Sorry.

Call you "Jack" then?

If you want.

With my hands and feet numb from cold, I trudge the stairs and enter the old room viscid with heat.

For now all is quiet. A pin dropped in the snow would shatter the silence for a thousand miles in every direction. A whisper could cleave the cold winter sun. You could hear the whirr of time or the whimper of memory. You could hear God paring his nails, such soft chaff.

BOOK IV

ONE

Today's my birthday, because Miki said so. Today's the end of the world. My heart flutters at the thought. I expect great fanfare. I expect trumpets, cloven hoofs pummeling the sky. Miki said a man entered a church in Dallas and, citing Revelations, shot the congregation with a rifle. She said a women in Miami plummeted from a five-story building, and a retired high-school Science teacher from Oakland rammed his car into a crowd on the Embarcadero. Chaos. It breeds everywhere. We try to contain it, but what's the use? Disorder is our natural state.

Earlier, I awoke to Blake's presence in the room, the unmistakable chafe of his boots against the hardwood, and parade of jangling keys, like horse bridles—*Youse comin' or gonna sit there like a pig's ass?* Blake's the white rabbit. The white rabbit grows to the size and shape of Blake. The room spins and the rabbit as Blake asks something of me.

Don't have eternity, shitless.

A chasm opens in the floor of the master bedroom and Blake slips through. I follow him. I fall through a rabbit hole. I pass through rooms that reek of failure. The walls are Rorschach blots, forming inky lizards, crows mashed up in leaves, all the land's vulgarity spinning on an axis. I am a child again. Thirteen. What do these sound-shapes refer to? "Thirteen," "child," "velocity"? We land in a summer where the trees posture in full bloom, their crowns bathed in silver. The hornets in the locusts shrill. Wally is dead, burned in that basement fire. It is the summer of '46.

The squeaky wheels of a service truck, Blake's Ford pickup, with its dusty bed loaded with garden tools. Drums flits by as we hurtle through the landscape of memory. The radio plays songs. Blake spits out the window. Screech of brakes. The Ford's viperous rattle. Having made it into downtown Conyngham, having driven up to Christ Church, parked at the curb, we walk past markers and gravestones that jut uphill like jagged teeth. Light in red lozenges pools in the gaps between the eucalyptus trees. Blake snorts, spits tobacco on the grass. I follow Blake down a flight of wooden steps, past the stonecutter inscribing numerals onto a stone slab, his left opal eye regarding me creamily. Blake lifts his knotted claw to the bill of his cap.

Keepin' busy, Wallace? he says.

War makes fer good business, Blakey.

Ain't that the truth.

Wallace hisses in laugher, as if his vocal cords are torn. Later Blake tells me a drunk with a knife slit his throat for reasons he never explains. It is 1946. Boys as young as seventeen have enlisted, flown to Germany, returned in pieces. We pass headstones and placards nailed to plywood embedded in the earth. Headstones drape with moss, punctured by water, veined by ice. Each set of numbers measures a fixed time that staggers the imagination—1796, 1799, 1812, 1883. The slabs and graves stretch flat, lichens cling to the stone, names vandalized by the weather. I wonder how James Quick, D. 1799, died, just nine years old. I wonder why Lena Settle died, being just sixteen in 1811.

We come upon a tall, sprawling maple tree, its crown dressed in sunlight. It is beautiful, so tall it seems to encompass the sky. We turn down a graveled path leading to the southern lots. Weedy gravestones, like poultice, an indeterminate grayish green. Ivy snakes the slabs. Mushrooms sprout along a small paling fence. We enter a copse. Down a short path stand two spotted headstones bearing the name *Vangaarden.*

Blake straddles a patch of clover set between the two graves.

Hello, Poppy. Momma.

Blake's eyes hold neither regret, nor love, certainly not compassion, but perhaps trace anger, for his eyes, open and glaring, glisten with redness, look unsettled and seething, still seething it seems with decades old resentment. He loads his lip with a big wad of loose tobacco, gyrates his jaws like a mule churning grass, then spits onto Obadiah's stone.

It's mah birthday. Come here every year and pay a visit.

Seems odd. Seems strange, but who am I to argue? He's a strange man. An odd man.

The trees lightly shiver in a warm breeze. My body shivers, but not from the temperature, because though it is humid, my body feels cold as a block of ice. Staring at the headstone, I feel no connection with it. Blake pats Geraldine's name then sucks his cheeks and pours a stream of tobacco onto the stone. It oozes down her name like molasses. I feel terror. Perhaps the terror I feel each moment in Blake's presence is an inheritance, like a trait, consummated in each generation and scarcely bred away. Over the next few years I would think back to what Blake said of Obadiah, that he invented the coal-grate a decade before Judge Jesse Fell, and that Fell had stolen the invention and patented it. What might the Vangaarden's fortunes have been had Obadiah mounted a spirited protest? Obadiah was a simple railroad engineer, descendent of Henry Vangaarden, a private first-class in Van Etten's regiment who died in the Sugarloaf Massacre, so our connection with this land ran deep as ground water. Obadiah was a drunk and… In the spaces of that ellipses I imagined the worst—a man whose hatred for his failed chances projected itself into hatred for his son.

The reek of old cold stone, the stench of hot summer grass, dust and shadows and the paucity of light, these are what I recall. From the inside pocket of his suit jacket, Blake extracts a tin flask, unscrews the top cap and gulps whatever is in it as easily as if drinking water. He wipes his hard mouth on his sleeve.

The Bible tells us to forgive, 'cause forgiveness frees, and it says other things 'bout sins and all and that ya gotta forgive yerself 'fore yas can forgive the other stuff. And I try an act ma forgiveness by comin' here ever year and rememberin' and forgivin'.

We stand beside each other, man and boy, united, it seems for a moment, over some injustice done to him, and I feel a pang of sympathy. The wind shivers the eucalyptus branches. Leaves fall in dry sprays across the lot. Blake wipes his neck with a handkerchief. He takes another long pull from his flask and clears his throat.

Have a swig.

No, sir.

Don't be a shitless.

The bourbon tastes like sweet coals in my mouth. I choke. The air holds no oxygen and I find it impossible to breathe. Blake giggles like a coyote. I hate him again.

If it burns it means it's working.

His teeth are yellow-stained. He has the eyes of a rabbit.

Yes, sir.

Snatching the flask away, he lopes toward a stone slab, clears the stone of leaves and crouches upon it. Thumbing out the tobacco from his lip, from the inside pocket of his suit jacket, he slides out a thin, black cigar, lights it with a match he strikes on the sole of his boot. A nice trick. I like him again. The tip of his cigar glows crimson and clouds of blue smoke clot then whirl in the air. The air no longer smells like hot summer grass, cold stone, dust. It turns carbolic—blue smoke ballooning with the heavy reek of tarnished leather and charred black oak and dung.

Happy birthday to me, happy birthday to me, happy birthday, dear Blakeeee, happy birthday to me.

He is sickness. He is volatility coiled, like a spring. I don't like him. I pity him. I hate him because of what he and Wally did to Pearl. *La-la-laaah-la-laaah-la, Har-Har!* I want him dead. No. He might haunt me in death as he terrorizes me in life. Little did I know then that the dead *did* speak, the dead sang and sputtered just like the living, and sometimes you heard their voices through the people and the objects they touched. We are ghosts of each other.

The stippled light blurs things. With my fingers, I trace each letter of the Vangaarden name. The old surname "Vangaarden" means nothing to me. It holds no texture. No depth. It holds no dimension.

The reek of Blake's cigar lifts skyward, polluting reverence. There he was, a guardian of secrets, protector of mysteries—*Blake got different after youse was born. He got hard on me. Blake turned to iron.* I feel heat in my collar. The weight of hot air. Sweat drips from my forehead and I taste salt and my knees hurt and my cheeks are flushed. I could choose not to feel these things by focusing on light, the memory of Pearl, but I could not eradicate my name. So what tied me to this land, I wondered then as I have been wondering since I returned, but the random fact of my birth on it? What is my responsibility but to reform my name? I shoot a glance at Blake. His eyes hold the sky. He lightly hums his birthday song. Blue smoke snakes and steeps, scatters in thin waves. I feel nothing for him. I feel no connection to his life.

A blue jay soars down from a eucalyptus branch and lands on Obadiah's headstone, clicking its claws across the topmost edge. It cheeps. It hops to Geraldine's headstone and cheeps again. In its black eye sits a tiny reflection of a boy, a pale flicker of a boy. *Cheep-Cheep*. I imagine Obadiah's face, blanched like a potato, a skinless mask of porcelain bones, rictus of tobacco stained teeth and crooked, eyeless sockets; and Geraldine, her bleached skull, her hairline cracks like corpuscles along her temples. Tremors of birdsong permeate tiers of earth, penetrate a jumble of bones. If my grandparents could reach up through the layers of time, diffuse their spirits through the soft blue grass to stand before me for a minute like waves of shifting smoke, what would they say? If they could pour a glass of water and drink or paint pictures of a landscape or run through the woods and rub their backs against the wrinkled bark of a pine, and if they could light a match or lift a shovel or even suffer the stings of an insult, would they not choose, if they could, life? The dead live in more than just graves. The dead occupy the spaces between the things said and unsaid, forever in the background, like the whitewash of the universe's birth song, like the pulse of a heart your ears cannot hear.

I brush away the lichens clinging to the old cold stone and I wonder, what had Obadiah's legacy become? What had Geraldine bequeathed? These sets of bones had once loved each other enough to produce Blake. Their love had armed him with a set of beliefs and sent him into the world. What was their legacy except hatred and violence and fear?

I rise from my knees like a supplicant, then I turn toward Blake and I say, *Can we go home?*

TWO

Turning the Bakelite's dial, passing static and fuzz until I reach FM 90. The radio snores. Dim and distant, Miki's voice, coated in smoke and honey and whiskey, pushes through the circuits. It's like hearing an old friend. She sounds excited. She has something important to say. After crashing into a school bus, a semi-truck slid off Route 80, toppled down an embankment, killing the driver, ten children, and wounding thirty more—*a crash blamed on black ice*—I worry for Armand, poor man—*Those of youse out there on our turnpikes, drive a little slower. Kindness might save a life or two.*

While we slept, the house bent itself askew. Now it leans backwards, the chimney against the old oak's trunk. Several walls fell down, cracked in thirds. The ceiling splintered. Those are lovely patterns. Maybe next week, these brazen winds will settle and the snow will cease and Drums will recede into its natural state of winter—washed white, battered and beaten. For now, the blizzard winds unsettle the old oak, tear apart the house and rend the Dutch barn plank by plank, post by post, beam by splintery beam. Bones have a tendency to break under less pressure than this. The weather terrifies. Terror returns us to our primitivism.

Is the world ending?

I hope so.

I switch Miki off and squint at Jack. He rubs his hands, then blows on them, and I say, Rub your chest to stay warm; the arms will take care of themselves. There are black circles beneath his eyes.

My head's hot.

The heat on his forehead is evidence of a suffering I cannot surmount. I know I can't do anything for him. I wonder why he's even here? He said he was lost. Maybe he's afraid? Maybe he needs a little push. Nature gave him two strong legs. If I order him gone, he'll go. If I point him in the right direction, he'll be fine. Youth is his defense. How would he make it? The old Hawthorne farmhouse is at least two miles down, and downtown about five miles or so, and not a soul stirring at this hour. Can't get to Hazleton by foot and not in this storm. Where would he go? Escape into the woods? Run toward the frozen creek, tramp across the frozen fields, scrabble up the hill slopes, skid down into depressions and into the flood of winter? He'll knock on the door of another house, a warm house, where there's a fire in the hearth and warm and dry clothes in the closet of a boy his own age, and hearty food warming in the oven. A gentle woman who smells sweetly like oatmeal cookies and every warm thing in the world will embrace him. The head of the house will call him son, might even have on a cream cardigan draped over his shoulders.

Come on, I say.

Where?

Come on, will you? Will you please come on?

Into a pillow case I throw in a box of cookies, a jar of peanut butter, a bread loaf, a box of matches. I work silently, choosing things at random, plastic forks, potato chips, a screwdriver. I push the bag on him at the front door. Outside a blustery wind moves the light.

Here ya' go.

Why?

Reaching into my back pocket, I find my billfold, remove a crisp twenty-dollar bill.

Consider it a gift.

Why?

Go on and take it, I say.

No.

Pointing toward the driveway I say, See that road? Just follow it down past the Mercury, pass over the bridge, till you hit the main road,

Deep Hole. Go left. You'll see a dirt road a few miles down that'll take you to a farm house. There'll be people there that can care for you. Get you some medicine for that fever.

He stares at me blankly.

I can't leave.

You can and you will.

Before I can stop him, he runs down the front porch, tears across the yard with phenomenal speed. His feet kick up sprays of snow. Before I can shout, Come back! he sprints toward the barn and before I know it I pursue him, shouting, Wait!

The fieldstone walkway that led from the back porch to the double leeward door is gone, sunk into the earth. Ankle deep, I stumble through the snow like a drunk, my face bitten by wind. Somehow I reach the barn. There's tranquility here. Hello? I say, my voice barely my own. Hello? My voice returns to me, hollow and wooden as if launched into a wooden barrel. A dull creak sounds across the empty barn like a ship's settling hull.

My chest is a furnace. A cache of damp hummocky smells steep the air like rotten lemons and damp hay. This space still contains memories of long nights spent, me locked up with my precious stoves. The shattered dormer leaks light like a tongue of water. I shiver as much from the cold as from fear. *Induced memory is when…* Shut up Armand! I fumble for a match. The flame hisses.

Where are you, boy? Come out, come out from wherever you are, I say, sing-songing—*Hush little baby, don't you cry, Mama's gonna buy you an apple pie.* From my body drips the rancid flow of false heat, unearned sweat induced by fear—*Somerset, help me, these ropes burn!*

A ladder leans in the corner by a tall, bisected window. I tilt my head to the hayloft.

I got no time for this, I say. Stop hiding.

A bird flies from the shadows, black or brown, I cannot tell. It lands on a windowsill. *Caws.*

Har! I say, *Har! Har!* This old man flaps his arms, pushes the air with his hands, stomps his foot like a madman when suddenly Jack appears out of the shadows, his hands in his pockets. I want to slap his face for running away from me. I want to shake him by his shoulders and roll him over my knees and spank him red and raw.

I got nowhere to go.

It's as if I've been punched in the liver. But you can't stay here, I say.

But I can't go either.

Jesus H. Christ. My anger (it isn't really anger; it's just a display of anger, like Palance reciting his lines in a soliloquy) dissipates, like kettle steam.

Don't make me go.

Don't? I say. My voice choked with concern. Don't?

I helped you and now you have to help me, he cries.

Stop sniveling like a girl, I say. I am defenseless. Helplessness always drew out my compassion.

Just don't run off again, you hear? What I say, I say for your own good. Suddenly my words launch me into the past—*Pops, is it for me or for you when you say those things that hurt?* The walls shape-shift and the rafter beams spin and light pours through the dormer more gold than white, filling up this space around us with such luminescence it hurts my eyes. I raise my hands to my face to protect myself. I cannot see what's in the light.

Strange. My hands look strange. Not mine, but mine. I am forty years younger, saying the same words to Cole—*What I say I say for your own good!* The room spins and the ground collapses beneath my feet. Switching places with Jack, I am reduced to the size of a twelve-year old boy. I raise my head to Blake's face knotted in rage. His right hand lifts The Bible to his temple. He's poised to strike me with it—*What I say I say for your own good!* Words are legacies.

The scene rearranges itself. The radiant smears and shaded tiles reassemble into the world I recognize. Jack stands before me in the barn. He wipes his nose. I kneel before him and with my two cold thumbs wipe away his tears.

It's okay. It's fine.

I'm sorry. I'll try and be better.

Whose words are these? His? Mine? *Mama, I'm sorry I'm always sick and slowing us down, but I can't help it.*

You sure are, I say to him. Just the sorriest little boy I ever seen.

He smiles and suddenly I am also smiling. Jack turns to the hayloft and whispers something.

What's that you said? I say. He sweeps the area with his arm. It's a strange gesture, like that of a carny introducing a circus act—*And now, ladies and gents, I give you Pearl, The Rocket Girl.*

Is this where you killed your family?

My heart seizes. I didn't kill anyone, I say.

But isn't this where you died?

Stop confusing me. I ain't dead.

He crouches, sits, crosses his legs like an Indian scout. He holds his knees, rocks back and forth. Is he waiting for something?

Prove it.

How do I prove my life? How does anyone prove what they meant to the world? I had thirty-three stoves in my collection, I begin. Exactly thirty-three, age of Christ on the cross.

That doesn't prove nothing, he says.

The curtain draws. Spotlights blast white circles on a stage. Outside, a camera moves on rail tracks, captures through its aperture the façade, windows, the steep, gabled roof extending almost to the ground. Left unpainted to preserve the grace of antiquity, the textured wood looks gray, but the roof, painted dark red and the trims in cinnamon brown, gleam. Wisteria climbs the façade and branches like capillaries. Bearded tendrils find purchase in cracks and nooks in the wood in an effort to authenticate secrecy. A pent roof provides some protection from the weather, but not much, for snow and leaves and rain, birds and bees and wasps always drifted in.

The camera moves inside. Pans across the space. Tilts up. The vaulted ceiling explodes, revealing a dark, starry sky. A moon squats in the center of that pinhole blackness, huge as a planet.

This space could remind you of a church—*Sing with me, Somerset. Can baby boy count the stars that brightly twinkle-twinkle in the midnight? Can you count the clouds, so lightly o'er the meadows floating by? God, the Lord, doth mark their number with His eyes that never slumber; He hath made them every one.*

The stars, Mama?

I inhale. Exhale. A blend of organic and metallic fumes that remind me both of my life's purpose and progress. Somewhere behind these noisy smells lies the evidence I existed. *A machine shows a man his limits, but*... Blake would say and struggle with the end thought. Later, decades later, I would tell Cole, *A machine can make a man fly; make him a bird, a fish, a god. Machines speed up and slow down time. Man is the machine-making animal. Man is the slave-making machine,* and he might have thought that the truest thing I ever said. Here and here and here, I spent my hours as if I had an inexhaustible reserve of time, working on stoves, or there, sitting for hours listening to things whirr and click-clack, clatter and hiss.

Jack laughs. His is such a human expression, like sweet breath on your skin.

Prove it.

Did you know that in the summertime, the branches of the old oak laden with light shone like a crown of gold, and the sunlight cut a path toward the barn's double doors, forming, what seemed, my road of light? A salvation road, I once told Nona, and she laughed and said, *Your salvation is your family, Dutch, that's the only light worth anything.*

In late-July, the trapped air felt like a balmy womb. Those were gaseous days, so viscid even the birds dozed in the trees.

Prove it.

In the evening, swallows and martins, and even a white hooded owl, entered and nested in the eaves. I found them perched on the rungs of the loft ladder, softly sitting on the old lifeboat's gunwales, roosting on the sills, burbling and cawing and trilling like a jury. I found birds' nests, complexities of chaos and order, intact, some still with the shards of pale blue eggs inside. I used them as kindling so that when they burned you could scent forested light. *Can you count the wings now flashing in the sunshine's golden light? Can you count the fishes splashing in the cooling waters bright? God, the Lord, a name hath given, to all creatures under Heaven.*

I tamp down bits of frozen straw, clumped like fetid hair. I slide my heels over the frozen dust. I shuffle my heels across the herringbone patches of amber tweed, then turn and stare long and hard at Jack. His face an imbrication.

Why did Cole go away?

I don't know.

'Cause if this place was as great as you said, why did he leave?

He didn't leave, I say. He's still here. He's always been here.

You're lying. He picks up a pebble and tosses it against the wall. He seems to be searching for something, some clue about Cole through my confessions, and I am not ready to oblige myself, nor him.

I'm hungry. You hungry?

Even I know that you haveta be honest if you wanna get better.

Let's eat. Let's work. We might try and demolish the kitchen later.
There's no food.
Then, let's listen to the news of the world.

THREE

Nona and I are in the kitchen. It's an ordinary day of the week. No occasion. We're preparing dinner. Just dinner. Cole plays by the old oak, wearing a feathered headdress Nona made for him by sewing a hawk's and crow's and loon's tail feathers. He's an Indian scout. A Brave. The scent of sweet scallions, of ginger, of sweet onions sizzling in the skillet. Sharp and sweet and lovely. Three Atlantic salmons piled up on the chopping block, their undersides glistening pink, their steel-gray scales seasoned with Nona's black pepper, cayenne, and salt rub. Just dinner. Nothing fancy. Together. An ordinary Tuesday, I think.

I lean against the porcelain sink, washing tomatoes on the vine—red and bulbous tomatoes that, when thumbed, leave no dent. It is hot. A floor fan blows tepid air. Nona looks grim-faced.

Up all night?

Again.

Painting birds?

A series on ravens for the Conyngham Library.

I feel good washing those cool tomatoes—so red, so red and cool. I glance over at her by the stove. Such a good, hard-working exhausted woman.

My armpits black with sweat. The revolving fan in the corner blows apart and mixes the aromas, of ginger, sweet scallions, sharp garlic. The muslin curtains pulled back from the half-closed window above the sink. It reveals the view of the old oak. A white lily in a brick red pot on the sill. Its petals flutter from the fan's tepid breeze. Cole tries his best to climb the rope ladder up to the treehouse we built the year before. *My time machine, Papa.*

A satanic breeze gusts now and again and the ladder swings. Cole pendulums like the arm in a grandfather clock. I don't open the window because the hinge is loose and because my hands are busy massaging the wax from tomato. I finger the leaves that droop from the short stems and cling to the red skin. Cole swings. Pleased with himself. He does this again and again—*To spite his father a son will risk everything, even his life.* And Cole swings and the board the ropes we tied to it the year we built the treehouse shivers like a leaf in a breeze. I tap the window. My wedding band's ruby clinks against the glass, leaves a wet stain. I wag my finger and I smile and shake my head no. Cole gestures with his hand *Okay.*

Okay. Danger is done. Cole has obeyed. Life returns to safety.

Did you say something, Dutch?

I didn't say anything.

Cole steps off the ladder. He runs circles around the tree. A strange and wild look to him. A wild innocence that suddenly reminds me of myself at his age. Ten? Is he ten? Cole looks free. He looks free in an insolent way, in a way I could never dare show. Not now. Not any time since. My hands shake. The wedding ring burns. I feel a pang of hatred—for him, no, not for him exactly, but for his expression. He has no right to it. No goddamn right.

I love him, I mumble to myself, convinced of it. He is my boy. Mine. And Nona's too. Nona says something behind me. Why is she always saying something when I'm doing something?

Where did you put the baking soda?

My eyes are transfixed on Cole—Cole running in circles around that old tree, his mouth agape, his eyes wide.

Where did you put the baking soda?

The tomato feels waxy in my hands as the cool water from the good faucet washes over it. My hands feel cold. There's still that hot fan breeze blowing hot kitchen air. A trickle of sweat rolls off my temple and I taste heat and salt.

Never mind, Nona says.

Did you say something?

Nona adds something to the skillet, potatoes, perhaps that sweet ginger? It sizzles and pops excitedly. New smells lift into the air, scents of my past when I stood in this kitchen and played housewife to Blake—*But the mouth of fools, shitless, feeds on foolishness*—cooking his favorite dishes—*And the glory of children is their father, their father, their father, har-har-har*—offering him at night, long after Wally's death, my body against my will as dessert, against my better judgment, late at night when a father cannibalizes his own.

Cole laughs. The skillet sizzles. The fan cycles through its revolution. Warm fingers of air stroke my face. My ruby ring glows hot. Cole, still running, still shouting something, still with that feathered headdress flapping. Palm to his puckered lips, he dances in that skipping, circling motion of Indians—*boo-boo-boo-boo-boo*. His feet kick up squalls of dust. Like an Iroquois warrior. Like a savage. A cannibal.

His dance offends me. *He is my son—And he sins who hastens with his feet.* I have created the condition for his freedom—*Whoever rewards evil for good, shitless, evil will not depart from his house.* I am responsible for his freedom and I can easily take it away—*Fun's gotta be earned. Pleasure's gotta be earned. Work's how we pay for our pleasures, now take down yer pants.* Blake, when you dragged my soul down into the darkness, when you left it to die, did you still believe your pleasures outweighed my pain?

Dutch, are you done with that batch?

What?

What has Cole earned? He climbs the rope ladder and then frog-walks across the low-hanging limb and jumps to the ground. I tap the glass again but he doesn't hear me. He doesn't want to hear me. He doesn't care to see me. He doesn't care. He climbs the rope ladder again and I am at the window tapping harder now, the ruby ring clicking against the glass and Nona behind me still asking something and the fan again with its tepid air and the things in the skillet popping.

Nona tugs at my sleeve and I turn abruptly as if she's slapped me.

What do you want? There is no honesty in life. No decency. No respect. No one cares about good hard honest clean thorough work. Nona shrinks from my expression, built out of deceptive, misplaced fury.

Easy boy, she says. Smiles. A good smile. Cool. She picks up her knife and cuts an onion. She sniffles, wipes her hand beneath her nose. *Chok-chok-chok* against the birch block, her knife goes. Half empty beside me, just a few tomatoes in it, sits the colander.

Do you need them all washed? I say finally. *All of them?*

She nods yes. Nona is tired and I am cruel for snapping at her, yet I don't apologize. I cannot. There is power in not apologizing. Heat in it that is pure.

Outside Cole climbs into the treehouse, leans out the window, still with his hand to his mouth *boo-boo-booing,* and he leans out of the window of the treehouse and I want him to fall. Let him fall. Let him hurt himself. He'll learn because I am tired of being a father who protects, who searches for his boy in the woods—*Pain'll teach yas much quicker than a kiss, shitless, Har-Har!* Blake's greedy laughter. Sick. I turn the tomato over in my hands when I hear Nona shout my name behind me, *Somerset! What are you doing?*

The tomato is a pulpy mass. It drips through my fingers. It clouds my inheritance, that old ruby ring. When I look up at Cole again, he is gone. Where did he go? I crane my neck to see. Where has he gone?

Throwing the pulp into the garbage disposal, I flip the switch and turn it on. Its mouth gargles. Little metal teeth gnash up the larger bits of pulp, the smaller bits of green leaves and pale seeds. A bloody froth. I wipe my hands with the dishrag that hangs from the stove handle and make for the screen door.

Where are you going? Nona asks me.

Where does it look like I'm going?

From the deck I shout Cole's name. *Cole,* I say, not loud, not angrily, just his name. A father has the right to call his son's name. Cole doesn't answer. He doesn't come. This is a son's right, too. To avoid his father. I descend the porch steps, thumping each board, making my presence known.

Cole. I tramp across the yard toward the old oak. *Cole*, my voice rising in pitch.

Cole appears beside me, making a gesture of a gun with his thumb and forefinger, *Bang!*

I stare at him long and hard.

You're supposed to fall dead when I say Bang!

Why was he hiding? Where? Did he not hear me calling him? His eyes glisten with excitement. His pleasure is a rebellion. His smile grows broad, and his cheeks, like his knees, are smudged with dirt. His hair, fine and coppery, like my hair, brushes over his eyelids like wet straw.

You're supposed to fall down, Papa.

Am I? Does this game demand that I die? Jealous of his ignorance, envious of his happiness, covetous of his freedom, I can think of nothing to say. I could have dropped down and made as if shot by his fake gun, dropped down mock-dead on the grass and granted him his victory, or I could have danced with him, but I didn't. I didn't choose to die. Together we could have climbed up to the treehouse, sat in one of its rooms together, and together pretended to travel back in time. But we didn't. Freedom, his, the freedom taken from me, felt like an insult to my sense of that so-called purpose-driven life.

What is the sum of six times nine? I say.

Cole gawks at me, puzzled. He lowers his gun hand. His grin fades.

Six times nine? Cole says. This is his undoing, as it was mine decades before.

Six times nine, I say. Stern. Resolute. He stares down at his feet, as if the answer might be there just beyond his toes. He stares up at me, confused, just the hint of a smile on the edge of his lips, as if to say, *Is this part of the "Bang, you're dead game?"* or, *Why ask this now? I'm playing, Papa, just pall-ay-ing.*

I see Blake's face in his face, the expression of unearned pleasure, the expression of perverse freedom to do anything, anytime, anywhere.

The vein in my temple throbs. Unearned pleasure upsets me. His homework lies unfinished. He hasn't finished his chores. He hasn't asked me about my day, how I had chased down a promise down a long forested road, a long forested road that led me to a house of junk. What right does he have to play when I have to work? I feel rage at his pleasure, for it held neither anger nor heat, no more the expression of ecstasy than that of shame, and I felt my blood surge.

Cole lifts his hands and mimes something—*fifty fo*— I strike him with the back of my hand. Where does it come from, this energy to hurt? It's as if from instinct, the old blood surging through my veins, without reason or sense.

Six times nine, I scream.

Blood erupts from his nose.

Is.

All I see is red. Red froth. The ruby ring.

Fifty.

All I feel is heat. The gray lid seals in the valley's heat. Teeth gnash.

Four.

I have started something I cannot stop. The old blood has dragged up from somewhere deep inside and it needs expression—*Har-har!* The world burns in slow motion. The trees pause from their bending and the wind freezes. Colors falter. Sounds diminish. *Die.* I don't hear Cole begging me to stop.

Six times nine is fifty-four, I shout. *Fifty-four, you goddamned idiot! Say it!* Perhaps he screams for me to stop, perhaps he repeats the answer I've just given him.

Stop! Stop! Stop! I hear his lungs in his voice, strained, stretched, ballooning to the point of bursting.

His squeals shake my rage. He turns to run away, but I have him by the wrist. I twist him toward me and hold him. I squeeze him.

My son, my son, I say, contrition in my tone that sounds false. A snap of bones. I don't hear him cough or struggle and I feel him grow limp against my body. *I love you, Son, I love you, I love you, I love you.*

Nona's voice reaches me as if from the silent depths of water. Nona pulls at my shirt, digs her nails into my arms. Scratches my face. Pulls my hair. Her voice is a shrill, *Let him go! Let him go!* Her screams shatter the sky. *You're choking him. You're killing him.*

Cole must have been ten years old when all that happened—*No, Papa, nine.* Was that afternoon the beginning of his hatred?—*No, Papa,* I never hated you. *You just didn't understand.*

FOUR

The boy plays with the ruby ring. He turns it over in his hands, lifts it to the light battering the windows, then slips the ring into his pocket. It's a joy to watch him, his expression a mix of wonder and pleasure. Before I can think of Cole again, a branch falls from the old oak. It falls, it clatters against the deck pile, and the deck pile sends tremors through the house and powder into the air. The powder dissolves into the falling snow. Our stomach growls. Our head throbs with hunger. We haven't eaten. We eat snow, tasting the faint sweetness of the earth buried beneath tiers of winter. What day is it? Whose life is it?

I light my last Hemingway, relishing the draw. I check my matchbook. Three matches left. No booze. Still no Armand. There's no hope for him now.

I was wondering why you won't tell me about Cole.

I've been telling you.

Didn't you say honesty's the only policy?

A piece of the house breaks away with a terrific intensity, like tires screeching across asphalt. The front of the house, porch and all, collapses onto the front yard—*The less you know the more you believe, Pops.* The room recedes, the boy in it. The curtain draws. The stage lights dim. A spotlight reveals an empty chair.

Sit down, I say, gesturing Cole toward the chair. A bench, scattered with hammers, chisels, saws, reaches toward pockets of empty space. Several stoves stand in various stages of repair. A poor light. Windows reveal a pensive summer, a silver sky so placid it seems as if painted with a brush.

Cole enters. He lopes into the barn, measuring his steps—heel-to-toe. He's seventeen, looking like a large version of a small boy. It is late-June, just three months before the end of our world.

Sit.

He sits. The chair creaks.

Fuzz on his chin replicates itself in a small patch of rust on his chest. His once coppery hair has turned a deep shade of auburn and falls into his eyes, fans across his shoulders like a plumed tail. He's as tall as I am with a taut, muscular body he hasn't earned. He's a failed promise. Fails to listen. Daydreams. He has my large hands, but his have the soft texture of laziness. He stares at me with Nona's deep unflinching eyes, unlike hers, a parrot green; his are a cosmic blue, like mine.

The skin beneath my overalls itches in the heat, but still I light a match. With the match I light a cigar.

Ivan put you up to it? I am referring to the fire at Christ Church. I remind him of his culpability, the kerosene bottles hidden in the woods. Sheriff Earley had found him half a mile from the church's façade as it flamed. Earley found Cole at Amber Daria's, eating a Sundae, his clothes reeking of kerosene. Cole led him to a crate hidden under a black tarp in the woods. Cole's face looked bloodless when I bailed him out of Hazleton County Jail.

No.

Then who?

He shrugs.

There is no punishment I can levy against him for what he's done. His adolescence has exhausted me. There is a pattern in it, a slow slide into hooliganism: cigarettes, whiskey, vandalism, and now this, flirting with arson. Having made his life an embrace of impenetrable abstractions, a rejection of Drums and of us, the fire he set is the last straw. There will be reprisals. I believe him: He believes in nothing. He's become what I fear most: Nothing.

What do you have to say for yourself? I say.

What do you want me to say?

The truth for starters.

For the past few years he's lived inside his head, in a world of music that sounds like noise, and in books whose titles bear witness to a search through realms of ideas I have no possibility of understanding: *Twilight of the Idols, Being and Time, Fear and Trembling.*

He shrugs.

I expected better from you.

He smirks.

You think this is funny?

His smile drops.

I tell him how afraid I am for him, that I feel he's squandering his life. I tell him how loyalty to family and faith in God and to one's community creates one's obligation to improve. I say it's about time he thought about his future, about finding his calling in life and utilizing the talents nature had given him. I tell him things I wish Blake, had he been a father, would have told me. Cole nods, less acknowledgement than impulse.

I pace the room, flailing my arms, my voice rising in pitch or dropping down to a whisper. This is the theater of fatherhood. I am fatherhood's performer.

You can't keep secrets from us. I know you too well. I know everything about you.

Cole shifts in his chair. He looks uncomfortable.

You don't know anything about me.

Is that so? What don't I know?

Cole clears his throat. Shifts in his seat.

Truth is, I'm afraid of you. It's like being afraid of the dark and it's this big fear, like I don't even know who I am when I'm around you, like I forget my own name when I'm around you. Do you know what that kind of terror feels like?

I am stunned. This is not what I expected. I want to tell him, *If you only knew Cole. If you only knew.* I had projected the image of myself as a pillar of strength, courage, virtue, but inside I felt weak and afraid and vicious.

Listen—

No, you listen, Pops. You have no time for anyone except for your junk. He stands. *I wanted to be someone great once, but what's the point? Nothing has any meaning. We're born and we get older and we die and the world goes on as if we never were.*

You have to try to matter.

There's no point in mattering. Cole rubs his hands as if warming them for a fight. I extinguish the cigar.

Son—

You wanna know the real truth, Pops? Truth is, I'm afraid of becoming you. You're so scared of living, that it—

I did my best.

Let me talk. He moves to the windows. In him there's that brooding intensity of corralled bulls. *You were always working, and when you weren't working you were trying to get me to do the things* YOU *wanted me to do. Your defense—you provided food, clothes, gave me rules to follow and chores to do and a religion to follow, but that doesn't make you a dad. Shit, when I needed direction, I got platitudes. When I needed understanding, I got sermons. When I needed guidance, I got silence.*

Who could ever know what you needed, Cole? It was a guessing game with you. One day you want to be a rocketeer, then a bug collector, than an actor in the circus, then a poet, then a goddamned guitar player, now what is it, an arsonist?

He shrugs. *Maybe.*

Maybe.

Maybe I wasn't meant to be anything. Maybe I'm already all I'll ever be, a great big nothing living in a nowhere town going nowhere.

Spare me your melodrama.

Maybe I want to burn down this town.

I could have told him that I know how he felt, that after Wally died, I lit a pile of sticks in the woods, stripped myself naked to the waist and danced around the blaze like an Indian, feeling an erotic pull toward heat. I wasn't alone then. Wally's ghost was with me. We jumped through the flames and the singe felt cool on my skin. We laughed and sang funny songs like *Pop Goes the Weasel*. Wally said to load the fire up with more than just sticks, also leaves, and I even rolled a log down from the hill. A fist of sparks floated up, ignited some low lying branches and one dry oak shot up in flames as if it were coated in a catalyst. Wally's voice said *Run* and I ran 'til my lungs hurt, and I stopped running after awhile and watched the forest burn.

Wally reappeared beside me, also breathless, and he whispered, *That what it was like when Pearl lit the woods?* And I said that I didn't remember. And what I said, *that I didn't remember,* was a lie. I punched Wally's ghost and his ghost punched me back, hard, and we tumbled on the grass kicking and biting and punching each other while the fire fanned and spread into the surrounding woods. No one ever knew.

Maybe burn down the world.

Stop! Other fires erupted that year. One fire I set ignited the poisoned creek entering Jeddo, where the old mining tunnels had long ago deposited chemicals into the creek beds. That was the worst of them. The woods burned all that day and the next while people battled back the blaze with pails. A great bulging cloud hovered above the mountain with raveled threads of shadow blue and saddle brown. Ash rained down upon Drums like snowfall. Blake found me in the basement of the house, my face blackened with soot. *What in the devil's name you done?* he said and I said, *It was beautiful, Sir. The flames were like water.* I could've told Cole that Blake taught me how to control my urge to burn things, that he gave me a code, saying *One mustn't believe too strongly in things that burn, but controlling fire makes you a sorta god.*

Cole snaps his fingers. *Pops, you there? Hello? I was saying something, I was—*

Kisenwether's kid's learning mechanics at the state college and Mike Danner's kid's going into engineering and George Muddie's kid, that dumb sonofabitch, half-wit, is on a wrestling scholarship to Penn State, even that penny-slut, Kelly Washburn's girl, is off to Princeton. And you? You were the best of them.

I didn't realize I was in a competition.

Everything's a competition. 'Bout time you realize it.

His expression turns distant. I can feel his retreat.

One day you'll know what absence feels like.

Shut your mouth.

He sighs. He stares up at the lifeboat hanging from its ropes and I wonder if he remembers himself asleep there, his tiny arm dangling down and me shaking him awake—*Come son, stop your shammin'. Shop's closed.* And inside me I hear Nona's voice, *Hold your anger, Dutch. Hold your tongue. Don't drive your boy away. Don't say something you might regret. Be kind. Understand. Listen. Believe in this miracle that is your son.*

Shut your mouth!

I reach Cole with an astounding velocity. Before I can stop myself, my hand slaps his face. Before it slaps him again, Cole has my wrists, his grip like a vice.

Not this time, he says. He pushes me backwards. I slip. My finger catches on the edge of the stove, slices the tip open.

Sprawled on the floor, I feel my lungs seize. I wince. I clutch my hand to my chest. Blood from my finger smears my ruby ring. Everything tightens. A sharp pain sears the length of my spine.

Can't breathe, I barely manage to say.

Quit yer shammin', Pops.

The curtain draws to a close.

Dad? You okay? Dad?

FIVE

Jack digs his fingers in the windowsill. He extracts something, a shard of wood, places it in his mouth. Chews. I twist up my face. Don't do that.

I'm so hungry.

Didn't your daddy ever teach you anything?

I can't remember. Remember?

I turn to the hearth fire and the flames resemble fish. Let's cook up some fish.

Jack raises his eyebrows, as if to say, *In this weather?* As if to say, *Aren't you just a crazy old fool?*

That's right, I say. We'll do a little ice fishing, just like the Eskimos. You like fish?

I can't remember. Remember?

I lift myself from the floor by my own strength and, by the force of my own will, cross the floor. The shovel leans against the wall where I don't remember leaving it. My joints creak. My spine feels rod stiff. This brumal life has hardened me. I am turning to stone.

All I need is a hook and some twine, I say. We can make a rod from a tree branch or something. I circle the room, dragging the shovel by its handle across the floor. Jack eyes me.

What're you doing?

There's a big pond on the other side of Nescopek where the fish might live in the winter, I say. "Might" is a big word. If I were writing this in my little memo book I might cross out ~~might~~ and replace it with "still." But "might" is all we have to get us through. Die of hunger or try to fish. We don't have much choice. Armand is absent. Jack stops and turns to the window.

It looks bad out there.

It's bad in here.

Snow falls in heaps and clumps from the sky, erasing boundaries, blotting distances.

Our boots crunch the snow. The crunch of our boots in the snow sounds like scraping ice from glass—*scraping ice from glass sounds like chewing pebbles the size of uncooked rice, and chewing uncooked rice sounds like grinding pumpkin seeds in a pestle, and that sounds like…* That's a game Cole and I would play.

When I was about your age, I say, I'd ice fish that honey hole with nothing more than a bent paper clip tied to a string and that to a branch.

How far is it?

Not far.

Jack and I pass the barn, pass the lean-to, pass the denuded orchard. We pass through a gap in the winter trees that looks like the mouth of a bear cave. The snow falls on us, around us, steadily, evenly, and the wind gusts, blasts of air so frigid it slackens time.

Over a short hill and into the woods—*to grammie's house we go. Papa, where's grammie? Pops, where's our past? You never tell me about our past. Ma told me her side but what about yours? You listening?* We're shin-deep in snow pack—*Papa, where is the wolf with the big teeth? Is that story you told about the Rocket Girl true?*

Everything slows. The world may appear dead in winter, the froglets buried deep beneath the creek-bed whose gray mud bulges stiff as stone, mud beneath which the aphids mock death, and the mosquitoes and bees and hornets lie as quiet as pebbles, but some insects only pretend to be dead, they hibernate like bears. Snow flurries blur our bodies. We are shimmers, like shifting centers of blasted atoms.

I can't keep up.

Go on and try. We'll dig up something and use it as bait, I say. Beneath a log or something, there might still be a little warmth where grubs might live—*Har! Har!*

Okay.

There's lampreys and minnows down there, I say. If we're lucky we might catch a winter trout. Hellfire, don't be silly, the winter doesn't bother the birds or the fish. No, the bears are safely tucked away and the wolves have their winter coats. The birds fly south not because of the cold but because there's no food.

I'm cold now. I can almost hear him thinking, *Is this necessary? Aren't there easier ways to find food?* No, I will not eat scavenger birds. I will not eat dead ravens. No beasts who chew their cud but haven't cloven hoofs—the hare, the hyrax, the camel, finless fish. I will not consume the kite, the falcon, the raven, the crow. No rats, no insects, however protein rich—*So sayeth The Lord.*

Tell me another story, Jack says.

I'm all out of stories.

Do like the Eskimos do.

Are we Eskimos, Jack?

We're snowmen. Snow beasts.

We're abominable!

I can't say that word.

I found a girl at this lake once, a girl who looked as if conjured up by all the wild grace in the woods. The year must have been '50 or '51, and I must have been seventeen and she must have been fifteen. It was at a clearing over by Four Seasons Lake that I set up camp that day. A giant bass was on my mind, a large-mouth rumored to be thirty or forty pounds, and I was going to lip it. All that week I dreamt of its ichthyic grace threading the deeper waters, a big fish, insouciant and free, ignorant of a boy dreaming of hooking it. Alone. Just past dawn. I pitched a tent. Alone, I nailed my pack to the trunk of an old oak just like Nick Adams.

Who?

Just a guy in a story.

I scooped a small depression in the earth with a small hand shovel, then made a roasting spit from the branches of a nearby elm. I made a little fire. With a mason jar, a jar meant for pickling things, for fermenting cucumbers or catching bait, I entered the woods. I kicked over the carcasses of old logs, fingered the pale undersides of maple leaves for caterpillars, plunged my hands into the soft brown earth and pulled earthworms thick as arteries, dropped them squirming in the base of the jar. As the light broke across the horizon line, bathing the sky silver, the soft heat decocted new fragrances—blossoms from trumpet vines, clover patches rimed with dew, the sodden silky mushrooms, garlic pods. I chased a salamander from the trunk of a redwood into the creek's mish-mash of sticks and rocks. That was half the pleasure in fishing, finding the bait, like half the fun in having an experience was discovering your capacity for it.

And then?

Then the forest ticked under the weight of sunshine. New heat released everything the woods had retained at night. Every tangled corner carried rhythms. A song lay between the trunks of the birch trees, waiting for you to discover it, and if attuned to it, the sounds mimicked the polyphonies of sacred music. Sometimes a branch like a crown of leaves fell to the forest floor, the dull breeze still strong enough to bash the limbs of centuries' old oaks, and in all that profusion of sound you heard the heartbeat of the woods. Sometimes a twig snapped. Sometimes an acorn dropped to the stony creek bed, then rocked in the current.

And then?

A sheltering trail leads us into the deeper woods. The wind cannot reach us here. There is abundant silence. Snow trickles through the thick lots. The snow diminishes. But it is darker now, much darker. There might be bear traps, holes dug in the earth and covered over with a thin membrane of leaves and snow, and who knows what might lurk in the shadows. This is dangerous play. These are the discarded adventures of youth, childhood adventures into abandoned bear caves, up trees, into foxholes, up Sugarloaf Mountain, into rabbit holes. This is like those insufferable afternoons spent flinging rocks from homemade slingshots through church windows, setting fire to tire piles in some old corn field; this is the omnium-gatherum of discarded selves, the mélange of who you were, the past jettisoned by unnamed roads as you made your way in life.

Are we there yet?

Not yet.

Through the white trees, Big Nescopek, olive-black, leers at us, grim as a lane of coal. We approach it, ignoring the signs of *No Trespassing* and *Private Property* nailed to the trunks.

Should we go back?

Just stick close.

I'm cold.

Frozen solid, the surface of the water looks ominous. From the creek's bed, stones poke out like a mangled mouth of crooked teeth. Small skittering prints maze their way into the woods. This evidence of small, mammalian life pleases me. Maybe there's a quorum nearby? A buck or an elk? Maybe a wolf? Wouldn't it be wonderful to discover a wolf? There's a trickle of water beneath the ice, though perhaps I imagine it, because perhaps that's just the wind brutalizing the bare branches. Even when we think of life as static, there pulses, imperceptible to us, the pull of a current, the fall of a leaf, vegetable life inching toward the light. Life, invisible, courses and expands, propagates. Buried beneath the silted beds, far, far below, perhaps dwell millions of hibernating eggs—fry, tadpoles, amber droplets of crawfish, doodads unconscious to the cares of men—and perhaps also colonies of nymphs frozen in shoals, and perhaps also infant wasps and blind worms brimming with larval health. It makes me smile to think so.

Cold? Are you really? Just think of someplace warm.

What about your story?

I roamed for a few hours with that mason jar, filled it half-full. I sang songs, my voice burnishing the trees with its timbre and the trees accompanied my voice with symphonies of reedy clatter, it swelled my heart, a swish of branches like a wave, those faint oceanic sounds. Birds trilled. Once or twice I turned toward the sky and shouted, *Who's there?* then waited for a reply that did not come. Just the birds in the branches. Just a chipmunk jittering, exploding across a branch, afraid of its own shadow. I moved on to a nearby stump and set the bait jar on the ground. I whistled. I practiced hooking my line—the Albright with its twelve turning wraps, the wedge knot, the Berkeley braid. I baited several hooks and let the lines dangle beneath my fist like swinging a pendulum.

And then?

Then returning to camp, I made several inarticulate tosses into the lake. Little dexterity or feel for the sport. Wedging the fly rod between a pile of chalky rocks, I stood and admired the hue of the water, olive-green near the shore, spreading to a rich confederate gray, then blue, like the gradations of a flame. The walnut trees beyond the shore looked deep chocolate; others, cinnamon brown with lime green or wheat colored leaves. A forest you could eat, vegetation on which to fatten yourself.

How much further?

Farther.

Whatever.

Further farther mother father—I whistled "Ring Around the Rosie," perhaps something else. I skipped a thousand rocks off the water, then loaded my hands with a thousand more. I paced around, because fishing was less about catching fish than testing your patience. Hell, fishing was about managing time, understanding the relationship between an effect and its cause. Fishing meant slowing your breathing, hearing your heartbeat, listening to the water's heart, the woods' pulse, the sky's rhythms, and that is all fishing meant—disappearing, becoming part of the soft, slushing water.

My legs hurt.

Stop your bellyaching.

And then?

Then maybe another hour passed. I checked my lines. Taut as piano wire. Feeling a pull toward the woods, I left my camp, because fishing also meant letting go. If the fish sensed your eagerness, your impatience, then they wouldn't bite, like a house senses you. The best fishers are those who don't want to fish. The fish come to them.

And then?

Then I found a clearing in the woods not far from the lake. It was dressed in wildflowers of such stunning variety that I thought I had stumbled onto Eden. I sought out Sugarloaf Mountain and named it Ararat. I pictured Noah's ship stranded there, its hull broken apart and leaking animals. Birds poured from its hull.

And so?

It was beautiful. Around me spread a carpet of near infinite variation—white nightcaps, creeping barberry with their spiked yellow clumps, bearded beggar-ticks that looked like hands cupped to receive the communion, and dandelions, and beds of clover, and fire-wheels. I lay down on a bed of marigolds and I chewed on a leaf stalk and I marveled at the colliding clouds. A bearded dragon battled a knight mounted on a horse. The knight's lance pierced the dragon's tail and then the dragon swallowed him up, horse and all. The cool wind kicked up peppery smells of hyacinth, heather, the piquancy of deadfall. I shut my eyes.

And then?

Then a twig snapped, like the crack of gunfire. The nape of my neck prickled. I propped up on my elbows and said, *Who's there? Come out come out from wherever you are.* If I had capacity for anything then, it was unearned fear. If I could imagine anything, I could imagine the worst, of a creature haunting the woods, monsters constructed from the mingle-mangle of my imagination. Mesingw.

I ain't fooling around. Come out or I'll, I'll… I had no threats to offer. I had no weapons. The woods responded with a rustle. Something rattled, honked in the crowns, a branch-end fell to the earth. Then it was too quiet. Then something sounded like a parting of bushes. Swallowing hard, I swallowed fear. I followed the memory of that sound into the darker woods.

My hands are going numb.

Pipe down.

I came upon a blue heath ringed along the perimeter by white oaks. Nothing to see here but still the air smelled rancid. A swarm of flies buzzed like a thousand small engines. Mosquitoes whizzed by my ears like bullets. I climbed over a pile of rocks assembled as if for a ritual, a partition or dividing wall, and landing on the other side, something rattled beneath my feet. I stopped mid-step, my toes at the saw-toothed edge of a bear trap, a blackened bear claw in its grip, oozing maggots and flies.

And then?

Then something flashed at the edge of my vision: a fawn, its caramel colored hide peppered with patches of white, its jaws curling, its obsidian eyes chinked with light. Stoically it stood. Absolutely still, bowlegged, as if invented by the woods, one of its delicate profusions of mystery and magic—a fairy book animal, some princess or witch transformed by a spell. Looking somewhat bewildered, what with its radar ears spiked to capture every soundless motion, as if by watching me I would transform into something other than a boy, I would transform, in its fixed, dark glare, a hedge or a bush, something viridian and unthreatening—just another emerald fixture in its familiar landscape. I stepped around the bear claw, closing the gap between the fawn and me by a foot or so, when it angled in that erratic way that fawns do, produced a frightened, acrobatic leap over a thistle and bounded through the woods. I glimpsed the flash of its white tail winding through the bush.

And then?

Then I ran toward it, my thighs snapping branches, feet crushing dry leaves and dry twigs. I was speed. The parade of trees blurred at the outer edges of my sights while my body surged with vitality. Intense and animate and possessed of meaning, mutated, I became a creature of the woods, a wolf or a bear. I might even have howled as I ran, howled like Mesingw, eater of children.

Is that it there?

That's it.

The pond, when we reach it, looks nothing like a body of standing water, but coated in paraffin. The embankments that circumscribe its boundaries look level with the height of the snow, so the only marker that determines pond from land are a few spindly trees leaning crookedly in the distance—black oaks, I think, stripped, standing at jaunty angles around the borders like wire. Jack pulls close to the edge and I spread my arms wide to keep him back.

Wait.

On the powdery banks, I lay the shovel lengthwise against the pond's surface. I step gingerly onto the ice, my legs still ankle deep in snow. Jack watches.

Careful.

It may hold, I say. I have no doubt that it will.

With the shovel in hand, I take twenty steps onto the pond, thankful for the laws of nature. I think of the gradations of color, the color of temperature and how this winter of white deceives. *Pops, black is not just the absence of color, but the hottest color. Pops, did you know that a black hole in space is actually a burning pit of hell? And did you know that red is the coldest color, then orange is hotter, then blue, then violet, then the hottest is black?* What good will knowing that serve, Son? *Pops, do only things of use have value?* That boy's head was crowded with useless facts.

We'll need to break down the ice to get to the fish.

What shall I do?

Don't just stand there looking pretty, find a branch, something not too stiff but bendable, about five or six feet long.

Jack salutes, *Aye, aye, Captain*, then turns and runs into the woods.

I don't have a plan. Plans are guidelines. Scaffolding meant to be abandoned. So I cross the pond's powdery surface and like a gravedigger, the shovel in my fist, I step lightly but firmly through the hard pack. Step-by-step. Achieve your goal, step–by-step. Claim your victory, step-by-step-by-step.

Reaching midpoint between center and shore, I drop the shovel. In a swirling motion, I push away the snow. I make a circle. An eye. The wind, that awful wind, like an accretion of verbs, pushes against me, buffets my body, whips my scarf. Maybe this is what Armand's Anil must have felt when plummeting from the sky?

I peer through the falling snow, looking for Jack. A blurred shape runs across the banks and I shout, Did you find it? He doesn't want to hear me, I think, or can't. The wind has erased us. I am a thing made more solitary by this winter washing over me, sapping my diurnal strength. Drums holds me in its frozen fist.

Summoning supernatural strength, I strike the ice cover with my shovel. Imbecilic effort. Puerile. Effete. What other words can I summon? Asinine—*Come on, Dutch, you can do better than that. Come on Pops, you didn't used to hit like a girl.* I have hardly enough energy to leave a dent, let alone burst through the ice. I would need Mesingw's strength to accomplish this, the power of a monster. I am no monster.

With the shovel tip, I stab, jab, poke the ice, leaning my weight into it with my foot. Snow crashes whitely against my face. I am cold, so cold, so frozen—*If you're cold you have to think of someplace warm.* Running, I am running through the green woods, my chest heavy, and the quilts of the afternoon envelope me in their heat. Panting. I hear my lungs whistle. Acrid sweat drips into my eyes but my legs still feel vital. I chase the flash of a fawn's tail.

My heart pounded with violence, the valves threatening rupture. On a small rise, I dropped to my knees and peered out through eyes rimmed with sweat. The far edge of Four Seasons Lake disappeared into a line of evergreens so expansive they seemed to reach into the sky. Beyond the forest, the mountains mutely undulated, and the ends of branches fanned black against gray clouds of molten tin. The cliff overlooked the blue expanse of water. The water, calm as a glade, suspended disbelief. Was it real? It was. My fisherman's camp, invisible from that angle, must have lay north of where I stood. A small ring of blue smoke curled up over the treetops in the distance.

Beside me snaked a narrow creek, no more than a sliver around which white and brown stones formed a low threshold of a wall. It trickled effortlessly through the woods. What was it once? What is it but a barrier now? Water, like a tongue of silver, emptied into the lake.

I strike the ice. I am less cold. Memory of that day warms my hands because the water emptied into the lake. That afternoon, my body bled heat. My lungs exhaled heat. I stripped off my shirt, then shoes, then socks, shorts, and left them in a heap by a willow tree. I fell into the roots of that tree, pressed myself into its cooling shadows, lulled myself to sleep by the sound of the spiraling jetties. The dark water churned, creating foamy cataracts. The water near the cliff's base looked the texture of pea soup. I settled my breathing and closed my eyes when a twig snapped nearby. *Who's there?* I said, barely above a whisper.

Through the thickets, on the opposite side of the creek bed, where stones of various gold and purple hues collapsed into pellets or dissolved to amber silt, stood a girl. Someone I'd seen before? A vague familiarity. But where? I rose out of the roots, dipped behind a low hanging branch.

I strike the ice. I stomp my boots against the ice. The ice is firm. It hates my effort.

Her hair fell in two long braids to her waist. Even then, in the fractured light of that day, her hair looked as if cured with oil. Her leather sandals clicked against her heels as she paced, heel-to-toe, undecided over something, questioning something, and the hem of her white skirt of some sheer material like organza or lace, swished against the floor. She touched her forehead, jingle-jangled her metal bracelets, and she recited something, an incantation or prayer, I could not tell. The feathers in her ears, brown plumes with spots of white, fanned outwards in the hot breeze, like the ears of a nymph. There seemed to be some glorious power emanating from her that pushed itself outwards, conscripted each and every thing that stood around her. It was a power just on the edge of revealing itself. The branch I leaned against broke. *Snap.* She turned toward my general direction. I crouched lower to the ground. She curled her fingers over her mouth.

Cacaw, Cacaw!

With the heel of my boot I stomp the ice. I raise my head, looking for Jack. Where has he gone? Abandoned me? Followed our snow tracks home? I want to call to him, but the wind rises up and pushes me forward. It howls. It screams.

I couldn't help but stare at her. A girl clothed in light, her jade eyes, like green nets, caught the sun streaming through the branches.

Cacaw! Cacaw!

Then she turned back into the woods. I thought of that fawn. A flash of white. Graceful legs kicked up the dust like explosions.

Thump-thump-thump! The sheet of ice is tough, unyielding. The surface will not crack. *Thump!* I feel claustrophobic. I feel I'm being watched, as if each snowflake falling is an eye judging my life. Jackhammering the surface with my shovel, stamping my dumb feet, I am, if nothing else, persistent, because fishing also means tenacity. I know the shallowest part of the pond is not its center, but its outer edges, like the shallowest part of one's life. Maybe I should have begun closer to the shore. This is a mistake of judgment. What else have I been wrong about? *Everything Dutch, you've been wrong about every*… A crack forms at the edge of my boot. The ice below me fissures. I wish Armand were here. He'd put an end to this—*Get yourself back to that warm room. Should I be working on the roof, Pops?*

Jack, I say. Jack, quick with the branch! I reach into my pocket for the nail and place it in the crack. I hammer it with the shovel.

Jack!

The ice screams. I look up from the ice bed and I catch a glimpse of a figure. Jack's body looks fractured, his atoms breaking apart. He seems as if spreading into the trees. The ice beneath my feet breaks. A black hole reveals itself like a splintered mouth. I step back.

Jack Frost!

Did I imagine that girl in the woods signaling to the birds, *Cacaw-Cacaw*. Get yourself back to camp, go back and check your line, go back and bait a few more hooks. Beads of sweat trickled down my temples. Go on and swim in the lake and drift over its surface like a leaf, go on and sway with the currents. Sweat snaked into my eyes, burning them. Sweat dripped from my nostrils, through my lips and onto my tongue. My underwear clung to my thighs like a soiled second skin. *Ca-Caw!* Things jostled in the trees. A leaf fell. A twig fell. A great tidal wave of wind shook the boughs.

A bird's squall, sharp and inhuman, rollicked from the sky. Two crows skated down from the treetops as if absconding from a crime, guilt in their wings, cawing in that blind disregard for melody. One landed near my feet, and the other where I saw the girl—*A crow ain't nothing but a flying rat. Caw-Caw-Caw.* Parched ejaculations pitched into the air without direction. Then rose the dim explosion of snapping twigs, of dry leaves chewed up under footfalls. The girl emerged from the woodsy shadows, emerged with speed and grace, her eyes locked onto a distant target ahead where the cliff ended. The lake was gravity, ready to pull her in.

Before I could shout, *Stop,* she launched herself over the cliff, her arms straight as spears, her legs scissor-cutting the air.

Jack's voice tumbles out of the air like a plangent bell, *Sir!* The cracked ice beneath me gives. I swallow a large gulp of air. Water grips my ankles, pulls me in, swallowing me up into a watery darkness that burns like fire.

But hers was a high parabola. A perfect arch. Not like my plumb descent. Time slowed and lengthened then altogether stopped and it seemed the girl glided through space, like a girl shot from a cannon. Without a splash, she ruptured the olive water, and the olive water opened to receive her, and the olive water knitted itself back again, then with the finality of an insult, the concentric circles of tiny waves rippled to the shore.

The water tears into me. An eye of light above shimmers like a tiny sun. My body is a line, without beginning, without end. The water is bleak, thick with murk, and I drift and I fall toward the bottom where the dead must display their bones. Are Cole's bones down here, somewhere deep below, clothed in the rank fibers of the water? I hoard each molecule of oxygen and tear off my jacket and peel off my trousers.

Then I am at the cliff's edge. Any second now, the girl would surface, swim to the shore. She might whip her hair in an arc of silver at the shore's edge, and then… A dull ache pushed inside my ribs. Something felt wrong, some tear in the fabric of space. The quietude felt wrong. Even the trees, no longer mute, but spinning their branches in the hot wind, testified to some crime occurring below the lake's surface.

And the world spun along, the curtain of night would fall, the birds would bandy about from limb to limb, singing their songs, and tomorrow the sky above the Poconos would once again turn stony gray, unmoving as dead planets, and the water would continue to reflect the stone gray sky. The meadowlarks in the fields would continue rocking their crowns, oblivious to me plunged to the bottom of a pond. My heart races. Do I imagine Cole's face, ice blue, black eyes in whose dullness emanates a vast nothingness, pulls upward from the pond's depths. Do I imagine an ice blue arm reached me, arms like wax mannequins, and ice blue fingers handled the balls of my heels? Fingers clamped onto my ankle like a vice, pulled me down. Was this death?

I broke through the thin dark membrane while the girl lay at the lake bottom. Silt stirred up. My eyes clouded. Sounds dulled. The distance between the surface and the lake bed felt immeasurable. I palmed greasy rocks as I swam, brushed against drowned trees, slipped past kindling saturated and flaking apart and slick with fetid weeds. Grass like a witch's hair, black and oily, brushed my chest. A water snake slithered by, its blank eyes like nail heads. I swam past oil drums, rakes, a hand bell used by small town sentries to ring the hour. Here lay the bric-a-brac evidence of Drums' distant past, memory distorted by time and the depths of water. A whitewall tire stuck in silt, oozed rubber bits along the trail of bicycle parts. Beside a filigreed rail, lay a bicycle frame, upended and rusted, with its chain snapped in two. A toolbox languished beside crates of mason jars, amber jugs, amber bottles and rusted oil cans. I swam, my eyes burning. I swam toward an outstretched arm, pale as a blanched stick.

Cole pulls me down.

Ahead, two braids whipped like snakes in the slow current. Panic coiled the girl's face. Fear. Mine. Hers. Her left leg was lodged beneath two corn bailers. Held down by junk. Taking hold of her wrists, I pulled. My lungs ached. I needed air. Planting my feet against the rusted iron hulk, I pulled again and her face twisted in pain. Bubbles escaped her mouth. My head throbbed and my chest tightened and I looked up toward the surface. Air, light, these can heal me. Don't leave. I pressed my lips to her cold lips. I blew warm air into her cold mouth. Was it enough?

And down.

Pull while I dig! I gestured. She nodded. She understood. My hands pushed away years of silt and rocks, pushed away the neglected underworld. My lungs felt as if ready to collapse. I unknotted time. She pulled her foot free. She rose. Her thin arms thrashed furiously toward the trembling light. Her thin ankle trailed a cloud of blood.

I yield. I float downwards into an amiable sleep. I shut my eyes and drift, warmed by the cold.

She lay face up on the shore, her braided hair loosened and fanned around her like a dark net. Her ribs expanded and contracted like bellows. On her face alternated calm confidence and the shock of luck, like athletes having snatched victory from the jaws of defeat. I coughed water onto the rocks.

I can see your seahorse, she said.

Covering myself with my hands, I scrambled into the woods, hid behind a young oak. At the water's edge she removed her skirt. *Come out come out from wherever you are.*

Later, we lay together on the shore, naked and unashamed, like Eve and Adam. Exposed to one another and to the woods, to the lake and to the sky and its pale light, we lay together, the late afternoon sun drying us, like Adam and Eve. Now and then, a warm wind washed over us, a cooling warmth that trembled the hairs on our arms, and in the whole of the universe there was no sin.

I was trying to fly, she said. Her teeth chattered. I took her hands in my hands and blew. She slipped them out. Her first refusal.

But you're shaking. So she was, her bare skin pimpled with cold.

Just a little.

We watched the surface of the lake, the plop of a fish's tail, circles of silence enfolding us, joining us to textures of sound, colors of the sun setting across the sky. The waning sunlight shimmered across the water like a molecular road, a path to Heaven.

I'm Winona.

No! I shout. My mouth explodes and bubbles drift like jellyfish. *No!* My eyes open. My mouth exhales water. *Light a match, Dutch, see if you can; Pearl walked into the woods with a candle lantern inside a hurricane and Wally made you hold his hand and drink the fire water, so simple, so simple the way the world goes dark and then grows light again, because Pearl's a whore and to kill the heat inside you is to kill the whore, and so Cole, Cole, you who never knew the depths of loss would learn it from me, and that was my gift to you, and I'm sorry, I am very sorry, I am…* Pulled down by the ice blue fingers of an ice blue boy, and yet I feel lifted. Is this death, to rise even as one falls?

Snow palms my face. Warm snow—*Snow is ash.* My insides feel cold, body bloated with cold, throat like a razor. Pain there. I taste blood in my mouth, like copper. I drag myself across the snow-banks. I cough up blood. Spit blood. Expel the useless ancient blood. I shut my eyes. My lungs rasp. Birds. I think I hear angels.

Later.

In the house. The warm room.

Rub your chest and your arms will take care of themselves.

I do as I'm told.

You're lucky I was around. Jack crouches before me, so close I can smell his teeth. His blue eyes sparkle. The hearth glows yellow. Steam, built up on my shoulders, coils, filament by filament and dissipates. I am like the last gasp of heat from a match extinguished in a water bucket. I cough.

You my guardian angel now?

Maybe I am or maybe not. His tone sounds wise yet playful, like the voice of an ancient tree, if it could speak.

Maybe, I say, the one word I can manage through my chattering teeth. Jack rises, moves to the door. Don't leave me.

You still cold?

Yes.

But you're burning up.

I am.

Just think of someplace warm and you'll be warm.

Okay.

SIX

A day of violent sunshine, Day-Glo, like the flash of light off a tin roof. I am twelve because this house is Blake's house and because it is too bright and too hot and the heat of this summer day is God wielding a weapon. I am twelve because I am sickly, gangly, and have to run laps to the mailbox and back as ordered—twelve times, because Blake woke up and said so. *Twelve apostles and twelve months in a year and the clock strikes twelve twice a day.* I am twelve because my life directs itself toward the constant upkeep of this house, my enemy. I am twelve because Blake has confused my obedience with love.

Reaching the end of the drive on my sixth lap, I want to crawl into a hole and sleep, let the worms carry bits of my skin away, let the millipedes burrow into my body. I want to sleep, because sleep involves dreams and in dreams Blake can't touch me. But something gleams at the base of the water tower. It's a bicycle, so pristine it seems surreal.

I had seen it in a Sears's catalogue down at the IGA, and I might have torn out the page and might have folded it into my pocket and walked out of the store with Blake. I must have tacked the picture up above my bed and stared at its spokes before falling asleep. Now there it stood, in cool candy red and cream vanilla, glowing under the pale light as if anointed by God, just like the picture.

Light flashes over the whitewall tires, and even the chain guard gleams in tin. Its curved buckhorn handlebars have a little trilling bell in chrome just above the right handbrake. I finger the lever of the chrome bell, graze my hands over the springer seat, so perfect, so fine, its rich leather the softness of cream. I will ride it every day, in secret, because if I told Blake about it he would surely take it away. Taking it from the water tower where it leans as if anointed by God wouldn't be a crime at all. It'd be like finder's keepers. It wasn't my fault someone left it here so new and shiny for me to find.

But still I search for its owner, because that's conscience talking. I part the brambles and scour the nearby bushes and search the trees. I even climb the water tower to the topmost ledge and peer across the wheat and cabbage fields, stare down the length of Deep Hole Road. I shout into the sky, *You've left your bicycle*, or maybe I didn't.

Several cars pass, a Studebaker black and shiny as a beetle, a Model-T like a hearse, an Oldsmobile, the sun reflecting off its hood ornament like a twelve-pointed star. Tires warble, roll along with too little air in the tubes. Faces behind the passenger windows regard me with sanctimony, or charity having reached its apex. They are like the faces I saw in the windows of train cars. No one will stop. I could be lost, for all they know. I could have bumped my head, forgotten my name.

I'll count to twelve and then it's mine. Someone left it here for me because I am twelve and because I am twelve it's meant for me, also because it's here under the ladder of *my* water tower, beside *my* Deep Hole Road, in *my* Drums. I push it into the bushes, cover it with some branches I pull down from the surrounding trees.

I make like I'm running back to the house when Blake's Ford pulls out onto Deep Hole. He says he's going to work on Mr. Bledsoe's rusted gutters, then Mrs. Park's leaky bathtub, then Mr. Jourgenson's broken faucet. He tells me he's left me a list of chores to do and I say *Yes, Sir* when he says he wants them done before he comes home, which is by six, but it's also a Tuesday and that means he'll be in Hazleton playing cards with some guys until past midnight. Blake speeds away, the Ford's tailpipe spitting smoke.

I wait for my wristwatch to tell me it's safe to leave, because clocks have a habit of being wrong sometimes. Once a clock told me it was safe to stop scrubbing the staircase and rest my head on the landing, and Blake came home and found me asleep and he slapped my head with his palm and twisted my ears. Another time, a clock told me it was safe to listen to *The Great Gildersleeve Show* on his Emerson. Blake pushed me into a bathtub and held me down until the air left my lungs. So I waited thirty-two minutes this time, because I knew that, if the half-hour passed, Blake wouldn't be back until when he said so, and even if he came home at six, I'd have done what I needed to do and done what I had to do—ride that bicycle till my heels bled.

The half-hour passes. The wristwatch tells me it's safe. *Hello beauty,* I might have said upon uncovering the bicycle. I might've kissed the springer seat, might've kissed the little chrome bell. I mount the seat and pedal down Deep Hole, to St. John's, riding over the single car bridge on Mundies and Kisenwether Road, the boards clattering cheerfully beneath my wheels, and I ride the sidewinding roads decorated with the June colors, pure excitement on my face emanating like light from the gauzy sky and my eyes sparkling with tears like the crystals shimmering off the ponds. I ride through Sugarloaf Valley, passing apple groves and fields of lush chard, and I ride through the golden cornfields that seem to summon all the endowed health and beauty of my world.

Taking a right onto Township Road I pedal through Markham's field, trilling my bell like a manic bird. Trilling my bell, passing cows that churn their jaws, their soft lazy eyes pause to regard me, a blur on a red and cream pony. In the distance, a silly tractor chugs and chugs, turning up the beet harvest. Farm hands are busy, crouched close to the earth, picking cabbage. Service trucks hauling garden equipment pass, and I trill my bell and they honk their horns. I'm seen, heard, and because they honked their horns and waved to me, I'm part of their world now, acknowledged for the sublime thing I am: A real boy with a new red and cream auto-cycle by Schwinn, the same one in the famous Sears catalogue whose picture sits above my bed.

I ride on, gritting my teeth as the road turns uphill. My legs burn. Heat collects in the crevices of my skin. I power my way up the foothills of Sugarloaf Mountain, pedal up the slivering trail to its summit, which is more a mound than a peak. Breathless, I lean the bike against the trunk of a giant willow—*sort of found you in a basket at the base of a willow tree, Son.*

The sunshine calmly leans into the afternoon; it has that softness you find in paintings of saints, where the light seems to emanate from within a body, say Christ's, or Sebastian's, and emanates outwards caressing objects in rooms staged as if for a blessing.

I climb the tree because its limbs reach to the ground and, above me, the arms fan outwards like the invitation of an embrace. Blake must be working on a toilet or cleaning out a gutter, but not me, I'm climbing a tree, just like a boy my age has to, because it's his right to. If I can reach the highest branch, shout into the valley Pearl's name, she might hear me and find me and take me to my real home up in Eden.

Dragonflies flicker below me, crank in air rife with the scent of honeysuckle. Mosquitoes buzz in the locust trees and, from the branches, the soft clatter of birds' wings sounds like comfort—downy beds, rustling blankets, all the hoarded warmth in the universe. From beyond the evergreens, a woodpecker clocks against an old oak. Squirrels chitter in the branches of a Douglas fir. There is the dim hum of bees. Serenity never sounded so busy. Quietude never sounded so wealthy. All that evidence of life, life and time, time and nature's blind singular purpose working in concert with play, meant God was a trickster who whispered from the gaps of trees—*Look not far and wide for I am here, all around and also within you, never far from reach.*

What is it like to be the sky, or light, or the wind, or the earth, or the water? What is it like to be a tree, or a bird nesting in a tree? Can I be someone else just by changing my words, my name? Did imagining you as someone else make you so?

Everything looks frozen in that saintly light: The rugged farm houses emerge from the joyful, bottle-green grasses, and the red barns with their steeply pitched roofs squat like mute monoliths, and a grain silo, far, far below, firm as a rocket, poses as if ready to lift off to some apple-red planet, a slow stodgy mist huffing around its base like the steam from an idling booster. Entombed behind the ramparts of thick trees, the dark creeks and silt ponds of this, my known universe, lay before me inviolate. Each tiny farmhouse or corral, barn or patch of field, looks manageable from this distance, yet harnesses a voltage that could shock you. The cornfields flexed in ordered rows from east to west, perfect parallels of man's power over the land that never quite belongs to him, regardless of titles and taxes and deeds, because ownership is chimerical.

Woods yield to fields then woodlots, a leavening of pattern duplicating itself mile after mile, then slipping into the Poconos. I imagine them as the peaks of Sinai. I imagine this land as the final battleground of the Apocalypse. Lifting my head to a view of villages, towns, boroughs, commonwealths: Black Creek Township to the south and west, Penn Lake in Dennison to the north and east, even the slim shadow of the Lehigh River curves there so far below as to render it a mute thread in a tapestry. Still, somewhere, and hidden by the tops of trees, a woodpecker clocks. *Tock-Tock-Tock.* Here I sit, contemplate all this human organization and natural order and disorder and feel, minute by minute and moment by moment, my soul leaking out—the borders between me and the furtive earth, me and the hills, me and the vast expanse of sky that hovers above like a gray lid, slowly erased. The tree exhales. The tree asks me what it's like to be a boy.

What's it like to be a tree? I whisper. What's it like to be rooted, guarding your own plot, leaking your roots into the supple earth, feeding on water and human pollution and light? If I become a tree, would God in all His glory return me to Pearl?

What's it like to be a boy? asks the tree again, and I say, *I don't know what that's like. I've never known.*

I shut my eyes and slow my breathing and hum the only song I know, "God is Nigh", because Pearl would always sing, *Day is done, Gone the sun, from the lake, from the hills, from the sky,* and then she would stop all of a sudden, perhaps choking back something—a tear induced by memory—and then continue, *All is well, safely rest, God is nigh.*

As my little voice carries across the big mountain, down into the big valley where that tractor chugs and those two service trucks hauling farm utensils work to till the earth, and where Blake, somewhere, fixes Mr. Jourgenson's such-and-such, my voice mingling with the buzz of bees, the *Tock-Tock-Tock* of the woodpecker's beak, carries itself already altered and capable of altering the world. A song or a prayer, just like a memory or a story, has the power to alter a life.

My spine is not a spine. My skin is not my skin but bark. Spine that is not mine melts into the bark as if sucked into it. My arms lift upwards, lengthen, my hands lengthen and my nails become long, translucent spears. My body stretches like rubber, reaches through the sparse canopy, reaches up toward the blue day and threadbare clouds, extracting light from the sun. The sun, how it shimmers in the gauzy sky like a coin in water, its light impossibly wealthy and splashing heat. My palms flatten and my fingers splay then twine and sprout leaves and shoots and seeds. My torso, pulled by gravity, pulls into the trunk, stretching my lower half into a gelatinous line. My feet unravel and coil like hissing snakes, and my soles flatten and spread over the willow's roots like spilled cream beneath the cool earth. My toes push aside mites and millipedes, or swallow them up, worm past rocks and ancient stones—dagger heads, tomahawks, the carcinogen waste of extinct insect empires—then nudge aside the roots of other trees and other shrubs and other bushes and other weeds and explode into root hairs. My hips crack, spin backwards and my rib cage splinters and my clavicle fractures in half—the two halves of my body coalesce into an inverse of itself.

I am turned inside out, exposing to the pecking birds my heart, lungs, spleen. My head falls into the loose shards of my broken chest, where the supple engine of my heart pumps, nourishing my taproot. Ground water passes up my flanks, pulls through my roots and limbs, nurses my new branches and penetrates my thickening crown. My skin, a lusterless sheath, striated and puckered, becomes grooved bark and hardens. Time as I know it is no longer time. I am not a boy but a tree. I swish my branches. My leaves thrush like waves lapping the shore. I am a willow tree.

An incredible thing to see oneself from two places at once, as if by looking at yourself as a tree, you look down at a boy who you vaguely recognize as yourself.

I will name the tree Somerset, the boy looking up at me says.

And I will name the boy Somerset, I, as a tree, say. We remain, each of me frozen in place, each of me guarding the secret of an imaginary self.

Seasons rise and fall like alternating waves of shadow and light. Merlins, mallards, and harlequins build their nests in my branches, frightful insects, squeaking their small purpose, skitter dumbly up and down my flanks. Skinks leap up and down and across my branches, tickling my trunk. Laughter shivers across my branches. Wood ticks burrow their wicked mandibles into my bark, and widow spiders construct their webs, catching mayflies, mosquitoes, green-backed flies as lovely as oily emeralds. I don't mind this. I have no reason to mind this. Our breath is the breath of the universe. Our eyes the eyes of birds and fish, beetles and crabs and butterflies. The bear and the wolf see with our eyes, even the heart of the white-capped mountains pulses with our stony silence, even the grainy seas churn our thoughts. The stars burn because of us and we weep because of their distance. This is all there is to the meaning of life. This is everything.

I am a city. Red ants tickle my spiny roots, building towns in my crevices, bees construct their houses between my leaves, delicate as paper lanterns. Worms construct cathedrals on my branches. Parks made by lichens cling to my trunk and in them walk ticks, bounce fleas, those miniscule vampires.

I am a universe. Beyond time. The ancient stars still furious at their isolation scatter, collide inside me, explode, forming infinite pools of gravity. A vortex siphons space and time. Years enter new years that resemble old years. A nearby pine tree tells me a joke about a blue jay and a hare and I shiver my limbs in laughter. An old oak shares with me his wisdom. Seasons mean water, heat, wind, color, ever punishing cold. Spring rains return each year and wash the valley clean. Storms arrive from huge blasts of dark sky, then pass away. The summer sun rises to heights of the atmosphere, blasts us with its creamy heat, steaming the puddles in the ruts and declivities, parching the fields. Windstorms spread our seeds. I languish in air made watery, air in which blend the aromas of unknowable flowers. My leaves glow brown. Birds fly from their nests and travel south, sensing some new sharpness in the air. The woodpecker that clocked its beak against my trunk falls dead from my boughs.

All turns white: The glassy treetops, stripped of leaves, stand thickly against the silver lidded sky like mute skeletons. Weathered branches clack and the snow-fleeced hills silently undulate. Fingers of ice decorate this newly minted city of white. Lattices of crystal hang from my branches, refracting rainbows of color, while chains of diamonds cling to my roots and elbows. The birds have mostly gone, except for a few crows that bark a dry banter—*Caw-Caw*—carrying the regret of all the hurt and joy, loss and gain of the world. I wait. My roots turn cold. I wait for the winter to pass.

I soften under spring rains, deluging the dead grasses with sweet water, and when the sun thaws the ice-hardened earth, I soften. Silvery drops shatter into pools of mercury that spread around my roots. What do I feel but summer's knife hot heat pass into my hollows, pierce my wrinkled skin? The heat pushes deeper into my heartwood, unfreezes my blood, liquefies my ice, makes me a boy again.

I am breathless, cradled in the tree's elbow, my arms and legs tingle. The late afternoon wind shivers through the branches. I am unable to move. I am dead, but alive, unborn, reborn, stillborn, frozen stiff as stone, and I want to lie here forever, because if I bicycle home, Blake will ask me to work, and if I try to tell him what I felt, that for a moment I disappeared into a willow and become one with time, he will tell me to work, and if I allow myself to vent the indignation rising from the pulse of my quaking heart, he will command me to work; so, I'll lie here, still and silent, folding my quivering arms across my chest, and I'll shut my heavy-lidded eyes and I'll count silently the seconds toward the long silent moments to twilight.

What happened to your bicycle?

I suppose I lost it.

I wish I had a bicycle.

I am not sure if it was ever mine.

SEVEN

A beam bursts and part of the second floor turns sharply downward. I feel spent. Useless. Worthless. My project, like my life, is undone. Armand hasn't come. He hasn't come to help me. But he might come. He might. I still have a little hope.

No, he won't come.

No, he won't.

A sharp tickle in my throat snaps my jaws shut. My chest rumbles. I cough. There are shards of glass in my chest. My nostrils hold the emanations of cold silt and pond scum. I can taste the irony ice.

A feverish cold quickly sweeps through me like a thousand volts. I shiver. My gums judder like a ventriloquist's dummy. Jack places his blanket over me and I rub my chest, but no warmth comes to my body.

You're about the last friend I have in this world.

I guess.

The burning candles set around us are a small comfort. The wax melts off the shafts like those geological formations Nona, Cole, and I saw vacationing in the Crystal Caves one year. A red candle sits guttering on the windowsill where several dead moths lay heaped in a corner. A tallow candle sits beside my suitcase, blue smoke spiraling upwards. It forms a gray, indecipherable language—lazy *C* and *S* and *G*. The last candle, in gentian, reminds me of the twilight, a deep purple with specks of silver in it like diamond dust; it stands beside my teeth effervescing in a glass of water. The fire ticks.

When Cole was eight or so, ten years before he vanished, he choked on a turkey's wishbone. I squeezed his sternum while Nona dug her fingers into his throat. We managed to save him then. As reward, I bought him ice cream, and as a double reward for having lived, I took him to a science exhibit in Carbon County. We studied a set of limestone cliffs, sheets of stone depicting the clatter of ancient sea life—ammonites, fish heads with teeth like vertebrae, trilobites, brittle stars. Ancient glyphs, strange spines and feelers, fins and tails embossed in sheetrock like runnels in a frieze. We seemed, he and I, like time travelers.

So our forested mountains, I said to him, *and the lands surrounding it, were once the geology of a great inland ocean. You'd have to take such things as faith if the evidence weren't there to convince you, but hell, some people in this town probably still believe that Jesus walked among the dinosaurs.*

What happened to them, Papa? Why did they—

Die? Who knows for sure.

Before us and around us stood evidence, frozen, sets of fossilized bones reassembled and mounted to recreate postures of fight or flight or nesting, scavenging or feeding. What sin had they committed to cause their extinction? Soon we'll be extinct. Soon our cities will turn to cinders.

Staring into the teeth of a raptor, I said, *Nothing is ever truly lost. Everything is always retained somewhere, or reinvented, or repurposed—in an idea, in a story, in a memory.*

Son, they say that forgiveness is the remission of sins, for it is by this that what has been lost and was found is saved from being lost again.

Papa? Will wishing people back make them come back?

~

Wally and Blake dragged Pearl through the mud, tied her wrists to the bumper of Blake's rattling Ford, while the no-name bitch brayed like a goat by the barn—*Youse help me hitch her down. Get'er hands, shitless, the whore, get'er before she runs away. Wally, youse get the muzzle on the whore. She's tarnished the good, goddamned Vangaarden name.*

That day, Blake and Wally, like two machines, worked silently, anticipating each other's actions—a nod of the head, a grimace, a two-finger tap on the shoulder. They bound Pearl's ankles and gagged Pearl's mouth with an oil-stained shop towel, and it's as though by binding and gagging her they changed Pearl from my mother into something beyond roles—her stiffened posture confused me, the hard snuffling of her breathing like a kicked horse was not the mother I knew.

She's sin, look upon sin. Look what sin does to the sinner. Blake's was the calm voice of malice, retribution, and malice was the voice of authority, and retribution was its engine. But what of my sin? My sin was to listen and to watch and do nothing. My sin was paralysis. Compliance was my sin. My sin was obedience to a man's voice I already hated.

That day, I stood rooted to the earth as if made of stone while Wally did his father's bidding—*She's a false mudder, shitless. Bakaak-bakaak! False as a three-dollar bill.* If she was a false mother, then I was a false son, standing over Wally's false mother, watching with dim, dusty eyes Wally and Blake bind her wrists—*I hereby sentence youse ta whorin', lyin', larceny, infidelity, gluttony, lycanthropy, vanity, pride… And I sentence youse to… Wally tighter, tighter around those wrists so this whore feels its sting.*

Pearl, brave Pearl, did not scream. She did not. Brave, stoic, lovely Pearl did not protest. She did not resist. Why did she choose to accept this punishment as if she had earned it? Why was my punishment to witness this unraveling? And the squeaky wheels of that old Ford ground the pebbly drive, like grinding bones, and the engine clattered down the rutted path leading down to Deep Hole Road.

All returned to quiet. The trees returned to their rightful places. Above me the clouds collected darkly and thunder clashed. Distant lightning. Black tears, the shape of wasps, rained down upon the mulched earth, releasing gnats and steam. Rain pelted me. Finally, the Ford rolled up the drive.

My eyes widened and my tears splashed with rain and mixed together with the cloud water and formed puddles at my feet. My bitten lower lip bled and mixed with the rain-tears. That was not my mother, when I saw her. Her skin, ragged. Mother of bone and blood and rags. That was not my mother. No, she was a new mother, a different mother, a mother transformed by Blake and Wally into pain and muffled screams. Mother of tears. Wally giggled while Blake hid his pleasure. Blake's lower lip bulged with chew. I rubbed my eyes. Soon I would awaken and Pearl and I would be at Delray Beach, making for the ocean.

I watched them like a spectator in a crowd, as if watching actors on a stage playing my father and mother and brother. They spun around her, kicking dust into her face. It was like watching a star die while they, one of its planets, spun at the outer edges of her vortex, pulled into her black heat, into her infinite gravity.

They dragged Pearl into the barn, her rubbery legs trailing blood, dragged her even as she implored me for help with her hands and eyes, and they tossed her like a disheveled doll into the center of the barn where the parts of bottled ships spread about on a worktable with tools meant for artful purpose, and from somewhere—How?—Blake emptied a jar of moonshine on her face and said—*Let 'er stew in its heat for a minute*—and still her eyes, those soft, doe-like eyes implored my help, whimpered help, cried out for some quick and silent mercy from a son too paralyzed by fear to hear her, her eyes full of wetness and salt—*Help! Help! Help me!*

You know I can't, Mama. Why ask when you know I can't?

Blake emptied his bladder on Pearl's face, then ordered Wally to do the same. *Let her soak in piss. Let the pisswater burn 'er body clean, the filthy whore.* Blake emptied his lip and lit a cigar. Wally squatted against the ground. Copying Blake he loaded his lip with chew. Idiot non-brother.

From somewhere between the folds of his jacket—How?—Blake pulled out a small pocket Bible and opened it at random. Silver spittle dripped like a long cord of venomous snot from his lips, then scripture, venomous, obscene, rancid, rained down on Pearl like his mouth was a cloud and the words were fiery water—*Hallowed be thy name, Thy kingdom come, Thy will be done on earth as it is in Heaven*—and he ripped a page from that book, gestured to Wally with two fingers and Wally understood. Wally ungagged Pearl, and Blake crouched close to her and crushed the page in his fist and stuffed it in Pearl's mouth—*Eat, eat you starving bitch, eat the words of our Father.* He screamed vile things into her face. Did I help him, the man I hated, defile the woman I loved? Did I slap Wally's snickering face?

Blake's voice altered, assuming some tenderness he had no right to.

Barely above a whisper he said—*Seeing they may see and not perceive, and hearing they may hear and not understand, lest they should turn, and their sins be forgiven them.* He cradled the back of Pearl's neck and lifted her up, and Wally giggled and said, *The sower sows the word, he do.* Blake balled up his fist and struck Pearl's eye, not just once or twice, not less than six times, then dropped her head where it bounced off the floor. Pearl was bloodied and wet with insult and Pearl's eye looked like a pulpy tomato.

Blake turned to me and said, *If summun' sins and commits a trespass against the Lord, or if she's found what was lost and lies concerning it, then it shall be because she's sinned and is guilty, guilty, guilty, that she shall restore what she has stolen, and she shall restore it to its full value. Amen?*

Amen, Wally said.

Why does she deserve this judgment? Because she saved me from the fire in the woods? Because she sang songs to me when I was afraid of the dark? Because she stole food for us when we hadn't two pennies to strike together? *Poverty, son, means God forgives your thefts.* Why deserve this, because she sacrificed her body to wolves in exchange for medicine, food, a warm bed?

A trickle of urine spread from her thighs, and dirt and blood mixed like manure on her broken face. Her lungs issued a rasped breathing, dry and asthmatic, like a saw blade entering wood, and I scented blood in the air, steaming up with the sweltering dust. Rain pelted the pent roof. Rain sounded like a crackling fire outside the window.

By the light of the gloaming, by the light of a single candle in a hurricane lamp guttering and steaming on the sill, Blake and Wally strung Pearl up by her wrists while I watched, confused by the depths of such violence. She hung from the rafter beam where Blake's lifeboat would dangle there like a cloud. She hung from the rafter beam, a naked bloody doll, dripping blood onto the barn floor.

Let 'er be, said Blake then spat. Wally spat and trailed him out the barn door, like his shadow. My mind churned. Maybe Pearl wasn't meant to leave like Blake said. Maybe no one who leaves deserves to return without punishment.

Come on, shitless!

I ran from a mother I no longer understood. I ran from the power who created me, sheltered me, protected me, to the power that could kill, following Blake and Wally to the house.

That night, Blake chained me to the porch rail because I hadn't earned the right to sleep inside, all while the no-name dog howled in the kitchen. Rain pattered the lee. My eyes held onto the barn. Pearl hung inside, just like Jesus flagellated on the cross. Blake and Wally were asleep and I was not asleep because punishing someone was hard work. Later, I worked my wrists through the shackles, and by morning, with a slow rinse of water that misted the trees, I entered the barn. I stood in the center, helpless as Job before his God, silently asking, Why? Why would leaving Drums warrant this, this... What was it? Hatred? Torture? Suffering?

I stood before this other woman, her blood, which was my blood, congealed on the face of this woman who had carried me inside her body, hardened blood on the arms of this woman who had held me and cradled me, blood clotted on the face of this woman who had pressed her face into my face and had rubbed her cheek on my cheek, and her blood, her womanly, motherly blood caked the barn floor, such good blood wasted, this good blood that once nurtured my blood and my cells, this good blood that once formed my bones, my brain, my skin, and whose good, nutritive blood once formed my soul.

Water, Pearl said, barely above a whisper. *Give me water.*

Yes, water, of course, water because water was the only cure that could end this, because water cleanses, cleans, water—*Because the Spirit of God hovers over the face of the waters*—water vanquishes sin.

Water.

It true you killed my twin?

Water.

It true, Mama? It true what Blake said?

Her body shuddered. He neck moved in an indeterminate direction.

It true what they said, Mama?

Wat—

I backed away, back into the shadows, backed out through the open double doors. I returned to the porch and I lay down and slipped my wrists into those shackles and I waited for Blake and Wally. But is that what I did? Didn't I help you, Mother? I helped you, didn't I? When Blake and Wally went away and told me not to come and look upon you, my dead mother, did I not untie your wrists and hold a cup of water to your quivering lips and save you, didn't I? Didn't I also give you clothes to wear and helped you with your slippers?

Without offering me a goodbye kiss, didn't you limp away, your heart bleeding in your chest, your blood trailing you into blackened woods, gone away, gone, away gone—*This time you can't follow*—but I did, I did, didn't I? How could I not? I followed so that I could protect you. Your one bloodied eye lay open, the other knotted shut, witnessing me witness your end without speaking. You slipped into the shallow depths of the creek. You forded the black water, spilling waves, and you waved me back with those red raw wrists, but I didn't turn back, because you needed the water to heal you—*Go back.*

I want to go with you. I want to go—and her voice said, *Hush, hush little one, don't you cry*, singing as she swam down the creek. *Day is done, gone the sun, from the lake, from the hills, from the sky.* And she sang, *All is well, safely rest.* And I stood on the banks, mouthing the words without sound, *God is nigh.*

Later, while Blake and Wally made several trips in and out of the house, returning again and again to drop Pearl's things into a pile on the back lawn, I stood, my arms hugging my chest. While Blake threw down her corselettes, girdles, stockings of sheer lace, bertha-collared blouses and puff-sleeved shirts, batwing sweaters and gingham dresses and petticoats, still on their wooden coat hangers, threw down her hairbrushes, tote bags and hobo bags and muffs, threw in her clogs and sandals and flat-footed slippers and all the framed pictures of her youth as a small town starlet, The Rocket Girl of the Wilkes-Barre County Fair—just all the mélange she had left behind and all the bric-a-brac of her small life—I stood by the old oak, rooted to my spot on the grass in the shadow of the old oak, watching, it seemed, an ancient custom of erasure.

Fire cleanses us of the sinner, shouted Blake, the keys on his belt loop jangling like a mule's bridle. He could not control her, and because he could not have her, he could not own her nor determine her, so what he could finally control was her memory.

While several crows circled overhead, barked and cawed, blackly watched me watching this ritual as tribal as any fire dance or rain dance or community harvest song, Wally poured kerosene over the pile. Blake said a few things out of the Bible. Then he snapped it shut. Then he threw a match down onto the pyre. Gouts of black smoke eddied, smoke the color of molasses reeked of anger. The flames licked the corners of a photograph of Pearl seated at a long wooden table, looking uncomfortable in a white dress, a lace collar framing her head like two halves of a pockmarked moon. The fire licked the edges of her hair, blackened her half-shut eyes and reduced her downturned mouth to a hole circumscribed by soot. Soon the edges of a book flexed and snapped, and paper scraps swerved into the air. Blake reached up and pawed a burning page and it crumbled at his touch. Wally held my glare through the flames and turned away, all trace of his insolence gone. Blake stood before the roaring fire, arms akimbo, legs apart. *You ain't ta speak 'a Pearl, youse hear?*

Frozen before the fire, frozen before the fire without an answer to my life, frozen, I felt darkness seal itself around me as a palpable, breathing, dripping thing.

Soon the crickets screamed. Blake's belt loop jangled. Wally *boo-boo-booed* like an Indian. The incessant cawing of the crows filled the trees and the last faint gasps of the flames smoldered, rolled toward the sky like the last faint gasps of the dying. I stood before the smolder and turned my eyes to where the woods began. The flash of a rabbit's tail bounded into the woods. Maybe a pale face held my stare. Where does a soul go? What remains in the world after a soul departs?

They might burn your things, Mother, but they can't burn your memory. All your things might be up there in the clouds, and one day it'll rain and we'll be coated by aspects of your petticoats and clogs, your horsehair brushes and lipstick tubes, and taste the rain perfumed with your apple-pie recipes and formulas to banish ghosts, but... Blake's incessant yelping of my name returned me to this life—*Come on shitless, let's get a supper in us.*

No, it wasn't so easy to extinguish a life, as if just by burning up all the things one ever owned you could erase a person. Though I couldn't articulate it then, I know now that the soul exists in the things people touched, used, admired—a scratch made by a thumbnail in the planks of a wooden bench overlooking the Baltimore Harbor, or a spot of dried spittle on a brass knob, or a scrawled dedication in the inner flap of a book, even a painting pondered in a museum for an hour holds all the gazes that gazed upon it—collected together, these were invisible evidence that fixed a soul into the world long after the body crumbled. The soul lives in things. This is all the soul is when the body is done. This is the whole meaning of remnant and return.

EIGHT

I am here amid spider webs and silverfish, amid the cold shells of dead snails and the frozen dust.

Jack says, *Is remembering the past really imagining it, like you said?*

I say, I'm not sure. Sometimes I think we need others to help us remember.

I think so.

Soon there'll be no one left to corroborate me. Soon there'll be no evidence of us—*It's strange that invention goes on after we complete life. Others invent us for their own purposes. They remember events that perhaps never were, making and remaking us in their imagination, making everything we are, everything we've done, a fiction.*

Maybe we're just someone's story, Pops, and people conclude our lives in any way they want. Maybe that's what dying really means, when everyone misremembers you, then forgets you?

I won't forget. I refuse to. Son, your disappearance, like Pearl's, was worse than death. Though I was too young to understand it then (too old now), I know absence is a form of presence. When sunlight feels warmest, it's on the cold skin that craves it. Symphonies sound sweetest after a long spell of noise. Silence and absence are also forms of beauty. And light. And darkness. Maybe the living aren't truly alive until they've gone, and that's a paradox. Memory makes them more alive, more real than even these palsied hands and this cold, insufferable house, or that goddamned tree outside. *That's all I wanted, Pops, really, just to be remembered.*

Son, you gave us no explanation, no cause, nothing to attach reasons to your absence, and because I found no note, I found no justification. You simply vanished—into the woods, into the lake, into thin air. Nona said it had to do with her—*If I had been stricter, Dutch, less forgiving. If I'd been more like you.*

You have a point there, Nona. But I knew that your leaving us had nothing to do with her and everything to do with me. It is my cruelty that led her to believe she was responsible.

If you had died, Cole, that would have been one thing. We would have buried you beside Obadiah and Geraldine, beside Blake in the Vangaarden plot in downtown Conyngham. We would have brought lilies to your gravestone, white lilies, for that seemed appropriate, and not just for their fragrance but for their color, too—white, the pure blend of all colors. We would whisper prayers to the grass that grew and the marble slab bearing the minute facts of your life—your name stenciling the veined stone, the numerals declaring the date of your birth, the date of your passing—and we would trace the inscription on the stone with our fingers made wet from weeping: *Day is done, gone the sun, from the lake, from the hills, from the sky. All is well, safely rest, God is nigh.* We would tell you that we loved you and that we missed you, because that is what parents do. We would smear our tears over your name. What vigils we would have made?

Perhaps in the veins of the marble, I would have glimpsed your face, and it would have been a good face, a blended face from all the years I knew you. There would be your young, wild, handsome face, without an ounce of adolescent anguish upon it, but of gratitude for life. Suppose you could see us, hovering above us on the pine green lawn, the emanations of death coiling from your eyes like smoke from a lit cigar. You would be for us a kind of audience, grinning to himself at our tawdry performance. Suppose you could watch the event of your commemoration become a yearly routine, and say you would be pleased at the words pouring down through the soil. What would you think, if you could? Would you think us silly for paying tribute to your bones? Would you have laughed at us—*What's all the fuss?* Our rituals honoring you would mean nothing to you, only to us, the living, we the bearers of grief.

In the end, commemoration of our dead makes nothing happen, but perhaps it returns something, like the understanding that we are also not long for this earth, nor alone, that in the end, our performance in life is just a stage play. Now, reaching the end of my time, I would like to know what you know.

What was the last thing Cole said to you?

Okay, Pops.

What was the last thing you said to him?

I can't recall.

NINE

I *can't, I won't stay here,* you said the day you left. *This place is—*

Is what? You have responsibilities to us and to this house and to this town, and you said, *What about responsibility to me, Pops?* It was a good question. In retrospect, an answerable one I chose not to answer.

When I close my eyes, Cole stands silhouetted against the barn door, leaning his shoulder against the jamb with that blithe grace of his, a coolness borne of his own making—the child of the woods, the trees, the collector of rocks and builder of crude rockets, the riddler, amateur poet, philosopher. I always saw in him the dazzling reflection of Pearl's wildness, the wildness I had briefly adopted when it was just Pearl and I together. His pose I recognized as my own before Blake crushed it beneath his heel like a roach. But I can't blame Blake for everything. Part of healing is taking some responsibility for myself. I could have left Drums, scoured the ends of the earth for Pearl. But I didn't. By my teenage years, I had rebelled against rebellion, conforming myself to a set of values, Blake's religiosity, I half-believed would make me whole.

Your child is a defense against oblivion, so your hope for them is to do better than you did. You water their roots and pour upon their heads warm sunshine, and you fill their minds with knowledge and their hearts with examples of courage and self-sacrifice in hopes that virtues will bloom. I hoped to provide Cole with advantages, preparing him for his great voyages, using words I barely understood, words like tools passed down like a set of traits. But I know I failed to tell him the stories and anecdotes, the myths and legends that create a life's foundation. When food and water and shelter are not enough, stories sustain us. *That's the best you can do,* Armand would say. *We tell our tales and that is all that legacy is.*

Go on.

The sky turned the color of ashes that September morning, threatening rain. Outside, everything sat awash in blue, as if some great sea had receded suddenly, leaving the elms and redwoods, oaks, and orchard to drip and drip. A wet wind drew strength from the north and carried in it the watery smells of small ruined towns—Black Creek Township, Nazareth, Weatherly. It was as if I were gulling water. Nona's hydrangea bushes had wilted in waves of summer heat that month, and the stillness in the air almost deceived us into believing that all was well with our household.

The black oaks beyond the barn stood caked in billows of satiny fog; the air, effervescent as beer, cool and clay-scented from the furrows of the surrounding hayfields, rose to magically distorted heights. It seemed even the clouds, if you could smell them, would smell of the tilled earth, the sweet corn harvest, oh! even the sky would smell of it. The unpainted posts and posterns of the unfinished fence Cole had abandoned before his arrest stood up like a row of mangled teeth at the edge of our lawn. Why did it seem that we always erected some new barrier to protect us from new breaches? Henry James barked. He was old by then, twelve or so. Half-deaf, he barked at imaginary noises. Half-blind, his glassy eyes were edged with small blue circles, but he still had moxie. He whined and squeaked as I approached, his tongue lolling out. His tail wagged off the late summer gnats.

Settle down, boy.

Crossing into the woods, we navigated over a log bridge. It stood against the flat stones like a concatenation of frayed cigars. Big Nescopek's current had not completely dissolved it into pulp. Reaching a patch of deadfall, I stayed Henry James. He whimpered.

Quit whining, I said. I lit a cigar with a match and blew smoke rings into the air. Henry James, scenting a muskrat perhaps, a jackrabbit, stood his ears up, his senses keen on something beyond my vision.

Controlling his freedom meant controlling his nature; it meant conquering his will. If only, Cole...

Easy boy, I said. I loved to tease out the moments. It was how I tested loyalty, obedience. If only, Cole... Passing a hand over Henry James' eyes, I unclipped the tether from his collar. *Go on, then, but don't stray too far.* He shot through the thickets like a missile, bounded through the brush, the heft of his body electric through the tall grasses. I trailed along, blowing clouds of sable smoke that held the shape of clustered towns before breaking apart, wondering what dogs sensed. Theirs was an altogether different world, invisible to us, manufactured from various decaying or fruitful scents that formed a picture of... of what?

My picture was complete, each corner filled in with sky or earth. I belonged to Drums, belonged to the earth, the water, the sky breaking apart above, belonged to the spears of light shafting through clouds the texture and color of mackerel, revealing plots of deep blue—blue lakes in which white anvils drifted—and it felt good. Somewhere high above, a jet threaded the clouds, its thunder falling in chains over Sugarloaf Mountain. A tractor tilled the hayfields, the mechanical *glug-glug* of the motor a pattern of work multiplied, reminding me that I was not alone, that somewhere a man who prided himself on work, also worked to provide for his family.

Passing a grove of Canadian maples, iconic in their distance, their black barks like spires of sable smoke, knotted branches sheathed in luminescent moss, I thought suddenly of Wally—that half-wit false brother who always sought Blake's approval, always served his will, pushing me to the margins. Despite the rising heat. My skin prickled, and I thought of life drawing to a close. The moss was a parasite, assuredly eating its way through the birch and the birch would die, incapable of fending off this passive attack. The moss was like a set of insidious beliefs that clung to a life. Cole's belief in nothingness was like a parasite to its host. Why believe in that when there was so much beauty in the world?

And then?

Then a breeze rustled the tanned fields, bending down the stalks of old hay, their golden fibers netting the light exactly like that of napped yellow felt. Upon finishing my song, it seemed even the trees erupted in applause. I might have bowed from the waist when something fell from the boughs, rolled toward me like a sentient ball of puff.

A bird's nest. Inside, tangled in the straw fibers and bric-a-brac of leaf stems and twigs, lay a birdling. Its pink beak and pink talons lay delicately curled (so small, so humanlike) and its body, barely a form at all, twitched like a broken machine. I watched it struggle, the frail inch attempt to free itself, but it couldn't. It twitched, *cheep-cheeped*, then collapsed, curling inward like a salted slug. It had hatched blind, fragile as a flake of snow. It had deafly screeched. It had patiently awaited its mother's return for a regurgitated worm, while the air, the very substance of its freedom had undone it. I stared longingly at its form, a small question mark, the light breeze still animating its down. I studied its eye, a buffed glass bead, and saw nothing of the beauty that surrounded me. It had briefly felt freedom, for seventy-odd plummeting feet. Freedom or fear? Seventy-odd feet of fear.

Cole had jumped out of the treehouse once, sprained his ankle, and when I asked him why he'd jumped, he said, *I wanted to see if I could.*

You could have broken your neck.

But I didn't.

Son, why test our limits and your own? Why take such risks? You listening?

Was your mother any different, launching herself from that lakeside cliff when we were too young and too stupid to realize that risk could kill? She had jumped just to see what it would feel like to fly. Was Pearl any different, rocketing through space and into a net, trailed by the smell of fire? Was Blake any different, whose risks turned him into a monster, or Wally, stupid Wally, unable to fathom the extent of play that could turn deadly in an instant?

Cole, you were always falling, from your bicycle, from the porch, from the treehouse, falling off your chair, always hurting yourself, and I was always there to pick you up, dust you off and help you—*When did you ever help?* Henry James barked.

Come on, boy.

With Henry James trotting ahead, we entered woods darker and deeper than the ones we'd left behind. Peaty smells populated the air where the sunshine spread unevenly between the gaps in the maple trees. On a trail patched with amber puddles, puddles reflecting the pines and sycamores, I came upon Big Nescopek. It riffled through the thin line of walnut trees and redwoods and ivy blossoms, its dim patter crowding out the forest, ticking like a manic clock. A thousand natural hues swirled. Countless sounds—whoops, yammers, the ululations of distant birds. A thousand scents—the lovely decay of dead wet leaves, richly sweet or savory. I suddenly thought of that afternoon, nearly a lifetime ago, when I had found a bicycle leaning against the water tower on Deep Hole Road, and how I had rode and rode across Sugarloaf Valley, pedaled up the sidewinding paths of Sugarloaf Mountain as if managing the hump of a whale. I had found a giant willow tree that afternoon, slept in its arching limbs and dreamt impossible things. I laughed at the thought. How far had I traveled from that imaginative boy? Who would I have been had I lived imaginatively and not chosen the safe path? Where was that boy now but buried under the heap of responsibility? Unknown, unknowable.

Was my anger at Cole really resentment? Did I resent him for being the kind of boy I had abandoned? The birdling, an image of the birdling, reflected within me, its mute eye, its twitching wing and I heard a voice not my own say, *The only things necessary on this earth are loss and return, loss and return, the cycle never ending, ever repeating, again and again for eternity*. The Indians would call that *samsara*. The Hindus would say *moksha* is our release from it, and the ultimate goal, *nirvana*. We lose ourselves and we must find our way back, we repeat our cycles again and again.

God, I muttered, *If You can take a life without cause, then You can surely protect it, too. Protect us from ourselves, keep us safe, provide us the means to achieve our dreams, help us find ourselves and return ourselves to us.* I waited for a sign from Him. I waited for some thunder, a flash of lightning, a breeze carrying on its shoulders the scent of ancient hyacinth, sage, myrrh.

Only the sharp scents of the creek in all its black fluorescence reached through the overhanging trees, and I thought how that little birdling should have a proper burial. I turned back and, as if reading my mind, Henry James trotted past me, padding the trail ahead.

I made a tiny barge. Using the type of care priests reserve for handling the host—*My body is bread and My blood is wine*—I gently lay the birdling on the leaves, then secured it in place with a foot of vine. I might have said a prayer just then—*Ashes to ashes and dust to dust*— because I struck a match and lit the raft. When the flames established themselves, I set the pyre adrift from the banks of Big Nescopek.

It took only a second for the dark currents to take hold of that rumple of sticks. White smoke poured from the tiny pyre. The little barge bobbed, weaved unceremoniously for twenty-feet or so before it sank, turned underwater, end over end. I crossed myself. Whistling for Henry James, I turned toward the trail for home.

After settling Henry James in his pen, I unlocked the barn and entered. The air inside held that morning's warmth, the pickled scents of work.

On a pedestal table stood my latest project—a Fairy Crawford II in rust and gunmetal black. It had a folded-down high shelf and swinging trivets. Three crates of stove parts labeled Wedgewood, Queen Atlantic, and Treasure Crawford stood against the far wall beside several parlor stoves, all ready for packaging. My finished goods, the Castle Crawfords, the Glenwoods, the Princess Atlantics with gas sidecars, stood along the far wall, clear-crated and ready for delivery. Every curve and line, every intricacy, every characteristic of each stove was known to me, as if I had formed them from my own blood. I knew their moods, could diagnose their ailments by sound alone. I had tools to fix them. But I didn't know you, Cole. I didn't understand you. Not anymore. I suppose I can admit that now. How could I admit I had no answers for your life's questions? *Pops, love's got nothing to do with understanding.*

Cole, even then I often thought of cradling you on my lap in the bathroom with the shower faucet running hot and steam building up around us like a fog—*Breathe it in, Son, breathe it in*—and like a perfect mimic you matched my rhythm. How the soupy air eased your dry lungs and settled your cough. I felt accomplishment then. I could heal what ailed you. I could use water and heat, air and light as tools to fix you. How that watery air made you my son again. No, I wasn't ever willing to let that feeling die, Cole, not even after your mother told me that *Part of parenting is letting your child go.* How could I let you go?

I picked up a claw hammer from the workbench and I promised myself I would try harder to reach you. I promised myself that while Lisa and Greggie ran about the lawn playing catch with a baseball, and the charcoal grill sizzled the steaks, and the sweet-corn salad bowl sat on the porch table, I would sit you down somewhere quiet and listen to what you had to say, really listen, and if you were unwilling to talk, I would embrace you and tell you that I loved you, that I didn't blame you for setting the fire to Christ Church, that we'd figure things out, together. All was forgiven. You were intelligent. You were sensitive. You were my hope and promise and my son.

And if you asked me things, I would answer you honestly, sincerely, as to the details of my past. And I would tell you about the history of this town and about Blake and Pearl and Wally. And I would tell you these things in hopes of reconnecting the broken circuits of our lives, because in the end, honesty wasn't just the best policy, it was the only one. *Clonk-clonk-clonk*, my hammer went.

Go on.

Cole entered the barn before noon. The wall of tin signs above my workbench blanched and a hard band of light reached across the floor, his shadow in it, a bowl cradled in his hands.

Clonk-Clonk, my hammer went against the cast iron panel. A thousand thoughts swirled through my head. Listen to him. Understand him. Reach him by sharing some small story about your life.

He moved into the room, set the bowl down on the pedestal, near the skirt of that old Fairy. He fingered a socket set, touched the array of parts catalogues, thumbed an unsorted dish of washers, screws, bolts. *Clonk.*

Guests here yet? I said.

No, Sir.

Clonk.

You think about what we talked about the other day?

Yes, Sir.

And?

I decided I'd go out to Frisco and see the country before I—

Where?

San Francisco.

Everything cinched tight around me. My wedding band with that damn ruby cut into my finger. My clothes felt tighter. The room turned small and I heard a voice say, *You have no right to play with your life. You daydreamer. You nothing-boy. You skulk the woods like a devil. You bring us shame. You rebel for the sake of rebellion. You are not the boy I sat with in the boughs of the old oak and stared out over Luzerne, naming constellations. You are not the boy who built that rocket in his room and sent it soaring over Sugarloaf Mountain, not the boy who collected rocks, not the boy who hid behind the curtains waiting for us to find him. You are not my son!*

Clonk, Clonk. Sparks. The beautiful reek of metal on metal. White sparks flickered, arced, faded, such delicate work, this destructive mending. The old rage stirred my blood.

Breathe, I thought. Breathe. Though my hands trembled, I did not strike you, Cole, and I did not lay down my hammer and I did not wipe my hands in a soiled cloth in anticipation of shaking your hand. I didn't cross the room and take you in my arms and tell you I was sorry you were afraid of me and sorry our relationship had soured and sorry you believed we lived in a nothing town going nowhere. I didn't tell you we'd get through your problems together and that I would try to see life from your point of view. Instead, without turning to face you, I said the words I most regret in life. I said them without even facing you, for to look at you then might've turned me to stone. You cleared your throat.

What's that, Pops?

You're a goddamned disgrace to our good name.

What?

Sonofabitch. I wish you were never born.

Maybe you couldn't believe the words tumbling from me, because it was worse than hitting you, strangling you, beating you until your thighs erupted in welts, because the pain of broken flesh would heal. This was worse than calling you "shitless," worse than all the names Blake called me when it was just him and me alone. Cole retreated to the open door.

You don't mean that, Pops. Please say you don't mean that.

I wish you were dead! I hope you die a painful death, you fucking piece of shit! Inside I could hear Blake laughing—*That's it boy, youse can't change the cycle 'a hate just by changing yer name.* I felt that ruby ring glow hot, that old bead of blood.

Cole, you may have stuffed your hands in your pockets then, and you may have leaned your shoulder against the side of the jamb, and you may have said, *I'm sorry I didn't turn out the way you wanted. Sorry I let you down,* but you didn't say it because I turned toward you then, my face coiled in rage. You might have shuddered, and you did. Your eyes might have held my glance, then swept across my workspace, settled on the pedestal bench with that Fairy stove sitting atop it, then rode over to the stairs to the loft where Blake's lifeboat hung from the same rafter beams where Pearl once dangled from her wrists, a gaze that revealed each last scrap of wasted effort in my life. You might have turned your eyes back on me, your hazels shimmering. You might have made a circle in the dirt with your boot and you might have nodded your head in hopes of reaching some conclusion.

You'll never change. Dad. You exhaled and, in that exhaled breath, I felt you strengthen.

Get out of my house! In the next instant you turned into a shadow against the hard light of the afternoon sun. Without saying, "So long," you walked away. No, those aren't the words a father says to his son, no matter how deep his disappointment, but there they were, hanging in the air like hooks the last time I saw you. The tall rectangle of light fell hard against the floor without a trace of you in it. You left open the door.

It is words that can heal or kill. It is words that can create or end a life. If I could travel back in time, I would have done things differently. I would have taken Cole in my arms and told him, *Son, you mean the world to me, because you're my son, despite your faults, and I love you and you should take all the time you need to figure out your own role in life, because it's your life and you're the one who's going to live it.* And I now know what your absence means: By staying away, you were waiting—for a retraction, for contrition, for an apology—but it would not come.

Clonk, clonk, clonk, the hammer went. A chip of metal shot up and struck my temple. *Clonk, clonk, clonk... clonk.*

And then?

I busied myself, stabbing a burner's portholes with the straightened end of a paper clip, when in the distance Cole's Scout roared to life. The gear shifter *plonked* out of neutral into first. I blew into a venture tube while the angle of Cole's departure sounded lean, clean as a struck crystal. While I cleared away from a burner pan decades of settled dust, Cole's Scout growled, tires spitting bits of gravel. While I fitted a brass valve onto a manifold, the final roar of V-twin engine surged into the air like an apocalypse, its dark exhaust notes draining into the wild late summer heat. While I leaned against my workbench crowded with tools, I pounded my chest, settling the fury of my beating heart. The world turned red. The posts and beams seemed tainted with the Vangaardens' ancient anger—*Har-Har-Har!* Cruel laughter. I swallowed air as pressure mounted behind my eyes, a pressure exceeding the compression in my chest, all this while Cole roared down the long, winding drive, the Doppler effect of his engine rising then falling, then fading.

I struck a match and held it under my palm while my son, my only son, my love, my torturer, my pain, my salvation, my heat, my fire, buzzed away like a hornet down Deep Hole Road. Some words, like some acts, are irrevocable.

TEN

Armand, what's the root word for stupidity? What's the etymology for regret? What would the Indians call stubbornness? And tell me, Armand, please tell me what's the Indo-European paraphyletic for malice?

I'm not Armand.

I know.

Cole, your disappearance—*Never to call it a death*—taught me a new language, a new philosophy of reckoning. Your absence distorted every sense. Your absence held a mirror up to my life in which I saw distortions. Maybe I was never a real father to you, not the kind you needed, because all those years I yoked myself to Drums, carried on with the farce that I belonged here, fiddling with restoration, I could never accept your hatred of this place. No matter how much I tried to excoriate my past or justify my present, I had nothing to show for my life except a collection of pretty, old stoves, a lost son, and a ruined wife. Now all I have is this—a broken house in an outsized landscape castigated by weather.

I'm not Cole.

I know.

I inhale the house. There's a beautiful wind trolling the house. I scent maple sugar.

Smell it?

No.

The storm smells like sugar.

Wind hammers the walls and something cracks and something falls. A rafter breaks, a beam bursts, a stile tongue snaps. Something screeches, like a kettle whistle. Something crackles like a conflagration. The banister collapses and the house shakes as if in paroxysm (thank you, Armand, for the word).

From above, there's a noise I think sounds like rainwater. A quick glance out the frosted window presents a white foamy sea—rushing, eddying, retreating—and I think of waves—lapping crashing, receding. A white rabbit tumbles across the yard.

Sir? You still there?

The following year, you left us, Cole, four days of cold rain then a week of cold sunshine unordered Drums. The clouded sky stretched across the horizon that week, like a giant sheet of hammered tin. Without prologue, the rain erupted in the middle of a dull afternoon. A relentless downpour, as if the sky had torn open and emptied a sea. The old oak shuddered in the rising and falling wind, its crown pulsing like a lung, threatening to topple the house. Water glutted the leaves and beads of silver skirmished off its mistletoe. Rivulets like braided ropes drove through the bark and thunder, heavy a sound as rumbling hooves, shook the house. Water puddled in the network of the old oak's roots. Pools of venomous soup formed in the yard in which collected fanglike stems, needles, milky mud the color of amber.

Soon the ceiling sprouted leaks and Nona and I had to run around with plastic pails and tin buckets, hubcaps, bowls, and cups. We angled them atop puddles already formed in the living room. Water left retinal stains on the sofa cushions. Nona and I, in our mad dashes across the house, broke down laughing. We spilled onto the wet floor like children playing in puddles. The storm gave us something to focus on besides losing Cole. We had not yet finished with blame, but we were unready to give up love.

There's another leak, Nona, I said, bursting with laughter.

We ran through the house covering up the bird cages, protecting her canvases, almost danced through the rooms, almost pirouetted up and down the staircase, cheerful as larks.

Nona stuffed a tea cozy into a wall crack to plug a leak, and that caused waves of laughter. I found a burgeoning cascade tearing down the hearth, spread a murky pool of ash and cinders across the hardwood floor, that I plugged with my cotton underwear. Cracks in the ceiling trickled water the color of diluted rust.

We lost power. Later we sat on the kitchen floor eating cold beans out of paper cups and white bread slathered with butter and honey. Later we tuned out the barrage of tinny, ticking sounds and thunder. That might've been the best meal we ever ate. We made love on the floor, awkwardly, by turns laughing or weeping. We slept tangled in one another's arms like vines.

Then the rain, as suddenly as it started, stopped, leaving the house to steam in a pale sun. Naked, we walked from room to room, assessing tea cozies and underwear in cracks, bumping our toes against pots and glasses and frying pans brimming over, all this while the steady *drip-drip-drip* accompanied the slow creak and jostle of the house.

On the third day, the sun shone again and all the clouds dissolved. While Nona pushed with a straw broom water from the family room into the hall, I stepped outside to find a sodden world. Nona joined me on the porch.

What do we do now?

We'll fix it, I said. *We'll make it better.*

It was balmy the rest of that week. When the sunlight finally broke through the clouds, it made everything too bright and too loud, hastening the evaporation of the soil and raising the temperature of the air. Even in the morning, tendrils of heat lifted from the lawn, and everything, from the old oak to the Dutch barn, smoldered. The trees exhaled wet oxygen and the dense clouds returned to seal us in, sealing in the moisture, so that even by late October, while Drums prepared for Halloween, the air flattened, laden with wet heat. When the mercury climbed past a hundred, we fought fatigue by leaving all the doors and windows open, turned on all the floor and ceiling fans. Took cold baths. Drifted through the house like nudists.

In those wild hot afternoons, Nona and I made plans to visit Amber Daria's for scoops of vanilla ice cream coated in caramel, but we never got further than our plans. Little did we know then that we would no longer swat at the green winged horseflies lapping vanilla puddles on the picnic tables. We would no longer meander through Whispering Pines Park, chasing Cole chasing the fireflies that blinked and faded, blinked and faded, like stars. We would no longer dance in the evening shadows, descending without disturbing the swelter, plunging us hot and sweating back into the Mercury already a furnace. Little did we know then that we had already cut our ties with Drums.

Each birthday that passed, each Independence Day, or Halloween, or anniversary I relived your vanishing. I tried putting your disappearance from my mind while your mother did all she could to live—*He's just lost his way, Dutch, just lost, like those kids on the milk cartons*—and I never once denied her those delusions. *I read about aliens abducting children, you think that—?*

Son, remembering you was reliving you. I know now remembering is not resurrection. Remembering is not return but only its apparition. What we retrieve in memory are ghosts. Your absence has become an unquenchable thirst, and the more I remember you, the thirstier I become. I am sure it pleases you to hear this, but it's what you need to hear.

Go on, Pops. I'm listening.

Cole, I want to hold you in my arms, hear your bare feet slapping the hardwood, running from one end of the hall to the bathroom. I want to wipe away your tears with my thumb, places strips of cottony cloth drenched in aloe over your poison rashes, smell your laughter and eat your rage and suck the toxins that poisoned your mind so that you wouldn't suffer. I want to be the man who had answers for your life. What I would give for you to hurl an insult at my face. Spit on me. Slap me. Kick me. What I would not give for your hard punch to my heart.

I'm listening.

Cole, in the years following your vanishing, language became a wall; it concealed everything, even me from myself. After losing you, I lost my words. Grief had withered my tongue. Even for years after, even after decades, my voice had died.

A terrific crack appears in the ceiling.

It's time. Come on.

Where?

Let's go.

Jack pulls me up by the sleeves. He parts curtains that never were and we enter a field of wildflowers that never existed. We enter a meadow so brightly gold it seems impossible—the flowers are made of brass and the trees are apricot-hued and every cloud appears brassy. The sky beyond the Poconos look steeped in amber and the citron sun throws spires of dull, brassy light onto the bright brassy earth.

They'll take good care of us.

Who?

You know who. Come on.

Winter returns. Long daggers of ice droop from the branches of the blackened oaks. The blistering wind sweeps the crowns, and the daggers clack together like muted chimes. But it is not cold like before. It is not cold. I think we are time-travelers, Jack and I. Each step delivers us deeper into an alternate past where my Cole is alive, where my Nona is young, where I am not an insignificant stove-junker, but the type of man my son respects, honors, loves. Jack and I cross a field of piebald oaks, and here Pearl is alive, and Wally is alive and glowing, and Blake is not the monster I took him for.

Not far now, Jack shouts. His legs lift and fall, lift and fall, such superhuman energy, and his arm pivots and swings, pivots and swings, precise as a metronome. He pulls me along with his voice. I almost stumble. I want to tell him to slow down, that this old rickety man can't keep up his pace, but I don't.

We arrive at a clearing blanched with light. It's bounded by evergreens, conifers, elms, redwoods. It's the redwoods whose height impresses me. Their peaks reach through the clouds. Such serenity. The blizzard cannot reach us here. No wind rises to attack us, and even the sun coldly shines like a moon. Crows in the trees sit eerily silent, inscrutable witnesses to this strange game. Cocking their black heads, they scratch their flanks. An unimpressed audience. A murder stirs through the air silently, flaps noiseless wings and hooks quiet talons into the denuded limbs like shadows.

Jack releases my hand, marches toward a depression in the snow.

This is where they'll land.

Who?

The Eden people, remember? You said they'd save us and take us to Heaven. Remember what you said?

Did I say that? When? I cough. I clutch my chest. Now I want to cry. What else have I said I cannot remember? This is child's play. This is the effect of words without a foothold in the world, where the pondering, teasing imagination of an old man makes for a child a

Heaven of Hell or a Hell of Heaven.

That's right, I say.

It all looks vaguely familiar. Is this the Lindberg Field where Cole launched his rockets? No, that was miles away, but now I'm not sure—*Look for a row of piebald oaks and a notched oak tree; an oak tree struck by lightning, its flanks seared black.* Perhaps it's the Bloodstained Field, exactly as I described it for Jack. Daniel Klader's cross stands camouflaged among the piebald oaks. But how is this possible? Armand might say, *It is possible for the objects of our imagination to come to life.* Jack flings his arms wide and twirls.

How long we supposed to wait?

I don't know.

I still have the beacon.

The what?

The ring. Remember you said to hold it up when they come?

A falling star glides across the sky. Jack points to it.

There.

Jack pulls the ring from his pocket. The ruby glows like a bead of illuminated blood.

Hold it up so they can see you, I say.

He does what I say. His eyes are adamant. He has a smile. The falling star falls across the horizon. Wind shakes the trees. The murder lifts and winter returns to us, cold and furious and terrifying.

Why didn't they stop for us?

Son, there's no ship to carry us to Eden. I made it all up.

Why would you?

I have no strength to argue. Let's go home, I say. Jack touches my shoulder, passing a current through my bones. I shiver.

I'm cold, I say.

You shouldn't lie.

Very cold.

I know.

ELEVEN

The curtain draws. The lights dim. The spotlight reveals a man on the dusty floor of an old bedroom. The hearth in corner is dark, a black mouth coolly steaming. The window in the wall shines like a vacant eye while the man lies in his cryogenic room and quakes from the cold. Perhaps he thinks of someplace warm, the tan sands of a Floridian beach, or maybe he dreams of Paradise? He folds his hands across his chest. *Moksha is a form of hell, Somerset. The soul's liberation from the endless circle of life and rebirth is a nightmare from which I wish to awaken.*

It's just gibberish, Armand.

Being means giving up your old forms of self, Pops.

Then I give up. Son, I give up the old coarseness, the hurting words that always tumbled from my lips before reason had opportunity to rein them in. I give up my capacity to hurt. I relinquish my sundry roles, my various functions and masks. I give up my *atman,* that mythical eternal soul. Abandon Eden. Avalon. Ararat. Resign the sort of love that bound me to a hope made useless by hoping.

~

Son, maybe we are just made up of words and memories, like you said. Like you said, though words are just sounds, words are all we are. A tentacle from the old oak crashes through the roof.

~

Son, most of us squander our talents in pursuit of dreams too large for us. We hope for our future self and sacrifice our present and ignore the past. We awaken one morning beached on the shores of our lives, naked and alone, having fought battles we couldn't hope to win. We fall sleep beside a spouse we no longer recognize, in a house that no longer fits us, surrounded by images of strangers. We leave detritus in our wake for others to sift through. We use words that hurt those we love most. Like amnesiacs, we stumble about, questioning who we are, how we got here, and why. We ask ourselves old questions. Tired ones. Unanswerable ones.

~

I want to sleep, but I am afraid of what I'll dream. If I sleep, I just might dream of returning to a home that doesn't include notions of leaving and having left, not a place of endings but of beginnings. *What's the point in it all, Pops? Our lives have no meaning*. Sure they do, Son, you were my meaning, my family, lives mean whatever you want them to mean.

~

The wall thrums like a muted string. The man presses his hand to the plasterboard and somewhere behind the conduits, the ice in the iron pipes crackles, sends conversations through his fingertips. Any sudden move might shatter him to pieces, pieces that might roll across the floor, melt in pools then enter the joints of the house.

~

The man's bladder bursts. A wet stain spreads over his inner thighs. This just might be the last insult in a life replete with insults. He slips off his shoes, removes his clothes. Naked, he stands in the center of the room, his body a loose geometry of soft rhomboids, cones and cylinders. His hands shiver. He inhales dust and coldness and dead memory and he jabbers words, unpronounceable gibberish—*quixatokl, slgrnumnuh dna vlqqwerr, hireathkl puh un un*. His nostrils flare. If he can just breathe and hold his breath he might suck up the darkness and make himself whole again. He longs for a match. He longs for the courage to squeeze the trigger of the gun. Bourbon. He listens for the clatter of hooves, a thunderclap, and waits for black mist. He has not painted his door with lamb's blood, or was it the blood of a goat?

~

A mass of swirling clouds multiplies on the horizon. It ranges over Sugarloaf Valley. Its serpentine tongue laps up the Great Swamp, the Lake of Four Seasons, drinks up the ponds and Big Nescopek. The mouth siphons farms, gulping red barns and steel silos. It churns Fern Maslow's daisy cows penned in his cattle barn, snaps in half the spines of Homer Danforth's Clydesdales. Tearing apart, limb by limb, the forests of cedar and pine. Branch by branch, the mouth sunders the maples, the redwoods, and pulls, root by root, the haggard pine oaks, whisking away their trunks. Arnie Sandewski's Craftsman and Fern Gibson's Georgian revival, and Robbie Hagstrom's Post and Beam, the pell-mell assemblage of stick houses, century-old bungalows, thrust upwards into the turbulence. Tractor parts spin. Tin signs. Rubber tires. Slate shingles from red barns collide with tumbling weathervanes, swirl with aluminum gutters and red brick. The vortex spins toward ancestral homes. Downspouts screech before breaking. The gabled skylight shatters. The roof rips away tile by tile, piece by piece, then the roof whisks away, revealing pink insulation in the attic that rips from its tacks. The exposed rafter beams burst and the king posts collapse and the struts and side beams snap like matchsticks. The walls, stripped to the beams and posts, crackle. The floor joists buckle. The electric conduits are next to go, torn from their junction boxes; they coil and whip and strike the air like snakes. The plumbing pipes jostle from their braces and break loose. Bit by bit and piece by piece, the house fractures and surges upwards like bubbles effervescing in a glass. The poor old oak puts up a brave fight, but it's no match against the spiraling gyre. Torn from its roots, the maelstrom propels the old oak's bulk, launches it a hundred feet into the air while the man clings to nothing but a malformed hole.

The pandemonium roils in the distance, churning its rage over Sugarloaf Mountain. It charges toward Hazleton, high on the hill. The curtain draws on a wasteland. The stage lights dim. I have to laugh. I do. *Swnhjklthm eu flkcxqdges.*

Where is Jack? I'd like to tell him that, in a million years, a meteor might barrel into Sugarloaf Mountain, and its irony nooks and ancient ice cracks might carry the cryogenic seeds of alien life. After another million years, new bracken might sprout. Armies of pollen might roll across this land, seeding new trees to replace the old. Pollen drifts might melt into the mineral-rich earth and seeds might sprout new forests, new orchards, a new vegetable kingdom with new species of flowers and fruit and peppers we have no names for, restoring this land to an Edenic state. I have to laugh. I cough.

~

I reach for the Bakelite, longing to hear a human voice. I twirl the knob and Miki's voice resurfaces. It's faint at first, but strengthens. She says things I don't care to hear, statements of loss and suffering that have quantifiable value: How many the storm has killed, how many disasters it's made, how many lives it's ruined. It is December 24th, she says which makes it Christmas Eve. The world spins along in space toward another revolution, then another. Her voice fades, replaced by music. Now a song plays that I faintly recognize. My foot taps in time while a watery piano plays stabbing, staccato chords. A haughty voice croons, a little melancholy voice, almost bird light in its soaring. *Tweet, tweet, tra-la-la–lala.* I think of Nona—*Hear it, Dutch? That's Cole's song.*

~

I hear it Nona. I hear it. The speaker fizzles and the radio fades. Nothing but that white noise of the universe.

~

Dutch, Nona shouts. *Dutch, what are you jabbering about up there in the dark? Come down here. Supper's on. It's Christmas Eve and Cole's here and he wants to tell you a tale of wandering.*

Pops, come on down, I need to say something.

Son, the past returns, sometimes in an altered form, but it always returns, because time ravages memory and memory ravaged by time reinvents itself. No, nothing is truly past. Nothing ever really dies. I believe we retain everything somewhere—in a house, in a memory, in a story.

~

Somerset, you listening to me?

I'm listening, Nona, I'm listening.

~

A cold draft slips through the cracks in the wall. The wind cuts into the room. I scent winter flowers.

TWELVE

The snow does not fall and the wind does not blow and the sky does not tear itself to pieces. I stand in the front yard on this cold new morning. Nothing moves. Neither air nor light. The landscape looks as if painted. No movement in the trees. No snow devils spin. No dog barks.

~

I love this time of the morning. The ants in their anthills lie asleep, the beetles and dust mites lie sequestered in their hiding places, and the finches are asleep, dreaming—*Do birds dream?*—of red-tailed hawks, wheeling and wheeling in the air. I wonder if hawks dream of being wolves. What do wolves dream of? Perhaps a glade upon which to run, a full moon, a quorum of deer? No, I may never stop pining for Drums, for *hiraeth*, believing in that shifting center of my brain, that the wholeness of a human soul depends on that quality of mercy that familiarity of home delivers. Pull a man out by his roots and fling him far and farther still, plant him in some other fertile ground, and though the soil be nutrient–rich, he never quite grows the same.

~

In a few moments, the sun will rise over Blue Mountain, and the woods will come alive with life. In a few moments, the old crescent moon will fade, the constellations will fade—*Pyxis, the ship's compass; Polaris, the North Star*—and return to wherever stars go. The morning sky will die, stretching from one end of the horizon to the other like a giant sheet of lead. And that seems right, because it is as it always was.

~

I reenter the house, reenter my old bedroom. The hearth is cold. A cold black mouth full of ashes and embers.

Jack, I say. You here? Where are you?

~

I smell heather, hyacinth, myrrh. In the frosted window, the warp of an old man's face reflects in the glass. He wears a hound's tooth pageboy cap like mine. His face looks haggard, like mine. His eyes are Cole's eyes.

~

What kept you? I say. Never mind, never mind. You won't believe what I've been through. An epic storm. Epic. There was a boy, stricken with fever… Jack? Jack? Christ, where's he hiding now? There was… is… Armand, are you listening?

~

Light cascades from the winter sky. The snowcapped Poconos burn blue. Birdsongs. Impossible. Scent of spring wildflowers. Green apples. Honey. Smoke. Rust. Between the gaps in the evergreens glows a winding, slivering road. The morning welcomes me, quiet as a crystal.

~

Who are you? Who-Who?

Acknowledgements

I am thankful to the University of San Francisco's MFA department, and in particular Nina Schuyler, Carolina DeRobertis, Lewis Buzbee, KM Soehnlein, Stephen Beachy, David Vann, Jason Brooks Brown, and Elizabeth Rosner for their influence, support, encouragement, and guidance.

To the town of Drums, PA, where I lived as a boy, and to the city and people of Hazleton, whose storied past I mined for the substance of this novel, I am deeply grateful.

There are too many influences to mention, so I will list several whose work has been a constant inspiration: William Faulkner, James Joyce, Rainer Maria Rilke, WH Auden, Cormac McCarthy, William Maxwell, Vladimir Nabokov, RK Narayan, Wallace Stegner, Ludwig Wittgenstein, the inimitable Marilynne Robinson, Alice Munro, Alice McDermott, James Salter, and Paul Harding. Their passion for words and ideas, perspicacity, attention to character and consciousness distilled in gorgeous prose, reaffirms my belief that literature is the greatest art.

Thank you to the good people at Little Feather Books, and fellow writer and editor Cynthia Ceilán. Also thanks to the numerous literary journals that have supported my writing: *The Gettysburg Review, Glint Literary Journal, Crack the Spine, Zouch Literary and Miscellany, Blue Lake Review, Glimmer Train, The Indian Review, The Faulkner Society, The Criterion International Journal,* and *Crack the Spine.*

I owe my gratitude to Chris Norsian, for serving as a beacon of truth in a city where posturing and illusion is the norm, and for keeping me grounded. May you rest in peace. To my wife, Jessette, whose quiet encouragement kept me focused even during my darkest hours, and most of all to my son, Suryan Emerson, my "little star": my light, my love, my universe.

About the Author

A "maximalist" writer, influenced by poets and musicians and philosophers, S.K. Kalsi crafts sentences that resonate with depth and power. In searing prose, he reveals the souls of loners and atheists, iconoclasts and dreamers, people turned inward by obsession, broken by love, crippled by heartbreak, illuminating souls shattered by loss.

S.K. Kalsi holds an MFA in Creative Writing from the University of San Francisco, a BFA in Creative Writing from Long Beach State, and a diploma in Screenwriting from UCLA. His short stories have appeared in numerous literary magazines, including *The Gettysburg Review, Glint Literary Journal,* and *The Criterion,* among others. His work has been nominated for a Pushcart Prize. He lives in Napa, California, with his wife, son, and two dogs.

Made in the USA
Middletown, DE
11 February 2015